MW01257954

ALSO BY SAM SWICEGOOD

Jack, the Worst End User (and other stories)

The Trust

The Wizards on Walnut Street

The Magician on Main Street – *Coming Soon*

"Death is a redhea has a dog."

Crow began to pick up some of the fruits ai
shelf, along with what looked a lot like salted pork. .
they had settled themselves at the table and Crow
way through some plums and a potato that she unab.

Gail stared at her and picked through an apr
particularly hungry.

"Please eat," Crow pleaded. "If you don't, you're g(
There's a thing called scurvy and it's really bad."

"My friend told me about that one. He used to br
weird bags of juice. And later, bottles."

"Your *bandit* friend?" Crow probably didn't mean t(
cynical.

"You know," Gail said after a pause, her eyebrows raised
a tone of voice delicate enough to stroke the wings of a but,
they are coming back, then we just stole from them." Crow
chewing and looked down at her fingers, now covered in plur.
"You say you don't 'get' me," Gail continued, starting to peel th
from an apricot, "but you seem to really hate thieves. Then, you
a bag of money—"

"They stole my stuff first!"

"—not the point." Gail repeated something M used to say: "We
all thieves. The trick is to not be an asshole, too."

Crow was stunned into silence and spent the next few minutes
avoiding Gail's gaze. "Again, I'm sorry. I have a bad history with being
robbed and mugged a *lot* because I have valuable things. So I'm sorry.
I shouldn't be judging anybody for what they do these days because
everyone's lives suck. Not just mine. I guess I somehow forgot that,
okay?"

Gail gave her a smile. "Okay. Friends?"

NO PLACE

Sam Swicegood

Dragon Street Press
Cincinnati, Ohio

Copyright © 2019 Sam Swicegood
All rights reserved.

All rights reserved. No part of this publication may be reproduced, distributed, or transmitted in any form or by any means, including photocopying, recording, or other electronic or mechanical methods, without the prior written permission of the publisher, except in the case of brief quotations embodied in critical reviews and certain other noncommercial uses permitted by copyright law. For permission requests, write to the publisher, addressed "Attention: Permissions Coordinator," at Elsewhere Media Limited, PO Box 12106, Cincinnati, OH 45229.

Ordering Information: Quantity sales. Special discounts are available on quantity purchases by corporations, associations, and others. For details, contact the publisher at the address above.

Orders by U.S. trade bookstores and wholesalers: Please contact Elsewhere Media Ltd at (607) 4-GAMES-4 or (607) 442 6374; or visit www.dragonstreet.press for further information.

This is a work of fiction. Names, characters, businesses, places, events, locales, and incidents are either the products of the author's imagination or used in a fictitious manner. Any resemblance to actual persons, living or dead, or actual events is purely coincidental.

Library of Congress Control Number: 2019942916

FIRST EDITION
1 3 5 7 6 4 2
2019 Hardback
ISBN: 1-7331225-1-6
ISBN-13: 978-1-7331225-1-1

Also available in trade paperback

To found family
who believed in me
when I didn't believe in myself

ONE

"I'm looking for a road," Gail mumbled. Off to her left, the sun had gloriously broken the horizon and was now beginning its upward creep across the eastern sky. Even the warm rays, however, could not quite pierce the chill that permeated the country air. They shone through leaves at the far end of what appeared to be the remnants of a field of crops, which had either been abandoned or recently harvested; she did not know very much about farming and couldn't tell the difference.

The sheepdog looked up at her.

"I'm looking for a road," the girl from the mountains repeated, with more confidence. This time she gestured to the faded map in her hand and practiced her opening pitch once again. "I am hoping you may be able to help point me in the right direction." No answer. She sighed. "Does that sound okay? Does that sound...normal?" The dog tilted its head and yawned before losing all interest and beginning to sniff the side of the road as they walked. "Thanks for listening."

As she rounded the next curve, the land out to the left glistening with the early morning dew, she spied what looked like a crossroads in the distance. A single large barn on the right side of the road was the only structure near the place, and as she and her sheepdog came closer, she could see that the crossing road was significantly wider and less deteriorated than the one she currently trod.

The sheepdog decided that this open crossroad was the proper place to stop for a break. He did so, plopping onto the grass on the dew-covered side of the road and making a half-yawning guttural noise in his throat.

Gail put her hands on her hips and looked down either side of this new road. Either direction could potentially have led to town, or to the road she was looking for. Why was it that all of these roads were so stupidly similar? The same dull colors, the same high grass on either side, and nary a road sign in sight.

She heard a cough from somewhere behind her and tensed. The sheepdog rolled to his feet, sniffing around, and before the mountain girl could start looking for the source of the sound herself, he was over the curb and dashing into one of the abandoned fields. Up ahead, no more than a hundred meters away, a large metal post jutted out of the ground, towering in the sky. The purpose of the metal structure wasn't immediately apparent; perhaps it was some tool to watch and measure the day, like a gigantic sundial. Even now, the rising sun cast a long spear of darkness across the field toward her, stretching far out of sight.

She approached it with caution. There, she discovered that the source of the cough was a young woman, tied tightly to the metal itself. She looked rather uncomfortable.

With the angle of the rising sun, it was hard to make out her features, but the woman appeared to be brunette, and she was mostly covered in dark clothing. She was tied, or maybe tangled, in a rope or binding material that secured her to the obelisk, and for a moment the mountain girl thought she might have misheard the coughing sound. She didn't know how long the woman had been tied up there; it was very likely that she was already dead.

The young woman coughed again. Her eyelids fluttered open, and she looked down at the mountain girl. "Alright," she said weakly, "death is a redhead. And she has a dog."

"I'm not death," Gail retorted as she looked around for a way to get the woman down. "Why are you up there?" It seemed a good question to ask. People might get strung up to die like this for perfectly reasonable reasons. Well, 'reasonable' was perhaps a little contextual.

"Bandit crew," the woman coughed, wriggling a little in her bindings. "Attacked me while I was climbing down. I got tangled in my safety rope while I was kicking them in their stupid faces—" she coughed for a moment in the dusty air and then let out a deep sigh. "I hate asking for help, but there's a ladder on the other side…"

"A ladder—oh." The mountain girl spotted the rusted ladder leaning against the side of the metal obelisk and started to climb up to get within reach of the ropes. "Hang on, let me figure out how to do this so you don't fall."

The woman said nothing and waited patiently. Not that she had much else to do, besides complain—but she didn't. She just sighed and waited, apparently accepting of her current situation. The mountain girl was glad she wasn't complaining. People tended to complain far too much, as though they didn't realize that everyone, everywhere, had a lot to complain about. The people who would deign to be so "special" as to think that their complaints were important enough to need vocalization were a pet peeve she never really could dismiss.

Gail reached the rope and examined them carefully. This woman had managed to tangle them pretty well, both around each other and around the protruding rungs that served as a ladder. "Are you okay? Did they hurt you?" she called out as she dug in her pocket for something to clamp onto the rope to stop it from slipping as she untied it.

"Not me," came the defeated reply from the other side of the metal obelisk, "but I dropped my bag, so they grabbed it. And since I was stuck, they left me here and stole stuff out of my barn."

"I'm so sorry," the redhead replied with as much emotion as she could muster, while her fingers undid knot after knot and she finally felt the bindings starting to loosen. She had seen the bandits pass her way the day before. They had seen her, too, but neither had had the will or the desire to fight. The bandits had awakened a den of wolves and foolishly ran from them—arousing their predatory instincts. "I should have stepped aside and let the wolves get them," she muttered under her breath.

Finally, the ropes loosened just enough to allow the helpless young woman enough room to wriggle out and hang from them. From there, it was a simple matter of sidling hand-over-hand along the outside of the obelisk until she was in reach of the ladder. The mountain girl slid down the ladder and back to the safety of the ground, with the other following behind and landing on wobbly legs. She tried to regain her balance but fell backward onto the ground. "Ack! My legs feel numb."

The mountain girl didn't move to help her up. Instead she crouched down on the ground next to her. "Are you alright? Do you need water?"

The other nodded slowly. "Please. I'm Crow, by the way."

"Like the bird?" The mountain girl dug in her pack and found a waterskin. She passed it over.

Crow took a long drink of the water and had a brief coughing fit as the liquid coated her insides. "Like the bird. You?"

"Gail." It was strange hearing her own name, even coming from her own mouth. It was strange hearing words coming from her own mouth at all; to be fair, she hadn't spoken to anyone besides the dog in weeks. "Are you hurt at all?"

Crow pulled her legs up to her chest and rubbed a spot between her shoes and the bottom of her pants while shaking her head. "Only my pride. But I can't stew on that too much. As soon as I can walk, I'm going right down that road to town and finding those thieves—"

"You know the way to town?" Gail looked at her with wide eyes, like a child told she was going to receive a gift.

"Yeah. It's a few hours that way." Crow tilted her head toward one direction down the crossroad. "You feel like joining me? I hope that sword's not just for show."

"It's not." Gail was very matter-of-fact and rifled through her bag for something else.

Crow looked over at the English sheepdog, who sat half-crouched with his ears at attention. "Is that your…um…dog?"

Gail glanced up. "Oh, yes. It's okay, Lukather." The dog relaxed and trotted over, plopping down near Crow and tilting his head while he considered her. Gail, meanwhile, fished a folded piece of paper from her bag and started unfolding it. "I'm looking for a road," she said as she passed it over.

Crow looked at the map up and down. "Ooh, a map. Okay, let's see. Where are you trying to get to?"

Gail pointed to the southernmost part of the map, on a peninsula.

"So which road are you looking for?"

"This one." Gail traced a finger down a light, smudged line that crossed the map vertically. "Once I find that road, I can just follow it. But I can't find it."

Crow nodded, the side of her mouth twitching as she contemplated. "I might be able to help. But I wouldn't be able to help without getting my things back from those assholes. I need my, er…tools." She raised her eyebrows knowingly, hoping that Gail might know to what she was alluding. From her expression, though, the mountain girl did not seem to understand. "No problem. You must be too young. What are you, sixteen?"

"No," Gail said, her voice slightly higher in pitch with frustration. "I'm seventeen."

"So you were only two or three then." The question was directed more rhetorically, it appeared, as Crow continued without receiving an answer. She pulled herself up, handing Gail back her water. "It's alright. Point is, I need to get my stuff. If you're good with a sword then that's a bonus. Hopefully, we'll just get it back without a fight…but you never know."

Gail narrowed her eyes, stuffing the waterskin back into her bag. "I don't want to fight people."

Crow glanced, momentarily, down at the sword. "Neither do I. But if you want to find that road, I'm happy to help you—especially since you probably saved my life just now…" She paused in realization. "Thank you for that, by the way. I probably should have said that first."

Gail didn't reply and slowly stood up, brushing the dirt off her knees. This was turning into a relatively uncomfortable conversation, and the added idea that she might have to get into another fight was digging into her.

Out in the mountains, she had her share of bandits and thieves and scavengers. They would show up and maybe, if they were skilled, spot signs of her presence and spend some time looking for her. Rarely, they would find her. When they did, they did one of three things. They would leave her alone, considering any interaction with her to be a burden on themselves. Or they would try to convince her to join with them and explain that the mountains were no place for a young girl all alone. Sometimes, particularly if they wore merchant colors, they would try to capture her or kill her. Sometimes they succeeded in the former, but even then, she had always managed to escape.

And then there were the Mori. She did not fight the Mori. She only ran from them.

Crow was looking at her with a curious tilt of the head. "I'm not trying to upset you or anything. But they took my stuff and they kidnapped my cat. We go find them and try to get them back without a fight. I can take care of myself if you really don't want to go, but I'd feel a lot safer if it was three-on-two and not three-on-one."

The dog barked, and Crow jumped slightly. "She meant three on three, Lukather," Gail said with a wry grin. "Alright, I'll go with you. But if we can do it without a fight, that's what I want." She thought for a moment and added, "And you owe me dinner."

"It's a deal," Crow said, taking off toward the barn. Gail cast one last long glance at the tower of metal and followed.

Up close, it was clear that the field here was abandoned rather than harvested. Vines and invasive grasses grew up in high patches, and piles of dried leaves dotted the ground here and there where they had been rounded up for burning. If this was Crow's farm, she clearly wasn't doing any work here. More likely, she just took it over, lived in the barn, and didn't care if the land had gone to seed.

Crow pulled open the barn door. The air inside had a musk and a certain dryness that made it, at the least, a windbreak from the chill. Within, several wooden crates filled with books and other strange gadgets littered the floor. Gail didn't recognize any of these things or know exactly what their names were, but they had a certain level of familiarity to her that she couldn't place. Beside the boxes was a bed— a real bed!—with a stained mattress—a real mattress!—on it pushed against a wall. The rest of the barn was empty.

Crow removed her jacket and replaced it with a hooded cloak she pulled out of a nearby cloth bag. It appeared that the limited wardrobe she owned was all black, from her blouse to her trousers to her thick studded boots. Gail observed her new companion carefully—she was short and wiry, with skin the color of coffee and cream and exceptionally curly dark hair that reached her shoulders. More interesting than her appearance, though, was the way she carried herself—quite confidently, despite the fact that a few hours ago she had been tied up and left for dead by bandits. She didn't seem particularly shaken by this fact. "Are you, um…alright?" she asked cautiously.

"Yeah," Crow replied, straightening her hood with a stilted, impatient movement of her hand. "I just want my cat back." She picked up a hunting knife and secured it to her side as she swept out the door. Gail was intrigued. Although Crow didn't seem to be much older, she had the beginnings of worry lines on her face that made her look, at a glance, a bit older.

I probably have those, too, she mused to herself. She hadn't seen her own reflection in a long time. Gail absently touched the wavy red locks that cascaded down past her shoulders and partially down her back, and as she followed Crow out of the barn, she secured it with a hair tie behind her head.

"You've been out here a while?" Gail asked as they started down the dusty road toward town. Trees and fields still spilled out on either side of the road, and the remains of what once were houses were visible off of short paths from their trail.

"A few months. It's been a great place to do my work. But I have to leave soon," she added with a furrowed brow. "Something big is happening."

"What kind of work do you do?"

She gave Gail a sidelong look. "I'm not sure you'd understand it. No offense." Gail shrugged and shifted her attention elsewhere; the redhead wasn't sure if she liked Crow very much. She was kind of a jerk.

Crow looked bothered by the silence and cleared her throat. "I do research, mostly. I connect with people and we talk strategy."

"What are you strategizing?"

"Fighting back. Against the Mori."

Gail's eyes went wide, and she took an involuntary step away from the girl in black. "I don't want to fight the Mori."

"Nobody does," Crow replied in defeat, holding her arms up above her head to stretch. The marks from the rope binding had begun to appear as yellow and blue bruises. "But we have to eventually. But yeah, that's what I do. I'm mostly an organizer. I don't do the, uh...heavy lifting."

Another brief silence descended, and again it was Crow who apparently could not stand to let it linger. "What's your story then? If you're seventeen you probably don't remember much of a time before the Mori, do you?"

Gail shifted her feet as she walked, trying to put her thoughts into words. She remembered a lot from back then, but those times were like secrets in her heart that were hers alone. The world had changed significantly in a short ten years. Those times seemed like a far-off dream she kept hidden and treasured as if by sharing them they might somehow slip out of her head and evaporate into the air like water on hot sand. "I don't."

"Well, that's fine," Crow continued as a chill wind rushed over them, shoving her hands in her pockets. "But after what I found out yesterday, something has to be done. If we don't stop the Mori soon, millions of people will die."

TWO

Everywhere around was the sign of two kinds of decay. The first kind, the temporary kind, was the draw of the season, inflicting its temporary gloom upon the land and changing the lively green to gold and then to brown and red. One might call it a temporary death. It was a death that gave promise of rebirth and return of the seasons. It was a decay with purpose and meaning. It was a cleansing of the sins of the year and paying penance with the cold so that a glorious resurrection might arise in the spring.

The second kind of decay was also prevalent: the permanent kind. Houses on either side of the road were collapsing from disuse and the vicissitudes of the seasons. Crops like the ones in the field they passed were rotting away in the soil. It was a death that had no return or rebirth, as though the evidence of man's passing through these hills was slowly disappearing to be reclaimed by Mother Earth.

In a way, Gail mused, it was still a part of the temporary death. The weather that washed away these buildings was using the slowly-crumbling remains of wood and stone to enrich the ground and reuse them to grow all the more boldly each year. Nothing lasts forever.

"I hate going into towns," Gail admitted as they started to pass crumbling buildings where people had set up shops. Banners that were probably once brightly-colored hung from windowsills and indicated places you could get services. This town was a traveler's town—a place to stock up but never really settle down. People shouted for attention, trying to sell the things most important to your normal mountain hermit, like food or tools or cooking equipment. These kinds of towns were scattered here and there through the mountains and hills. Outposts far away from the grand cities of the Mori.

The thing about these towns was how much they both loved and hated passers-by. If you were coming in to refill your bags or wagon, and you weren't planning on staying very long, you were practically a celebrity in towns like these. But the moment you decided that life in one of these places actually sounded like a good idea, the whole town would turn on its heel. Resources as scarce as they were, it made a sort of sense: An extra person in the town would be one more person prying gold out of the pockets of travelers. That left less to go around in the long run. It was a fragility that made the whole thing seem fake—as if the town itself was just a painting without any real substance behind it.

Gail had tried to join one of these towns once a few months back. She didn't have anyone else to turn to, and she showed up in town and tried to build a life. But they didn't want her, and eventually she was turned out on her ass because she didn't have much skill as a merchant. She was dragging everyone else down.

Crow shrugged. "I guess it depends on the town. This one is alright. I've only been here once or twice." She pointed down the street. "And there's our destination. Bet you our bandits are in that pub."

They were. It was late morning, and the pub had not really gotten up and going for the day, but that didn't prevent it from being the most obvious target for bandits traveling with bags of stolen goods through the chilly mountains. The three of them were near the fireplace, their feet up and pointed toward the flames, chatting in just-slightly-too-loud voices about heists from long ago. They knew that the pub wouldn't throw them out so long as they kept the tab running, and they clearly didn't want anyone to think they were anything less than cold-blooded killers.

They passed through the door without great to-do, and Crow walked over to the bar, speaking in a low voice to the bartender. He looked concerned for a moment, and afterward seemed placated by whatever she told him. She pointed to the pile of gear up against the far wall and the bartender nodded. She passed him money. They shook hands.

Gail, meanwhile, hung around the front door with Lukather. She wasn't sure what to expect quite yet, but she was perfectly happy dashing out of here and down the road if necessary.

"Okay," Crow said with a clap of her hands. "Let's make this really easy, guys. I get it, you're really happy about whatever job you did and that's cool, but you took *my* stuff and I'm not happy about that. So give me my stuff back and I think we're good."

They all turned bleary eyes on her. Not a single one of them was anything close to what could be considered "sober" and it was apparent from the vacant, unfocused gazes. The bowman who had threatened Gail spoke up first. "Heeeey. It's the wiiiiitch. She's done followed us."

"Seems a pretty witchy thing to do," another added.

"Witch?" Gail said under her breath.

Crow tried to look relaxed. "Look guys, I really don't want to make this a thing, alright? I'll let you keep the money. Just give me my box back. Then we're out of your hair and you can keep drinking until your bodies give out."

"Finders keepers," the other man said. Gail spotted a red-stitched nametag on his jacket: "Dirk". He gestured to the gear with a hand. "If you wanted to keep it you shoulda fought harder."

Crow glowered. "I've been pretty polite now. So I'm going to walk over there and pick my stuff up and walk out. If you try to stop me there's gonna be trouble."

"Trouble?" The bowman put up his hands in mock fear. "Oh dear, the witch is gonna put a curse on us. I'm not—" he hiccupped and belched in quick succession. "I'm not Mori. Your curses won't work on me."

"Again," Crow replied impatiently, "I *know* that. It's pretty obvious that you're not Mori." She took a cautious step toward the pile of bags, her body posture appearing relaxed and nonthreatening. "So are we alright then? No prob—?" As Crow took another step forward, the bowman made a lightning-fast move. In one swift motion, he grabbed an arrow, nocked it, and let it fly.

At least, that's what he tried to do. But as deep into his cups as he was, the bowman only succeeded in grabbing an arrow, failing to nock it, pulling back on the string and slamming the bow's body into his own face. He let out a squeal like a wounded animal and thrashed about a moment before slipping off the chair and hitting the floor.

"Pathetic," Crow mumbled as she darted for the bags, her hand closing around the handle of a box. Before she had even a moment to grab these two things and step back, however, she found a knife at her throat. The man with the bright red-stitched lettering had risen to his feet in an instant, his blade grasped tightly in his hand. Gail's hand found her sword but had no chance to intervene before Dirk had ordered Crow to drop the loot. She did, and the thrashing canvas bag let out a yowl.

"I am a lot less drunk than he is," Dirk said softly.

Crow sighed. "Come on, man. I'm making this really easy for you. I don't want a fight. I just want a few things back. Not even all of it. I feel like I'm being really reasonable here."

"I know. But that doesn't mean I'm just letting you have it. I'm open to some negotiation."

Crow glared. "Negoti—really? I am literally letting you have everything except these two things. What more negotiation do you need?" Dirk's eyes went down to her shoes and back up again. Crow seemed to understand that answer. "Oh, gross," she said with an audible cringe.

Behind her, Gail heard Lukather's soft growl rising, and her ears perked at the sound of a bow being drawn back. She looked down to see that the bowman had succeeded in readying an arrow, and she let out a frustrated cry and stepped forward to try and land her foot on the weapon's curve and throw off its target. The movement caused Dirk to look away, for just an instant. In that instant, Crow's fist landed a sucker-punch across his jaw, and sent him careening to the side—

The moment seemed to slow down, and Gail watched with absolute clarity as the arrow was loosed, rocketing upward and finding a fleshy target. Her leg exploded into the lightning-crackle of pain, and she stumbled forward. She threw her right arm out, trying to find balance, and at the same time, Dirk was in the completely wrong place.

The sound of bandit footsteps played over in her head. The sound that had woken her, and led her to follow the bandits, echoed mercilessly as the blade of her sword slipped in between Dirk's ribs and out the other side. His torso crumpled into her, and he took in a surprised breath that immediately became a cough full of lung blood. His eyes went wide, and he hit the floor.

It was suddenly very silent in the tavern, Gail noticed, though a growing ringing in her ears made her wince. The bowman was staring, slack-jawed, at his compatriot on the floor, his drunken state apparently numbing his ability to process exactly what he was looking at. Crow, too, was in shock, her hand slowly moving to her throat to be sure that it hadn't been sliced in the tousle. Even Lukather was silent, crouched as he was and ready to pounce.

Gail ignored the searing pain in her upper thigh. "Grab your things," she said through heavy breaths. "Quick." She reached down and, swallowing the taste of bile rising in her throat, pulled her sword from Dirk's chest with a sucking sound that made her bones hurt just to hear it. She could feel hot blood running down her leg and she hoped that the veins and arteries had not been severed, because that would mean a death sentence for certain.

The box with a handle and the canvas bag filled with angry feline were in Crow's hand, and she dug with the other hand to find something. Gail kept her eyes on the bowman on the floor, making sure he wasn't going to make any other sudden moves, but he appeared to be paralyzed. He did not dare move.

Crow found what she was looking for, and as she headed for the door she grabbed onto Gail with her free arm. They stumbled out of the tavern together, panting. "Wagon!" she screamed as they broke out into the dazzling sunlight of the town. Dozens of townsfolk turned to look. "I need to hire a wagon! *Fast!*"

Someone was already acting. A nearby carriage driver steered toward them. Whether it was out of a sense of business or understanding of the urgency of the situation, he stopped right in front of the two young women and leapt down to help Gail into the back. "You got money?" he said in a thick accent, pulling a box from under the seat. It was full of bandages.

"Yes, just get us out of here!" Crow climbed in and grabbed a roll of bandage cloth from the box and starting to unroll it. The driver climbed back up and lashed the reins hard just as Lukather bounded in after them.

Gail was trying to stay calm—a difficult proposition with a punctured leg. The bleeding was steady but slow, and the arrow still stuck within appeared to be staunching the flow quite well for the moment. Crow, meanwhile, had trembling hands and heavy breaths that made it clear about her level of panic. "Here," Gail said, taking the bandage. "It's not as bad as it looks. Promise."

"O-okay," Crow said, sitting back and trying to reclaim control of her breathing. Gail examined the wound. The arrow had gone into the skin and emerged out again a few inches around the circumference of her thigh, missing bone by a significant distance and barely impacting muscle. Even more fortunate, the head was not flared, but had been sharpened to a simple fine point.

There was little to do right now in the back of a bumpy carriage. Reaching forward, Gail grabbed Crow's hunting knife right out of the belt and used the serrated edge to cut most of the excess arrow off. She began bandaging around her leg, trying to ignore the hot pain that was crawling across her skin. "It's not bad," she assured Crow, who

21

had gone rather pale as she watched. "Did you get everything?" Crow nodded but said nothing. Gail finished tying the bandage around the wound and leaned back in the seat. "That's all I can do right now. Take a breath, Crow."

Crow shuddered and opened the leather-bound box and removed a set of spectacles, setting them on her face. "Oh god, that's so much better." She turned her gaze onto Gail. "Hey! I can see your face now. You're not just red hair and a sword." She gasped slightly. "Oh my god, you have *freckles*."

Outside, the road they had spent hours walking down was now rushing past, the horses thundering along ahead of them. Gail was entranced by the sight and sound of the things and she concentrated on their tawny and grey manes to get her mind off the wound in her leg. A smile crept over her face as she looked out the front window where the driver was perched, controlling them with a stick lashed with ropes.

"You look like you've never seen horses before," Crow observed. "Where on earth are you from?"

"The mountains," Gail replied absently, still fixated on the powerful creatures in front.

"That doesn't really narrow it down...never mind." Crow closed the box as there was a tap on the window. "Ol' Marty's the name, Ma'am. How far are you going?" The driver asked.

"421 and Raven Rock," Crow called back. "And thank you for being so...um..." she seemed to be searching for the word.

"Johnny-on-the-spot?" Marty grinned a smile full of gold and silver teeth.

"Yes. That."

"Yes'm. It's what I do. You said you had money, by the way..."

"Oh! Right!" Crow set the cat-in-a-bag aside and dug in her pocket, pulling out a pouch. "What do I owe you?"

"Five, normally. Let's call it seven for the fast exit?" He raised his eyebrows a few times for emphasis.

Crow counted some small bronze tubes out of the pouch. She passed them through the window and turned back to Gail.

Gail was eyeing the pouch. It was a faded golden color. "Is that the bandit's money?"

Crow put it away in her bag. "Why would you say that?"

"The bag's not black."

Crow's mouth twitched as though she as trying to suppress a smile. She was unsuccessful, however, and burst out into a few mirthful chuckles. "Alright, you got me. Seemed fair though, didn't it?"

Gail shrugged and looked back out the window. The face of Dirk, with blood running down his face from his lips, was stuck in her mind. She had just left him there. Would someone come to his aid? Would there even be any kind of aid? She tried to tell herself that someone had shown up just after the girls had fled and was even now in the process of stopping the blood and sealing the wound. She looked down as a wet nose poked her in the side. Her eyebrows knitted guiltily. "It was an accident," she told the dog.

Lukather tilted his head. Crow glanced back and forth between the redhead and her sheepdog. "It...I'm sorry that happened—" She opened and closed her mouth without words for a moment and chose to remain silent.

Gail broke their silence after a minute. "I don't like hurting people," she said with more than a little trepidation in her voice, "and I've never killed anyone. At least," she sucked in a trembling breath. "I hope I haven't."

"You haven't," Crow assured. "Town's probably got a doctor fifty feet from the bar. Any town worth anything has at least one because you never know when something will, you know...happen. A fight, or a bandit raid, or the Mori..."

Gail patted Lukather on the head and felt the horse-drawn carriage begin to slow down. They were already arriving back at the intersection. Crow gathered her things as the carriage rolled to a stop. They stepped out, thanking Marty for his help, before easing their way to the barn. Crow threw the door open and helped the redhead to the mattress.

Lukather sat nearby looking calm and quite still, like a furry statue. His only movement was his flaring nostrils and continued glances at Crow, who had begun to search through the boxes of stuff in search of medical supplies. Gail gave the dog a brief smile and began to unwrap her leg and examine the bit of arrow shaft still lodged under the skin.

"I don't have any medical training," Crow was saying, finally locating a box with unreadable markings on it, "but I have a lot of, um, instructions." Crow set the box of supplies on the bed and started unlocking her black leather case—her "tool", Crow had called it. Gail was more than a little curious, and leaned to the side to see what this item might be.

Within the box she glimpsed a pane of glass and a small sea of lettered buttons, all attached to a sleek black base that Crow unfolded to stand up. The sight of it ignited deep feelings of recognition from her very early childhood. "I've seen one of those before," Gail said before she could stop herself. "It's a…um…My mom had one. It's a…" she tried to search for the words.

"It's a computer," Crow said gently, and turned the contraption on.

INTERLUDE: THE INVASION

Shhhhhhhhhhhhhhhhhk. Shhhhhhhhhhhhhhhhhk. Shhhhhhhhhhhhhhhhhk.

Danielle was hardly awake by the time the third digital tone had finished. Rubbing her eyes, she pulled herself up in bed and looked over her husband's shoulder. He was perched, quite still, on the edge of the bed, his eyes fixated on the screen. "Rhwhu—" her question immediately became a yawn, "—going on?"

He didn't say anything. The screen was playing a low digital tone. The screen was blue, with bright yellow text: A PRIMARY ENTRY POINT STATION HAS ISSUED AN EMERGENCY ACTION NOTIFICATION.

"This message has been made by national alert and warning authorities," a voice said in a garbled tone that sounded as if it was being spoken through a loud hallway, "Please stand by for a message."

The message repeated itself. Anthony shrugged. "It's been like this for a little bit. I couldn't sleep and my phone was blowing up. Sorry to wake you."

Dani shrugged, reaching for the shawl near the foot of the bed and wrapping it around her shoulders. "Is it too early for coffee?"

"Never," he said with a peck on her cheek. They both watched the screen repeating its message for a long moment.

She cleared her throat. "I was asking you to make coffee."

"Oh, were you?" he said with a light jab of his elbow, "I thought you were offering."

"And you're not going to be gentlemanly and do it yourself?"

"I'd never want to deprive you of the honor making it, or my eternal gratitude for doing so."

"That almost sounds sexist," She said with a playful grin and moved her feet to the floor, shoving him almost right off the bed. "Fine, I'll go make it, and you'll have the *honor* of…" she whispered something in his ear, "…when I get back." She sauntered out the bedroom door toward the kitchen. A glance in a hall doorway told her that their raven-haired daughter was still fast asleep, and a bleary look at the kitchen clock told her that it was actually probably too early for coffee. But what the hell.

A few minutes later, she returned with a cup of steaming wakefulness in each hand. The screen had finally changed to show the face of a balding, sickened-looking man in a suit. Dani didn't recognize him. "…have not made their demands known as of yet," he was saying, "but we are awaiting the results of the conference with the president. It is advised that you remain indoors at this time."

She offered him the cup but he didn't take it. It was a moment, in the slowly-flickering light of the screen, before she realized how ghastly pale he had suddenly become. The grin she had left on his face was now replaced by utter confusion and the playfulness in her stomach vanished. "What happened?"

He shrugged—a slow, almost mechanical movement as if his brain hadn't quite remembered how to express emotions. "Aliens," he said simply.

She rolled her eyes. "Ah, of course. Here, take your coffee."

He looked up at her, down at the coffee as if he had forgotten what coffee was, and back up to her. "I…sorry, yeah…not joking. Aliens."

She set the coffees down on the bureau next to the small television set. "Wait, seriously? No way."

"They arrived an hour or so ago," he said quietly. "They're already in back rooms with world leaders. They're just…appearing places."

"Appearing?" Dani's fingers were shaking.

The man on the screen was handed a piece of paper. "We have just received word that..." he took a deep breath and tried to retain his composure. "We have received word that the visitors who call themselves the Mori, have made demands to the people of our planet. There will be an address by a world leader within the next four hours. Please be advised to remain indoors at this time."

The screen briefly returned to the Emergency Alert screen before changing back to the local station it had been on. It was playing a late night live infomercial, but the host was standing off to the side of the screen with his mouth agape. Someone mentioned to him that they were back, and the host looked at the camera with a completely blank expression, unable to even form words and leaving the channel in awkward silence.

Dani slowly turned to look at her husband. "It's going to be okay."

Anthony took a deep breath. "I don't...I don't know what we're even supposed to do."

"Stay inside," Dani said with finality. "And we will wait. And we will make sure our daughter is happy and healthy."

Anthony nodded slowly and reached for the cup of coffee. His hands were trembling so much that instead of grabbing the handle, he knocked the cup clean off the table, where it fell to the floor with a thundering crash.

◦

It was almost 6 am by the time the Emergency Broadcast system buzzed across the screen again. Mira was still snoozing soundly in her bed, and Dani had just finished making two bowls of oatmeal that she carried to the bedroom. She had discarded her nightgown within the last few hours, the uncertainty and fear of the early broadcast having let both her and Anthony to decide that—what the hell—they might as well try to work out some of their anxiety together while they still had the chance. They felt a bit less shaken as the second broadcast came on, and gave each other brief encouraging smiles between bites of oatmeal.

"Please stand by for a message from the Prime Minister of the United Kingdom."

"The UK?" Anthony said with furrowed eyebrows. "Not the President?" Dani shrugged.

A moment later the Prime Minister of the United Kingdom was on the screen, looking very calm and resolute. It was a reassuring sight—such a respectable lady in gentle repose, gazing out from the other side of the world. Her audience was, presumably, the entire planet. "The Right Honorable, The Prime Minister of the United Kingdom" blazed at the bottom of the screen.

"Greetings to the people of all nations," the Prime Minister said with soft and reassuring depth to her voice. "This is a broadcast from 10 Downing Street, and is being simulcast on most emergency broadcast systems available in every country in the world."

Anthony set his bowl down carefully, his fingers shaking again.

"At 6:15 AM, Greenwich Mean Time, this morning, the planet which is our home—an incredibly large place populated by billions of people, but in a grand and inconceivably vast universe, only a miniscule grain of sand floating in endless space—was visited by another world. I speak to you today not only as the Prime Minister of the United Kingdom, but as a representative appointed at the request of our guests to serve as a liaison and representative of our planet."

She paused, as if allowing every single viewer a moment to realize that each of them had been holding their breath for the last 30 seconds and needed to breathe and take the last few poignant words in.

"These people who have come to us have traveled here to make a new home. We have met with them with talks of peace between our people. They have agreed."

Around the world, another collective breath was let out. Every person in front of a radio or television felt a simultaneous wave of relief.

"…and have presented certain terms to us which must be met to ensure such peace for the future. We, the people of Earth, have accepted these terms."

That collective breath was again taken back in.

"We recognize the superiority of our new neighbors. In the name of peace—the peace they have offered us—we therefore, the people of Planet Earth…" She paused, the words coming out her mouth having momentarily overwhelmed her, but quickly recovered. "…have surrendered our governance to their authority."

Dani and Anthony looked at each other for a moment. Anthony's mouth still had oatmeal in it but he had stopped chewing.

"We will cooperate with their leaders and meet their demands. Namely…" Her eyes moved slightly, indicating that she was now reading from a card or prompter. "We shall surrender our accursed weapons to them, evacuate the cities which they have claimed as their new colonies, and follow their direction in all matters. In return, we are promised peace and prosperity."

The Prime Minister took in a deep breath. "The cities which the benevolent and revered Mori have chosen as their new homes shall be disseminated soon. They shall soon begin the…" her eyes narrowed as she read the next words carefully. "Ritual of Homecoming to prepare our world for their rule."

The Prime Minister reached the end of the page, and her eyes focused on the camera again. The emotions in her voice were very well-disguised. One could barely even hear the sheer disgust as they left her lips. "They are grateful that we have chosen to cooperate with them, for the alternative was…undesirable."

Tony and Dani looked at each other again, and both knew exactly what was on each other's mind: their daughter, still deeply lost in dream only one room away. She had gone to sleep in one world and would wake up in another. She would grow up without much understanding of what had just transpired. Great decisions had been made in such a short time, by so few people! It was an injustice that made their hearts break. They did not need to communicate their fears to each other; it was simply known between them that the little girl's welfare was the most important thing moving forward.

The broadcast was nearing its end; there was a certain finality in the Prime Minister's last statement before the screen went blank: "People of Earth: be well. We are one people now. Do not despair."

THREE

Gail scraped back and forth across the end of the arrow sticking out of her thigh. One hand was holding the shaft tightly, keeping it from wriggling in the wound and causing even more pain. The pain she was already experiencing was hard to ignore, even if it had been slightly reduced after she had choked down some medicine from inside Crow's medical kit.

Crow was tapping away at her computer, bringing up things that looked like anatomical charts and medical diagrams. Luckily, Crow had explained, the arrow appeared to have missed all of the major arteries entirely. The biggest problem now was that the shaft had pierced the quadricep muscle of Gail's thigh and without an exceptionally careful extraction it might cause a rather awful tear.

After that, it was supposedly a matter of cleaning the wound and applying pressure. Crow's computer had a large library of reference materials and downloaded data, from which she was able to double-check her work in a multitude of medical journals and books.

Gail continued to file the end of the arrow, making sure there were absolutely no burrs on the tip. "How do you even have that at all?" she asked, trying to take her mind off of the painful vibration of the file across the embedded debris. "I thought the Ritual of Homecoming destroyed most computer things."

"Computers, guns, missiles, gas-powered engines," Crow added through gritted teeth. "But for some reason it missed a lot of things. Basically—" Crow held up a grey block of plastic with a silver label on it. "—anything that wasn't on when the ritual went off, especially stuff that runs on batteries like this, had some kind of chance of making it through. Small chance, mind you, but it means that there's a handful of these out there. This thing is worth more than you can possibly imagine. Along with a lot of this stuff." She gestured back at her box of gadgets.

Gail stopped filing and her eyes widened. "All of this stuff *works?*"

"Most of it. A few things still need fixing, but I'm working on it." She returned to her typing.

Gail put the file down and ran her thumb across the top of the filed-off end of the arrow. It was quite smooth. "Another question. That one bandit called you a witch."

Crow snorted. "Yeah, anybody that collects this stuff is a witch. At least, according to the Mori. They think our technology—and science in general—is witchcraft. We're actually kind of a loose confederacy of people that use whatever technology we can find that still works, and we communicate through a delicate radio network called the New Internet." She looked over. "Do you know much about them? The Mori, I mean?"

"I run from them," Gail said instantly, as though it were the most obvious thing in the world.

"Well, sure, of course. They're way too powerful and as far as I know they can't die. But you can *scare* them."

Gail opened a bottle of a foul-smelling liquid—iodine, Crow had said it was—and started brushing it onto the arrow shaft next. "How? They're really powerful. And they have magic."

"It's not magic," Crow said abruptly, and she caught herself and took a mental step backward. "So it's sort of a…it's a…It's *not* magic," she repeated, with a softer but more deliberate tone. "I'm not good at explaining what exactly it *is*, but there's a guy I know who can and I'll have to have him explain it later. But basically: it's *not* magic."

Gail shrugged. "Okay, it's not magic. But how do you scare them?"

"These." Crow gestured to the boxes of gadgets. "The Mori don't understand them. They think they're witchcraft. If you wave something around that lights up and makes a lot of noise, they'll call you a witch and then usually they'll go away. They're really superstitious about that stuff."

Gail was dubious, and had more questions, but there was a far more pressing matter at hand, so she nodded her head and looked down at the arrow. "Okay. What next?"

"Well," Crow said with a grimace, "we need to pull the arrow out and then flush the whole...hole...with clean water. With these." She rummaged in her box of things and produced a bottle of water and a plastic surgical syringe.

The arrow, apparently, had already begun to settle comfortably into its new home, and to attempt to remove it with any amount of gentleness was simply not possible. Crow suggested turning the shaft of the arrow while they pulled, and that finally loosened it from the flesh. Sweat beaded down Gail's face and she let out painful grunts as the arrow finally came free, leaving two holes a few inches apart on her thigh.

Crow filled the syringe with water and, with no lack of trepidation, shot a steady stream that went in one side of the wound and started to dribble out red on the other side. Gail howled again with pain as the water, while cool and clean, irritated the membranes and torn muscle. A few more syringes full, shot into both ends of the wound, cleaned it thoroughly enough that Crow decided it was time to bandage it. This task, comparatively, was easy—the pressure from the bandages gave her thigh a bit of a numb feeling overall and when it was finally secured, she let out a breath that felt like she had been holding it for days.

Crow snapped the medical kit closed. "Okay, best we can do. Now we've got to keep it clean and dry. And by that I mean, making sure the bandage isn't seeping through." Gail gently massaged the bandage.

The pain was very mild. "And don't do *that*," Crow said sharply. Gail pulled her hands away and shifted into a sitting position. "Okay, so…what now?"

"Nothing right now," Crow replied with a sigh. "I have to climb that tower next. I was hoping to do it before noon, but there goes that plan."

"Why do you have to climb the tower?" Gail shifted a little on the mattress to keep from putting too much pressure on the wound.

"I have to fix something, and then I can get a better signal for my computer." Crow snapped her computer shut and moved it into a padded bag. "I don't want you to stress yourself out or anything. You just stay here."

Gail shook her head. "No, no, I can get up. Really. It's not so bad." She tried to stand up to prove her point, and winced slightly as she put her right foot down and straightened up.

Crow's glasses slipped slightly down her nose as she gave Gail a stern look. "You can come over to the tower, but you're not coming up. Doctor's orders."

"You're not a doctor."

"I could be, you don't know," came the acidic reply as Crow swept out of the barn. Gail stood and watched her go. She actually *didn't* know anything about Crow at all, other than the fact that she collected old gadgets and for some reason had a death wish to rebel against the Mori. It wasn't a particularly encouraging image of her new friend.

Lukather sniffed at her bandage and sat down, looking up with a tilted-head gaze. "She could be anyone," Gail said quietly to the dog. "We should probably be cautious. We don't know what she's capable of."

The dog blinked.

"But she *did* help me get back here. And helped me with the arrow. That's a good sign, right? That I can trust her?"

Lukather's ear twitched.

"Well, I'm not very good at trusting anyone. Except you, boy." She patted the dog's head and followed after the departing witch.

"What is it?" Gail asked, looking up at the steel pole with growing curiosity. The top of it was a cluster of grey plates bolted to the top and suspended out a few feet from the center.

"It used to be a cellular tower," Crow explained as she unpacked several ropes, clasps, and pulleys from her bag. "Back before the Mori, you used to be able to connect to a cellular network over radio signals and—" She stopped as she caught a glimpse of Gail nodding but clearly not understanding what was being said. She took a moment to reorganize her explanation into something more palatable. "You used to be able to communicate with people around the world using invisible signals in the air."

The redhead swallowed that morsel of information a little bit better. "So what are they used for now?"

"Well," Crow said, securing one end of the climbing rope to her belt, "it's basically the same concept now, but the signal strength is very weak to keep the Mori from interfering with it. There's a pretty big group of people that maintain these towers, and they communicate with each other through these networks. That's the New Internet I talked about. It's sort of an invisible army." She grinned and gestured upward. "I'm Crow, and this is my Crow's Nest."

Gail didn't seem to acknowledge the pun; her head tilted a little at the final part of the explanation. It was clear, though, that Crow knew what she was doing and was quite pleased with herself.

"Of course," Crow continued, "if the nest gets damaged then the network goes out. So I have to go up there and fix it, and hopefully I can reconnect with everybody and see what the plans are."

"I understand." She didn't understand at all. "Is there anything I can do to help?"

"Well," she said as she began her climb up the short ladder at the base of the obelisk, "you can keep this ladder steady and while I'm up there keep an eye on things." She seemed to remember something and dug in her bag to retrieve a handheld device which she handed to Gail. "Here, if you need to talk to me, hold down this button here. But don't hold it down the whole time. You have to release the button to listen. Got it?"

Gail looked at the device. It was small and black with a black tube sticking out of the end. "I think so. Um…" she tried to look encouraging. "Be safe."

"Always," Crow said, starting her climb upward. At the top of the silver ladder, there was a set of protruding spikes that formed an upward row all the way to the nest. Crow secured herself to a metal wire that was bolted to the side of the pole and began to climb, using the protruding spikes as handholds.

Gail watched her ascend, taking a seat on a nearby upturned bucket, and tried to keep from shivering in the cold. Lukather trotted over and laid down on the ground beside her, nudging her hand in expectation of head scratches.

Her eyes swept the field and she thought about her little detour here. If Crow wasn't lying, whatever she was going to do in the Crow's Nest would allow Crow to look up information about how to find the road. But then what? She was not going to get far on an injured leg, even more so if she was going to do it alone.

The device in her hand made a crackling noise. "Almost to the top," an out-of-breath Crow's voice came from the speaker.

"Be careful," Gail replied, pressing the button down. Up on the tall pole, Crow held out a thumbs-up as she reached the cage at the top. She was hard to see, untangling part of her climbing gear from her belt and pulling herself into the nest area of the pole, before disappearing from sight. "Everything okay?"

"Just fine," Crow replied through heavy breaths. "Okay. Hang tight down there, it's gonna be a while. Now I just gotta…" the device crackled and went quiet again.

Gail took out her sword and examined it. The bandit's blood had caked onto the blade. Dammit! It would need some extra care to clean it now. She touched her fingertips across the flat of the blade, tracing the swirls etches into the surface: a stylized letter "M" and the shape of a coiled serpent.

From her belt pouch she took out a small bottle of oil and a cleaning cloth. As she dabbed the oil cloth on the blade and watched as the rust-colored stains began to lift from the surface, she daydreamed about the first time she had seen this sword. She had been far more frightened then than she was now. But then, as now, this sword was the thing standing between her and certain death out here in the open wastes of the world after the Mori.

It occurred to her that she hadn't really ever looked at this sword up close since it had come into her possession—what, two weeks ago? M's sword. Her stomach twisted a little. In her mind's eye, she pictured him. M—his only name, he had told her. M the runner. The only one who could be trusted never to discard her or sell her off. M the not-easily-caught. M the pain-in-the-ass.

When M had first found her, he might as well have been M the monster. The trees and hills were close around her like a labyrinth, and when she glimpsed him coming down a lightly-trodden path toward her, the shiny sword on his belt and his stocky reinforced jacket made her think he was just a looter or a thug. He was just like the others: wandering around and trying to prey on the weak. She ran from him immediately, but her little-girl feet weren't as coordinated as they could have been, and she became tangled in a branch and hit the ground hard. She yelped, immediately covering her mouth, hoping she hadn't been noticed. It was too late; she could hear the sound of boots moving in.

Then, he was telling her not to be afraid. And his voice was calming. He helped her to her feet and asked if she had been separated from a group, and where her parents were. And when she told him exactly where her parents were, he deflated instantly.

"Well," she could almost hear his voice ringing softly in her head, "you can come join my family. We have enough to share. What's your name?"

"Gail." Crow's voice on the radio startled her from her reverie, and she reached up to click the button.

"Yeah."

"Everything okay down there? I'm almost done." The sky had somehow clouded over while she wasn't paying attention, and as the thick grey blanket swirled above a heavy wind gusted across the field.

"Yeah."

"Anything I need to know? Anything you want to talk about?"

"No."

"You're a lovely conversationalist." The radio went quiet again.

Up above in the nest, Crow was edging her way off the ledge and back onto the ladder. Gail tapped the button nervously. "Please be careful up there…"

Crow began her descent, inching down each rung. Gail slowly stood up, watching and feeling a dull ache in her leg and a tense knot in her shoulders. If Crow started to slip and fall, there would be absolutely nothing the redhead could do about it. So she just continued to watch, her fingers trembling a little bit.

There was a flash of lightning and the sound of thunder that made her jump, and Crow appeared to be startled as well; she stopped climbing for a moment, and adjusted her climbing gear, before collecting herself and resuming her descent. She was almost halfway down now. "Please don't start raining yet," Gail said to no one in particular. Crow came down another few rungs, then a more, then a few more, and as she came to the last few just above the metal ladder, another flash of lightning split the sky. Again, Crow hesitated, but gingerly edged her feet to the top of the leaning ladder.

Gail held the ladder tightly, looking out with concern at the approaching storm. With probably less than a minute to spare, Crow reached the ground and, grabbing Gail under the arm to help support her movements, took off toward the barn. They reached the cover of the roof as another roll of thunder rattled the metal sheets above them. A torrent of rain hammered on it, filling the barn with a sharp din.

Crow grinned. "Made it. Now, we can get some research done!" She practically danced over to a covered piece of furniture and whipped the blanket off to reveal a chair—a plush black leather thing on wheels. She dropped into the chair and, perching her computer on her lap and tapping away at the screen. Lukather stomped in from the outside, the rain having soaked into his fur so as to give him the appearance of a very fuzzy swollen sponge. He stood there and panted with a grin.

Gail limped to the bed and sat down to catch her breath. "What kind of research? You said something big was happening. That millions of people were in danger."

"Exactly. I was trying to get more details when I got cut off." Crow kicked off with her feet and sent the chair rolling across the dirt floor. She stopped in front of the bed and showed Gail her screen. It was mostly blank, with a bit of text displayed. Gail didn't understand exactly what it meant, but Crow pulled a small device out of her pocket which was displaying a short string of numbers. She typed them in, waited for the numbers to change, and typed in the next set.

The screen flashed for a moment and then changed. Lines of text scrolled down the page with a list of names on the right hand side. Gail was transfixed.

Crow looked at her as if expecting her to ask "What is that?" but after a few moments of silence she answered the question anyway. "You probably don't remember the Old Internet, but it was basically a big network where people could communicate with each other from all over the planet. Well…this is all that's left of it. A clustered network of people like me, with computers like this, and a really *really* basic text software. This is the New Internet."

Gail nodded, finding herself able to mostly-parse the explanation. "And you all just…you plan? Against the Mori? How do you know they aren't listening in?"

The witch held up the small number device. "Authentication token. You have to get one from the rest of us, and we don't give them to just anybody. Catch is, you have to check-in regularly, and if you don't, they wipe your authenticator…" the rest of Crow's explanation was rather detailed, and while she didn't really pay attention to the words—something about packets and intervals—Gail watched as Crow's face cycled through a myriad of excited emotions which finally resolved into a look of slight worry. "…and I probably shouldn't have told you all that, but it's immensely interesting and I figure you probably couldn't explain it to anyone else if you tried so it's safe." This was clearly not meant in a rude way, and Gail smiled.

"Well," she replied, "I'm impressed you know so much about it. And to be fair, I didn't even realize all of these things survived at all. I've been living—"

"—in the mountains," Crow said with a raised eyebrow. "Really far out of the way, I guess? Nothing wrong with that, mind you. Keeps you far away from the Mori. It's the same reason I live here."

The sound of the rain stopped with a suddenness that made both of them and the dog jump. Outside, the raindrops had halted in the air, suspended like a sea of tiny diamonds. Crow and Gail looked at each other and immediately understood the significance: the Mori.

Crow glowered. "Well, f—" She tapped a few words into her computer, her fingers scrambling over the keys with a rapid chatter. Gail pulled her sword out again, heaving herself to her feet and listening, straining her ears against the sudden quiet outside. In the distance, she could hear the static sound of rain, and she suspected the Mori had perhaps only stopped the rainfall in the general vicinity. But that general vicinity was far too close for comfort. "Come on," she said, gently tapping Crow's shoulder. "We have to run."

"Two more seconds." Crow was staring at the screen, apparently waiting for a response from the people on the other end of her connection.

Gail limped over to the door and peered around the corner. Through the shining droplets, she could make out a moving form, dazzling and white, stalking toward the barn from across the road. The Mori was already far closer than she usually would ever let herself get to one, and her rapid heartbeat seemed to double in its cadence. "Crow…"

"Got it." Crow snapped her computer shut in its leather case, grabbed a bag and threw some gadgets into it. "Get ready to run when I say, okay? Forty-five. Forty-four."

Gail gritted her teeth. "Why can't we run now?"

"Because," Crow said as if it was the most obvious answer in the world, "then all it will do is chase us. Thirty-nine. Thirty-eight."

Gail remembered Crow's explanation of being a witch. "You're going to scare it off?"

Crow nodded. "Thirty-six. Thirty-five. You have to trust me. Thirty-Three."

"I'm not good at that, you know," Gail whispered to herself. Lukather was suddenly at her feet, his fur still sopping wet. He was staring at the thing in white, which was becoming more and more detailed as the raindrops parted around it. The Mori had made it halfway across the large road to the median, and Gail could see that it was probably a male, judging from the shiny golden beard on its angular face. There was a chance it hadn't spotted them at all. There was a chance it would just pass them by.

Crow took a deep breath and pulled one last gadget from her bag, continuing to count down under her breath. "Get its attention," she said.

"What?"

"Quick. Get its attention. Twenty-six."

Gail let out a frustrated noise and shouted out into the frozen rain. "Hey! You!"

The Mori suddenly moved in a burst of speed, gliding along the surface of the road and over the curb in one smooth movement. Gail could see it approaching, fast, and even Lukather was trembling against her leg. She could see its black eyes and pale, corpse-like face and knew it would be upon her in a moment—

"Stop where you are!" Gail saw the dark, cloaked form of Crow move in front of her, holding something in her hand. It was pink, with

41

a clear star-shaped tip on the end of it. She pressed a button on the side, and the wand lit up with an array of little lights and a high-pitched, musical sound. It was clearly a child's toy.

The Mori stopped. The movement sent a shiver down Gail's spine at how unnatural it was; rather than skidding or stumbling to a halt, it simply stopped as if all of its momentum had simply vanished, but it stood there, its golden hair swirling about its face and looking at Crow with suspicion.

"I am the Witch of Raven Rock!" Crow announced, swirling the toy around her head. "And you are not welcome here! Run while you can!" The Mori growled—an unearthly, echoing sound that made Gail's fingers tingle—and it looked like it might lurch forward and attack, but at that moment Crow pointed the toy at it and cried, "Be gone!"

Then, something incredible happened. The toy made another squealing musical noise, and all at once the rain began to pour again. It slammed into the ground as if it had never stopped at all. The Mori was instantly soaked, and it screamed. It made some motions with its hands, flailing about in the torrential downpour, but its magic appeared to have completely gone.

It turned and ran.

Gail had never seen a Mori run away before. It no longer glided smoothly across the ground. In fact, it stumbled a few times in the way a young child who still had not completely mastered the art of running might do. It was a pitiful sight that quickly vanished into the sheets of rain.

Crow took a deep breath and put her toy wand away and gazed around the barn that had all of her personal effects. "That'll keep it away for a bit. At least long enough to get out of here. We're leaving. Because they might come back with hunters."

Gail stammered, not completely able to articulate words. She was able to get out "…what?" and hoped that summed everything up.

"I will explain. But right now we have to leave."

Gail furrowed her eyebrows. "We?"

The witch stopped and considered her for a moment. "Yes. We. If you want to. If you don't want to, then that's fine too…but you're going to get soaked as shit. And if I'm honest I could really use backup where I'm going."

"Where?"

Crow picked up her bag and handed Gail a roll of wide, grey tape. "Here, tape this over your bandages. As for where…You're looking for I-95, right?"

The tape unrolled easily and Gail wrapped it tight, securing it to the skin in a way that looked pretty waterproof, if she said so herself. "Right."

"Okay, come with me then, and you can figure out if you want to stay with me once we get there."

Gail looked down at Lukather, back at Crow and around the barn which had been so cozy just a little bit ago. Now, it was suddenly an unsafe place and they would have to flee. "Okay."

They covered most of the boxes of gadgets in a tarp and stuffed them into a back corner. Crow packed up a backpack full of necessities and produced an umbrella. They left, huddled together under the umbrella, and started off down the wide and empty highway away from the crossroads. Outside, the rainfall had already begun to wane, and Crow expressed her hope that it would be sunshine again within an hour or so. And that, hopefully, the Mori would not follow.

FOUR

"Okay, so how'd you do it?" The pain in Gail's leg was starting to subside a bit. She had been able to lean on the umbrella for a little while since the rain had stopped. At that point they had stopped to change Gail's bandage, which had already seeped through with blood. Crow assured her that this was normal.

"Do what?" Crow was being exceptionally smug. Gail's ignorance about a plethora of subjects brightened her friend's mood a little bit because it gave her things to talk about and explain. Or maybe it gave her a feeling of satisfaction or superiority. On the other hand, Gail thought, it also made her look like a major asshole.

"You know what I'm talking about." Gail probably didn't mean the words to come out so gruffly, but there it was.

Crow rolled her eyes. "Alright, so some of us in the resistance discovered that the Mori technology—"

"—the Magic?"

"—the *technology*," Crow insisted, "gets disrupted by certain kinds of radio waves. It only works for a little while and the range isn't that good, and you need a massive transmitter—like the Crow's nest," she added. Gail nodded. "and since we make it a habit of adding any cell

44

towers we reactivate to our network, it means that a handful of us can actually control them and make them emit this anti-Mori-tech sound."

Gail nodded again, hoping Crow didn't get into the technical specifics. "I think I understand. So you can control it at a distance?"

"Unfortunately no—at least, not yet," Crow said with a tinge of disappointment in her voice. "but what I did is tell the people online where I was, and that I was going to scare one of them off. I asked if they would wait 60 seconds and then send the signal from my tower."

"That's why you were counting!" Gail smiled. "You were literally counting down the seconds until the…the…thing went off. And it turned off the Mori's power."

"Exactly." If it was possible to look even more smug than before, Crow did so. "Wave of the wand, yell a few words, and *bam*. The Mori thinks you're a witch, and he runs." Lukather let out a wide yawn as he trotted along next to Crow. "Nobody asked you," she chided.

Up ahead they again saw the rusting sign for Lillington, the town where they had caused such a ruckus before. Gail was nervous about returning to the tavern, for fear that she might learn of the fate of the young man who she had impaled on her sword. Of course, she might discover that he was quickly saved from death, but the more likely scenario, she reasoned based on the severity of the wound, was that he was dead. Somehow, the idea that she might discover the truth was more frightening to her than simply dreading the consequences of her actions—as though by living in a limbo between what she feared and what had really happened she was somehow absolved of guilt.

Lillington, however, was far quieter this time around. No one shouted from windows or waved flags to get their attention. In fact, there was no one in sight at all.

Crow slowed her pace as she approached the edge of town. "Do you think…?" She didn't need to finish her sentence. Gail knew that she suspected the appearance of the Mori earlier had put them all to flight or into hiding.

"Do you want to stop here?" Gail asked. "We can just as easily move on. Especially if you're afraid the Mori might come back."

"That's fair." Crow stood there, taking in the vision of the quiet, empty town, and considered her options. "I mean, for all I know everybody's just hiding somewhere and they'll come back. But we don't particularly *need* anything here either."

Gail sat down for a moment to rest her leg and they had what felt like a silent conversation, glancing at each other and around at the empty street, for a few minutes. Then, as if they had come to an agreement without words, Gail rose and they started off through town without another word.

Without the hustle and bustle of commerce in the town, it was far easier to focus on their surroundings. The buildings on either side, despite their crumbling state, were still beautiful to behold in their own way. The names of places that once were, and were no longer, flanked their steps.

As they reached a big intersection in the middle of town, they stopped to rest beneath the awning of a two-story faded grey building bearing the sign "Buzzard Law Firm" in large black letters bolted to the brick. Gail removed the tape from her thigh and changed the bandages beneath, examining her arrow wound. She found, thankfully, that it had remained clean despite the mud. Crow offered a container of some kind of medical ointment of which she applied a small amount to both the entrance and the exit wound before re-wrapping her leg in a clean part of the bandage.

"Have you eaten recently?" Crow asked as Gail finished securing the linen strip around her thigh.

"Yesterday."

"Okay, here." Crow passed over a bar of something wrapped in a faded wrapper. She unwrapped it, and within was a block of some sticky, crumbly stuff packed tightly into an edible thing. "They're safe to eat, I promise," she said, taking a bite of an identical bar. "Grains and nuts and stuff. It basically doesn't go bad if you keep it well."

Gail wasn't entirely sure that was true, but Crow's confidence in the matter, not to mention her own stomach, outweighed her doubts. She took a bite. It tasted salty and sweet and also kind of ashy, like chewing on a piece of burned wood covered in honey. "I don't know why that Mori came all the way out here in the first place," she wondered aloud.

"Exploring, I think," Crow replied. She had already practically wolfed down her own food bar and was opening the water canteen. "They keep expanding out. From what I hear, their cities are getting more populated and they need room to expand."

"That's not what we agreed to, though."

"Exactly. We agreed to give them a bunch of cities, and in return we all would be permitted to live everywhere else. Which is unfair enough on its own, but now they're trying to encroach outward even more. It's messed up—hey. Don't you dare put that food bar in your pocket." Crow was suddenly scowling.

Gail stammered. "But…but what if we—" She tried to express into words why exactly she was hiding the food away.

"I have more food bars, *Necia*. Eat the damn thing before I sock you." Gail quickly obeyed, unwrapping the rest of the bar and taking a few bites quietly. Crow watched her. "I don't really get you yet, girl. And I mean, I figure you're good people because you saved my life, but I don't really…I don't really *get* you. Where are you from? Why are you traveling by yourself?"

"I'm not by myself." She glanced at Lukather, who took this as a cue to immediately drop into the mud and roll around in it.

"The dog doesn't count. Where's your family? Do you have a traveling group?"

"My parents are dead," she said after a moment of thought. "And I…I had a friend. But he's dead now, too." She looked down at the food bar in her hands. "He's the reason I'm looking for that road. He told me to follow it but I don't know why."

Crow nodded and seemed to be debating her next words carefully in her head. "Okay, so when you lived in the mountains, did you live with your friend?"

"No. Well, sort of. He was part of a group. He would come by and check on me at my house in the mountains, but he didn't ever really stay long."

Crow brushed some dust off of her pants. "Okay, that's something. What did the group do?"

"They robbed people." Gail swallowed the last of the food bar.

Crow stiffened. "Okay, so you're bandit. Great. I have the best judgement of character, apparently."

The redhead bristled. "I'm not a bandit. I never robbed anyone. I just…I just kept to myself."

"But you used supplies your 'friend' gave you," Crow pressed, "You know where those supplies came from. You're complicit." Her face was sour all of a sudden, and Gail stammered out confused and apologetic sounds that had no words attached to them. There was a tense moment, and Crow was narrowing her eyes and opening her mouth to say something when suddenly Lukather rolled to his feet and barked.

They both looked. It was hard to tell what exactly Lukather had seen at first, but Crow, too, had noticed it. "What is that?"

Gail hoisted herself up with the help of the umbrella, and they headed northward. A block or so north, a set of steel tracks crossed a hill running east to west. The crossing was still in use, it appeared—the power of steam apparently still a viable option for locomotion—and on the tracks a single figure stood, unmoving.

At first glance it might have been a junkyard statue of some kind, Gail thought. Standing slightly over her own height and covered in green and black plates, it appeared to be a suit of armor fitted with all sorts of gadgets and wires. The person inside was completely encapsulated, and the letters "USMC" were stamped on the left arm plate beneath a striped flag that Gail was sure she had seen before.

"Whoa," Crow said, taking a step forward and examining the armor, "this is some awesome military stuff. I wonder what it's doing out here. Has it been here this whole time?" Gail looked at the dust and dirt, and gestured to a set of faint, but visible, footprints. Crow's eyes went wide. "No way. No way that this thing still works. Do you think there's a person inside or that it's some kind of automated thing?"

Gail gave her a look of scorn, as if to remind her that of all of the people who might have had an inkling of an answer to that question, she was not one of them.

"Right. Sorry." She moved to the back of the armor and looked at some of the plates and wires on the back. "Whoa," she said again, "this thing has a massive battery. Like, military-grade. And it looks kind of…hacked together…" She looked down the street and spotted a tall, fading sign. "Hey look, a junkyard. I bet we can grab a new battery. Maybe we can turn it back on."

"That sounds like a bad idea." Gail's voice was nearly a whisper.

Crow shrugged. "If there's a person inside, I'd love to get them out. If it's automated, maybe it can help us. As much as I hate wasting time…" Crow didn't wait for any further objections before turning and jogging down the road toward the junkyard. Gail watched her go and debated not following at all, because a moment ago she was sure Crow was about to completely lose her cool.

It wasn't her fault M was a thief. He did what he had to do to get by, and sometimes doing something that was *legally* objectionable was necessary when the alternative was *morally* objectionable.

M killed people. Gail knew that much. He told her so, late one afternoon a few summers ago, when she spotted a rust-colored stain on his boot that he had apparently forgotten to clean off. She had asked him directly if he had ever killed people, and he didn't deny it. He did tell her, however, that he only killed people when it was necessary to protect someone else.

"Or yourself?" Gail had asked, pulling a few stray locks of red hair out of her face. M once told her that when she was mad she looked like a volcano spewing lava.

"No," M replied simply. "My life has little value. Other people…like you. That's a different story."

Gail stopped, her mouth hanging open in shock. "Did you kill someone to protect me?"

M didn't answer.

⌂

The "junkyard" turned out to be a small concrete lake of vehicles, lined up in rows like soldiers. Each one was busted or damaged or faded over a decade and a half of disuse; even so, a few vehicles under a rusty but still-standing canopy appeared mostly intact, despite the fact that the Ritual of Homecoming had destroyed a lot of their internal parts.

Gail found Crow next to a big green vehicle. She had popped the hood and was now touching various internal parts with a metal probe. "Nope, this one's dead too. I don't know much about car batteries and how long they last." Crow moved onto the next vehicle, opened its hood, and continued probing. Gail sidled up behind her.

"Can I—"

"No."

The redhead took a deep breath and clicked her tongue. "Come on Lukather. We're going." She turned, walking back toward the road and stopping at the curb, trying to figure out which way to go. Finally picking a direction, she started heading back towards Lillington.

"Wait!" Crow was scrambling to catch up. "Wait, wait, wait. Stop, Hang on."

"What?" Gail rounded. "I don't even *know* you. And you're being really…really…" her words were acid.

Crow put out her hands. "You're right, sorry. I'm in a bad mood. I'm hungry and tired and I'm very easily distracted, okay? Just…give me a second here." Crow dropped into a sitting position on the curb.

Gail tapped her foot. "You keep asking me all these things about me, and you've told me pretty much nothing except that you're rebelling against the Mori and that *millions of people will die* and you haven't told me why. And then you don't really tell me anything, and you keep telling me that you'll explain later, and your explanations are really hard to follow and—" she took in a breath as she realized she hadn't inhaled, "—and I am already pretty alone out here and my only *person* friend in the world is dead and I really don't want a reason to not like you anymore, okay?"

Crow was gazing up at her with astonishment. "You…that was a lot of words."

Gail put her hands on her hips and said nothing else.

"Okay, I understand. I'm not so good with people either, in case you didn't notice. My stupid mouth gets me in trouble. So…alright. Let's do this, okay? It's afternoon. I would *really* like to take a nap. Let's find a house, get some sleep and maybe some food, and then I'll fill you in."

"And we're still going to the road I'm looking for."

"Yes, we're still going to the road you're looking for." Gail nodded and offered her hand; Crow took it and stood up. "Okay. Small town, but plenty of houses."

"We don't know if the townsfolk ran or if the Mori killed them."

Crow licked her upper lip in thought. "Well, I can have hope that they saw the Mori and ran. All of them. At once. But realistically…" She let the sentence trail off and Gail grimaced. "But anyway, I saw a street back that way that looked like it led to houses. Let's go."

They walked back across the tracks and stopped at the suit of armor. As a last ditch effort Crow tried for a few minutes to see if there was some kind of release switch but none could be found, and as there was no further indication that anyone was in distress underneath the green and black metal plates, they abandoned it and headed down a side road.

They passed a lot full of faded yellow vehicles which were quickly replaced by trees. After a few minutes the right side led to a driveway, with a red brick house perched at the top of a small hill. Crow had said surprisingly little, but Gail did not press her to speak. Instead, Gail led the way up the driveway to the house and, with sword drawn, gently knocked on the door. There was no answer.

"Is it unlocked?" Crow said under her breath, and she reached out to grasp the door handle. It opened with a click.

Inside, the house was dark but clean. The walls were a stained wood paneling, and the floor was hardwood that had frayed rugs scattered here and there along with a mismatched couch and loveseat. Farther into the house, the living room spilled into an open dining room with a table and chairs, and beyond that, a kitchen.

Crow walked straight through the living room and foyer to the kitchen without stopping. There, several jars of marmalade sat on the counter. Gail was inspecting them when Crow opened a north-facing door and exclaimed, "Oh, nice!"

"What is it?" Gail sidled up behind her. Behind this door was a pantry with a strange, wrinkled metal wall. The air from inside the room was noticeably colder than the rest of the kitchen.

"It's a cool pantry. They sort of became the rage when everyone's refrigerators went out—" She caught a glimpse of a scowl from Gail. "—I mean, it's for keeping food fresh for a few days. And since it's pretty cool outside, there's probably good stuff in here, assuming someone was here today…" She considered the pantry for a moment and flashed Gail a smile. "So we'll assume that everyone's fine and that they're coming back. We'll take a little bit with us but leave the rest."

The younger girl brightened considerably and nodded. Crow began to pick up some of the fruits and vegetables on the shelf, along with what looked a lot like salted pork. A few minutes later, they had settled themselves at the table and Crow was munching her way through some plums and a potato that she unabashedly ate raw.

Gail stared at her and picked through an apricot. She wasn't particularly hungry.

"Please eat," Crow pleaded. "If you don't you're going to get sick. There's a thing called scurvy and it's really bad."

"My friend told me about that one. He used to bring me these weird bags of juice. And later, bottles."

"Your bandit friend?" Crow probably didn't mean to sound so cynical.

"You know," Gail said after a pause, her eyebrows raised and with a tone of voice delicate enough to stroke the wings of a butterfly, "if they are coming back, then we just stole from them." Crow stopped chewing and looked down at her fingers, now covered in plum juice. "You say you don't 'get' me," Gail continued, starting to peel the skin from an apricot, "but you seem to really hate thieves. Then, you stole a bag of money—"

"They stole my stuff first!"

"—not the point." Gail repeated something M used to say: "We're all thieves. The trick is to not be an asshole, too."

Crow was stunned into silence, and spent the next few minutes avoiding Gail's gaze as she finished her plate of plums and wiped her face on a nearby rag. She stood up and took the garbage to the kitchen to dispose of it. When she returned, she seemed to have pulled herself out of her own thoughts. "Again, I'm sorry. I have a bad history with being robbed and mugged a *lot* because I have valuable things. So I'm sorry. I shouldn't be judging anybody for what they do these days because everyone's lives suck. Not just mine. I guess I somehow forgot that, okay?"

Gail gave her a smile. "Okay. Friends?"

The word stopped Crow in her tracks and made her head tilt back as if Gail had just shouted at her. It was clear she hadn't decided yet whether or not the redheaded wanderer and her goofy dog could be trusted, but after a moment her shoulders untensed and the witch grinned. "Yeah. Friends."

⌂

"Gail!" Crow's excited voice came from downstairs. Gail turned away from the mantelpiece, where she had been examining the faded and framed photographs resting there. Each was of someone's children—the original homeowners, or the current one's, it was impossible to say—and were of happy times: children in the park, a family in front of an impossibly large building, a family in front of a mountain with four faces on it. It had given Gail a sinking feeling in her stomach to look at these moments frozen in time, as the realization hit her that, no matter what happened, she would not get these kinds of moments with her own family. Even if the Mori were to leave the planet tomorrow, her parents would still be dead.

She headed down the stairs into the basement of the house, Lukather in tow. Here, in the gloom that was barely illuminated by a basement window streaming in the last dregs of evening light, Crow had discovered a large square basin filled with water. The contraption had been heavily-modified with extra tubes and pipes, but Crow seemed to already know what to do with it. She was rapidly turning nozzles. "They have a bath. A steam-powered bath! We can take a bath." She grabbed Gail by the front of her shirt. "I can take a bath!"

Gail couldn't help but smile as Crow returned to the dials, allowing steam that was connected from somewhere to fill the pipes with a hiss. "I used to use a hot spring," she said. "It was nice."

"Ooh, a hot spring." The idea made Crow shiver. "That sounds good too. Some towns have a big spa or showers or something. One of the things I hate about this place is that I only get a shower when it rains." The water had started to bubble as jets of steam were forced into the pipes. "Okay, now we just let that warm up. You're not a prude, are you?"

"A what?" Gail cocked her head to the side.

Crow gestured to the water. "The bath's big enough for the two of us. I don't know how long the steam will last."

"Right." Gail still hadn't caught on to the question.

Crow lifted her shirt a little. "I'm going to get *undressed*. Does that bother you?"

"No. Why?"

"Okay then." She shrugged and started to remove layer after layer of black clothing: cloak, shirt, pants, even black long underwear. Then, with a stretch and a bend, she climbed into the water and let out a deep sigh and a string of curse words under her breath.

Gail tilted her head in a manner highly reminiscent of the sheepdog at her feet. "That good, huh?"

Crow opened one eye and gave her a look of mock annoyance. "No, it's terrible. You joining me or are you going to sit there and stink in your own sweat?"

Gail disrobed, folding her clothes and setting them off to the side. She unwrapped her bandage and looked from the wound to the water. "Do you think the water's clean enough? I don't want this to get infected."

"Hmm? Oh right. Uh…" Crow shrugged. "We'll make sure to clean it again once you're out." Gail nodded her assent before climbing into the water. It was warmer than she had expected; she let out an involuntary sound, like a puppy whose tail had been trodden on, as the water rushed over her thigh wound. It only took a moment or two to become accustomed to it, though, and she sank down into the opposite side of the basin.

"My grandma used to have something like this," Crow said with a dreamy tone to her voice. "It was good for her arthritis or something, but it was also just…awesome to sit in. Also it was electric, of course."

Gail nodded and leaned her head back to look at the ceiling. "It must have been nice back then. All of your old magic."

"My what?" Crow chuckled through half-awake bleariness.

"Your old magic. Computer things. Elect…rity."

Crow lifted her head. "It's not magic. It's just science."

Gail closed her eyes. "What's the difference?" She could almost feel the look of scorn from across the tub.

"Magic is stuff that's not explainable," Crow said with enough condescension that it might cause the water temperature to rise a few degrees, "and it *doesn't* exist. Science is explainable. It's testable." She reached over and turned the valve, making the steam jets stop and eliciting some clunking noises from the pipes.

"The things the Mori do," Gail replied, sinking slightly deeper into the water, "can you explain them?"

"Well, *I* can't, no, but—"

"Then it's magic."

Crow considered her for a long time before laying her head back again. "I...am too tired to argue with you."

A long silence descended between them. Gail was sure, from the lack of conversation, that Crow had fallen asleep on the far side of the tub, and after a little while she slipped out of the water and began to dry herself with a towel hanging on the wall nearby. She took particular care at handling the wound on her leg, and after another application of the ointment she headed upstairs. A bathroom closet in the house furnished a first aid kit with fresh bandages for which the mountain girl was grateful, and when she finished, she came back into the living room to snag a glance at Crow's long black cloak disappearing up the stairs with a sleepy "Dibs on the biggest bedroom. Night!"

Gail stood there in the living room with Lukather, who was gazing up at her in expectation of what to do next. She considered following Crow upstairs to find another bedroom, but as she looked around she spied the brown plaid couch and dropped onto it without a word. It was the most comfortable thing she could ever remember sleeping on.

FIVE

Gail didn't expect to dream of M. She didn't expect to dream of anything, to be honest, as tired and sore as she was. Nights of tired soreness tended to be harbingers of dreamless sleep, in her experience. In her experience, the fact that one knew that they were dreaming was a rare gift in itself.

Even aware that this was a dream, she was frightened. Her body didn't give any of the outward signs of it—no trembling fingers or worried creases across her face, or heavy breaths. But inside, she felt a frantic need to run.

M was there. He was there exactly where she had last seen him: walking down the trail away from her treehouse and whistling a happy tune, his shoulders back and his gait practically a skip and a dance.

Gail's mountain retreat was well-hidden, she was proud to say. M had selected it for her because, from the main paths down the mountain, it was particularly difficult to find. From the main path, as it curved around a rocky bend, the trail ended in a steep drop-off straight down the mountainside. In reality, though, if a person were to go and investigate, they would find that there was a ledge slightly below. A person could climb down to it, walk around a jutting boulder, and find a small space between two rocks that led to a tiny space and an overhanging rock fixture where the house was situated. It was a tiny home where a child, and later a young woman, might be able to make a cozy home. It was a place where M would meet her, and teach her things. How to read. How to fight. How to talk in M's secret silent code with her hands. How to forage and how to identify dangerous plants and animals.

M had given it to her when she was young. He told her that if she ever heard someone coming, she should stay quiet and duck behind rocks and escape out the back side of the house and vanish into the woods.

Gail watched herself, a few weeks younger than now, as she waved good-bye to M after he had dropped off a box of supplies. He had invited her to dinner down with the other people in his traveling band later in the afternoon. He said he would see her soon.

The Gail who was watching—the real Gail, if the concept made sense in this dream world—watched and screamed out to M. She tried to tell him that two Mori scouts were coming up the mountain path, looking for a way to alleviate their divine boredom.

But the M in the dream heard nothing, and vanished down the path—

—and Gail woke, feeling hot tears in her eyes. Lukather was awake, too, and immediately upon seeing her distress he began to lick emphatically at her cheek.

Gail scratched his ears and patted his head. They both stopped, however, at the same instant as the sound of footsteps echoed from the other side of the front door. Lukather rolled off the couch and sat with his ears alert, staring at the front window, while Gail tried to make herself as invisible as possible.

Something was outside. Something glowing, she noticed, since she could see the shifting shadows across the ceiling as whatever it was moved in the front yard. She rolled from the couch, landing without a sound on the hardwood and rugs. Hand-over-hand, she crawled toward the stairs and, once out of view of the front window, scampered up toward the bedrooms.

Crow was sprawled out in an entirely undignified fashion across the down comforter, completely lost in dream. Gail looked at her for a moment and moved to the bedroom window, sidling up to the edge of it. She peered around the windowsill and into the front yard.

The armor, previously frozen on the train tracks, was moving around in the front yard. It had a dim red light on its shoulder that was softly blinking as it moved, methodically, across the yard and toward the front door. Gail stepped backward toward the bed, and gently tapped Crow. The witch let out a snort from the back of her throat. Gail tapped her again with increased urgency.

"Whaaaaat is it?" Crow said without opening her eyes.

Gail shushed her. "The armor is alive and it's outside."

"What?" Crow was alert and on her feet almost instantly. "What? How?" Gail opened her mouth— "No, it's not magic," Crow added, and stalked to the window. The armor had made its way to the door, just barely visible in the moonlight. "It might try and force its way inside…"

It knocked.

Gail and Crow both look at each other, and out the window again. The armor was waiting, unmoving, at the door. A few long moments passed and it raised its arm to knock again.

"What do we do?" Gail said, edge rising in her voice.

"No idea. The Mori sometimes reanimate our technology to do things. I bet that's what this is."

"But why is it here?"

"No idea." Crow watched with narrowed eyes as the armor stepped away from the door and out into the yard. It looked downward at the muddy front lawn and started to move its hand across the dirt. "It's writing in the dirt. Hang on. H….E…L…oh no."

Gail peeked over the windowsill. "HELP" was written clearly on the dirt, and the armor was now like a statue again, facing the house. "It needs our help."

"It's a trap, Necia."

"It might not be."

"It is. It's a Mori trap."

"Hang on, what did you call me?"

"Necia. It means 'stubborn girl'—but *not now*, Gail—"

The armor was back at the door and knocked again. It turned, walked back to the mud, and started writing again.

"P…" Gail read out under her breath, "L…E…A…It's writing 'please'. Come on, Crow, we have to at least check."

They stared at each other across the dim light of the window. Crow, dressed all in black, was practically a floating angry head.

"If I ran from everybody who might be a threat," Gail whispered with a sour look, "then there would be a metal pole not far from here with a dead Crow on it."

The words made Crow recoil and she rolled her eyes. "You are really, *really* unfair. This is a completely different situation."

Gail straightened up. "Then stay here." She backed away from the window and headed down the stairs. Drawing M's sword from its scabbard, she approached the door. "Who's there?" She demanded through the panel of wood and glass.

The armor didn't respond. Through the glass pane, Gail saw it raise a hand and wave hello.

"Who are you?" she demanded, putting as much force behind the words as she could.

The armor again didn't respond. Its shoulder light flashed a few times as if it was losing power or the bulb was burning out.

"Are you armed?"

The armor didn't move. Its light blinked again.

"It's trying to talk to us," came Crow's voice from over Gail's shoulder. The redhead hadn't heard her come down the stairs. "Morse code. I think." She raised her voice. "I don't know Morse Code, okay? So blink once for yes and twice for no. Do you understand?"

A pause, then—*blink*.

"Are you here to hurt us?"

Blink blink.

"Are you here to make us leave?"

Blink blink.

"Are you armed?" Gail repeated.

Blink.

"I can disable you remotely," Crow said with boundless confidence, "so if you try anything I will disable your power source immediately and use you for spare parts. Do you understand?"

"You can?" Gail hissed.

"No," came Crow's voice in her ear. "Shut up."

Blink, came the reply.

"Okay," Crow breathed. "Open the door."

The door made a horrendous creak and moonlight streamed into the living room, illuminating the suit of armor in an unearthly glow. The only detail visible was a blazon across the shoulder: *U.S.M.C.*

Crow gave a dubious look. "You're a U.S. Marine."

Blink.

It moved deliberately, cautiously, as it fumbled with something on its belt. The armor held it aloft, and revealed a box of plastic, with numerous brightly-colored buttons on it. Gail could see the full alphabet, numbers, and a few other buttons. A label proudly designated the device a "Type-N'-Talk".

Gail and Crow looked at each other and back at it. The armored creature held out a finger and pushed a button. No sound came out. Crow looked down at the device. "It's broken?"

Blink.

"Is this how you communicate?"

Blink.

"And you want me to fix it?"

Blink.

Crow gestured to the letters. "Do you have a name, Marine?"

The armor put his fingers on a few of the useless buttons. N-I-C-K. Then, perhaps on a whim, he raised his right hand and made gestures with his gloved fingers.

Gail gasped. M's silent code! She sheathed her sword and made a gesture with her hands the way she had been taught. "Do you understand me?" She signed.

Nick looked at her for a long moment and held up his right hand, making a knocking gesture: "Yes."

Crow looked back and forth between the two of them. "Okay, okay, everybody hang on just a second here. You—" she pointed at Nick, "—are a suit of military power armor with no ability to speak, and you—" she pointed at Gail, "—are a mountain hermit that doesn't even know what a computer is, but you can speak *sign language?*" She threw up her hands in defeat. "What is my life right now?"

Gail had no reply. Nick offered Crow the Type-N'-Talk again and Crow took it. "Can she fix this?" he asked with deft hand movements. Gail translated.

"Maybe?" Crow turned the thing over in her hands, squinting in the darkness. "But not right now, it's too dark. This is gonna sound really rude, armor-guy, but can this wait until morning? It's kind of the middle of the night."

Nick didn't reply. Gail wasn't sure if it was possible for an emotionless suit of armor to look deflated, but in the light the armored man had an air of disappointment.

"Hey," Gail offered suddenly, "you said you were armed. Can you keep watch for us until morning? Then Crow can fix your magic box."

"It's not—" Crow stopped herself from speaking too loud and took a deep breath. "But yeah, that's actually a pretty good idea. You keep guard out here, and I'll fix your thing if I can. Deal?"

Nick offered his hand. Crow shook it before taking a hold of the door handle. "Okay, good. Good night." She snapped the door closed and glared at Gail, opening her mouth a few times wordlessly. Finally, she found nothing of the slightest usefulness to say, and she dropped her shoulders. "Great. Random armored stranger is keeping watch. I don't even—I just can't even. I'm going back to bed."

Gail smiled at her. She didn't mean to look smug. Or maybe she did, just a little. "Good night!"

Crow said something unintelligible as she stomped back up the stairs.

SIX

"Get off of me, you dumb dog!"

The shouting woke Gail, and she sat up and rubbed her head. She was curled up on the floor of the upstairs bedroom. Light was pouring in through the front window, throwing the whole room into a tangle of shadows and glows as it filtered through the trees in the front yard. Lukather, meanwhile, had bounded up onto the bed and was currently licking Crow's face "Gail! Come get your—stupid dog—" She dove under the cover to hide.

Gail laughed and patted the floor beside her. The sheepdog dropped from the comforter and onto the floor beside her. Gail looked around; she was on the floor in the upstairs bedroom. How had she gotten here? And when? "Uh…morning?"

"Morning," Crow replied with the voice of someone who wanted to snuff out the sun and go back to sleep. "Guess it's time to get up and go."

"You have to fix Nick's box first." Gail pulled herself to her feet. She had discarded her pants somewhere in the night, probably from the humidity of the evening. She pulled them back on.

"Oh, right. Him." Crow stretched, pulled on her cloak, and trudged across the floor to the stairs with Gail falling in behind. "Hey! Robot boy! Are you still out there?"

He was. Nick had barely moved; he stood with his arms behind his back, his right hand loosely grasped by his left. Crow eased the door open, looking the armored Marine up and down. "Hey. You." He turned to face her. Crow stiffened a little at his gaze—if the blank look of his helmet could even really be called a gaze—and she stepped aside. "Come in or something."

He stalked into the living room and gestured to the couch. Crow nodded, and he took great care as he settled himself onto the antique furniture. When he had almost completely put his weight on it, the couch let out a worrisome creak and he stood back up again.

Crow, meanwhile, picked up her backpack from near the door and rifled through it until she found a small tool kit. Taking the Type-N'-Talk and the tool kit to the dining room table, she proceeded to perform a surgical procedure on plastic box, removing pieces one at a time and inspecting them. A few she cleaned with a tiny cloth. Each piece was sorted methodically into rows on the table.

"Thank you," Gail signed to Nick, sitting down on the couch to put her boots back on.

"You're welcome," he replied. "I didn't know the—" He made an unfamiliar sign, "—had come through."

She repeated the unfamiliar sign questioningly. It was like the sign for "crown", but the fingers, instead of resting gently on the sides of the head, were curled up menacingly.

"Mori," he lettered the word. He followed this with the signs for "Crown", "Monster" and then the new sign again. The clear implication was that the Mori were the "Kings of Monsters". Gail nodded.

"We aren't sure if the people ran away or if the Mori killed them," she signed.

He didn't reply for a moment. "Do you live here?"

"No, I'm just passing through with her." She gestured to Crow.

"Leaving soon?"

She nodded.

He was unresponsive again for a minute. "The people will probably be back." Gail knew he was lying, but seeing the words made her feel a little better. She got up and headed to the kitchen to see if the homeowners might have something she could dig into for breakfast. She found a box on the counter stamped with an unfamiliar sigil and the letters "DOTE". Within, she found practically brand-new packages of several expensive commodities, including— "Hey, Crow, there's coffee in here, do you—"

"For the love of god, yes. And I'll forgive you that you even had to ask that question."

Oh, coffee. M drank a lot of coffee, she recalled, and he had taken particular care to explain in a particularly haughty manner exactly how to brew the perfect cup. This house, unfortunately, lacked several of the silly-shaped pieces of equipment that M had owned, but she did locate a porcelain pour-over funnel and a few mugs. She found a match and lit a fire on the wood stove. She was surprised to find that the sink faucet had running water, but she recognized that whether that water was drinkable was an entirely different matter altogether, and she collected some to boil it.

"EIGHT." came the sound of a croaky digital voice from the dining room. "EIGHT. EIGHT. EIGHTEIGHTEIGHT."

"Well, that's promising," Crow mumbled, and started her reassembly of the device. "You had dirt in a few places dirt shouldn't be. Nothing corroded, so that's good." She screwed a few pieces back together. Gail came in from the kitchen with a cup of black liquid in a mug. Crow gulped it down without hesitation and a satisfied sound erupted from the back of her throat. "That's awesome. Today is going to be a good day."

"I hope so," Gail said, sipping her own mug. The taste was alright, but she was sure M would have considered it unsatisfactory. She looked over to Nick. "Can you drink coffee?"

He held up his arm and tapped his thumb and two forefingers together on that hand: "No."

"Are you stuck in there?" Crow said, narrowing her eyes at him. He nodded. "For how long?"

He didn't reply. Crow grumbled and finished snapping and screwing the last piece of plastic on the device. "Alright, it's all fixed," She said, standing up. "Now—"

"We're looking for a road," Gail said, picking the Type-N'-Talk up and carrying it over to him. "Where are you headed?"

Nick took the device and tapped on the keys. "EAST," the device announced.

"Where did you come from?" she asked with sugar to her voice that she was sure was further infuriating Crow.

Nick shrugged.

"Are you from Camp Lejeune?" Crow said, still not moving from her spot at the dinner table.

"YES."

"What happened there?"

"MORI."

"Dammit. I figured they'd take out our military installations eventually. Was this recent?"

"3 MONTHS."

"Huh. Weird, I didn't hear about it." She grimaced. "How are you still running? Some kind of new power source?"

A pause. "YES."

The witch was to be adding things up in her head. "The kind of power source that might get knocked out by a radio disruption?" Nick did not reply. Crow rose, her muscles visibly stiffening. "Are you powered by Mori technology, Nick? Don't you dare lie to me."

He fumbled with the Type-N'-Talk. He appeared to be writing, erasing, then writing again. Finally, he simply said: "YES."

"Dammit," Crow said, dropping her tool kit into her bag and picking it up. "Fine, we're leaving right now. Come on, Gail." Gail backed up from Nick, who was looking at them and not daring to move. Very slowly, and deliberately, he typed on the device.

"I'M NOT MORI."

Crow scoffed. "Forgive me if I don't believe you."

"MORI DESTROYED LEJUNE."

"You said that."

"MARINES ENGINEERED MORI TECH."

"They *what?*" Crow took a step forward. "That's impossible. It's too advanced. Nobody's been able to do that."

"MARINES DID." He tapped out more. "LOTS OF SCIENTISTS."

"And?"

"MORI FOUND OUT."

"Shit." She paced around the living room for a second, her eyes darting wildly at nothing in particular. "So the Marines found out how to use Mori technology. That's big. That's huge. No *wonder* the Mori are moving into phase two. I bet when they found out, they started seeing us as a bigger threat. They probably thought it was witchcraft on steroids."

What do you mean, 'phase two'?" Gail said, crossing her arms.

Crow ignored her and rounded on Nick, a fire burning in her eyes. "I want to be abundantly, categorically clear. You're saying that, despite the fact you are running on some kind of Mori power source, you are *not* working for them? You're not a spy, or an enforcer, or anything? Because I am *not* in the mood for any more…" she seemed to be looking for a non-vulgar word. "…shenanigans. So answer me *very clearly*. Yes or no: Are you a bad guy?" Her breathing was particularly heavy, and Gail was unsure if the witch might leap up and start strangling his metal neck in search of answers.

Nick didn't even hesitate. "NO."

"How can I trust you?" she demanded, jabbing a finger into his metal chest plate.

"PLAN."

Crow took a step back "What plan?"

Nick reached to his belt, unsnapping a belt pouch and fishing out a faded card. Gail looked over Crow's shoulder to read it. *Professor Avery Glen, Department of Celtic Studies.* Below that, written in pen, read the words *Campbell University, Buies Creek, NC, September 20, 8am.* Crow sighed in apparent defeat.

"Who is this?" Gail asked. "Does he have a plan?"

Crow let out a defeated sigh. "That's what I've heard," Crow said, still eyeing the armored man suspiciously. "He's been traveling up and down the east coast with some kind of seminar, and he's giving one tomorrow morning. That's where I'm headed, too, since he's nearby. With that, uh, *information* I told you about."

Gail pointed at the words *Buies Creek.* "Where is this place? Is it near here?"

"Relatively," Crow said under her breath.

"Is it on the way to the road? We're looking for a road," she added to Nick.

"Gail's trying to get to I-95 for some reason," Crow explained. "I agreed to take her there."

"Is 'Campbell University' on the way?"

Crow shrugged. "Gail—"

"YES," Nick interjected.

"Great!" Gail walked to her bag and picked it up. "Let's all go. You can come with us."

"What?" Crow's voice was a high-pitched squeal by this point. "I didn't agree to that," she balked.

The redhead shrugged. "Okay, well it *seems* like we're all going the same direction. And didn't you say you wanted to go there anyway?"

Crow looked between the redhead and the suit of armor before heaving an incredible sigh. "You know, Necia, I liked you better when you were quiet."

"Well," Gail retorted, "I liked you better when you weren't a..." She seemed to be searching for an appropriate curse word. "*Jerk.*"

Crow opened her mouth to reply, but Nick interrupted. "COUGH COUGH." Crow looked at him, back to Gail, and walked past her out the front door.

◌

The road north, out of Lillington, seemed much bleaker on this particular morning. Gail couldn't tell for sure, but the brown and red leaves in the trees almost looked greyer than before. There was no sign of any of Lillington's population returning yet, and Gail was pretty sure that, despite assurances, they never would.

That was the way the Mori left things. Empty and abandoned— not even a body or signs of a struggle left behind. They cleaned up after themselves.

As they reached the bridge north of town, Gail stopped and turned to look back. "What do you think happens to them? When the Mori take them, I mean?" Crow looked at her for a moment and then at Nick, as though trying to figure out the exact level of tact needed to answer and not be a complete asshole. She didn't have to respond, however, as Gail continued: "Sometimes people tell children that the Mori take them away and eat them. 'That's why you don't go wandering', they tell them. Be a good child or the Mori will eat you." Gail hadn't seen many children while growing up; just the small few traveling with their families through the mountains. They never stayed long enough to become friends.

"That's terrible!" Crow blurted. "Why would you tell a kid that? The world's already scary enough as it is."

"But I mean," Gail said, finally tearing her eyes away from Lillington and starting off down the cement highway, "does anyone really know what happens to them? Do they just die, or..."

"No idea," Crow shrugged. "Nick? You have any clue?"

Nick was silent.

SEVEN

They continued north for a short while, passing many abandoned buildings on either side but paying them little attention. When they reached an intersection next to an old and overgrown cemetery, they turned east and began down another, wider road marked by a single rusted sign with a white painted diamond on it which declared it to be "EAST 27".

Crow flexed her right arm a little. "Hang on, something feels weird." She stopped and walked over toward the cemetery, where a stone bench sat near the edge, inscribed with a name that was no longer readable. She pulled off her cloak and lifted her shirt. "I don't see anyth—hey. Gail. Come tell me if you see anything here on my lower back."

Gail came over and looked. There it was: a piece of something sharp and metallic lodged in Crow's lower back. The skin surrounding it was an angry red. "Oh no, this doesn't look good. I didn't notice this last night—"

"What is it?" Gail described the bit of shrapnel. "Dammit, that's what I was afraid of. I must have gotten scraped while I was stuck up on the pole. Can you pull it out?"

"I can try," Gail said, kneeling beside her and examining it. It was a relatively small puncture and not very deep. With a steady a hand as she could manage, she grasped the piece of glass between her fingernails and pulled. It came out in one piece, and the wound immediately became a small bead of blood. "Got it. Pass me one of those sticky bandages."

Crow dug in her bag and handed over one of the paper-wrapped sticky gauze pads. Gail put some of the antibiotic ointment on it and put it over the wound. Crow, meanwhile, didn't seem bothered at all, nor was she in pain. It was astonishing. "How are you able to be so…*calm*? This must hurt." Gail inquired.

Crow didn't reply; she just shrugged and put her cloak back on.

"You were up on that pole for at least an hour yesterday, too, and you weren't the last bit sore when I took you down, but you've got those rope marks all over your arm."

"And?" Crow said, the slightest bit of edge rising in her voice.

Nick's head turned and there was a click inside his helmet. He looked at Crow for a long moment and picked up his talking device. "NERVE DAMAGE?"

Gail tilted her head, and Crow reddened in the face. "Did you just *scan* me? That is so gross." She stood back up and stalked farther down the highway.

"What does that mean?" Gail said, jogging slightly to keep up with her.

"I don't want to waste time talkin' about it. I hate wasting time."

"It doesn't seem like a waste," Gail insisted. "Remember how I said you needed to tell me things?" Gail pressed. "This one seems important."

Crow slowed her pace with a deep sigh. "Fine. I'm just embarrassed, okay?" She was silent again for a long minute.

Gail insisted. "About what?"

Crow rolled up her sleeves and touched the rope marks visible on her skin. "I can't feel the pain. I can feel the sensation—the touch—but I can't feel the pain."

"That doesn't sound so bad—" Gail said, and the resulting look from Crow told her that this was apparently the completely incorrect thing to say.

"No, it *is* bad. See, I ran into a Mori a year ago. Some kind of doctor-type. She was capturing people, doing things to them, and letting them go. 'Releasing them back into the wild', she said. I was one of her *experiments*." The final word was spat out and Gail looked at her feet.

"Okay, that sounds very bad."

Crow nodded, breathing in a very controlled manner with her gaze still fixed on the concrete ahead. "So I have to keep checking myself for injuries. And I know that when I get hurt, it's definitely worse than it feels, and I am pretty sure one day I'm going to die of infection without even realizing that's what it is. It's a mess. I'm a mess." She was quiet for a few agonizing minutes.

Nick tapped Gail on the shoulder and gestured to Crow. Understanding, Gail reached out and touched her arm. "You're not a mess. I promise."

Crow rolled her eyes. "Anyway. You haven't really told me your story yet. You mention this friend you had in the mountains. And you—" she jabbed a finger in Nick's direction, "still haven't told us what the hell happened to you."

"Nick should go first!" Gail blurted.

Nick continued to walk as if he hadn't heard, before reattaching the Type-N'-Talk to his belt and signing toward Gail, occasionally stopping to define or spell out words where they were unfamiliar to her. "I am Gunnery Sergeant Nick Harvey. When the Mori invaded, I was stationed at Camp Lejeune I've been stationed there since. 15 years. The military was officially disbanded after the Ritual of Homecoming, but in reality, it simply stopped being as visible. Many military installations continued to operate independently or in very loose communication.

"One of the major tasks at Lejeune was a research group that was trying to understand Mori technology. The researchers made a lot of breakthroughs. They figured out how to tap into the Mori power source and make things work."

"How did they do it?" Crow demanded excitedly as Gail's translation left her mouth. "That's amazing. That's, like, *world*-changing development. We could fight back and—"

Nick held up a hand. "That was the plan, but the Mori found out somehow. I think someone at Lejeune sold us out. But the Mori attacked and as far as I know, I am the only one who made it out alive."

Crow stiffened at this revelation. She chewed on her words for a moment. "Well that doesn't explain your suit of armor. Do you ever get out of that thing? You probably really have to poop."

"Crow!" Gail looked shocked.

Crow shrugged. "I mean—"

Nick held up his hand. "An experiment," he signed. "I volunteered to test it. A suit of protective armor. Mori technology seems to impact kinetic energy in a way beyond human understanding, so we built a set of armor that encapsulates and can cut off the outside world and try to dampen the impact of that energy. Like a turtle." Gail was amused by Nick making the sign for turtle, his hands over each other and his thumbs twiddling. It was an adorable gesture that was a stark contrast to the massive beast of metal making the sign.

"And?" Crow was sounding impatient.

"The suit…" he paused, as if trying to find the words. "It connects to my brain and is controlled directly, like an appendage. The down side to that is that I can't take it off without help."

"That's awful," Gail replied out loud. "So you haven't eaten or drank anything? How long have you been going like this?"

Crow stopped dead in her tracks and spun to face Nick. "You said Lejeune was attacked 3 months ago."

Nick didn't reply.

"So you've gone three months stuck inside a power suit? Without food or water?"

Nick didn't reply.

"How did you survive that?"

Nick didn't reply.

Crow's eyebrows went up high and she took a cautious step back. "You didn't survive, did you? But somehow you're still connected to the suit. Like...your brain is in it somehow."

Nick reached down and fumbled with the Type-N'-Talk. Gail was sure that, if he had been flesh-and-blood, he would be trembling. "YES. BRAIN ALIVE."

"But the rest of you is..." Crow gestured silently at him while she tried to figure out how to sum up his condition. "...dead."

Nick typed "YES" but didn't press the button to speak it aloud. He deleted it and typed "NO" but also didn't say it. Eventually he lifted his arms in a shrug.

"I don't really know what I'm supposed to think about this, but I'm not going to lie—I am really creeped out by the idea that an armored zombie powered by Mori technology is following us," she said to Gail.

Nick did not reply, but he somehow seemed to appear wounded by her words.

"He's helping us, Crow," Gail reminded. "And he hasn't hurt us thus far. He's had a lot of opportunities, hasn't he?"

Crow sighed deeply and began walking again.

◌

They approached a place on the side of the road—a bright yellow building with a faded and partially-collapsed sign. There were people inside.

"No way," Crow said, her pace picking up. "No way. It's been 15 years. No way."

"What?" Gail increased her gait to catch up with her. "What is it?"

"It's a Waffle House."

The restaurant had, like everything else, certainly seen better days. Many windows were replaced with boards or riveted street signs, but on the whole it was still apparently operational. It was also not particularly guarded—most establishments of this kind would have one or two thugs outside to keep bandits at bay, but there didn't appear to be any.

A small bell chimed as Crow pushed the door inward and entered the place. The sticky smell of sugar was on the air, along with the fine odors of bacon and eggs that made Gail's stomach feel like it was suddenly six times larger than a moment before. "Hello," came a call from the griddle, where a plump older lady with curly hair was busy flipping a row of sausage patties. "Just sit anywhere, dearies."

Nick looked at the cramped booths and elected to step back outside to act as security. It made sense; he had no need for food, after all, in his condition. Crow watched Nick and Lukather leave through the glass door as she settled in her seat. "Okay, so I have a theory about him," she said with wide eyes. "I don't think his story adds up."

"Why's that?" Gail picked up the menu, which was laminated but quite faded. *Emergency Menu*, it declared at the top under the restaurant logo. *We are only able to serve a very limited menu during this time.*

Crow didn't even look at it. "So someone at Lejeune betrayed the Marines there, supposedly, right? But Nick's the only one to survive, because he has armor that just *happens* to be powered by a Mori…battery or something. And he just *happens* to come across me. And I'm fighting against the Mori. And he tells me there's someone who has a plan to stop them. And we should come along."

"But you knew about it already," Gail whispered back, not yet understanding the implication.

"So," Crow said with additional gruffness to her voice, "I know how this story goes. This is a trap, Gail. We're being led into a trap."

Gail looked over her shoulder. Nick was standing outside as he had on the porch, his hands behind his back and unmoving like a statue.

The restaurant's other occupants paid them no mind. A trio of denim-and-leather thugs were huddled in a far booth, while the only person at the bar wore a long studded trench coat and a low, narrow-brimmed hat with skulls printed on it.

The waitress finally came over. "Welcome to Waffle House, dears. Know what you want?"

Crow blinked at the menu and looked up at her. "Okay, I am really confused. How on earth are there still Waffle Houses working? This makes no sense." She gestured at everything around her as if it was somehow a brilliant façade.

"You ever heard of the Waffle House Index?" the Waitress said with a cocked, penciled eyebrow.

"No."

"Back in the day, the government used to use it as a sort of informal scale to determine how bad a natural disaster was. If your local Waffle House closed, you know it was bad, because most Waffle Houses had generators and everythin'."

"Okay..." Crow's tone indicated that she was catching on.

"Well, when the Mori came, we all just...kept going. I mean, we had to change things—our secret emergency menu basically became our permanent menu...but it's generally the same as it's always been."

Crow's mouth was open, like she wanted to respond, but she couldn't seem to find the words; Gail had to say something instead. "Where do you get all your supplies?"

"Merchants, some local warehouses. When we're really in need we buy from the Duke." she said with a grimace. "A lot of stuff is local, but he gets us a lot of the equipment, a few ingredients here and there."

"Who's the Duke?" Gail asked.

The waitress balked. "Who's—I guess you folks aren't from the area."

"She isn't," Crow said, having found her voice. "I am. The Duke is this businessman that basically kept production going. He built a lot of steam generators that are inexpensive and easy to make. Then, of course, he marks them up and probably gets rich on slave labor and indentured servitude. He's basically become king of the whole east coast. And somehow, he keeps clear of the Mori. Word is, they think he's a great and powerful wizard and they leave him alone by choice."

"Speaking of being from town," the waitress interrupted, "I heard that bad things happened in Lillington yesterday. You all come from there?"

Crow lost a little bit of color in her face. "Um…" She looked up at the waitress. "The town's deserted. I think…"

The waitress patted her gently on the shoulder. "I understand, dear. It's been happening more and more these days. Towns vanish overnight. A few weeks later it's a Mori encampment. I've been hearing things, ya know…" She sighed. "I used to work out in Cedar Creek. There was a whole group of restaurants, and a hotel, all in one little bundle. Great place for folks moving from town to town. But it was too close to Fayetteville, apparently, and one night we were given a four-hour notice to vacate."

"You got a notice?" Gail sounded hopeful.

The waitress nodded. "They gave us four. They showed up in two." She cleared her throat. "But I've been jabbering on here enough, you ladies look hungry. Might as well get a bite here now, since we'll have to close down if Lillington's gone." She sounded only mildly disappointed. Gail wondered how many restaurants and places this woman had worked at before now. How many times had she had to travel on and try to find work somewhere else? How many others like her were out there, just drifting from collapsing town to collapsing town? How many weren't lucky enough to get to the next one?

Crow finally picked up her menu. "Oh man. I need one of these ham and cheese sandwiches. Make that two."

"Three," Gail said. "Do you have coffee?"

"We do," The waitress replied. She didn't write any of this down and Gail wondered if it was a lack of pencils or if she was just really good at her job. "We get beans delivered by the Duke every Tuesday." She rolled her eyes as she again referenced the king of the east coast.

"You have coffee. Oh my god, you have coffee." Crow looked like she had just been told that she had just won a ticket to paradise.

"You had coffee an hour ago," Gail said with a raised eyebrow.

"So?" Crow retorted. "Can we get some of that to go?" she asked the waitress.

"For sure," the waitress said with a grin. "But rules are rules here: money first, dears."

Crow nodded and pulled up the gold-colored purse she had stolen from the bandits, counting some brass tubes out of it. Gail saw one of the people in the corner watching, and he gestured at the two women before returning to his conversation. She didn't like that; she put a hand on her lap not far from the hilt of her sword.

The waitress took the money and headed back to the grill where she started her work composing the sandwiches. Gail tried to calm her nerves with more questions. "Dumb question here. What are those, anyway? I don't know a lot about money."

Crow took one out. It was a slender tube with a dark cap on it. "These? They're bullets. Used to be used in guns before the Mori destroyed them all. See, when the Ritual of Homecoming happened, all of the fake money people used to have in computers was worthless. In some places, paper money got replaced. Someone—the Duke, I think—had the idea of using a resource we no longer needed—bullets, since all the guns were gone—and making them currency. And since you can use gunpowder for stuff like fires and wound treatment...well, I don't get the whole economic idea behind it, but the idea was that since people could use bullets for things like fires or wound treatment, they had value and that it could be economically stable because there's no way to make new bullets." Gail was just staring at her. Crow wasn't entirely sure if her eyes had glazed over. "What's wrong?"

Gail shook her head almost imperceptibly. "You are so...smart."

Crow's face scrunched a little bit and before she had a chance to reply the waitress dropped off two chipped mugs of coffee and a dish of what looked like fresh cream. "You still haven't told me your story yet. Am I going to get to hear it or what?"

Gail looked past Crow and straightened up. The crew of people from the back of the restaurant were walking over. "Hey. Hate to interrupt you lovely ladies but I have a special invitation for you both. See, the Duke is coming into town and is throwing a big shindig."

"We're busy," Crow said without looking at him.

"Oh, I don't think you're too busy for this one. See, you wouldn't happen to have talked to a fella named Dirk yesterday, would you?" Gail's heart sank in her chest, but she said nothing.

"Name doesn't ring a bell," said Crow. "But if I run into him I'll tell you that you're looking for him."

"See, that's the thing," the guy said, leaning on the table. "You ain't gonna run into him. He's dead. And for some reason you seem to be walking around with his coin-purse."

"This?" Crow pointed at the tan bag. "I found it on the side of the road. You want it back?"

"Don't lie to me, witch," he said with a rising voice. "The Duke's got a bounty on one of you for killing his brother."

"His *brother*?" Gail gasped. "We didn't—it was—" She was trembling.

"Now you're going to come with me. Easy-like, out the back, so we don't alert your bodyguard outside." He put his hand on Crow's shoulder and pulled.

Gail stopped trembling, and as her eyes darted from Crow's hand, now carefully closing around a fork, she had a burst of clarity and took action.

What happened next was blindingly fast. Her sword was in her hand. Crow's fork was in the man's eye. Gail's sword was up and deflecting a blow from a woodman's axe that one of the back thugs was swinging downward toward the table. Thrown off-balance, he tried to turn and swing again, but Gail was too fast, slapping the flat of the blade against his face and knocking him headlong into a metal bar stool where the man with the narrow-brimmed hat had been sitting.

That man, in fact, had also sprang into action, grabbing the third guy and putting a knife to his throat. The third thug was smart enough to not resist, watching with terror as their leader dropped to the ground, howling with pain and thrashing about while blood poured out of his eye socket. He tried to crawl to the door, but out of his good eye he was suddenly staring at the metal boot of an armored Marine.

Crow kicked him lightly with a boot. "Are you done?"

"Yes!" he cried. "Please! I'm sorry! Please don't kill me!"

"I'm not going to kill you," Gail said in protest. "I don't kill anyone. And Dirk attacked us first! And—"

"He doesn't care, Gail," Crow hissed. She nodded to the man in the narrow-brimmed hat, and he slowly let his captive go. Now freed, and taking survey of how easily he and his comrades had been dispatched, he took a quick seat in a nearby booth and tried to look as innocent as possible.

"The Duke has a bounty on you," the fork-faced thug blurted, clambering into a sitting position. "It's high. You won't get far. Not with that bag on you."

"Good point," Crow said with a sneer. She opened her own bag, poured the remaining bullets into it, and threw it to the side. Then, she turned to Gail and Nick. "We have to get out of here. Fast. Dammit, I was looking forward to those—"

"I made your sandwiches to go," the waitress had reappeared behind the counter and was putting several paper-wrapped items in the paper bag. "And I tossed in a few extra things in there that probably won't get used up before we close up shop."

"Where will you go?" Gail said, picking up the bag. "You just lost your whole restaurant in a day."

"There's others," the Waitress said with a tone of voice that suggested she was resigned to this life. "And this isn't the first time, like I told you. But if the Duke's coming after you, dear, you probably do want to leave, and soon." She looked over the counter at the thug who was bleeding next to the candy machine. "Are you going to cause any more trouble while I clean up your mess, young man? If you and your boys sit and be quiet I'll even give you some medicine for that eye. But cause me any trouble and I swear I'll scrub the toilets with your face."

Both Crow and Gail shuddered at the imagery and excused themselves from the restaurant. Gail had been so taken by the sweet smell of the air that she was hit with a profound sense of loss as she exited into the grey, cold air of the outside.

EIGHT

Crow devoured her first sandwich before they had gotten even a hundred meters from the Waffle House. She realized that she was now left with greasy, cheesy fingers, and dug around in her bag for something to wipe them off but was not successful. She eyed Lukather, who trotted alongside happily, but he immediately sensed her desire to use him as a napkin and retreated behind Nick for safety.

"We're being followed," Gail observed as they passed the first major sign indicating that they were approaching Campbell University. She jabbed her thumb back behind her, and the other two turned to look. There he was: the man with the narrow-brimmed hat, stalking back about a quarter-mile behind in his long black coat. "Should we say something?"

"He helped us back at the restaurant," Crow mused, finally wiping her greasy fingers off on her pant leg, "but I don't know why. Or who he is. We didn't ask his name, did we?"

"We could stop and wait for him and find out." Gail's optimism was like nails on a chalkboard to Crow's cranky ears.

"Or we could tell him to screw off."

"He helped us."

83

There was a tense pause between them, and they both stopped, sat down on the curb in the shade of a tree while passing a bottle of water back and forth for a few minutes. Crow convinced Gail to eat half a sandwich while the man in the coat made his slow, almost melodramatic approach toward them. So slow, in fact, that Gail had a minute or so to check on her bandage. It had bled far less than she had expected, and she was relieved to see it had not turned any worrisome shades. She finished pulling her pants back up and buckling them as the stranger finally got close enough to see clearly.

Gail could see that he was somewhat older than both she and Crow—maybe in his forties, around M's age. His hair, visible in wisps that hung out of his hat, was at one time a twisted black color but how had strands of white here and there. His dark face was unshaven with a patchy beard, and he had a smoking pipe hanging out of his mouth. Dark sunglasses rested over his eyes, while over his chest he held a bandolier of throwing knives, the surface of which was an array of rainbow colors in the metal. Lukather immediately made his dislike known, crouching down with his ears flattened and growling at the stranger.

"Thanks for helping us back there," Gail said as he came into earshot.

He slowed his pace a little. "No thanks necessary," he said, removing the pipe from his mouth. "It just…needed to be done."

"We didn't catch your name," Crow said, crossing her arms.

"I don't think I threw it anywhere." His voice was smooth, with a little bit of grit, like a fine soap scrubbed across granite.

Crow rolled her eyes. "That doesn't even make sense. Also, you are *so slow*. All you're doing is wasting *so much* time." His jacket rippled as a breeze blew by, and he struck a match on his coat, lighting the pipe. The witch remained unamused. "Suit yourself. Why are you following us?" She stood up and crossed her arms.

He took a long puff of his pipe. "I'm protecting you," he said, pushing his sunglasses up his nose with his middle and ring finger in one smooth motion.

There was a long pause in which Crow and Gail expected him to continue. When he didn't, Crow cleared her throat. "Protecting us from…?"

"You don't want to know." He let out a cloud of smoke and continued to stand there attempting to look important. It was almost pitiful to watch.

"Okay," Crow said, putting her hands out toward him as if to push him away, "I have had it up to here with people's crap. His, hers—" She pointed at Nick and Gail respectively, and both looked at her with some level of reproach, "and I'm certainly not going to put up with yours. So stop acting like some anime hero and answer my god. Damned. *Question*."

"Anime hero?" He visibly softened a little bit, and the pitch of his voice increased noticeably. "Would you say I'm more 'Kirito' or more—"

The sound that escaped Crow's mouth took all of them by surprise; it was a mixture of frustration, realization, and disapproval that came out as one single guttural noise. She hoisted up her bag on her side and turned. "I'm walking away. Please stop following us, creepy anime dude."

"What is 'anime'?" Gail signed at Nick.

"Not relevant," he signed back. "It's stupid. Trust me."

The stranger coughed on his pipe smoke. "Wait! Wait, please don't go. Hang on."

"What." Crow spun so hard the edges of her cloak cut the air with an audible *whoosh*.

He fumbled with his glasses. "I sometimes get caught up in the…persona, okay? I didn't mean to piss you off."

Crow waited, staring with such contempt that Gail expected the stranger to start charring where he stood.

"I'm an entertainer," he said with pride. "And I have been traveling by myself a little while, so I have to act tougher than I am or I'm risking getting robbed."

"An entertainer." Crow raised her eyebrows. While she was still clearly impatient, she at least looked somewhat less angry. "Terrific. But what do you do?"

"The knives," he said, gesturing to his bandolier. "Knife tricks. Knife throwing. I also tell stories, and play music, and—"

"What's your name?" Gail interrupted.

"Leonard, to my friends," he said with a sweep of his hat from his head, revealing a large balding patch, "and to everyone else it's Leo, Hero of Eastern Shore."

"I'm going to call you Leonard—not because we're friends," Crow's face had twisted into a mirthful smile. "But because the other name is *stupid*. Now, why are you following us? You still haven't gotten that far."

"I'm not following you. Not all of you, anyway. I'm following *her*." He pointed to Gail.

"Me?" The redhead put her hands on her hips. "What on earth could you want with me?"

He sighed, another puff of pipe smoke coming out of his mouth. "I've been following you since you left Roanoke."

"Roanoke?" Crow repeated, casting a sidelong glance at Gail. "Virginia?"

"The same," Leonard said, settling his dark sunglasses onto his hat. "And before you go off on me for thinking me to be some kind of creep—"

"—too late—" Gail and Crow said in unison.

"—you should know that I followed you because you have my brother's sword on your hip. The last time I saw him he told me about you and I came to find you." His eyes glanced down at the brass hilt of M's sword.

"Wait, hang on," Gail said, stepping forward. "You're not 'Uncle L', are you?"

He put out a hand. "Gail, it's lovely to finally meet you up-close." She didn't take his hand.

Crow looked from one to the other. She turned to Nick. "The day before yesterday it was me and my computer. Why is this my life?" Nick shrugged.

Gail tapped her foot. "M told me that you and he didn't get along. He told me that you were the bad kind of thief."

Leonard's face fell rather hard, and he scratched at his beard. "Did he now? I...I don't know what to say to that, if I can be honest. I mean...no. he and I didn't get along well. But I think we just had different ideas about...about what we were doing out here." He lifted his hat and ran a hand through his thick dark mane. "I actually have just been trying to protect you. Who do you think called over a carriage when you started a bar fight in Lillington, eh?"

"That was you?" Crow's eyebrows knitted.

"No," Gail said, puffing out her chest. "I could not possibly go this far without knowing I was being followed. It's not possible."

"If you say so," he said and took another puff of his pipe. "But I'm still here to offer to help you if you want. I have a few skills that would probably be useful to you. And even if not, a few extra knives can't hurt if you meet more thugs. Especially if the Duke really does have bounty on your head."

Gail's mouth was a frustrated thin line. "If you are who you say you are, then you're no hero."

Leonard's tongue tapped the top of his lip. It reminded Gail of a thing M used to do when he, too, was thinking deeply about how to respond. "You're right," he finally said. "But I have every intent to be."

There was a long pause as both of them considered the other. Crow finally leaned, her elbow resting on Nick as if he was a lamppost. "Okay, so I need an answer here, Gail. Does he stay or does he go? If he goes, then he goes, but if he stays we need to *get a move on*. Before more of the Duke's men show up on our trail."

"If you'd like, I could just accompany you up to the University. I have business there and we can part ways." He looked at Gail, his eyes suddenly wide like dinner plates, giving him the appearance of a lost puppy.

"He stays," Gail said after an extended consideration, her eyes still locked into Leonard's. "For now."

Crow didn't need a second affirmation, and she immediately started off down the street again, grumbling to herself. Nick followed.

Gail stood there, still considering Leonard with narrowed eyes. "If you hurt either of them, L," she said, her voice low and her hand resting almost casually on the sword's hilt, "I will kill you myself."

"Great!" He grinned widely, showing two silver teeth. "Then there should be no problems!" He tipped his hat and strode around her after the others.

⌂

Campbell University, Leonard noted, had been one of the first universities to renew itself after the Mori's appearance. There had been a few years of relative economic stability before the massive economic collapse, and during that time a handful of universities had been able to weather the transition away from electricity. Campbell was one of these, with large storerooms of books from years back that were put into distribution almost immediately. The school, he said, had only closed briefly the semester of the invasion and again during The Riots.

"What are 'the Riots'?" Gail asked as they passed a stone sign indicating the entrance to the campus.

"You don't know about the Riots?" Leonard said, his head snapping to look at her so quickly it popped audibly.

"She's been a bit sheltered," Crow said. "No thanks to your brother, I guess. I still don't know why some rogue might be interested in keeping a young girl captive."

"I wasn't captive," Gail said in defense. "I could leave whenever I wanted to."

"And?"

She frowned. "I never wanted to."

"The Riots," Leonard explained, "happened a few years after the invasion. Lots of young men and women in their early to mid-twenties—college age, I suppose—all decided it would be a good idea to rise up and take on the Mori through protest and political action. 50 universities across the United States and Canada all joined in forming a largely-peaceful movement. They petitioned the Mori for more rights. They peacefully disrupted trade. They sent letters and manifestos, urging our 'benevolent new rulers' to accept peaceful co-existence instead of subjugation.

"They staged three major protests: New York, San Francisco, and Chicago. They were planned far in advance, and scheduled to be simultaneous—indicating the solidarity of the youth voice. It was beautifully planned, if I must say. Some of the finest artistic minds came together to create a tapestry of words and colors that expressed in the finest of terms exactly what the people of the world felt, and how they didn't want to take back what had been taken from them— they wanted to share it." Leonard took another long draw from his pipe and let the smoke out in donut shapes. Silence hung in the air, the only major sound around them being the *clank-clank-clank* of Nick's armor on the asphalt.

"What happened?" Gail was intrigued. She also realized that she had been pulled into this story by the dulcet tone of Leonard's silky voice *exactly* the way she used to be pulled into M's. *His brother, indeed.*

"It was a disaster," Leonard said finally. "The Mori first ignored the protests. Then, after three full days and nights, something happened. It started with the protesters, first. They all just…they all just laid down to sleep. Then it spread—anyone in that 18-25 age group. They all just laid down to sleep."

"Alright," Gail said, caution in her voice. "That doesn't sound so terrible…"

"But they never woke up," Leonard continued. "They just slept. Nothing could rouse them. And they wasted away. After a few days, even if food and water was forced on them, they would simply…they simply stopped. Their hearts, their minds…everything just stopped. They all died within the week. 35 million people. The Mori dubbed the event 'The riots' and no one has tried to resist since."

"Not true," Crow said under her breath.

Up ahead, at one of the larger buildings, a few people were milling around a door. The slope of the lawn had permitted them to see Gail's traveling party from afar and they had begun to gather weapons. It was probably Nick, Gail supposed, who was the cause of their fear—a large metal man was likely one of the stranger things to see coming up a hill. "Stop! Hands up!" one of them called out. They stopped at once. Each slowly raised their hands, and several uniformed people with crossbows dashed down the hill toward them.

A young man with a trimmed brown beard took the front position, slowing until he was a short distance from them. He was wearing a blue uniform and a shiny badge. "Please identify who you are," he said, pronouncing his words fully and using his whole mouth as if talking to a child.

"We are here because we were *invited*," Crow said, shooting an icy glare at Nick. "Or was this a trap all along?"

The man with the crossbow looked confused. "What are you here for?" He said. It wasn't particularly aggressive, and Gail imagined that he was just a man doing a job rather than a person who actually wished them harm.

Crow was about to say something most assuredly snarky when Leonard's silky voice cut the chilly air. "Professor Glenn." He took a confident step forward, "He invited at least two of us—the gentleman in the armor and me. The two ladies are…" he gave Crow a sly wink, "very important persons." He reached, painfully slowly, into his jacket pocket and produced a business card similar to the one Nick had shown Crow and Gail earlier.

The uniformed man lowered his crossbow, walked over, and examined the card. "Do you have any identification?" He asked, some dubiousness in his voice.

Nick reached down and pulled a laminated card from his belt pouch and the man examined it. "Marine, huh? Nice suit." He nodded back at the others who lowered their weapons. "Come on, I'll explain while we go inside."

NINE

"I appreciate your cooperation," the man with the beard said as he led them up the hill and toward the winding brick pathways that covered the campus, "but we've had issues with infiltrators. I'm Green, by the way. Carl Green."

"What kind of infiltrators?" Crow asked, pulling her bag higher on her shoulder. "Like, Mori disguised as people, or—?"

"Not that bad, thankfully," Green said. "But there's a large number of wannabe Advocates that keep coming around trying to pry."

"What are Advocates?" Gail whispered to Crow.

"People who work for the Mori," Crow returned, in low breath, into Gail's ear. "They get protection, and some of them get taught how to use Mori technology. And now…" She sighed. "They're getting promises they'll be passed over when the Reclamation starts."

"Betrayers of the whole human race, if you ask me," Leonard added from Gail's other side. Crow looked at him for a moment and reluctantly nodded her agreement.

Green walked past a stone building with a high steeple and an enormous wooden door. Crow fixated on the metal crucifix on top, and Gail could see that a slim wire was running up the stone and was attached to it. "Please tell me that's a cell antenna," she said to Green, as he moved to unlock the front door.

"It is," he said, eyeing her. "Are you looking to connect?"

"If I can," she replied with obvious relief in her voice. "I got attacked near the one I used to use and had to burn it with a disruption signal. If you know what I'm talking about," she added.

Green nodded, continuing down the road toward a faded brown brick building. A sign outside the front door read "Marshbanks Dining Hall". They proceeded up the sidewalk to a peeling white door, which he unlocked, finally opening the entrance and leading to an anteroom decorated with sparse faded paintings. "There's a few other witches here, by the way. They might want to say hello—something about putting a face to a name?"

Crow grinned. "Oh, hell yeah. I almost never see any of these guys in real life."

"There's also some other armed forces," Green added to Nick, leading them down the hall and into a side chamber. "I can let them know you're here."

"THANK YOU," Nick said through his talking device. They headed downstairs and emerged into a large dining room filled with circular tables and easily a hundred other people, all conversing in low tones. Gail was taken aback by the sheer diversity of all the people around—people in suits, people in riot gear, and people in leathers or denims. There were a few ladies in fancy dresses and others in practically nothing at all. She felt terribly out of place in her stained white blouse and tan pants, and she slinked back behind Crow a little as she looked about.

Green disappeared into the crowd and returned a minute later with a grin. "The rules here are pretty reasonable: don't cause trouble. If you do, you will be escorted out. You can camp onsite overnight, or the dorms over across the quad are open, so you'll have a place to stay for the night and the man at the front desk will charge you for the service. Dr. Glenn's seminar is tomorrow." They all nodded their assent. "The military people I mentioned are over there," he told Nick, gesturing to a table full of people in various military uniforms. Nick thanked him again and stomped off in their direction. "And the other witches are over on that end." He gestured to a table on the opposite side, where a small crowd of people clothed in black were all conversing in low voices, each one carrying a bag that, like Crow's, must have contained a computer. Crow bounded over to meet them without another word.

And so Gail was left with Leonard. She didn't look at him. She didn't want to be anywhere near him. She couldn't quite place why he gave her a deep, sharp feeling in her stomach, as if she had swallowed a can of thumbtacks; but whatever the cause of it she wanted any excuse possible to get away from him. She saw her opening along the far wall: the restrooms. Without even any consideration as to whether or not they had running water here, she headed toward them. She felt Leonard reach out toward her but she slipped her arm out of his grasp, and at her feet she heard a low growl. Glancing behind her, she could see that Lukather was now between them, his ears flattened and standing in defiance of old Uncle L, who was taking the otherwise goofy dog's threats seriously. Satisfied that he wasn't going to follow her, she swept past a few tables, including the one where Crow was now sitting, and vanished into the ladies room.

The room was surprisingly clean. The polished floor was a sparkly grey color, and the stalls on either side of the wall appeared to have been recently painted. Even the mirrors were unmarred; not a single crack even ran along the surface. Gail tried to remember the last time she had seen an uncracked or unbroken mirror, and she honestly could not recall a single instance.

Stepping in front of that mirror, she considered the woman before her. The red hair around her face was loose and wispy—certainly on account of the bath the night before—but it was still tangled in places. Ultimately, she felt, it made her look like a mess.

Her eyes were drawn to her shirt, where a spot of rust-color was splattered across her neckline. She hadn't noticed it before in the dim cabin, nor had she seen it in the last couple of days' travel. She pulled

93

the neckline down a little, to see if she had some kind of wound, perhaps across her collarbone, which she hadn't noticed before. No, there was nothing. This wasn't her blood.

It was Dirk's. *The Duke's got a bounty on your head for killing his brother*, she heard the man from the Waffle House's voice echo in her ear. She had killed him.

"It was an accident," she pleaded to her reflection. "He stumbled and fell on my sword."

Then, she had left him there. She had been terrified and overwhelmed and injured and had left a man behind to die.

"There was nothing I could do."

You're a killer, her reflection seemed to say in return. *You killed another human being. The one thing M told you never to do.*

Tears were now streaming down her face, finding a home on her chin and in droplets on her shirt. She was holding onto the sink now, for support, and as her head started to feel dizzy from her sudden and uncontrollable sobs, she stumbled into a stall and took a seat on the commode, slamming the stall door and burying her face in her hands, trying to get the image of M's disappointed face out of her head. She could almost see him now. Shaking his head and refusing to look at her. Telling her how he had tried to raise her to be good and compassionate. She had thrown all of that away.

It was an illogical sadness, she knew in the back of her mind. She knew M killed people when it was absolutely necessary. It was something that happened behind the scenes, in a land far away from her. It was alright, she told herself, because it was a chore M had performed so far outside of her bubble of existence that it might as well have not happened at all.

But now, the solemn thought of death had been spilled into her own hands and, lost in a world she didn't understand, she sat, shaking, in a toilet stall.

Knock knock. "Gail?" She looked up and saw a familiar set of buckled black boots under the door of the bathroom stall.

"Crow," Gail coughed, and tried to follow it with some kind of explanation or reasoning, or even perhaps an excuse—but her words became jumbled and she couldn't force any of them to pass beyond the knot in her throat.

"It doesn't sound like you're doing okay," Crow replied. "And it doesn't sound like you're really able to talk right now either."

Gail put her face back in her hands and let out a whimper.

"Okay, so I'll talk. You're upset about that guy at the bar. But we don't know his story. We don't know what he did, especially if he's the Duke's brother. You don't know about the Duke, so let me tell you. The Duke tells people he's there to protect them. 'All people, under one flag,' he tells people. Protection from the Mori. Maintaining trade and influence. It sounds really peachy.

"But in reality, he's exploiting fear. He's exploiting desperation. People are willing to give up their dignity and their own rights just to jump on the Duke's promises. They know he can't keep them. And you end up with whole communities devoted to a man who is using them to support his own tyrannical regime. He claims he's protecting them from the Mori. And some people believe him. But whatever he's doing, he is making life worse for everyone else."

Gail had stopped sobbing, and now just listened. Her face was still glued to her palms, and she tried to recover her breathing.

"And then there's one more thing you don't know: The Duke's thug squads. They terrorize people. They show up and take their things, confiscating them for the 'common good'. They take people. People, Gail. They take people they think aren't good for society and they sell them to the Mori for experimentation. And in return, the Mori give them resources like food and building materials and tools and the like, and he gives them to his supporters, who then treat him like a god. Now, nobody's got proof of this," Crow said, and Gail could see she was now sliding her back down the door of the stall to sit down on the shiny tile floor, "and if you try to tell people that's what's happening they'll call you crazy, or a conspiracy theorist, or attack you, or whatever. But I saw it firsthand. I got kidnapped by someone wearing the Duke's colors. I got sold to the Mori. I got experimented on. And then I was left in an unfamiliar place to pick up the broken pieces of my life. And no one *believed* me."

Gail was completely quiet now. Crow was on the floor, holding her legs up to her chest with her back to the door.

"You want to know why I got so upset when you said your friend from the mountains was some thug? That's why. I was afraid he was working for the Duke…and I, and a lot of the other people I talk to online…we all know the Duke is working for the Mori. We know he's secretly an Advocate. A betrayer. So…it hit me pretty hard. And I got upset at you, and I shouldn't have and I'm sorry. I'm just—I'm just suspicious of everyone, now, because I don't want to end up being at the tail end of another Mori experiment." She sniffed and shuffled slightly on the floor, and Gail was certain she was wiping her face. "I feel numb all the time, Gail. Like…I can feel hot, and I can feel cold, but I can't feel pain. And somehow it makes it feel like I'm walking in a fog. It makes you think…" she paused. "It makes you think that the world really is just pain, because without pain, you just don't feel anything at all."

Gail reached out and unlocked the stall door, pulling it in toward her and seeing Crow there, curled up on the floor against the side of the doorway.

"And it's just—" She seemed to realize something, her eyes going wide as she looked back over her shoulder at the redhead in the stall. "Oh my god, you're upset about what happened and I was trying to be comforting and I made it all about me. I'm *so sorry*, I don't know what—"

Gail put up a hand. "You're fine. Your…your point is that the people who work for the Duke are bad guys. And so it's…what I did is okay."

Crow knitted her brow together. "I…I guess that's what I was getting at, I'm just really… I'm terrible at being supportive."

"It helps," Gail said with a shuddering breath. "For now. It…it helps."

"Is there anything I can do? I feel like I'm being a terrible friend."

Gail shook her head. "I'm happy to have a friend at all. Terrible or not."

Crow gave her a little smile. "I kind of feel the same way. I'm not good with people."

"Neither am I."

The witch shifted her weight and pulled herself to her feet, dusting off her cloak before offering Gail a hand. "Are you going to be okay? For real, now. You've had a bad couple of days."

"So have you," Gail reminded, gesturing to the bluish-colored rope-marks on her arm before taking Crow's hand and standing up straight. She looked over at the mirror, at her tear-stained, flushed face and her matted red hair and her blood-stained shirt. "I don't like her," she said, gesturing to the mirror.

Crow looked over at the reflection and looked like she was unsure how to respond. She looked back to the real Gail and examined her hair which reached down her back. "Well, your hair's a mess, for sure. Do you take care of it?" The redhead shrugged. "You have a lot of…tangles and things. Stuff looks like it's dried in here. Blood, and dirt…It could use a good wash. Or a cut."

"A cut?" Gail took a step toward the mirror. "Short?"

"If you want." Crow dug in her bag. "I have scissors. Not that I want you to ditch your hair, because it's a really pretty shade of red—"

"No," Gail insisted. "I would like to cut it. Please."

Crow found the scissors and snipped them in the air experimentally. "Would it make you feel better?" She asked firmly, gazing over her black-rimmed glasses.

Gail nodded. "I think so."

"Okay," Crow said, taking off her bag and setting it down. "Come over here and sit on the sink at the end."

TEN

A short while later, the two of them left the restroom. Gail had scrubbed the bloody stain from the neckline of her shirt with water from the running tap, while Crow snipped away delicately at her red locks and by the time she had successfully purged the rusty splatter from the fabric, she looked up to see her hair significantly shorter. It wasn't as short as Crow's, but it was now shoulder-length and, with the help of a comb the witch had in what seemed to be an endless supply of things from her bag, it was less tangled and framed her face with crimson waves. It was just long enough, Crow demonstrated, for her to pull it back and tie it into a ponytail if necessary. The witch offered a black silk ribbon, and she tied a neat black bow, securing the hair behind her head and making her look less like a scared young girl—"and more like a warrior," Crow had chuckled. "A lovely, gorgeous, badass warrior."

And she felt like a warrior, too. She was standing taller and more confidently as Crow led the way over to the table with the rest of the black-clothed people. Well, they were almost all in black—one girl was swathed in a deep midnight blue.

"Hey guys," Crow said, setting her computer bag on the table, "Gail, this is Falcon, Thunderbird, Hawk, Canary, and our resident lady in blue is Bluejay. They're witches like me, and help maintain the cell network for this area. Though to be fair, I've never met any of them in person before." They chuckled a little bit, "Guys, this is Gail. She's the one I mentioned rescued me from that cell tower I was tied to. And Gail: Bluejay is the one who told me about the Reclamation."

"And Eagle sent us here," Bluejay said in an accent Gail didn't recognize, "I also heard that you killed the Duke's younger brother."

Gail didn't tremble or cry and her stomach didn't tighten very much. She simply nodded.

"Good," the girl in blue replied. "I didn't know the Duke had a brother at all, but I bet he was just as bad. Rotten, the whole lot of them." There was a general murmur of agreement around the table and Gail's face began to flush.

"Come on, though," Crow said, a pained expression on her face as she pulled a chair over. "Join us."

"But I'm not a—"

"A witch?" the young man who had been introduced as Hawk said, brushing his hair out of his face where it dramatically covered one eye. He was wearing eyeliner. "Not yet you're not."

"I don't really think I could be," Gail protested, but she sat down anyway. "I don't know anything about your magic boxes."

"Gail is a bit too young for computers," Crow explained. "But she did help me scare off a Mori."

"Scaring Mori, helping someone repair a cell tower…And then of course pissing off the Duke. That's a pretty good resume you're building there. So don't count her out just yet."

"Why are you all named after birds?" Gail asked.

"It's symbolic," said Thunderbird, an androgynous-looking person with very short-trimmed hair on their head. "The cell towers are sort of 'nests'. And since we share a lot of information back and forth it gives us a particular 'birds-eye view' of the world."

"It was also our founder's idea," Bluejay added. "Her name is Eagle. Like, that's her actual name. Eagle. Speaking of which…" She turned her screen so Crow could see a conversation where Bluejay had been filling in Eagle on the details of the meet-up. "Eagle says hi and reminds everyone to be safe."

The conversation turned to something technical, and almost instantly, Gail tuned the conversation out and she started looking around the room. Her eyes landed on Nick, over at the other table, sitting like a statue while the other armed forces people laughed uproariously around him while drinking from dark-colored glass bottles. She also looked around for Leonard, and she finally found him in the corner of the room. Lukather was still guarding him, and she uncomfortably realized that the strange man was watching *her*. She was not one to be intimidated, however, and she politely excused herself from the table of tech-babbling witches to walk over to him.

"What do you want, Leonard?" She demanded.

He grinned. "I like what you did to your hair."

"Why are you staring at me?"

"Like I said," he said, pulling his pipe from his pocket, "I'm keeping an eye on you."

She grimaced. "Can you do it without... *staring?*"

He shrugged. "Sure."

She turned away, satisfied, but something caught a memory in the back of her mind and she turned back. "M told me you were a bad thief. What does that mean?"

He started to light his pipe but stopped. "Do you really want to know?" Gail nodded, unafraid. He leaned back in his chair with the unlit pipe in his hand, "You know that M used to be in jail. That he broke out of prison after the Mori invaded."

Gail raised an eyebrow.

"Oh, you didn't know that? Okay. Well. There you go. Revelation one." He moved to finally light his pipe but then apparently decided not to. "Revelation two: he was in prison for tax fraud, impersonating an officer, evading arrest, perjury, trespassing...oh man. What a list. Never killed anybody, though. See, M and I used to be a team. Con men. Grifters. You get me?"

Gail put her hands on her hips, her lips pursed tightly together.

"We had this con," he continued. "It was a great con. Online scams, fake contests—oh, we'd be stealing credit card information and making a few thousand dollars a week. But I had this great idea…see I wanted to go big-time criminal. So I plotted to rob a bank. M said no. He wouldn't back up that kind of operation. It was one thing, he said, to steal from strangers on the internet, but he wasn't going to dip his fingers into physical coin. That was his, uh, moral line."

Gail still didn't reply. She was standing, defiant and tense, awaiting the next revelation about her adopted father.

"Anyways. I did it anyway. I planned a heist without him. But, you see, I planned it as a two-man job. Then, when everything was ready, I guilted him into working with me in the end. I don't even remember what I said, but he agreed so we pulled it off. Made lots of money. Only—" He finally lit his match and began to puff the pipe. "—he got really guilty afterward and snitched on me. Turned himself in and when I heard about it, I booked it. He went to jail and I disappeared."

Gail took in a deep breath. "You basically sent M to jail because of your greed. He was right, you are the bad kind of thief."

"Is there a good kind?" Leonard said, a puff of smoke trailing from his mouth. Gail didn't need to hear any more; she turned on her heel and walked over to Nick's table, with Lukather on her heels.

The table of military members was rather loud, and none of the uniformed people paid the redhead any mind as she walked up to the armored man. "Hi Nick," she said with a smile.

Nick looked at her and waved.

"I wanted to thank you for coming with us. I'm sorry for everything that's happened to you and I just wanted to say I appreciated your company."

"Happy to join you, especially after you fixed my talk box," he signed. "You are looking a little less stressed. Feeling better?"

She nodded.

"Do you know where you're going to go after the seminar?"

"The road I'm looking for. The one Crow mentioned."

Nick contemplated this for a moment. "I would be glad to escort you there. I would like to be sure you get there safely."

"That's awfully kind of you," Gail said. "I'd appreciate the company." She leaned in and gave the armored man a little hug, trying to push the idea out of her mind that she was, in fact, hugging an armored dead body. "I'll see you later," she said with a smile.

Nick gave her a thumbs up, and she headed back to Crow's table.

For the next couple of hours, Gail sat at the table with the witches and listened to them talk about things she had never heard of before like "sequel server" and "javascript". Somewhere in there, they all set up their computers and began talking not only to each other, but also to people somewhere else. The cell network, Crow explained, covered much of the east coast and Midwest, as well as connecting as regular intervals to access points in Europe. So long as the signal was transmitted through radio signal, it was difficult for the Mori to pinpoint and intercept it.

Gail yawned and felt herself drifting off. At some point she apparently began to doze, because she soon after felt a finger prodding her nose gently. "Hey. Are we losing you?" Crow asked. Gail opened her eyes and found that she had rested her head on Crow's shoulder. She straightened herself up. "Yes. Sorry. I'm fine. Just tired."

"Maybe we should find a place to sleep." Crow looked at Bluejay while she closed her laptop. "That one guy, Green, said that the dorms are up for rent? How much is it?"

"Not much. They're old student dorms, so they're small but comfortable. The campus board of trustees is trying to attract people to the area, I think, and get younger people to start coming back to school."

"Fat chance, after the Riots," Crow grumbled, standing up. "Well, I guess I'll see you all tomorrow morning."

"How many people do you think know I killed Dirk?" Gail said softly as they passed from the dining hall out into the hall's main lobby. The cool night air was rushing through the cracks under the front door, a stark contrast to the lower level's heat from the crowd.

"Hopefully, not many." Outside, the wind let out a moan as it swept past the open doorway. It was quickly becoming dark; the evening shades of sun were vanishing behind the campus buildings. Gail shivered; it was partly due to the cold but also because of the overwhelming realization that this had once been a bustling campus full of young people before the Mori had killed them all in a single violent action.

Lukather was waiting outside. He barked once, and stood up to follow them. The brick path through the campus had been painted with yellow arrows which pointed toward the dorms. The two girls strolled through the campus, where a groundskeeper was lighting the many streetlamps that ran through the quad ahead. It gave the shadowed parts of the buildings an unearthly glow.

Hedgpeth Hall was apparently their destination for the evening. It was the only dorm building with lamp lights visible in the rows upon rows of windows. It wasn't a particularly tall building—it was rather plain and shaped like a large brick box. Gail and Crow followed the yellow pattern across an asphalt parking lot and up to the back door. A round, sunken-faced woman sat at the security desk with a lockbox. "Evening," she drawled.

"Evening," Crow replied, taking out her bag of bandit money. "How much for two rooms?"

"Fifteen each," she replied, unlocking the lockbox with a key from her pocket.

Crow counted the tubes in her bag and frowned. "Alright then. I guess we'll have to do just one room then. That okay with you?" she asked with a sidelong glance to Gail. The redhead nodded.

The woman took the ill-gotten money and exchanged it for a room key. Gail let out a grumble of pain from her leg as she trudged up the stairs, and by the time they'd reached the third floor she felt more exhausted than she could ever remember.

The room, to its credit, was a nice shared apartment layout. The common area—unfurnished—would have certainly fit a large couch and a few chairs. Off to the left was a kitchen, and in through the portal beyond lay a bedroom. Lukather spun around a few times and flopped down onto the carpet, while Gail walked straight through to the bedroom without a word, finding a lumpy but comfortable-looking mattress on a rusting frame.

"Check your bandage," Crow reminded.

"You check yours," Gail shot back sitting down to remove her pants. She looked at her thigh wound; despite all the jostling from walking, it had remained clean as ordered, and Gail went through the motions of unrolling additional linen from her bag and preparing to re-bandage her wound.

Crow, meanwhile, was having no such luck. The puncture in her back was just out of reach, and despite discarding her cloak and shirt, no amount of flexing or twisting would allow her to reach it. Gail watched her, perhaps a little amused, as she tried, but eventually the witch gave up. "Here," Gail said, securing her thigh bandage and moving over to sit by her. She peeled away the sticky gauze pad and saw that, while it hadn't grown any worse, the jagged puncture wound was still inflamed and red. She worked quickly, adding new ointment and securing a new sticky pad over it without a word.

On the subject of silence—Crow was being very quiet this evening. Once the bandage was secured she peeled away the rest of her clothes and flopped down on her back. In the lamplight, Gail could barely see the prickly texture of goose bumps which covered Crow's exposed skin. "Cold?" She asked.

"Yeah."

Gail stood up and checked a closet. Sure enough, it had a couple of tan blankets with tattered shiny edges.

"I want to trust you with something," Crow said finally, as Gail took one and unfolded it. "I found something out a few months back. Someone on the New Internet intercepted a radio message between two advocates. The Mori have big plans coming up the beginning of November. The next phase of their plan. They call it the *Reclamation*." She shuddered. "It's going to be the Riots but worse. They're going to wipe out people altogether, Gail. A massive genocide of everybody except a small few hand-picked by the advocates. That's what this seminar is about—Dr. Glenn is part of a plan to stop it. Bluejay, too. We're going to stop the Mori before it's too late. That's why I'm here. I want to get involved."

Gail handed Crow the blanket. "I want to help, too. But M told me I have to find this road."

"But you don't know why." Crow sounded dubious again.

Gail didn't respond; she just sat quietly, cross-legged on the bed beside her, while Crow shrugged and turned over. The witch sank into sleep in what felt like an instant, but Gail remained awake long after the sun had gone down, leaving the lamp in the window as the only source of light in the room.

ELEVEN

For the first time in a while, it was not a nightmare that awakened Gail the next morning. It was the first light, rudely streaming through the slatted window onto her face, which made her force her eyes open and draw a shuddering yawn from her mouth.

She was unusually warm, she noticed, and she discovered that at some point in the night she had crawled under the blanket and curled up beside Crow, who was still quite asleep. It was a comforting feeling, and one she did not want to pull away from, but at the same time she didn't want to be late for the morning's seminar. She carefully detached herself from her friend, who shuddered against the sudden rush of cold and pulled the blanket in around herself without waking. Gail stretched, headed to the bathroom, and returned to get dressed.

Crow still hadn't awakened. Gail patted her blanket. "Crow? It's time to go."

"I don't wanna," Crow said, pulling the blanket over her head so that she was completely covered.

"I don't want to waste time, do you?"

Crow let out a groan at her own words being used against her and threw the blanket off, gasping as the chilly air in the room came into contact with so much exposed skin. "Holy f—Jesus, Gail, it's freezing in here."

"I know," Gail said with pursed lips. "That happens when it gets cold."

Crow scrambled to put on her clothes, especially her black cloak that she tightened around herself. "I hate the winter."

"It's not even winter yet." She checked her sword, threw her jacket over her shoulders, and headed through the common room and down the stairs. Lukather was waiting by the door, ready for the next day's adventure.

Outside, the sky had lit up in swirls of red and purple, making the whole campus look like a muted painting done in two or three tones. People milled about outside, smoking cigarettes and talking in low voices next to buildings which served as breakers for the wind. A few of these people stared at the pair as they passed, and Gail wondered if her reputation as the murderer of the Duke's brother had made its way through the grapevine yet.

The seminar was taking place in a large lecture hall a few buildings down. The number of visitors appeared to have easily tripled overnight; the dozens who were down in the dining hall the night before had grown to one, maybe two hundred people now finding seats and waiting. The stage was empty save for a simple lectern and a white screen, which was apparently set up for the antique glass projector halfway across the auditorium.

Crow led Gail over toward the other witches and sat down with them. "Morning, guys."

"Morning, you two," Bluejay said with a wry grin. "Did you sleep well? Or did you skip sleep altogether?" Her eyebrows were high enough to risk disappearing into her hair.

"Oh hush, you," Crow said, pulling down one of the theater seats into a sitting position. "It's not like that."

"I mean," Bluejay continued, "you are sort of hanging all over each other this morning, so…"

"It's not like that," Crow repeated, and Gail continued to stand there, looking quite confused. It seemed to be some kind of inside joke, and upon seeing her face Crow unhelpfully explained, "She's suggesting that we're sleeping together."

"But we did sleep together," Gail said softly, taking a seat. "Is there something wrong with that?"

Crow's eyes went wide, and her face went through a cycle of several shades of red. "No! I mean, well, yes we did—but not like *that*."

"Like what?"

Crow looked helplessly at her. "You—you are really—" She gave up and put her head in her hands while Bluejay and a few other witches laughed uproariously at her expense.

Up on stage, a man with a shock of white hair finally stepped out from the curtains and up to the lectern. From here, Gail could see a web of wrinkles on his face that danced in unison as he spoke. "Good morning, people of Earth," he said with a big, toothy smile, resting a glass of water on the lectern.

"Good morning," came unenthusiastic replies from all over the room.

"I am appreciative of the attendance here today. I have given several talks such as these over the last few months, and I've only one more stop on my journey. Some of you have followed me in my task and I am thankful that you are here. Together, we have a chance to finally be free of the Mori." He took a sip of the glass of water. "I also would like to thank Mr. Green and the Central North Carolina Police for their help with security and vetting. Your devotion to protect people who need your help is always deeply appreciated. Even if law enforcement these days is a very different job than it was before the Mori."

"I'll say," Crow muttered. "Self-important glorified mercenaries…"

"Please allow me to introduce myself." He shuffled a card on the lectern. "I am Professor Avery Glenn. Director of Celtic Studies at Boston University. I am a noted academic in the field of Irish

Mythology, European proto-history, and cultural anthropology of the British Isles prior to 1500 BC." None of these words made any sense to Gail, but he sounded rather knowledgeable all the same.

"Let's talk about the Mori, shall we?" He nodded to a stage assistant, who lit the candle in the back of the projector and set the first slide into place. It showed a seashore, with a crashing wave frozen in the moment it touched the land.

"I assume that most of you are familiar with the biblical tale of Noah's Ark." There was a general nodding of consensus. "What you may not know is that the idea of a Flood Myth is not exclusive to Christian mythology. In fact, nearly every major culture has a myth about flooding, or rising sea water. In Ancient Sumeria, for example," he said as the slide changed to show a sandstone tablet covered in unintelligible symbols, "a tablet discovered in the early 18th century by scholar Hermann Hilprecht lists the ancient kings of Sumeria. These kings are divided into two classes—Deluvian and Antediluvian: Pre-flood and Post-flood kings.

"The Burckle Crater Hypothesis is a theory that these flood myths all have a single *real* historical event." The screen showed a map of the Earth, with a red arrow pointed off the coast of Madagascar. "This crater is evidence of an impact about 3200 years ago."

He took another sip of his water and the screen changed again, showing a blurry image of men in armor landing on a shoreline in boats. "The flood is also mentioned in the oral history of Ireland. This historical account, originated before written records, was passed down word-of-mouth until being collected as ballads and poems such as the *Libor Gabala* and the *Tain Bo Cualnge*, which document several of the mythological invasions of Ireland. There were several of these, along with tales about folk heroes and highly fantastical accounts of wars fought with might and magic."

There were a lot of tilted heads and furrowed brows in the audience. "But why should you care?" he asked with emphatic gestures of his hands, "What does this have to do with the Mori? Well…among these invasions: the Fomóraiġ, or Fomoire. Mythological creatures with magic and power unimaginable." He let the moment hang in the air while the gears turned in a hundred listening heads. "Ladies and Gentlemen," Glenn said with gravity, "This is not the first invasion of the Mori. *They have been here before.*"

The crowd erupted into excited and horrified whispers. Gail looked around and noticed that Green and the other police officers were gesturing excitedly. One of them pointed straight at her, and Green nodded. She shifted uncomfortably in her seat.

"According to these ballads," Glenn said after allowing some of the reaction to his words to sink in, "the Fomóraiġ, under the command of Cíocal Gricenchos arrived in Ireland shortly after the biblical flood—one which I assert was caused by the landing of the Mori space ship—in about 2800 BC. The Fomóraiġ asserted an iron rule on the native inhabitants of the island, using fantastical powers to control them and bend them to their wills."

The next slide showed a different scene of different people crossing the sweeping hills of the Irish countryside. "Over 300 years later, Muintir Partholón arrived as part of the second settlers. Partholón's people started a slow rebellion against the oppressive Fomóraiġ, and after a decade they launched an all-out war. The *Libor Gabala* describes the mythical Battle of Mag Itha. In this ballad, it is noted that it was fought 'with magic on both sides'. In other words, Partholón was able to harness Mori technology—their magic—and turn it on its owners.

"The Fomóraiġ, taken by surprise at their own magic being used against them, fled and took refuge off the island. Depending on which history you read, the Fomóraiġ became pirates or sea monsters. Partholón's people then died mysteriously of plague. This only left some of the descendants of Partholón, led by Neimheadh, a descendant of the biblical Noah."

Gail glanced over at Green again, who was now starting a slow walk up the side of the auditorium. She tapped Crow with a finger and gestured to him as discreetly as she could. "Green's acting weird. I think he knows."

Crow glanced over, pushed up her glasses, and nodded.

"The Fomóraiġ returned to the island and tried to assert control over Neimheadh's people. Neimheadh and his sons gave the Fomóraiġ battle and killed their leaders. Despite this victory, the power of the Fomóraiġ was too great, and their newly elected leaders Conand and Morg erected a tower from which they were able to derive great magic. They killed Neimheadh and three of his sons and enslaved the rest." He took another sip of water and the slide changed to show an artist's depiction of a massive tower. "But the myth does not end there."

Green had slinked behind the crowd and was now moving along the row. He took a seat beside Gail and nodded to her. "Do not move and do not shout," he said in a soft voice that Gail was sure only she could hear, "but you should know that the bounty on your head has more than doubled in the last 24 hours. So, this is what we're going to do: as soon as the professor is done speaking, you will follow me out the back and we'll have a conversation."

Gail trembled as she nodded her head, too afraid to look at him or even at Crow. She focused on Glenn, who seemed to be reaching the climax of his tale.

"The last son of Neimheadh was Fergus Red-Side, a strategist of great ability. He was able to free many slaves, make treaties with neighbors…he gathered together a mighty army, crossed the hills to Conand's Tower, breached its walls, and put the Fomóraiġ to flight. *Without* their magic," he added knowingly. "Fergus Red-Side drove the Fomóraiġ back to the sea, when a mighty wave rose up and swallowed all of them. And they were never seen again."

Gail raised her right hand as if to scratch her head. She didn't see him anywhere, but she hoped that Nick might be able to see her as, just out of Green's field of view, she began to letter-sign over and over: H-E-L-P. H-E-L-P.

"We won once," Glenn concluded, as another slide, this one of a modern-looking tower over a city, appeared on the projector screen. "And we can win again. I give you the Tower of Peace, built 15 years ago by the Mori in St. Petersburg, Florida. The capitol of the Mori here on Earth. Four thousand years have passed, but the Mori have not changed. Now, for our plan to put an end to this invasion of our old enemies, I will turn the floor over to my friend and technical expert, Mr. Bohr."

Gail's jaw dropped as Leonard, now dressed in a sharp grey suit, ascended the stage stairs and replaced Professor Glenn at the lectern. He was still wearing his narrow-brimmed hat. "Good morning, folks," he said with a grin. "My name is Leonard Bohr. I am formerly a networking and security specialist for a major bank. Today, I am one of the foremost authorities in the area on the Mori. I am here to talk a little bit about Mori technology—what some of you younger folks believe to be magic. With Professor Glenn's expertise and my skills, we…"

"Let's go," Green said, tugging on Gail's jacket.

"Come on, Crow," Gail said, straightening and slowly rising to her feet. Crow looked up and at Green, spotting something behind Gail's back that she couldn't see. She nodded and stood up to follow. Green took Gail by the arm and led her casually to the back door of the auditorium and outside, beyond the range of hearing from the inside. Around the corner, several uniformed officers stood with weapons in their hands.

"Now," Green said as one of them took Gail by her other arm. Another seized Crow, who let out a frustrated grunt. "What's your name, princess?" he demanded of the redhead.

"Let me go! I didn't do anything wrong," she pleaded in response.

"You killed the Duke's brother."

"I was there," Crow interrupted. "I saw it happen. Dirk, right? He threatened us, and then he fell. It was his own stupid fault."

Gail sighed. "It was an accident. He fell on my sword. He was drunk. You have to believe me—"

A right hook made Gail's vision explode into dazzling light for a moment. She sputtered, something salty tracing its way along her upper gums. "I don't care," he growled. "I want to get paid. And I don't want any trouble." He looked at Crow. "As for her…there's no bounty on her." Gail's heart leapt in her chest—maybe they would just let Crow go. Maybe Crow would get help? Or she would just run away and be safe? Either of those options were satisfactory as long as Crow remained unharmed. Green dismissed these thoughts with his next words, however. "Just kill her."

Crow, however, was looking above Green's head, behind where Gail was standing. A grin unrolled across the witch's face, and she stared right into Green's eyes. "Go fuck yourself," she said with a smile.

A rapid clicking sound erupted from her pocket, and the thugs holding her both stiffened and let out anguished cries before letting her go and dropping to the ground. Green raised his crossbow at her, but before he could even get his finger to the trigger, a massive armored body slammed into him from above. Gail had no idea how much Nick weighed, but from the sudden splatters of blood that left trails outward across the sidewalk, she figured it was certainly enough to crush the man's ribcage in a single stomp.

Gail lashed out, throwing an elbow into the face of one of the men holding her. The other one tried to sink his knife into her belly, but she threw herself backward, and his knife only sliced at air. She drew her sword, and in an explosion of nerves and adrenaline she swung the blade against the back of a knee, severing tendons and crumpling the thug to the ground while the last one, realizing all-too-late that this was not the right fight, took off across the quad. He got about twenty feet before an arrow split the chilly morning air, entering one side of his head and lodging there. He slowed, swayed, stumbled, and hit the ground with a sickening thump.

Crow was still standing where she had been, but after a moment she shook herself as if to shake off rain and proceeded to stomp her boot into the faces of the two people at her feet until they stopped moving. "How did you do that? Was that some kind of magic?" Gail gasped at her.

Crow pulled a black, curved tool out of her pocket and clicked it, making an arc of light crackle at the end. "With this. They both grabbed me, and I shocked myself, so it shocked them. Unlike them, though—"

"—you don't feel pain," Gail said, nodding. "Also, Nick…you are amazing."

Nick shrugged, pushing himself off of Green. The man didn't move, but his injuries remained covered by his coat. It was clear, however, that he was dead.

From the other end of the quad, a familiar blue-clad woman stepped out from her hiding spot. "You didn't think I would trust police officers walking away with my new friends, did you?" she called.

"Bluejay!" Crow grinned, walking toward her. "I'm so glad that you're such a—"

Bluejay screamed. It was an odd sound, like a scream from just below the surface of water, and as she dropped to the ground, Gail could see red pouring out of her mouth and ears.

"Mori!" Crow screeched, her feet frozen in place.

"Warn everyone inside," Gail commanded, dashing toward the fallen Bluejay. Crow took off while Nick followed Gail, looking around for the source of the spell that was now making the poor woman wretch and writhe on the ground. Gail grabbed her collar and hefted her out of the open area of the quad toward the archway of a building. Bluejay was still alert, but her breathing was becoming far more distressed as her throat and mouth continued to drip blood.

"Bluejay!" Gail said, pulling the woman's head into her lap. "What can I do! Where is it coming from?"

The woman could not answer. Her eyes were becoming red from suffocation. She grabbed the front of Gail's shirt with a bloody hand, and then with the other she started to trace a finger on the sidewalk, leaving a mark in the blood.

"What is it? How can I help you?" Gail cried through tears.

Bluejay traced a few letters and numbers on the ground: *1L9F0B0*. Once satisfied with this, she smeared the letters so they were unreadable and pointed to her bag, laying on the ground a few feet away. Nick picked it up and brought it over instantly. Still heaving

114

massive amounts of blood, the woman shoved the bag into Gail's hands. She coughed up more blood and forced herself to inhale, filling her lungs with just enough air to cough out a single word. "Osbourne." Her eyes, now red with lack of air and beginning to bleed on their own, rolled back into her head before she slumped back and stopped breathing.

Gail shook, unable to move for what seemed like an eternity. Her mind was filled with the image of her own parents, faces and hands bloodied like this, the last time she had seen them. Her mother's eyes, open and staring forever at nothing just like Bluejay's now were. Bluejay was another victim, just like they had been. Another victim of the Mori.

A far-off scream pulled her from her thoughts, and as she felt Nick's powerful hand on her shoulder, she knew she had to rise. She had to find Crow. She had to get out of here. She had to get Lukather—poor Lukather! Wherever he was, he was in such danger right now!

Stumbling, she drew her sword into her bloody hand and made her way around the side of the building back toward the auditorium. She saw them then—three of the tall, golden-clothed aliens floated a foot off the ground and were laughing as they threw balls of energy and shouted occultic words at the fleeing people as they poured out the doors. The people, unaware, ran right into their line of fire.

"We have to *do* something," Gail said, and before she could figure out exactly *what* to do, she had thrown herself forward. A scream—full of rage and originating deep in her wrenching gut—came from her lips, and the closest Mori to her had but a moment to turn and acknowledge her presence before M's sword came down in his face, and everything was darkness.

INTERLUDE: THE BANDIT

Gail dreamed that she was Dirk. She dreamed that she was the man she had killed.

It was dark in the forest, and his ears were keen to any sound that might give away his position to others. He was being careful. Even so, he winced as the tip of his scabbard scraped against the stone.

It should have been a fleeting sound that vanished into the darkness and went entirely unheard. Dirk himself would have heard it, and after a moment of consideration he should have shrugged it off and continued on his path through the trees, never again even considering the brief moment where the metal tip of his sword's scabbard had glanced off of a jutting piece of stone near the path where he walked. Yes, for sure, no one should ever have heard that tiny scrape of sound, because the bandit band had been very careful to avoid making any noise whatsoever. They had walked in patches of wet leaves and grass, where their very footsteps were swallowed by the mud that seemed to stretch on into infinity.

This mud! It was an awful thing that stung the tips of his fingers. No matter how well-secured his boots had been, the cold and wet always found its way in, through the tiniest holes and from all directions, soaking the leather through and leaving the foot beneath icy and numb. He yearned, even now, for a fireside, and if the boss had been truthful, it would only be a few more short miles of woods before they could escape the trees and brave the open countryside for a few *more* miles before finding town. Then, maybe, he could put his sore and cold feet in front of a steaming pot of stew and just sit there with a bowl of brown, bubbling gravy and meat in his lap. Maybe there would even be a hunk of bread to mop up the stew from the bowl before being chewed down on and releasing the savory liquid like a sponge into his waiting maw. And, of course, there would be wine and maybe fair company.

All of these things that were tumbling warmly around his skull should have been reality. They would have been—and even were expected to be—so long as there wasn't trouble. It had been a clean job so far, evidenced by the long leather sack tied over his shoulder: the fruits of their labors. It had probably been a mistake for the farmer to have had such a bounty just out on *display*, for any passer-by to see and gawk at. Of course, the passer-by would have had to have been up close to the farmer's window. And the curtains would have had to be open. And to be fair, the person would probably have had to be inside the farmer's house in the first place, which was exactly where Dirk was when he and his crew spotted the massive bounty just sitting there against the wall. Dirk and the other two had considered it for some time and agreed that such things should not be kept for the rare and privileged. The boss was calculating in his head before signaling that this was going to be their big haul, and he grinned the kind of grin that only ever graces the boss's face when he discovers the thief's trifecta: something that is valuable, in demand, and stealable.

A house, for instance, is both valuable and in demand. But one cannot easily steal a house. Not without kill the owners and their friends, and maybe even bribing local officials to report that the previous owners had "run off" leaving a perfectly good house for the taking. Such things lead to curious constables to answer the call of "I think a murderer just moved in next door", which inherently decreases the value of the house in the first place.

On the other hand, a box full of diamonds is valuable and stealable. But to find a buyer for those diamonds? Not so easy. One would practically have to trade diamonds for mere necessities, and eventually try to find some very wealthy person who might want to buy a few. But then there are those questions like "Where did you get those diamonds" and "What stops me from just killing you and taking them for myself" which are equally problematic to the unstealable house.

Then, of course, there are the things that are in demand and stealable, but which lack inherent value. Food, for instance, would fall into this category.

Dirk had stolen food throughout his entire life. More than likely, he mused, he had eaten more stolen food in the last ten years than food he had paid for. But it was a way to survive and he felt justified in his actions, at least, knowing that while food was in demand and stealable, there was a lot of it just growing everywhere, especially out here among the wheat fields. Food theft was practically a societal norm at this point: either you ate fruit off trees, or you stole handfuls of crops, or you munched on tall grass if you were desperate. Or maybe you were lucky and more than a little unscrupulous, and you stole livestock. Oh, what Dirk would have given for a nice breast of chicken or a slab of pork belly right now. But soon! Oh, he could almost smell it already…

All at once, in her dream, she was herself again. She was reclined, curled up in dry leaves in the off-road camp she had set up securely in the woods, she was awakened by the smallest of sounds. It might have been drowned out in the chirping of insects and the rustle of leaves in the night, but this night was peculiarly quiet. The sound of steel, to be sure, was a contrast to the sounds of nature, and is pierced her senses as though it had been heard from just in front of her face. Her eyes snapped open, and her fingers tensed, closing around a shaft made of leather and metal. It was an expert movement that brought her to her feet. It was as silent as a single breath. And with this movement, the mountain girl was alert and, despite the looming darkness that pressed in from all sides, she could just barely see the bandits in the darkness.

She was relieved that it wasn't one of the Mori, but bandits were just as dangerous. She readied her sword and waited to see if they had noticed her.

But they had not. They continued to traipse along through the wet leaves and grass in the other direction. She might have just laid her head back down where she had been lying but she was far too awake now. Her heart was racing. Sleep could wait until later.

She grabbed her blanket from the ground with one hand while sheathing her sword with the other. Her pack was within arm's reach, and as she pulled it across her shoulder she glanced around for the shaggy form of Lukather. But he was off somewhere already, and he would be able to find her if needed.

There was a long moment where she stood there, barely breathing through her nose and taking in the chilly and damp air. The sight of the bandits had made her stomach turn in a way she was not expecting. How long had it been since she had heard a human voice? Not that the bandits were saying anything right now—even so, the thought of them, after being free of the oppressive darkness and silence of the forest, breaking into gruff conversation about who they had robbed and murdered recently, gave her a moment of consideration.

It was a strange moment there as she considered her current position. She wasn't necessarily *condoning* the behaviors of the thieves. They had probably robbed and pillaged for years and would probably end up at the end of a hangman's noose before too long. It would be just and deserved. But for this moment, despite their crimes, she somehow...appreciated their existence.

She took off after them.

Unlike her, they looked like they knew where they were going. The ability to survive in the wilderness is one thing, but to navigate was something altogether different, and it was an infuriating trait to lack. She had managed so far but already she could see that this was a shortsighted plan and eventually she would have to recalibrate her path. Road signs only helped so much, especially ones that had been left to the elements for many years.

More to the point, the nights resting in beds of grass and hard stone was starting to gnaw at her. Back in the mountains, she had a bed made of stuffed linen that met her needs. It was comfortable. Or at least, as comfortable as one could find in the wilderness. All in all, she didn't mind the empty forest or the open plains or the mountains in the slightest—but that didn't mean that the idea of a warm bed wasn't an enticing one.

And so she became like a shadow, being careful to keep quiet as she trailed the roving rogue band by a short distance. Just close enough to keep them barely in her view, but not close enough to alert them.

The night was beginning to wane. She glanced up at the canopy in the hopes of stealing a glance of the moon. She spotted it, up ahead in the sky through the slowly-thinning canopy of leaves. Were they starting to escape the forest already? A relief.

A sound to her left pulled her from her reverie, and she stopped to concentrate, straining her ears hard enough that she could almost hear blood pounding in them. Something was moving nearby—something on four legs. For a moment, she thought it might be her own dog, having caught up to her, but another set of soft footsteps sounded behind her and to the right. The bandits—and the mountain girl, by proxy—were being stalked. Clearly, the echo of Dirk's sword against stone had stirred more than just the traveling swordswoman and her dog.

She raised her arms above her head. The wolves, she knew, were watching right now, and waiting. Wolves did not like to be around people if they could help it, and by appearing imposing it was likely that they would leave her alone. As long as no one panicked or—

"*Wolves!*" she jumped at the sound, as the man in the middle immediately panicked. But maybe it would be alright—in fact, the loud sound might give the wolves more reason not to approach. Just as long as no one started to—

"*Run!*" another shouted, and the pack of rogues took off into the darkness. Dammit. A moment ago, the wolves were watching with curiosity, and perhaps even fearfulness. Now, as far as the wolves were concerned, the bandits had been demoted about a hundred ranks in the immediate hierarchy. Now, they were *prey*.

She let out a frustrated shout at the top of her lungs, the sound coming out dry and raspy and unfamiliar to her own ears. She shifted her weight downward and broke into a run, nearly sending her tumbling into the last person in the group, but she dodged him at the last moment, continuing her agile sprint through the darkness.

It really would be a fool who would travel without the expectation of fleeing at any given moment. The land was so fraught with perils these days that attack could come from anywhere. The bandits, being one of those perils, knew this as well as anyone, and at the slightest hint of danger were off, abandoning any attempt at stealth and tearing through the trees toward the edge of the woods. It was a long moment and many precarious footsteps before the cool and humid wind of the forest was replaced by the stinging chill of a hillside breeze. Four sets of wild footsteps tore downward from the woods toward a town just visible in the distance, and as a heart-wrenching howl pierced the night air, the pack of beasts broke the edge of the woods and charged down the hill in pursuit.

Gail knew that they wouldn't make it to the town before the creatures had caught up. Out to her left, she saw a dark streak darting across the hills in a sidelong charge, and, knowing she had backup, turned to face them. Her sword found its way to her hand in an instant, and with a shift of her weight she reversed direction. Her boots slid in the mud a meter or so before she regained her footing and charged the leader, swinging the sword high above her head and screaming loudly to make herself as imposing as possible.

The sword came down hard, cleaving into the shoulder of the leading wolf and sending it to the ground off-balance. At the same moment, a massive English sheepdog collided into a second wolf, snarling and biting as they tumbled. The dog knew all too well that the wolves would be intimidated by a dangerous piece of prey, so it was likely that the growling and snapping was more for appearance than an attempt to maim. The wolf escaped its far-furrier attacker and tried to scamper off.

The leader of the pack howled, a red stain forming from the wound in its shoulder, and it rolled back to a standing position. She waved her sword above her head again, screaming loud, guttural noises at it while stomping loudly. It was a tense moment while it considered her, snarling and puffing hot air out its nostrils that hung visibly in spirals around its face.

It looked from the mountain girl to the sheepdog, and then past her, over her shoulder. Somewhere in its predatory brain it did some canine math, and with an angry grunt it turned to dash back toward the tree line, its pack mates in tow.

As soon as the wolves had cleared the hill, she spun to run toward town. Instantly she found herself facing a long arrow nocked on a metal bow pointed straight at her eyes. "Back off!" the bandit shouted. "You brought the wolves down on us!"

"*You* brought them down on you," she said with a cautious step back. "You *never* run from a wolf. It only makes them chase you. Didn't you know that?" He didn't reply, but his face told her everything she needed to know. "I guess not," she said, slowly and deliberately lowering the tip of her red-streaked sword, "and since you caused the wolf problem and I solved it, I figure the least you can do it put your bow down and keep walking. We're both headed the same direction."

Dirk snapped his sword into a sheath. The bowman shot him a cold glare, but Dirk only shrugged. "I don't want a fight this close t' town. You do what you want." Dirk turned on his heel and started off toward town. The other followed. The decision having been made, apparently, the bowman relaxed his bow and took off after them, throwing an angry glare over his shoulder as they vanished over the hill toward town.

TWELVE

"Shhh, it's okay," a voice called through the void. The void was endless before her, swirling with light and mist and flashing lights. As she stood there looking out at eternity, reality rushed up at her from below and threw her backward. Her head was spinning. She wasn't moving at all, it turned out; she was reclining, her head resting on something soft.

Her eyelids were terribly heavy, and it took an immense amount of energy to open even one of them. The first thing she saw was Nick, silhouetted against the moonlit sky, his features flickering in and out of view. The flickering, she realized, was that of a campfire, casting shadows across the armored man. He waved hello.

"Where's Lukather?" her first question to the armored man elicited a yelp from behind him, and the shaggy dog ran over to lick Gail's face and plop down beside her next to the fire. Satisfied that the dog was unharmed, she forced another question out. "Are you okay?"

"Yes," he signed.

"How about Crow? I sent her right into the Mori…" She coughed and a hand reached out to pat her from above. The soft surface her head was lying on, it appeared, was Crow's lap.

"I'm okay. Actually if you hadn't sent me there it would have been a lot worse. They had us surrounded. And they were going to just kill everyone, but I warned everybody and we were able to arm up and scatter. And then *apparently* some feisty redhead came out of nowhere and cleaved one of their heads in half." She smirked. "I can honestly say I've never heard of that happening before."

"I killed...I killed a Mori?" It hit her that she wasn't entirely upset with the prospect the way she had been about Dirk. "What happened afterward? It's all black."

"Well, there was a big fight. Professor Glenn is dead. I only saw part of it; I was trying to get people out of there as fast as I could. By the time I got out to the front, the Mori were gone and you were already out cold."

Gail reached up to feel her head, which was now throbbing. "Thank you," she coughed. "Thank you for getting me out of there."

Crow's eye twitched a little bit, and the sparkle drained out of her face. "I didn't," she grumbled, gesturing with her eyes. Gail turned her head, trying to avoid sparking more pain in her head and neck. There, sitting near her feet, was Leonard.

"You!" Gail shouted, jerking backward and almost toppling Crow over. "Get away from me!" Leonard didn't even react, save for a tiny confused wrinkle of his eyebrows. "Why are you following me? I don't know who you are! M's brother? Some expert on the Mori? An entertainer? A Bandit?"

"Yes, yes, yes, and...sort of?" He replied, scooting away from her. "I generally don't have the stomach for thug work. I'm a face man, if you catch my drift."

"Aren't face men supposed to be likeable?" Crow retorted. She patted Gail gently. "Breathe, Necia. All I can say is that he did save you. And it was...messy. Besides, if he tries to hurt you, me and the tin can will protect you." Nick looked at Crow and nodded before making a knuckle-cracking gesture in Leonard's direction.

"What do you mean, 'messy'?" Gail was regaining control of her breathing, but the salty taste of blood was still lingering in her mouth.

"When I saw you, one of the two Mori was about to cast some spell in your direction. You were still up and fighting, but I don't know what it would have done. So I did the only thing I could—I pushed you out of the way." He lifted his arm, and Gail gasped.

Leonard's arm ended just above the wrist. It wasn't maimed or even scarred; it was simply a cap on the end of the stump as if an arm had never been there in the first place. "How—what did they—" Gail choked out.

"It doesn't hurt," he said, returning his gaze to the fire and covering his arm with the tatters of his jacket. "I mean, it did. They didn't lop it off or anything. They just...it just *ungrew*. Might be one of those things they do to make people disappear." He shivered for a moment, and Gail wasn't sure if it was from the cold. "My throwing arm, too. No more knife tricks. I am now useless in a fight. So it's up to you if you want to trust me at this point," he said, casting a dark glare at the mountain girl, "But if you don't, I'm pretty sure that's entirely on you."

Gail shifted her weight a little, pushing backward into Crow. "I don't...I..." She couldn't find the words she was looking for.

"Look, Leonard" Crow said, and she appeared to understand what Gail was feeling, "I'm appreciative. *Very* appreciative. And I think I can trust you, but you have to fill us in on what's going on. And that goes for both of you," she added to Gail. "I need to know who you are and what happened. Leonard, you seem to know Dr. Glenn, so I'm hoping you know some of his plan? And Gail, you're involved...somehow. I haven't pieced that together yet."

"I don't want to tell your story for you," Leonard said, shifting uncomfortably in his jacket. "But I know a lot of it. Telling stories is all I have right now, so if you want, I'll share what I know."

Gail looked him up and down, hoping to see something that might give him away. If what he said was true, he would know M's story and perhaps even hers. She didn't know how much M talked about her when he was away. And if he was lying, she would know because his story wouldn't match up with her recollections. Glancing up at Crow, whose scornful gaze upon the crumpled man was still going strong, she nodded to him.

Leonard began with a retelling on his history with M, and their failed bank heist that landed him in jail. "It was a light sentence, though," he finished, putting more sticks on the fire. "And I expected that I'd see my brother again within a few years. I just had to keep low in that time. It wasn't even three months into his sentence, however, when the invasion happened. And it was M—Marion, as I knew him—who contacted me."

"Marion?" Crow asked.

"Yeah. He was named after Marion Mitchell Morrison, better known as John Wayne."

"I know John Wayne!" Gail chirped. "M gave me a book about him."

"I'm sure he did," Leonard laughed, "because he was obsessed with that guy. Being the good guy even when he was being bad. And if you know Wayne then you know his nickname—"

"THE DUKE," Nick said through his device.

"Exactly. See, the whole idea of somebody being "The Duke" and being a pillar of the community was M's idea in the first place. After he broke out of jail, he met up with me. We met a guy named Hamilton out near Washington D.C. and started this whole community activism group to try and make sure people that were being relocated by the Mori would be well cared-for. Hamilton took charge, and in the end, it was Marion who ended up giving him the title. Hamilton, then, took all the resources he'd amassed and started the empire you see today."

"You and M worked together?" Gail asked. "He told me you shouldn't be trusted."

"And I don't really think he trusted me either, to be fair," he replied, scratching his beard. "But he trusted me enough that when I told him I wasn't sure about what the Duke was doing, he thought it'd be a good idea to exit stage left. See, Marion wasn't all about that life. He just sort of let Hamilton do his thing and took off on his own, Robin Hood style. He went from town to town trying to see needs and fit them on a local level. By the time he heard that The Duke was starting to abuse his station, it was too late. Then, he found you." He looked over to her, and his eyes were softer than Gail had ever seen them.

"When he told me about finding you, he was so proud. It's like a piece of the puzzle fell into place. See," Leonard shifted a bit to talk more directly to her. Gail didn't move away this time—she was interested in the tale and besides, Crow had begun to softly stroke her head with delicate black-polished fingers, and it was an incredibly nice feeling. "Marion had a daughter before the invasion. He had to leave her behind when he went to jail and when the Mori came, he got separated from his ex-wife and never saw his daughter again. He didn't know if they'd made it, and he always held out hope. But it was weighing on him, and he came pretty close to giving up after a while. Then, you came into his life and he found another reason to keep going. And he found that mountain retreat where he took you, and he came and checked on you every chance he could, and brought you regular supplies, and taught you things. Because he wanted to keep you safe."

"Don't you think it would have been better to raise her with people, though?" While Crow's fingertips remained gentle against Gail's head her voice was not so much. "I mean, no offense, but she's completely lost out here. Everything's new to her. And now we're running from the Duke, dodging Mori, and—"

"The problem is," Leonard interrupted, "she was already in danger. Marion wanted to be sure that she didn't fall into the wrong hands."

"What does that mean?"

"You heard the seminar? Muintir Partholón was the one who turned the Mori technology against them. The way the legend goes, most of them mysteriously died of plague, but Dr. Glenn's theory is that the Mori tried to eliminate them because they had something…something about them that made it possible to resist the Mori magic. It's sort of accepted that the Mori can't be killed—when's the last time you heard of one dying? But as we saw a few days ago, that's not the case."

"A few days ago?" Gail said, the throbbing in her head slowly returning. "How long have I been...?" she asked Crow.

"About three days," Crow said, patting her head. "But I think that was mostly exhaustion. You didn't have any signs of a concussion so we all just...let you sleep."

Gail sighed. "Okay. Thanks, I guess..."

Leonard continued, stoking the fire with a stick, "Partholón and his people, the Partholónians. They were able to fight and kill Mori. They were able to use their Magic. And they didn't need any of the Mori's magical fuel sources. It just worked...somehow. And Dr. Glenn has found that in some people alive today, that's still the case. It's a small percentage of the population, mostly people descended from the British Isles. Your family..." he glanced to Gail. "Were they from a place called New York City?"

The name sounded familiar. It called back memories of tall buildings and busy streets. "I think so?"

"I figured as much. Largest population of Irish-Americans in the whole country. And, as it happens, the largest number of what Glenn thinks are descendants of Muintir Partholón."

Crow shook her head. "What made M think she was one of these Partholónians?"

"When he found her," Leonard replied, "she told him her parents were dead. After he got her situated in the house in the mountains, he went looking for them and found them. But he also found a dead Mori there—killed by one or both parents during the fight. He shared his findings, and they got back to some of Dr. Glenn's people, who got involved with others, and M realized that people like Gail would probably be hunted down if it got out they existed."

He looked over at the redhead, and in the dying firelight there was a burning anger she had never seen before. "They killed my brother, Gail. I need to stop them. I need you to help me. I won't force you, but I'm asking. So…while you sit there recovering, please think about it."

The crackle of the fire was the only sound for a few long moments, as all four of them sunk into their own thoughts. Gail looked down at her hands. It was hard to see them in the flickering orange glow, but she could see that they had stopped trembling. "Where are we?" she softly whispered to Crow.

"Outside of a town called Dunn, about 10 miles southeast of Lillington. Leonard went and bought some supplies since he didn't think the Duke's men would recognize him. We decided to set up here until you woke up."

Gail nodded. "You said other people made it out?"

"Yeah. Lots of them." It was hard to tell if she was telling the truth.

She bit her lip. "I'm sorry about Bluejay."

"Not your fault." Crow was looking upward into the blackness above the trees. There didn't seem to be any stars out tonight.

"It is," Gail breathed. "She wouldn't have been there if I—"

"Not your fault," Crow snapped, her gaze dropping to meet Gail's pleading eyes. Gail jumped at the sharpness in Crow's voice and shuddered uncontrollably. "Oh god, I'm sorry. I'm sorry, I didn't mean—" She pulled Gail closer and put her forehead against Gail's red locks and whispered more apologies.

Gail didn't move. She closed her eyes and tried to hold her tears in. Leonard and Nick were quiet on their side of the fire, and she felt a burning in her cheeks to think that they might be judging her. "I just want to go home," She said, trying to suppress the sob in the back of her throat.

Crow lifted her head. "Home? I thought you were trying to get to Florida. But you just said you're from New York."

Gail fumbled in her pocket, her fingers closing around the folded map. She pulled it out and unfolded it, tilting it so the ink would catch the light of the dying fire. The map was faded, but she could still see the line that was I-95. "When M died…he told me to find a road. This road. He told me to follow it. I think…he said to follow it home."

Crow squinted at it. She traced her finger off the Atlantic coast. "So North is this way. So…when you find your road, you'll be heading this way. Toward New York."

"And we're heading south," Leonard said with a sigh, finally joining in with the conversation. "Florida is where we're going. Toward St. Petersburg and the Peace Tower. I don't know why M would want you to go north."

The redhead's face contorted. "But that's where home is." She looked at Crow. "I guess that we'll split up once we find the road? How far are we?" Crow didn't reply; she just looked up. Gail followed her gaze and, as her eyes adjusted more, she could see that the sky wasn't starless—it was obscured by a massive stone structure far above their heads. "What is that?" She asked, but she thought she already knew the answer.

"I-95 overpass," Leonard replied. "Miss Gail, you have been delivered to your road."

THIRTEEN

In the morning, Nick and Leonard set about cleaning up the camp, covering their tracks and saying nothing to each other. Gail was quite sure that, despite assurances, Nick didn't trust the rogue in the slightest, especially given the way he seemed to be making sure that good ol' Uncle L was never left alone with either of the two women.

"I have to do something before we decide where we all are going," Crow announced, passing out stale crackers that would serve as their breakfast. "It's something related to witches and the online access points, but I would appreciate it if you guys wouldn't decide anything without me."

"What is it you're doing?" Leonard asked, zipping his bag back up and throwing it over his shoulder.

"Fixing another cell tower. Rainfall turned a local stream in a river last year, and a storm knocked one of the towers out. If I can fix it, great. If not, I'm going to try and salvage some parts."

"Can I help?" He sounded quite sincere in his question.

"No." That was the end of it.

They trekked under the overpass and about an hour westward across failing farms and fields. Here, the swift Cape Fear River divided parts of the landscape, with masses of trees lining either side of the current. Gail could hear the sound of the water all the way from the road which ended in a cul-de-sac surrounded by abandoned homes. They headed down a faded forest path and arrived at the shoreline. Just on the other side of the river, a large grey pole like the one where Gail had found her friend jutted out of the ground.

"Weird place for a cell tower," Leonard remarked.

"River's swollen, I think. Plus it's possible that it changed course a little bit." She pulled off her bag, took a few specific things from it, and started across the river, where a neat path of stones formed a bridge.

"Stay here," Gail commanded the other two as well as the dog before following her. This cell tower was far more rusted than the one before. Although it was still a massive piece of architecture, it was also shorter than the last one. Gail thought it looked sad, as though it, like many people in this world, was just ready to give up.

Crow took off her cloak and bag. She handed Gail the black radio like she had done before and headed to the base of the tower, shimmied up the side, grabbed a hold of the jutting rungs that formed the side of the tower, and began to ascend. "Back in a bit," she said, casting Gail a bright smile as she ascended the monolith.

It was interesting, she thought as she sat down, how different she felt from the last time she had watched the witch climb up a tower. Last time she was lost, scared, and utterly confused. Currently, she couldn't say that she was not scared or confused—those two things had simply become a part of her general existence—but she could say that she somehow felt a lot less lost. The idea that she might end up separated from the group terrified her.

But then again, there was a home to go back to, wasn't there? M had said so, and she had to trust his judgment. She doubted her own reasoning, but deep down she also knew that her decision to head north would be putting additional distance between herself and the Mori peace tower.

The radio made a garbled crackle. "Hey. Looks like everything up here is pretty useless. Maybe a couple small parts. So I won't be long."

Gail took the time to check her bandage. The wound in her thigh was not hurting at all this morning. The outside of the linen appeared quite clean, and she wondered if Crow had changed it in the day or so that she was asleep. Upon unrolling it from her leg, however, she was astounded. "Crow?" she said into the handset.

"Yeah."

"The hole in my thigh. It's gone."

"Wait, what? What do you mean, 'gone'?"

"It's gone. Vanished. No blood, no scar…it's just gone."

"Okay, that's really weird. You'll have to show me when I come down."

"Okay," Gail replied. "And then what will we do?"

There was a long silence. "I guess we keep moving. I hate wasting time."

"So you've said," Gail muttered without pushing the button.

"Why can't you just come with us? Stupid, stubborn, adorable, frustrating—" Crow's voice sounded muffled.

"What was that?"

There was a pause. "Sorry, my finger was on the button. My bad."

Gail smirked. "Did you call me 'adorable'?"

There was no response then, as a loud creaking noise emanated from the base of the cell tower. The whole thing shook for a moment. Gail hammered the button. "Are you okay?"

A longer pause. "Yeah, just a bit startled. I think I'm gonna come down now. Must not be as sturdy as I thought." Gail saw her friend's form crawling over the side of the 'crow's nest' of the tower. She had not yet even begun to descend when a second noise, followed by rapid popping sounds, filled the air and the whole tower began to fall.

"Crow!" Gail screamed, leaping to her feet. The tower stopped its bending for only a moment it looked like it might hang there precariously and allow an escape for the poor girl trapped at the top, but before she could even consider the possibility the bottom of the tower snapped and the crow's nest went straight into the water.

The rushing river threw the metal chunk to the side, and it began to slide along the slick bottom of the shallow river's bed. Gail leapt atop the broken part of the cylinder and dashed down toward the nest at the end, but she had to stop midway as it lurched back. "Nick!" she screamed. "Leonard!" The two had already seen what was going on, and as she glanced back she could see Nick thumping across the rocks to their side of the river.

There was no time to lose. Gail used the exposed ladder rungs as handholds as she shimmied along the pole. Thirty feet. Twenty. The pole had become stuck against a large rock and seemed to be stable for a moment, but she knew that one unbalanced movement would dislodge it and send it rolling deeper into the water.

Ten feet. She could hear Crow cursing at the end and her heart leapt to know that the witch hadn't yet been carried downriver with the current. She finally reached the basket of poles and wires; taking a firm hold on one ladder rung with a foot, she threw her arm forward. "Here!"

Crow's hands both held onto handrails in the basket, and the water's current was pulling too hard for her to attempt to let go with either. "I can't!" she screamed back.

Gail scooted forward, found a different foothold, and was finally able to grab onto Crow's wrist. She pulled, and Crow let go of the handrail with one hand, holding instead to Gail's arm. She pushed with a foot, trying to get free of the rushing water's surface, but it was too strong. Gail grabbed her with her other hand, relying solely on her foot to hold her steadfast to the metal pole, and she strained her muscles to free her. She was able to lift—just enough to grab another handrail and extricate herself from the rushing water.

The pole, too, began to move, but not in the direction of the river. As she grabbed tight to Crow's belt, Gail looked back to see that Nick, the armored juggernaut, had grabbed the end of the metal pole and was now wrestling it back onto the shore of the river. "Hold on," Gail shouted to Crow, and they both held onto the ladder and the handrails and each other as tightly as they could as the shore came closer and closer. Finally, after what seemed like hours, the cell tower was free of the water. Gail and Crow leapt off the pole and onto the bank.

Crow dropped to her knees, coughing up vomit and murky water. Gail rushed to her, patting her back and noticing that both of them were shivering uncontrollably. Before she could even choke out any words, Leonard had appeared from nowhere, unrolling a large emergency blanket and throwing it over them. "Are you two alright?"

"No, Leonard, we're drowning." Crow had regained her snark. "Somebody grab my cloak from over there…this blanket isn't big enough for both of us."

Leonard ran to grab it while Nick's head made the same clicking noise it did when he had scanned Crow. "HURT?" he typed out on his belt.

"I don't think so," Gail said, rubbing her arms with her hands under the cloak to try and get circulation back. "Just cold. We need to get inside somewhere."

"The town is too much of a risk," Crow reminded. "The Duke's lackeys are—"

"We don't have a choice," Gail replied. "We're going to get frostbite."

"Gail's right," Leonard said, handing Crow her cloak. The witch slipped out of the blanket and wrapped herself in the thick black fabric, allowing Gail to close off more of the chilly wind that felt like it was seeping through her clothes into her bones.

Crow gritted her teeth. "Fine, but we'll have to have a plan for quick escape."

"I always have a plan for a quick escape."

◠

Crow had been right about the Duke's lackeys. They were all over the streets in Dunn, and Crow brought her cloak in tightly to her face as they walked, hoping to keep her face hidden. Gail, still wrapped in the brown blanket, tried to do the same, but it was difficult to keep the blanket over her head while trying to reduce the amount of cold washing in over her legs. "Where can we go?" she aked.

"I have an idea," Leonard said, heading toward a tall, beige building with outer paneling and windows that had somehow withstood the test of time. *Fairfield Inn*, the sign read, and as they crossed the parking lot to the door, Gail was entranced by how well the property had been taken care of—the grass was neatly cut, and the parking lot had been patched up several times with pitch.

Inside, it was warmer, likely due to a roaring fire in the stone fireplace across from the information desk. Gail and Crow made a beeline for it, while Leonard went over to the desk to check in. Nick and Lukather came over to join them.

"Good afternoon," Leonard said, drumming his fingers on the front desk.

The woman behind the counter sounded unnervingly cheerful, as though somehow the front doors of this hotel did not lead to a slowly-crumbling world of pain and suffering at all. "Checking in, sir?"

"Not technically. Do you have a laundry? These poor ladies fell in the river and need to dry off."

"*Fell?*" Crow grumbled. "Like we're just silly girls who happened to fall in the river?"

Leonard continued his negotiations in a low voice before walking over to the fire. "They're going to let you dry off and give you a spare set of clothes while that's happening. In the meantime, there's a Waffle House down the road and we could go get food."

"That's awfully nice of them," Gail remarked, still shivering under her blanket as she stood up, "and I hope it wasn't too expensive."

"Not at all," Leonard said, leading the way out of the lobby and toward the laundry, leaving Nick and Lukather behind to stand guard. As soon as they had passed out of earshot of the front desk, he added, "Especially because the Duke is paying the bill."

"How?" Crow said, jabbing Leonard with her finger.

"I told her that I was working for the Duke, and that we were requisitioning use of the facilities in return for additional supplies next week, and that the Duke would pay out a stipend for her loyalty." He grinned.

"And she believed you?" Crow stopped at the entrance to the laundry and sneered over her glasses at him.

He shrugged. "I am persuasive. And I did in fact give her a real promissory note from the Duke. Well, a real forgery, but real enough."

"You're terrible." Crow went through the laundry room door and let it slam behind her.

Leonard looked rather deflated, and Gail patted him on the shoulder. "That's her way of thanking people," she said with an encouraging smile, and followed Crow in.

The hotel laundry was full of steam and heat and the salty-sweet smell of detergent. The whole operation appeared to be entirely steam-powered, with a massive boiler in the far corner providing what was necessary to make the modified laundry machines work.

Crow had already stripped out of her clothes and into new ones from a pile that had been laying out on the laundry table. She scowled as she dug a few things out of her wet pockets and dropped them into her robe's pocket. When she was done, she put her wet clothes into a dryer, still shaking a little in her light-blue scrubs and fluffy white bathrobe on it with the hotel logo embroidered over the breast. Gail stopped and let out a loud giggle.

"What?" Crow demanded, looking up at her.

"You're not in black."

"So?" Crow's skin turned a little red and Gail could not tell if it was anger or embarrassment.

Gail pulled her own shirt off to start loading another dryer. "So, you look cute."

"*What?*" Crow sounded like she had never been so insulted in her entire life.

Gail continued to chuckle to herself, removing her wet things and replacing them with hotel-branded dry ones. As she went to pull on scrub pants, Crow stopped her. "Hey, hang on. You said your thigh wound was gone, right?"

Gail stopped and ran her fingers across where the two holes once were across the side of her thigh. "Yeah. See?"

Crow came over and bent down to examine. "Holy shit, you're right. It's completely gone. Not even a scar." She ran her finger over where the wound used to be and Gail shuddered. Crow withdrew her finger immediately. "Sorry—"

"It's fine."

"—but how—?"

"I don't know." It was Gail's turn to flush red, pulling her pants on again and heading for the door. "I wonder if it has something to do with…" she tried to remember the word. "That thing Leonard was talking about."

Crow followed after her, drying her glasses on the towel fabric of the white robe. "Maybe. This is the first time I've heard of it. Which is weird, because I'm usually pretty well-informed." She sighed.

"But without Bluejay," Leonard was telling Nick, "we have lost all of our maps and resources. She's the one who had the plan and the details."

"What plans?" Crow said, strolling over to them. "And if either of you makes a comment about what I am wearing I will break your face."

Leonard raised his eyebrows at her outfit but didn't comment on it. "Bluejay knew details on this plan to stop the Reclamation. She had contacts, maps, diagrams…Beyond that, she had notes about the Partholónians, and supposedly she knew someone who had insight into the Mori. Dr. Glenn knew more about it than I did. See, we sort of kept the pieces of the plan separate, in case one of us was to be captured. Unfortunately, now three of the people with the *whole* plan are dead—Glenn, Marion, and Bluejay."

"What happened to her computer?" Gail asked, sitting down in front of the fire. The thin cloth of the scrubs was allowing more warm air through and she felt less like she was submerged in a bucket of ice. "I remember having it after she—she—" Gail swallowed hard and didn't complete the sentence.

"I have it," Crow said, walking to her bag and patting it. "But I can't use it because her authenticator…" Her eyes went wide and she pulled her own tiny number device out of her pocket. "Oh no…"

"What is it?" Gail got up and walked over to her. The little device was blank.

"It…the water…" She took a shuddering breath. "I've broken my authenticator. That means I can't go online anymore."

"Can you get a new one?" Gail said, putting a comforting hand on her shoulder.

"No," Crow said, shoving it back in her pocket. "They only get issued by Eagle. I was really lucky that my dad knew somebody…" She sniffed. "I got into computers pretty young. When the Mori invaded, I just kept doing what I had been doing at 8 years old—being a nuisance. And then my dad—he worked for the government, you see—when he helped put the New Internet online, he gave me an authenticator to keep me safe."

Leonard was suddenly on his feet, pointing to the front door of the hotel. "Come on."

Crow looked taken aback. "What? Come on where?"

"You are getting a waffle right now."

"Why?" Crow still didn't seem to understand Leonard's sudden movements.

"Because," he said with a wide grin, "you are having a shitty day, and shitty days are made better with waffles. And then you and I are going to figure this out."

FOURTEEN

Gail would have hardly believed, from the way Leonard and Crow were walking back and forth so excitedly, that this was Leonard and Crow at all. Crow, still in her light blue and white clothes, was "geeking out", as she called it, about things related to security protocols and scripts and automation.

It did also seem to be lightening her mood after the destruction of her authenticator. And Gail was surprised to see that Leonard, for all his faults, was exceptionally talented at getting people to open up— even Crow.

"So my dad," Crow said between bites of waffle, "worked for the government, in network security. Like I said, he helped put the New Internet together. Like, he knew Eagle personally—she was a coworker of his. But then, this was a few years ago, he got captured by the Mori, and they pried all his knowledge about the system out of his head. Then they gave him two choices: either become an Advocate and try to shut down the resistance from the inside, or die."

"Nice to have a choice," Leonard said with raised eyebrows.

The Waffle House here in Dunn was slightly cleaner and tidier than the one back in Lillington. All of the windows had somehow survived, and the other booths here had multiple groups of people in them.

These people looked to be from all kinds of different backgrounds, from farmers to salesmen to law enforcement to a booth full of what clearly were some kind of criminal gang; even so, they all respected the hallowed walls that were the house of waffles and paid each other no mind. No one even looked at Nick, sitting quietly in his power armor, so still that he might as well have been an armored mannequin.

"Well, the Mori didn't realize my mom and dad were partners in crime. My mom was a radio tower technician in the DC Metro area. Her skills with the hardware made the whole thing work. And since my dad knew that if he was an advocate he would probably have to give up information about his family…well, he did the 'noble' thing and died." The way she said *noble* made Gail think that she lamented his decision nonetheless.

"Your mom taught you how to do that stuff with those towers," Gail said, and Crow nodded, pushing the chunks of waffle around her plate. "What happened to her?"

"She's still alive, as far as I know," Crow said. "Last I heard she was down near Jacksonville, still working. She said once she got everything set up she'd contact me on the New Internet. I haven't heard from her since then, but I've got hope. She's a tough woman. She can cope."

"Sounds like a fun lady," Leonard said, pushing his plate away to clear some space. "Okay, let's see if we can get Bluejay's computer up and running."

Crow pushed her plate away as well, most of her waffle and eggs untouched, downed the rest of her glass of milk, and opened the slick blue machine. Gail, sitting on the opposite side of the table from them, couldn't see what they were doing—not that she would understand it if she could.

"What distro is this?" Crow asked.

"Looks like a really lightweight Ubuntu," Leonard remarked, tapping some buttons.

"I can see that," Crow replied, pushing Leonard's fingers out of the way. "Also no touchy. I'm the witch here."

Leonard bristled. "And I have more technical certifications than you can imagine."

"See this face?" She pointed at herself. "This is a face that doesn't care about your technical certifications. My computer, my rules."

"Technically it's *Gail's* computer, since Bluejay gave it to her."

Crow rounded on the redhead. "Gail—"

"Crow can have it," Gail said flatly.

Leonard cursed while Crow scooted the computer toward herself with a smug grin. "Now the problem is that we have Bluejay's authenticator but not her passcode."

"What does that mean?" Gail asked, trying to remain at least somewhat tagged-in to the conversation.

"Well," Crow said after a moment of thought during which time she was probably dumbing down several paragraphs of techno-babble, "in order to log into these computers you need two things: the number on the authenticator and a personal code. We have the authenticator, but in order to log in we need to figure out how to bypass the personal code."

"We could try some kind of brute force method," Leonard suggested to Crow.

"Please don't damage the computer," Gail interjected, imagining Leonard trying to brute-force the machine open with a prybar. Both Crow and Leonard shot her a glare so contemptuous that she resumed her waffle-eating without further interruption.

Leonard made some kind of other suggestion that Gail was unable to understand and had something to do with a magical device called a 'rainbow table'. "But she might have some kind of scorched-earth protocol that if we make too many attempts it deletes everything. I know I would."

"And if we wait too long, the authenticator will get flagged and disabled and no one will be able to log in."

Nick gestured for the computer, and Crow turned it so he could reach the keyboard. Gail leaned over to watch as Nick typed out "1 L 9 F 0 B 0" followed by the number on the authenticator dangling from

Bluejay's bag. The screen went dark for a moment and then lit up with text, images, and—perhaps most importantly—a text connection to the New Internet.

"How did you—" Crow was practically choking.

"Bluejay told us before she died," Gail explained. "I didn't know what it was, or I would have said something sooner. I'm glad Nick did."

The New Internet chat had already begun to light up. "*Bluejay just logged on,*" someone named Magpie observed. "*someone's got her computer.*"

"That's Magpie," Crow said aloud. "Bluejay's second in command. I think he lives in Mississippi."

"Hopefully he can help," Gail offered. Crow's expression at this statement suggested otherwise.

"*This is Crow, from Raven Rock,*" she typed. "*My authenticator is broken. Bluejay gave us her password before she died.*"

"*We don't have a way to know that,*" Magpie replied. "*You've been logging on the past few days on your own account.*"

"*I fell in a river while trying to fix a cell tower.*" Crow's fingers were angrily clicking as if the extra frustration vented on the keyboard could somehow translate into text. "*Authenticator destroyed.*"

"*Again,*" Magpie replied, "*we don't know that.*"

"*Then send someone here to confirm,*" Crow replied. "*There's a dozen witches who came to Campbell. Send any one of them to confirm.*"

"*No, that goes against protocol,*" Magpie retorted. "*if you are Crow, you know that.*"

"*Then what am I supposed to do?*"

Someone else named Canary butted in. Gail vaguely remembered him as one of the people at the table at Campbell. "*@Magpie: I saw Crow get away and we know she had Bluejay's computer. She's been keeping it safe.*"

"*Doesn't matter,*" came Magpie's reply a moment later. "*Security protocols.*"

"*My dad and Eagle WROTE those protocols,*" Crow said, and Gail was worried that several keys on the laptop might just snap right off from being hit so hard.

"*Doesn't matter*," Magpie said again. "*Maybe things will change in the future. Bluejay is dead so it's my responsibility to terminate these credentials.*"

The text from the window stopped updating, and a single line appeared at the bottom: *You have been banned from this server. Connection Terminated.*

"No!" Crow shouted, typing something in to try and reconnect, but the same message appeared again. She did it a third time, which returned the same result. "No, no, no, no!"

"We still have the computer," Leonard offered. "We have all the data we need to find out what Bluejay was doing."

"I just...I just got...I just got *banned*—"

Leonard laid a hand on her shoulder. "You know he was just doing what he thought was right. You'll get back online."

"How?" she demanded, scooting slightly away from him.

"We'll have to find Eagle," Gail said.

"*How?*" Crow demanded again. "I don't know Eagle. I've never met her."

Leonard smiled, the sparkle returning to his eyes in an instant, "But you know someone that does." He raised his eyebrows.

It slowly dawned on Crow and she took a deep breath. "My mom."

"Jacksonville, you said?" Gail stacked the empty plates, leaving Crow's uneaten waffle where is lay, and the waitress came to collect them.

"Mhm." Crow clicked a few things on things in Bluejay's computer. "Okay. Well that's one part of the plan, then. Oh man, there's so much stuff here. History on the Mori, studies on their technology...there's gotta be thousands of files here. I don't know where to start with her plan."

"Can you search for things?" Gail asked, craning her neck to see the screen better.

"Yeah, why?"

Gail looked at Nick, and he typed out Bluejay's last word: "OSBOURNE."

Crow looked between the two of them and opened a search box. The computer took a minute to sort through the files, but finally returned a folder: *Osbourne_final.* "Alright, let's see what we've got."

The folder contained a single document, titled *Notes.* Crow opened it and it had a name and an address of someone named Harry Osbourne who lived in Orlando. *Glenn says he's an expert on Partholónians,* Bluejay had noted under the address. *And he might know how to shut down the tower.*

They all stared in silence, reading and rereading the notes on the screen. All of a sudden, it was as if a world of possibility had been opened up. There was an actual plan to take down the Mori.

To Gail, who slumped back in her seat, the idea was terrifying. The world was already unknown to her, and the idea of trifling with it further made her stomach seize, potentially risking sending the warm waffles in her stomach back up her gullet. She had spent her life isolated, away from the danger. Now, in the span of a week, she had been thrust into the middle of the fight—and an overwhelming feeling of inadequacy now filled her. M had saved her and protected her for a reason. Was she really some kind of mutant? One of a handful of people with something special about them that could prove useful? More and more she wanted to run, to head north, and away from the fight to take back their world.

And of course, what was this world they wanted to take back? Gail had never really lived there, and the small things she recalled were nothing but distant memories and echoes of a life she might have had but for the Mori.

"Gail?" She shook herself mentally as she heard Crow's voice. "You okay? Or were you zoning out again?"

"The second one," Gail said, leaning forward again. "So what would you like to do? You seem to need to go to a few places."

Crow tilted her head. "*We* do? Are you not coming with us?"

Gail gave her a little smile. "No, I'm still going north."

"But we need you—" Leonard said.

Gail put up a hand. "I'm going north. You said there are other people...like me. Find someone else. I'm going *north*."

Crow's face was briefly pained, then, but she quickly recovered, pulling up a map of the southeastern United States. "Right. Of course. So here's Dunn, where we are," she said, tracing the cursor down it, "So...Jacksonville. Then Orlando. Then St. Petersburg."

"MANNING," Nick said.

Crow raised her eyebrows. "Manning?"

Nick reached over to the computer, opened a new note pad, and typed: "*I need to go to Manning, South Carolina. I have some personal business. It's not far out of our way. Is this OK?*" He gestured to the map, to a small town about forty miles south-southeast of Florence, South Carolina.

"You guys missed the last part of the seminar," Leonard said, "which is an invitation to a big summit outside of St. Petersburg. Dr. Glenn had been setting up a sort of encampment there in a cluster of RV towns called Sun City. It's just outside of the Mori capital's perimeter. I don't know who's in charge down there, but Glenn's been giving everyone a date of November 5. So that's our deadline."

"Not bad," Crow said, closing her laptop. "Gives us just over two months to get there. It sounds doable."

"Sure does," Leonard said, rising from the table. "We better start getting packed up. Let's go get your clothes."

◌

It was midafternoon by the time they started up the structure that led to I-95. None of them—including Crow—really said anything as they trudged up the ramp to the place where it met the wide, yellow-lined road.

Gail looked down both ways and stepped off the curb onto the grey asphalt. She had been seeking this road for such a long time, and she had kept getting turned around. Now here it was...and the empty stretch of black and yellow seemed cold and empty.

146

"Well, here's your road," Crow finally said as they stepped out onto it. The air was still, and a warm breeze wafted over them briefly. "I guess you and Lukather are off?"

Gail gave the witch a smile. "I feel I should thank you all for everything," Gail said, rocking on her heels a bit, "but I have nothing to offer you."

"I'm gonna say it," Leonard said, shifting uncomfortably in his jacket, "I would rather you come with us. Marion would—"

"M told me to find the road," came Gail's firm reply. "Now I have, and I know which way I want to go. Please—" she held up a finger to silence Leonard's next attempt to argue, "—don't try to change my mind." She walked straight up to him, leaned in, and gave him a tiny little peck on his cheek. "I'll be okay."

She turned to Nick and kissed him on the cheek of his helmet. He raised his hands as if he wanted to sign something to her, but them put them down. "BYE."

Finally, she turned to Crow, who was suddenly quite interested in the flaking bits of black nail polish on her fingers. She stepped up to her, and before the witch could protest she had thrown her arms around her and lifted her up as if she was made of straw. Crow squeaked as the air left her lungs, and after recovering her composure she hugged Gail back, and held her for a long minute.

"Go on," Crow finally said, pushing Gail away a little bit. "Follow the yellow lines and you'll be in New York in no time. I hope you find…something there. Be safe, Necia."

"Thanks for being my friend," Gail whispered. "I…I really didn't have any when I met you."

"Me either," Crow admitted. "Not in real life anyway. I'm not good with people."

"So you've said." She stood there, biting her lip, and looked down the empty stretch of highway.

"Go on," Crow said again, stepping back. "You know how much I hate to waste time." There were tears rimming her eyes and Gail opened her mouth to reply, but Crow turned away and started to walk the other direction and she thought better of it, instead whistling to Lukather to follow. Gail walked, her whole stomach feeling like it had been transformed into a cement brick, and didn't look back for some time. When she finally did, her three companions were tiny dots in the distance.

◌

Gail walked through most of the rest of the afternoon, and even as the sun began its descent down the sky to rest in the western landscape, she felt a desire to keep moving. It was perhaps a profound sense of loss that drove her onward through the evening and even part of the night, since she had become so briefly accustomed to the general bickering and chit-chat of companions that the silence was almost painful.

Not that Lukather was not a lovely companion. He yipped and barked occasionally, chasing a butterfly here or there and often looking up at Gail in expectation, but she didn't have a happy thought to share to the sheepdog. She was simply the mountain girl again—the loner, the perfectly-capable-and-independent girl who had learned a lot in a short time and now had to get back to just surviving.

Did she really need to leave, though? The thought was gnawing at her as the hours droned on and on, and she felt the burning pain of blisters forming at her heel. Still she persisted onwards, following the dim outline of the yellow stripe along the road. In the distance, she thought she saw a light heading toward her, but as she continued on it dimmed and disappeared and she wasn't sure it wasn't entirely part of her imagination.

She stopped. "Lukather," She said to the dog. "I think I've made a mistake."

The dog's head tilted to the side, ears perked.

"I'm just running away. M'sent me to this road because he wanted me to follow it *toward* the fight. Not run from it." She put her hands on her hips. "He would want me to go with them."

Lukather, of course, did not reply, but he did lean in to nuzzle her with his head. Gail took that as a sign of agreement, and she turned on her heels to start southward again. She would have to catch up.

A buzzing sound above her caught her attention, and she looked up. The night sky was bright, and in the moonlight she caught a glimpse of something hovering above her in the air. It had some kind of blade—no, several blades—and was following her quietly in the darkness. She stopped and kept looking at it, turning to try and discern more detail about what it was.

Lukather barked. Gail tore her eyes away from the thing in the air but it was already too late—they came from all directions, grabbing her and pulling her. She didn't even get a shout before a rag was in her mouth and a hood was over her face. She struggled, lashing out with whatever she possibly could—a bite, a punch, a kick—but it was to no avail. There were too many.

They carried her, still fighting, and began to bind her. Something went around her legs, first, holding them together tightly by the ankles. Then her arms were behind her back and something metal was being slapped onto them. She screamed into the rag but it was too muffled.

"Quiet down," A voice said. It was female. "You're perfectly safe right now, so do me a favor and calm down." Gail stopped struggling; completely confused, and with no way out, it made no sense to keep burning energy when she knew she was already so tired. There was something in her head, too, that made it seem like her muscles were moving through syrup. It was a sweet smell, like cinnamon and sugar. The darkness inside the hood and the darkness in her mind started to merge, swirling into a void that sent her reeling into unconsciousness a few moments later.

FIFTEEN

"Wake up." Her return to reality was far sharper than her journey out of it, coming as a pointed slap across her face. Stars danced in her eyes for a few moments as her senses regained function one by one. As her eyesight came into focus, most of her vision was a single person's face. She was tall, blonde, and painfully pale—or perhaps it was just the light, Gail thought, as a glance around the room told her that this dim room was lit almost entirely by holes drilled in the ceiling to let in sunlight. It washed out all of the colors in the room and cast it into shades of grey.

"Who are you? Where am I?" Gail asked, though with her ears still ringing from the slap, she couldn't be entirely sure that it hadn't come out a garbled mess.

"You are the guest of His Grace," the woman said, grabbing her by the chin, "the Duke of the East. And as a guest of his *hospitality* you should be thankful for the privilege."

Gail let out a confused sound.

"Now that you're awake, and he's awake, I'm sure he'll want to have a conversation with you. But I thought I'd take my turn first." She slapped her again, harder. At least, it felt harder; Gail's eyes exploded into stars again and she coughed loudly, but she couldn't hear it over the ringing in her ears. She felt the warm drip of blood coming out one ear and trickling down her neck.

"I'm s…I'm sorry…" she sputtered.

"Not yet, you're not," the woman said, seizing Gail by the throat and squeezing a little, limiting Gail's access to air. "But you will be. By the time I'm done you're going to be the sorriest—"

"Stop," came a deep, booming voice that echoed off the metal walls. The woman let go immediately and stepped back, but her face indicated a deep, burning desire to continue her abuse. The source of the voice was a man, dressed in clean tanned leather, now crossing the room with an icy scowl cast in the direction of the woman. "How dare you," he spat at her. "I said to bring her so we could talk to her. I did *not* say to capture her and beat her. What is *wrong* with you?" The man reached around Gail, grasping her by the waist in one big arm, and reaching up to undo her restraints above her head. When they unlocked, Gail was unable to find her feet and would have dropped to the floor if not for the man's gentle grip. "Get out of my sight," he growled at the woman, who left without further argument.

Gail tried to bring her rescuer into focus, but it was difficult. "H-help," she croaked.

He put a finger to his lips and helped her to a nearby chair. "I am so sorry," he said, and his voice was full of concern. "This shouldn't have happened. I didn't realize…I didn't realize you're only a girl. I'm such a fool."

Gail shook her head a little, not understanding. "What's…where am I?" she said, looking around the space. It was a large room, almost all metal, and was mostly empty save for a few tables and chairs.

"Raleigh," the man said. "The last great bastion of mankind. Here, please let me help you out of here. Please, please let me help you." His voice was so calming, and Gail could hear what sounded like guilty sobs building up in his throat. She allowed herself to be picked up again, and she rested her head against him. Her head was still foggy, and she closed her eyes. "I'm such a fool," he repeated, and as he carried her out of the room and into another one, she could smell something savory on the air. "When is the last time you ate? Never mind that. I'll handle it."

He set her down and she opened her eyes. The room was the most lavish she had ever seen in her life, with a gorgeous patterned wallpaper and several antique pieces of dark brown furniture along the walls. A mirror hung nearby though she couldn't see herself in it, and from the ceiling an ornate chandelier hung adorned with lit candles. She was seated on a bed; it was a massive, sprawling thing covered in thick down blankets, with tall wooden posts at each corner.

The man returned, pushing a little wheeled cart bearing a serving tray. He moved it in front of her, pulling the silver cover from it and revealing a platter of coffee, bacon, sausages, toast, baked beans, eggs, mushrooms, grilled tomatoes, and fried potatoes. "Please, Gail. Eat."

Her stomach, which felt suddenly like it had been emptied in an instant, growled loud enough that the man had assuredly heard it. She grabbed a hunk of toast and shoved it into her mouth, washing it down with the still-hot coffee. As the warm mash went down her throat she took in a deep breath. "H-how do you know my name? You're not the Duke of the East, are you?" She shoved a whole sausage into her mouth and chewed wildly.

The man walked to the far end of the room, grabbed one of the chairs that looked like it weighed a ton, and picked it up as easily as if it was made of air. He pulled it over to her. "Please, I don't want you to be frightened by what I tell you, Gail." He waited until she had swallowed her food. "I am indeed the Duke. But you have no reason to fear me. I already know that what you did was in self-defense."

Gail stopped. It couldn't be. She had been running from him for the better part of the week and had been *attacked* so many times! It simply wasn't possible. "I…I didn't—I don't—"

He held up a hand. "You don't need to apologize."

"You put a bounty on me!" She gasped at him.

"Yes," he said, running a hand through his hair. It was silvery and accented the delicate lines on his forehead. "I thought at first that you were a hired assassin. They come after me all the time and…I thought—" He exhaled and appeared lesser than he was before. "I overreacted. I found out later that you were just a girl, and I found out from the bartender in Lillington what actually happened…Oh Gail, it is I who owes *you* an apology."

Gail stared at him, completely lost for words. She grabbed a chunk of bacon and chewed while she thought of a response.

"And as soon as I found out I tried to get the word out. But it was too late. My more…*eager* mercenaries were already after you. So I knew I had to get to you myself before anyone else did."

Gail took a shuddering breath. She pointed toward the door where, presumably, the woman had disappeared to. "Who was—"

"My sister-in-law," the Duke explained. "She is still grieving the loss of her husband and is having trouble coming to terms with how wretched my brother was. She wasn't supposed to be here at all. I'm so sorry for that."

Gail's head was swimming. She picked up a large curd of scrambled eggs with her hand, completely ignoring the silverware, put them onto the toast, and took a messy bite of the whole thing. The Duke was watching, his somber blue eyes digging deep into her. She avoided his gaze as she finished her egg sandwich and followed it with the remainder of her coffee. The thought occurred to her that the food might be poisoned, or drugged, but on reflection she found that she didn't really care anymore. She had returned to the way she had been before meeting Crow, and Nick, and Leonard; she had lost all sense of purpose.

Her purpose, she tried to remind herself, was to get home! But even that made no sense any longer. New York was such a faraway place and one which she certainly didn't remember, so what use would it be to get there and be just as lost as she had been before? The plan to take down the Mori had been a sense of purpose—albeit a suicidal one—that she could get behind. Again she felt a pang of guilt at using her excuse of "going home" as a vehicle for her own fear.

But it wasn't as if she didn't have a choice. There were other Partholónians out there, Gail thought as she finally picked up the spoon and wolfed down a few handfuls of beans. Surely, they would find another person with the special abilities needed to complete the designs that Glenn and Bluejay and this mysterious "Harry Osbourne" had cooked up.

Her eating slowed and she set the spoon down, still lost in thought. She finally looked up at the Duke. "You knew my friend. M—or Marion. Right?"

The Duke raised his eyebrows high. "I sure did! M is the one who told me about you in the first place. Which is why, when I found out the truth of what happened I worked so hard to make sure you were alright."

"What did he tell you about me?"

"Lots of things. You were growing, you were learning to read, you were learning to fight…Oh, he was like a doting father. He would ask me to find things like clothes and books if I could for you. Books were hard to find, though…the Mori didn't like them."

"What is your thought on the Mori?" Gail asked, spreading politeness over her words like butter.

"They…" he stopped and considered his words. "Culturally, they don't understand people. They don't understand our ways or our technology. Now, practically, they are superior in every way. So I've long been of the opinion that we can coexist with them if we help them understand us."

Gail wasn't sure what to make of this answer. "But they…they came onto a planet that wasn't theirs. They pushed people out. Controlled them. Killed them. How is this okay?" She tried to keep her rising anger out of her voice. If the Duke was, in fact, an Advocate, it was all the more important that he not get angry at her.

"It's a cultural difference, that's all," the Duke explained. "What they're doing is only wrong from a certain, narrow, viewpoint. We see it as wrong because our culture reflects it as wrong."

"Don't you think it's *morally* wrong, though?" Gail persisted after downing the glass of orange juice on the tray.

The Duke chuckled. "Morals are hard to define sometimes. I do what's best for everyone. I try to help people because I *care* about them. I provide shelter. Food. Warmth. Supplies. Do I do it because it's *morally* right? Or do I do it out of compassion? It's the difference between an internal compass and an external one. Take the Mori for example: they are doing what they believe to be the best for their people. Does it hurt others? Sometimes. But they're doing what they believe to be the right thing. That's all anyone really wants to do—the right thing."

Gail continued to listen. The Duke's words were passionate, and she found it hard to refute his logic for a moment, until she realized how completely insane it was. "So what about me, then?" She said, finally pushing the tray of food away. "What is the right thing for me?"

The Duke grinned. "I need your help, Gail."

Her brow furrowed. "Me? What could I possibly do for you? You have…you have everything."

"I have some things, it's true," he said, standing up and wheeling the tray away from her. He stalked back to the chair and sat down. "But I don't have everything. You're special. You know that."

"How so?" Gail expected that the Duke knew about her 'special' lineage, but she didn't want to overplay her hand.

"Your blood," he said, and he reached for her hand, lifting it and holding it like it was a fragile butterfly. "It's very special. It's something the Mori have been seeking, for a long time. It might be the key to peace between our people."

She pulled her hand away. "What do you mean?"

He didn't reach for it again. "You already know what I mean, Gail. I'm assuming Leonard told you. I know he was spotted traveling with you. It's the reason M kept you secret for so long. You can use The Magic."

"I don't even know if it's true," Gail said, finally relenting to fact that the Duke knew an uncomfortably large amount about her already. "I haven't been able to do anything magical before in my life."

"Because you have no training," the Duke said. "Luckily, I know someone who will train you."

She tilted her head slightly. "Train me to…use Mori magic?"

"Yes."

She had never considered the possibility, even after Leonard's explanation. Mori magic? Her? She had seen the terrifying things the Mori were capable of. Weather control. Balls of fire. Whole towns wiped off the map. Whole towns—

Like Lillington.

Gail cleared her throat. "You said you talked to the bartender about what happened to your brother." The Duke nodded. "When was this? Because I came back to Lillington a few hours later and a Mori had already come through and killed everyone." It hurt her to admit, out loud, that the whole town had been slain, but she knew the truth was the most important thing here. No room for errors.

The Duke nodded again, much more slowly this time. "I was in the area already," the Duke said evenly, "and I have a carriage. I arrived, claimed my brother's body, and left before the Mori had arrived."

"And what brought you out to a small town like Lillington?" Gail asked, trying to act calm as she walked to the windows and touched the silky curtains with a finger.

The Duke was quiet again. A glance at his face showed he was depressed, and having a hurtful recollection of that tragic day. The pain was evident on his face.

He was a fantastic actor, Gail decided in that instant.

The Duke decided on his next narrative. "I was looking for you, in fact. I had heard you were traveling. Good sources, you know. And I wanted to meet you and make sure you were safe."

Gail inhaled deeply. "I don't believe you." In an instant, she had thrown the curtain aside, finding a sliding window that she began to force open. The Duke was behind her, and she kicked out as hard as she could, hoping she could make contact with his stomach or groin, and she hit something and caused him to stumble backward. She lifted the window, looking out at a street several stories below. It would be a rough fall, but she could survive it...in theory.

There was no time to decide. Hoisting herself onto the window, she forced herself through the hole, feeling herself falling—

Then, everything stopped. She hung in the air as if on invisible strings, halfway out of the window and unable to move. She couldn't even scream or move her eyes. The shape of the windowsill entered her field of vision as she was pulled back through the curtains and into the bedroom by two pairs of hands. She felt the constraints loosen around her, and she tried to lash out, which elicited a sharp slap across her face. Her body was twisted, changing to a sitting position before she was laid on the foot of the bed and the Duke tightly bound a rope around her wrists. He stepped back and leaned against a piece of dark furniture, a grin plastered on his face. "Now, now, we're all friends here."

The woman the Duke had called his sister-in-law was back. She looked at the Duke with concern. "I've never seen anyone resist that."

The Duke looked like he was going to reply angrily to her, but there was a sharp knock at the door. He crossed to the ornate wooden portal, pulling it open, and Gail, had she been able to, would have screamed and ran again.

There, in all of its white-robed glory, stood a beautiful female. Her robes and hair billowed as if in a gentle breeze even here indoors, and as she floated through the doorway the smell of flowers and warm summer rain filled the room. Gail felt the restrictive magic relax its grip, but by now it was too late to run. The Mori could destroy her with a single blink.

"Miss Gail," the Duke said, gesturing at the floating humanoid being. "Allow me to present Bláthnaid Clíodhna." His tongue trilled around the name, and he bowed deeply.

157

SIXTEEN

The creature, its long silvery hair continuing to twirl about her head, looked over at the Duke. He nodded, as if she had spoken to him. "My Lady Clíodhna wishes me to explain why you have been brought here, to me. You see, Marion and I fell out of sorts a few years ago. But by then he had already told me about *your kind* and how important you were. So I started looking for you, and others like you. There's no way to really *track* you so it's been a tough search. We even tried experimenting on others and seeing if we could alter their genes to make them…more like you." Gail swallowed a lump in her throat. Had Crow been the subject of one of those experiments?

"But now you're here. One of my men reported that you were in Lillington and that you'd caused a fight with some thieves and I came down as fast as I could. But you had already left."

"Y-your brother—" Gail choked

"I don't have a brother," the Duke laughed. "But it made a fine excuse for a bounty nonetheless. Then we trailed you, but your little witch friend made things a little complicated."

"She scared you off." Gail had found her confidence again. "The Mori that found us ran away like a little b—"

A sharp slap from the woman shut her up for the moment. She had crossed the room in an incredibly short time. "The Lord Aonghus let you live out of *mercy*," she sneered. Gail wondered if the woman actually believed this, or was simply playing up the part in the presence of the alien overlord.

"Be still," the Duke commanded, his voice serene. "But in any case. Despite the interference of your friends, we kept an eye on you. We almost had you at Campbell."

"I killed one of you at Campbell," Gail spat at the Mori. She tilted her head, still not speaking. Her eyes were an inky black.

"Yes, you did," the Duke agreed. He was still grinning. "It was a loss my Lady accepts so long as you are willing to fulfill her wishes."

"What wishes?" Gail demanded. She wanted to dash for the door, or back to the window, or really do *anything* but sit here and wait for the murderous bastards' designs to play out. They had killed everyone in Lillington, and it had been Gail *herself* who had lured them there. It was all her fault. She sank into herself, then, tears streaming down her face.

A voice played through Gail's head. The creature did not speak, but the voice resounded as if it had been shouted directly in front of her face. *You will be a mother to the world.*

"One thing the Mori cannot do," the Duke said, leaning back again on the furniture, "is sire new young. Their bloodlines are so *pure* that it is dangerous. But *your* kind," the Duke said, taking a step nearer to her, "are gifted. You can carry the magic. As such, you offer the opportunity of genetic diversity. And in return, you will be spared in the great Reclamation on the Feast of St. Áed mac Bricc."

"The Reclamation?" Gail said, raising her voice. "When you kill everyone?"

"Not everyone," the Duke said, his voice singsong. "Those who the Mori and their servants have chosen will survive. You can be among them."

Gail shuddered. "Genetic diversity…They want me to…*mate* with them?"

159

"With *you?* Of course not," the Duke chortled. "No, no, the Mori would never debase themselves in such a way. They wanted to harvest your maternal DNA. The ova, from your body, to fertilize and grow new half-breeds. Half-breeds filled with magic, able to perform great feats and survive. They will be the progenitors of a new race. New Humans."

The Duke's eyes rolled back in his head, and his voice became softer. The creature was speaking through him now. "They will be raised by the Mori, taught the old ways. Taught the magic of their forefathers. They will be loyal followers." The Duke was approaching in small steps. "And then we can teach you the Magic. To bring life. To heal the sick and wounded. To dispel the darkness and the evil. To make the world beautiful once again."

"And what if I don't consent to this?" Gail said, scooting backwards a little bit on the bed.

"You didn't need to," the woman who was not the Duke's sister-in-law laughed. "We harvested what we needed from you while you were asleep."

Gail's heart sank, and her hands went to her waist. There was no pain or mark, but a profound sense of violation washed over her. "How *dare* you—"

"However...you have more information that we need," the Duke continued, sill possessed by the Mori's commands and continuing as if she hadn't said anything at all. "You have information about the people planning a resistant move against the Mori's plan for the Reclamation. But what you do with that information..." The Duke's eyes snapped back into place and he completed the conversation himself. "Now that is the most important thing. If you share it with me, then My Lady can make you very comfortable. She can fill your days with joy. Imagine, Gail—you need never be lonely again. And then, when the New Children grow, you will raise them as their mother. You will be esteemed highly as the progenitor of a new species of people. You will be deified."

Gail's eyes went wide, unable to reply.

"M told me," the Duke said, having finally reached the edge of the bed where she was sitting, "He told me how his one regret with keeping you hidden away was that you had no real friends or family. Such a sad, lonely life. And your only friend, M, is dead now. Don't you want to know what it's like to have a family?"

Gail stared into those eyes. They had depth, and age, and were truly awash with sincerity. The Duke believed the truth of his words, He believed that this offer would ring true to its target. He believed that she was just a silly girl, trying to find her way home to a family she had never known. He believed she would be taken in by her desire to belong. He believed that her only friend in the world was gone, and that she was alone.

One person's face flashed across her mind, and she knew he was wrong.

The Lady Clíodhna suddenly looked rather uncomfortable, and she dropped onto the floor with a thump. She appeared unsteady, and the swirling of her hair and robes stopped entirely about her. She looked terribly confused, and the Duke swiveled his head to look at her, as if her telepathic connection to him had suddenly been severed. Gail had seen that look before: the look of a Mori rendered impotent. "Witch!" The Mori screeched.

Without hesitation, Gail slammed her foot upward into the Duke's face and tumbled from the bed. Once again, she dashed for the window, throwing the curtain aside. She was halfway through the open hole when a hand grabbed at her foot—the woman that the Duke had called his sister-in-law was trying to hold her in place. Gail let out a blood-curdling scream and kicked as hard as she could backward. This only succeeded in dislodging her foot from her boot, and as her foot slipped out she fell, writhing, out of the window.

She knew the fall was going to be great, and she fought against her every urge to tense up and prepare for the impact. "Feet first," she could hear M say in her head, as she tried to twist herself into an angle that would be less deadly to hit the ground from. She hit an awning, and the force of her caused the entire thing to collapse, wrapping her in a tattered plastic blanket and sending her reeling—

She hit something mostly soft, but even though it definitely muffled the blow of her impact, her body still convulsed in pain for a moment from the shock. Something—someone—was pulling the whole awning upward, with her inside it, and she thrashed about. "No! No!"

"Gail! It's me!" It was Leonard. Gail finally tore through the material and saw his face smiling down at her. "Quick, we don't have long."

A pair of arms lifted her out of the mess she had landed in. It looked like a mattress had been pulled across the sidewalk for her to land on; not the nicest thing to break her fall, but enough that it had probably saved her from more severe injury. "Leonard?" Gail coughed as he pulled her into a carriage waiting nearby. Leonard leapt atop the driver's seat and thrashed the reins, sending the vehicle careening forward without warning. Nick was in the backseat, looking strangely stationary, much the way he had been when she and Crow had first found him on the train tracks in Lillington.

"Nice ride," Gail called, still trying to unshake herself from the fall but having sudden clarity from the adrenaline that was coursing through her veins. The redhead couldn't help but plaster a wide grin all over her face.

"Courtesy of the Duke," Leonard called back.

"No way!" Gail shouted, trying to reorient herself in the back seat of the carriage. "How did you even know I was—"

A sharp bark answered, and Lukather poked his head into the slats of the driver's seat. "The dog found us," Leonard explained. "And we knew something was wrong. We started after you and noticed the Duke's drones were everywhere. Your pup led us right to you."

Lukather leapt into Gail's lap and licked her face over and over. "You are such a good boy," she said into his furry neck, hugging him and scratching behind his ears.

The carriage was making its way down a busy road. Buildings on either side swept past as the carriage went up a ramp and onto an elevated street.

"Where's Crow?" Gail asked.

"On a cell tower," Leonard called back. "She had to set up the disruption signal manually since she can't access the internet. The dog led us to the building and we saw you try to get out of the window and get pulled back in with magic, so Crow suggested we knock the Mori's magic out and hope you tried to escape the same way a second time."

"Good guess," Gail said with a satisfied sigh as they pulled off the ramp. Up ahead, she saw a familiar girl in black, leaning against a silver cell phone tower with her cloak's hood pulled up.

The carriage hadn't even pulled to a complete stop before Gail had dropped out of the vehicle and was running to her. Crow stepped up to meet her in a hug, but at the last moment she put out her hands to stop her. "Wait, wait."

Gail's face fell. "What is it?"

"I just…I wanna say something." She shuffled from foot to foot.

Gail looked down. She wriggled her toes in her boot-less sock. She was frustrated that she had let the dreadful woman snatch it off her leg, but at the same time that boot was probably the reason she made it out of the window at all. Crow made a sound like she was about to speak but Leonard interrupted. "We gotta go," he called.

"Right, right, wasting time and all that." Crow slipped past Gail and climbed into the carriage. Gail followed after, her jaw tightening in confusion. Crow pulled Gail onboard as the carriage took off again, and as the streets of Raleigh slipped away behind them, Gail settled in the chair next to her. "Where to, Leonard?"

"Train station," Leonard replied. "Since we're in Raleigh already."

"Train?" Gail understood the concept, but the application here didn't make sense.

"Yeah, there's a few trains that still run. Steam-powered."

"Expensive," Crow retorted. "But I guess you have 'ways' of making that not-a-problem?" Leonard just laughed. Beside her, Nick once again flared to life. "I guess they either shut the signal off or knocked out the tower," Crow remarked.

Gail, meanwhile, kept staring at Crow. She was avoiding the mountain girl's gaze. "Crow—?" she said as delicately as she could muster.

"It's my fault," Crow snapped, and Gail flinched rather hard at the interruption. "I should have convinced you to stay. Are you hurt?"

Gail shook her head. "I found out it's probably *my* fault," she replied. "The experiment the Mori did on you. It might have been because the Mori were trying to make more people like me."

Gail went on to explain the plans that the Duke had revealed to her. Crow listened silently, looking rather smug when Gail revealed that he was definitely an Advocate. She looked far more concerned, when Gail explained what they had taken from her.

"I'm so sorry," Crow said finally, as the carriage slowed to a stop in a parking lot beside a disused railway station. They got out, reorganized their bags, and began to walk along the side of the railway. Gail continued her story about how the Duke's brother wasn't really his brother at all, and that everything had been an elaborate hoax made to coax her out. Finally, she explained how the fight in Lillington had been the spark that had lit the Duke's fire and ultimately had led to the Mori slaughtering all of the denizens of the town. By now, she was sobbing through her words.

Leonard finally butted in. "Gail. You can't blame yourself for this. You didn't do it—the Duke did. It's not your fault."

"Technically it's mine," Crow reminded, "since I brought you to them in the first place to get my computer back."

"No," Leonard insisted. "It's the Duke's fault. It's the Mori's fault. It's not any of yours. Stop taking the credit for their evil."

◊

They came to a small abandoned town an hour or so later down the track. Their pace had slowed considerably after they had left the city limits, fairly confident that they had not been followed, by Mori or otherwise. Crow mused out loud how strange it was that for all their magical abilities, the Mori still couldn't track one missing girl.

"Because the Mori magic is based around sight and sound," Leonard explained. "The pervading theory is that for some reason a person needs to be able to see or hear them in order to be affected. The only exception is the spell they used during the Riots. No one knows how they did that."

"That's right," Crow said. "that's why the Marines built that super suit, right, Nick?"

Nick nodded. He had been carrying Gail for a little while, the rough terrain being terrible on the girl with only one boot. It only seemed right, given the recent events, to give her a little bit of a break.

They came around a bend and found an abandoned railway stop, with a small guard house a little bit behind it. The door was locked, but one heave from Nick's fist smashed the aging lock apart and they went inside to find a single room with a bed and a desk. "Let's stop here," Gail said, sitting down on the bed without much of a thought. "I am really exhausted. I need sleep. Is that okay?"

"Train comes in the morning," Leonard said, stepping back outside. "Clear night, too. I'll probably go build a small fire. Let me know if you need anything…" His voice disappeared around the corner as he and Nick stalked off away from the guard house.

The witch looked out at the setting sun. "Yeah. Good night…"

Crow was about to pull the guard door closed, but Gail leapt up and stopped her. "Wait. Stop. Please."

Crow turned. "What?"

"Are you upset with me?" Gail said, her eyes already red from tiredness and more unreleased tears. "You're acting really…"

"I'm feeling weird," Crow replied. "Nothing to worry about."

"I missed you." Gail pulled the door open wider. "And I like being your friend. And I know I upset you when I decided to go north instead of south with you, and I regretted it pretty much instantly, and

I even changed my mind and tried to turn back, and…and…" Gail dropped back into her seat on the bed, sobbing.

Crow's arm was around her. "Hey. Shhh. I don't…I just…" She took a deep breath. "I'm no good at this."

"At what?" Gail said, lifting her head and giving the witch a pleading look. Her cheeks were stained red.

"At this. I've never, ah…I've never had a real-life friend before. I think I mentioned that." Gail nodded. "And I realized when you were gone that I sort of…I missed you, too." Gail nodded again. "And you saved my life. Twice. And I just…" The witch's brown eyes were just visible in the growing darkness. She didn't seem to want to finish her sentence and she stood up.

Gail sniffed and reached out for her. "And I d-don't want to be alone anymore."

"You're not alone. Do you want me to stay with you?" Gail nodded. "Okay, then I will." Crow began to take off her cloak.

"You're not, um…" Gail started to remove her only boot, untying the laces delicately. "Weren't you concerned when other people knew we were sleeping together?"

Crow laughed. "No, no, they didn't think we were sleeping together. They thought we were *sleeping* together." She raised her eyebrows as if to drive the point home.

"What do you mean?" Gail stretched out on the lumpy mattress.

"That," Crow said, lying down beside the redhead and pulling her close, "is a conversation for another time."

SEVENTEEN

"Okay, Leonard, I get that you've done this before and everything, but Gail and I haven't. So...please stop saying it's easy."

"I didn't say *easy*," Leonard hissed back. "I said it's *simple*. There's a difference."

Down the tracks, the sound of the train's whistle could be heard, carried along the wind to the party now crouched down near the rail. Gail could see the billow of steam pouring out of the front of the machine as it barreled down along its course. Leonard had advised they would need to be sure the front cars had passed before trying to jump onto the train.

"My foot hurts," Gail grumbled under her breath, her non-booted foot tingling with the chill of the morning air.

"We'll get some shoes soon," Crow promised, rubbing the small of her back with a hand.

The massive engine rounded the bend toward them. It made a screeching roar as the steam engine swept past them, and the moment it had cleared their position Leonard was up and running toward the track. Crow and Gail followed behind with Nick pulling up the rear. He was holding a terrified, but excited, Lukather in his arms.

167

Leonard paused at the track for a moment and let Crow and Gail jump on first. He pointed to a jutting ladder flying towards them, and as it came within reach, Gail grabbed it and pulled with all her might, finding a foothold with her only boot and hanging on for dear life. She looked back and saw that Crow had caught the ladder from the very next car, and Leonard had grabbed one a few more cars down. Nick wasn't visible, but Gail had no doubt as to his ability to do anything physical whatsoever. Satisfied that her friends had latched on without problem, she began to ascend the ladder and pull herself to the roof of the train.

"The hardest part of walking on a train," Leonard had said in a way that reminded Gail far too much of M, "is the air. Once you're moving along with the train it's not hard to keep your balance because the train is moving as fast as you are. The problem is that the air isn't." This was abundantly clear as Gail pulled herself up onto the steel roof of the train car, and she almost slipped instantly as the flow of air struck her. The one remaining boot she had was much more helpful than her tattered sock on the other foot, but she was finally able to pull into a crouch and start to walk like a goblin across the roof toward the back of the train.

She caught up with Crow in a few minutes. "Nothing like a blast of cold air to wake you up," Crow yelled over the wind, and Gail laughed with her as they made their way back along the train as slowly and carefully as they could possibly manage. When they had reached the caboose, Crow climbed down between the last two cars and began to jimmy open the lock while the other three waited above.

The door opened before she had finished. Crow froze. "Hello," said the tired-looking train guard. He had a nightstick on his belt but wasn't brandishing it. Gail was sure he had to be somewhere in his seventies.

"Hi," Crow said, waving with a few fingers. "This isn't what it looks like."

"It looks like you're breaking into the back of the train to get a free ride," the guard said, stroking his wrinkled chin. "Which means you're either broke, or on the run from somebody. So if it's not that, then what is it?"

"Actually," Leonard said, climbing down between the cars as well as he could with only one functional arm, "We're part of the security detail. See, the Duke—"

"I don't believe you for a second," the guard interrupted, and he gave Leonard a very knowing look. "But I might be willing to say I saw your ticket anyway." He opened his hand expectantly and stepped farther inside so the people still clinging to the roof could start coming down into the car, which was currently filled with boxes and bags. Crow sighed, dug in her pocket, and produced some gold tubes. The guard laughed. "No, no, no bullets. Where we're going that's not coin of the realm, if you catch my drift."

"Does Florida still use bills?" Leonard asked, searching his own pockets.

The guard nodded. "Most places still do. Don't know why the mid-Atlantic changed it up."

"I bet that's the Duke's fault, Leonard said as Gail, Nick, and Lukather finally made it through the compartment door. "It made it easier since he controlled so much of the currency himself. Here." He put a green bill that read "50" into the man's hand. The guard appeared satisfied and turned to leave, but Leonard stopped him. "That's our ticket," he said with that sparkle in his eyes, and put another bill into the guard's hand. "Like I said, we're your security detail, courtesy of the Duke." He put yet another bill into the man's hand. "You're putting us up in an empty cabin you have? That's so kind of you."

The guard took the bills and laughed. "See, I wish all stowaways were this reasonable," the guard said, pocketing them. "Well, it's a pleasure to have you. Can I have your names for the passengers' list?"

"These is Corporal Head and Corporal Lady," Leonard gestured to Gail and Crow respectively, eliciting a frustrated sound and wide eyes from the witch. "The man in armor is Sergeant Beast, and I," he said with a wink and a tip of his narrow-brimmed hat, "am Lieutenant Fireball."

The guard noted the names and didn't seem to be at all fazed by their absurdity. With a nod, he took out a notepad and wrote a few numbers. "Your cabins. Glad to have you here." He winked back at Leonard, as though he was somehow excited by the thrill of being involved in this crazy business, and turned on his heel to leave. Gail wondered if this man, on the giant monstrous steam machine, had seen much excitement in his travels at all.

"Corporal *Lady*?" Crow said as soon as the guard had snapped the door shut. "What is *wrong* with you?" she punched Leonard in his good arm.

"And I'm Corporal *Head*?" Gail crossed her arms.

"Yes, fine, I've never been good with code names, alright? But at least we're not in trouble."

"Yet," Crow grumbled. "Where did you get all that cash anyway?"

"I've had it in my pocket for years," Leonard explained, pulling out a wad of bills. "I used to have a lot of cash on hand because of my line of work. I kept a bunch on me just in case, somewhere, someone would still take them as legal tender. Also they're good for starting fires. I'd be a much richer man right now if I didn't spend so much of this on staying warm."

Gail was looking around at the bags. She was wondering about the contents and weighing her chances. Without a word, she started zipping open the bags, and found, as expected, lots of clothes. "You think there might be shoes in here?"

"Oh, definitely," Leonard said, grabbing another bag.

The four of them went through the luggage bag by bag. Gail was insistent on putting the bags back together and leaving them otherwise undisturbed. Crow, meanwhile, rummaged around and zipped the mess back up when done. They found a few pairs of shoes, none of which fit particularly well.

Finally, Gail happened across a pair that mostly fit her feet. In a black gym bag full of socks, undergarments, and cans of some foul-smelling deodorant, a pair of silver boots with bright yellow stitching on the outside lay wrapped in a towel. They were impeccably well cared-for, and she admittedly felt a little guilty when she put them on, because she knew she was about to steal them and would likely never be able to pay the person back. She demanded a 20-dollar bill from Leonard and shoved it into the bag where the shoes had been. She felt a little better after that.

Out in the main train, the compartments were cramped and open, with rows of bed after bed. People gawked at them as they walked past, toward the front of the train—particularly at Nick, who certainly stood out more than the others. Gail felt oddly vulnerable here on this massive moving machine, and when thunder rolled outside she leapt involuntarily. "I've never been on a train before," she whispered to Crow.

"I used to ride the subway with my dad," Crow said back. "This is kind of like that, I guess. Are these the old Amtrak lines?" she asked Leonard.

He pulled open the door to the next car. "Yeah. They mostly run from Raleigh and go as far as they can without hitting any of the Mori towns. Sometimes they go right through them instead without stopping."

Crow nodded. "That begs the question of where exactly we're going, Leonard. I should have asked that about seven steps back in our plan."

They crossed into another set of compartments. These had doors and privacy curtains, and Leonard checked numbers against the piece of paper. "Oh, right. Our destination is the lovely and scenic Columbia, South Carolina."

Gail wondered if there was going to be anything particularly lovely or scenic about the town at all; she had not seen much beyond the greys and browns of the failing towns she had passed through. Even Raleigh, with its tall sprawling buildings, had been nothing but a study in shades of earth tones. The whole thing was far too depressing to think about.

"Looks like we've got this compartment," Leonard said, patting a door, "and one a couple doors down. So we should probably sit down and relax for the ride. Back when this was the Silver Star line it used to be about a four hour trip. Steam trains go slower though so it's gonna be more like six."

"Ugh." Crow leaned against the compartment doorway. "What am I gonna do for 6 hours? I'm gonna get antsy."

"The alternative is walking for a week," Leonard said. "I thought you hated wasting time."

"I do!" Crow protested. "I've just got to figure out how I'm going to be productive now. Maybe I'll go through Bluejay's computer…" She took a seat in the compartment.

Nick got Gail's attention. "I'm going to look around the train. I don't need to sleep." Gail nodded and Nick went off to the end of the car and disappeared through the portal.

Leonard tipped his hat in a slightly-creepy way and slipped into his own compartment. Crow pulled out Bluejay's computer, and her own, and set them both out in the seat next to her. Gail closed the compartment door and closed the curtains before sitting down opposite her. "I lost M's sword," she sighed.

Crow glanced up. "Yeah. I'm sorry. I'm sure we can find you another one somewhere. But I…I know how much it meant to you." She resumed typing.

"What are you doing?" Gail asked, trying to distract herself from the thought.

"Copying files. I didn't secure my computer with an authenticator like Bluejay did. But to be fair, my computer is a lot faster than hers, so I'm copying all of her files to my computer and then I can reformat her hard drive and maybe sell it."

"Sounds reasonable," Gail replied, knitting her fingers together over her lap.

"Then I can try and do more research into Mori technology. It's like…it's like they're able to manipulate kinetic energy with transmitters. But the disruption signal we put out from the cell towers scrambles the signal and kind of nullifies it. It looks like Dr. Glenn and

172

this Dr. Osbourne might have developed it, and Bluejay perfected the signal. I can see her notes from various experiments."

Gail listened and looked out the window at the North Carolina countryside that was sweeping past her window. She started to arrange her thoughts and experiences from the last couple of days into some semblance of sensical order but it was growing increasingly difficult. They had invaded her body, while she slept, and had taken her eggs…to fertilize them and create a new species that they could control. It was insane. It was monstrous. The Duke's speech about 'morality' rang in her head for a little bit and cemented her feelings that the Mori were truly monsters—but more to the point, they were monsters who truly believed that what they were doing was the right thing. It was the most benefit to their people, and humans were simply there to receive the shortest possible end of the stick.

Crow continued typing and clicking for a while. Occasionally she would stop, and Gail would glance over to see Crow looking at her, and the witch would return to work without a word.

Nick finally dropped by again, tapping gently on the compartment glass. Gail answered the door. "Everything looks clear," he signed. "Nobody that looks particularly strange. Lots of older and richer people, probably headed south for the winter."

"Like birds," Gail signed back with a smile.

"I'm going to go see if I can find some dinner for everyone. You all are terrible about your health. You don't eat or sleep nearly as much as you should."

"I appreciate you caring so much," Gail said out loud, gently patting his shoulder. "I wanted to ask you. What are we going to Manning for?"

He paused, considering his words. "My wife," he signed, "She doesn't know what happened to me. I don't know if I will ever be back to normal. So I would like to go home, and let her know that Gunnery Sergeant Nick Harvey died. And deliver my remains home."

"That's terrible," Gail signed frantically. "There has to be a way that we can—"

"No need," Nick interrupted with his hands. "I would feel better giving her comfort than giving her false hope."

The redhead stared at him, unable to figure out something appropriate to say. Finally, she simply signed "OK."

He continued, "You should talk to Crow."

"What about?" she replied.

"Crow is very fond of you. She was very upset when you left but she would probably never tell you that to your face. She was asking questions like 'Do you think she liked me' and 'was I too mean to her' and Leonard and I both saw how much she liked having you around."

Gail couldn't help but smile at the idea of Crow overthinking her crabby exterior. "She's a great friend."

"I think she might think of you as more than a friend."

Gail's mouth opened and closed. She looked through the compartment window at Crow, still tapping away at the computer with a face crinkled in deep concentration.

"You mean—"

Nick nodded.

"But what do I—"

"Do you like her like that?"

"I don't know," Gail signed back frantically. "I like having her around. I like listening to her talk. I feel safer when she's there when I sleep." She stopped signing and started talking out loud. "But what does that *mean* because I don't know."

Nick shrugged and turned away. Gail found this to be exceptionally unhelpful, and stared after him for a few long moments before heading back into the compartment.

EIGHTEEN

"So," Crow finally said, snapping the two computers closed and putting them both in her bag, "I feel like we should talk, or something."

"If you don't want to, we don't have to."

"I want to."

"Okay." Gail knitted her fingers on her lap again, waiting. Crow, meanwhile, fumbled with the clasp of her cloak for much longer than was strictly necessary. Finally she pulled the cloak off and set it to the side, looking down to brush off her black pants. "What do you want to talk about?"

Crow took a deep breath. "So, no matter where I go it's the same, right? Towns full of people that only care about themselves. People who don't want witches in their towns because they think they'll attract hunter Mori or something. It's a mess. And I've never fit in anywhere. I tried a few times. Like, before I lived outside of Lillington I lived in a few other places after my dad died. But I'm not good with people as a general rule. In fact, I don't really think I like people at all, do you follow?"

Gail nodded.

"Good. That's good that you follow that I don't like people. I think people are self-serving and hateful and when you find someone who really just wants to do something positive they leave and you never see them again and—" she stopped, caught her breath, and continued, somewhat slower this time. "I don't like people, but I like you."

"I like you too," Gail said with a smile.

"Like, I want to protect you because you sometimes come off as really vulnerable," Crow continued without missing a beat, "but then you also kick ass on your own and you keep on saving *me*."

"You saved me," Gail protested. "You helped me take care of the arrow, and now you saved me from the Duke. So we're pretty even."

"Even?" Crow sounded frantic now. "It's not about getting even, Gail. It's about the fact that I *like* you and I don't want to see you get hurt and for some stupid, misplaced reason you keep putting up with my attitude."

"I think your attitude is charming." Gail's face was a wry grin. Nick's words were still tumbling around in her stomach and Gail knew that this conversation, however currently jumbled it might be, was coming to a particular conclusion that made her smile to think about.

"It's *not* charming," Crow insisted. "I'm an asshole."

"I don't think so," Gail said with a shrug.

"I don't like people," She said again, as though the times she had said it before somehow had less meaning.

"You've said that."

"But I like you!" Crow iterated, throwing her arms out helplessly. "And I don't know what to do about it!"

"Okay," Gail said with a shrug, "what do you *want* to do about it?"

The compartment was suddenly very still. Despite the fact that the witch was sitting reclined in her seat, Gail had the strange feeling that she was tensing up to pounce like a cat. Crow was weighing her options. Then, in an instant, she pushed off her chair and practically leapt forward to grab Gail by her jacket collar—

The compartment door slammed open, and Crow changed her trajectory at the last instant, turning to land beside the redhead instead, looking up at a train security guard with wide eyes. "Yes? Can I help you?" she said, and her voice was sharp enough that Gail half expected the man's ears to start bleeding.

"I need—" He looked down at his paper. "Lieutenant Fireball, urgently. Something's happened."

"Two compartments down," Crow said, jabbing a finger in the direction of Leonard's door. The guard tipped his hat and Crow pulled the compartment door shut with an anguished groan.

Gail was now twiddling her thumbs. "We should probably check that out."

Crow's expression indicated, on no uncertain terms, that she didn't want to check it out at all at the moment, and her eyes scanned over Gail's face as if pleading for some kind of reprieve from the constant drama that swallowed them at every turn. "You're right," she finally relented, starting to get up from the seat. Gail stopped her, though, and leaned in to plant a kiss on the witch's cheek. She smiled. Crow smiled back. Grabbing their bags—for fear of them being as easily ransacked as the bags back in the rear car—they exited the compartment to check on what was going on down the hall.

"And then," a woman was saying. "They came up and tried to kill him while he was sleeping."

She was sitting opposite Leonard in the tiny train compartment. Her long brown hair was tied back in a messy bun and her clothes— pajamas—were impeccably clean save for the fact that her right arm was splattered in blood.

Leonard was taking notes in a notebook with his good hand. Gail could see that his off-hand handwriting was absolutely awful. "The train doctor's going to take good care of him," he said, "I'll need you to tell me everything you can about who tried to kill him. And why they might want to. Where are you headed?"

"Miami," the woman said, Leonard's calming assurances helping to allay her sobs. "Then we're planning on visiting, um…" She bit her lip as if unsure whether she should say the next few words.

"I think I understand," Leonard said, raising his eyebrows so she understood. "If you're headed where I think you're headed then I also understand why someone might want to hurt you and your husband. Who knew you were coming?"

"A few close friends, only!" she insisted. "We were very careful to not let it get out that's where we were headed."

"I understand." Leonard stood up and turned to the train guard. "Thank you for alerting me to this situation, officer. If I can get a list of everyone headed all the way down to Miami I would be greatly appreciative. We only have another hour before we reach Columbia, so we have to act fast." The guard nodded and headed out of the compartment. As soon as he was out of earshot, Leonard took the woman's hand. "Is your husband an Advocate?"

The woman nodded, more tears spilling down her face. Leonard patted her hand. "Alright. We will investigate and try to find the perpetrator. Stay here." He rose, closing the windowed door to the compartment. He addressed Gail and Crow. "Ok, first thing—"

"First thing, you're not in charge," Crow snapped. "Second thing, are you really going to investigate this?"

"No," he hissed. "But if there are Advocates on this train we need to act like we are who we say we are. So let's move around, act like we're investigating, and then slip off in Columbia."

"We're not going to actually ask around?" Gail said. "What if—"

"We're not having this discussion..." Crow said, but she trailed off, leaning against the compartment door and swaying.

"Crow?" Gail put her arm around her, and without her cloak she could feel something in the small of her back—something very warm.

"I don't feel so good," Crow said, putting her arm around Gail in return. "Kinda dizzy."

"You," Gail hissed at Leonard, "go do your stupid investigating, but while you're there grab that train doctor and send him here if you can." Gail helped Crow back to the other compartment and set her down. "Take it easy. You're all worked up."

"I guess..." Crow sounded like she was half lost in dream.

Gail turned Crow away from her slightly and lifted up the back of her shirt to find the source of the heat. Her bandage was dirty and yellowed. "Crow…did you change your bandage after you fell in the river? Have you changed it at all in…in days?"

Crow shrugged. "I just kind of…forgot. It wasn't hurting…"

"Of course it wasn't—*Crow*. Oh no." Gail pulled the bandage off. Below, the skin was an angry red, surrounded by yellow and blue bruises. There was also a sweet smell—the smell of infection deep in the skin. "Crow, we need to have the doctor look at you."

Crow shrugged again. "I'll…be…fine…" she was shaking.

The door of the compartment slid open. Nick stood there, staring at Crow in her state, and his head clicked loudly as he scanned her. "This is very bad," he signed to Gail.

"How bad?" Gail gasped at him.

"Very bad," he signed again. "She needs a doctor."

As if on cue, a woman with dark braids slipped past Nick into the compartment. "Hello, I'm—oh god." She knelt down and looked Crow over, reaching out to feel her skin and examine the wound in her back. "How long has she been like this?"

"She's had that wound a week or so," Gail said. "She hasn't been taking care of it…"

"It's badly infected. She's showing signs of sepsis—it's gotten into her bloodstream," the doctor explained. "She needs medical attention or she's going to die of septic shock. Help me lay her down." Gail helped remove Crow's shirt and clear the compartment seat to lay Crow face-down. The doctor listened to Crow's chest with a stethoscope, shaking her head. Crow was making unintelligible noises. "Dammit," the doctor grumbled. "Fluid in her lungs…she's already going into septic shock. This is very bad. I don't think I have anything here that can save her. If she makes it to Columbia we might be able to get her to a hospital. But even that would take a miracle—"

Gail stood up. A miracle… *And then we can teach you the Magic*, the Mori had said in Raleigh. *To bring life. To heal the sick and wounded.* Had she healed her own thigh wound somehow when the Mori had attacked Campbell? If she had, she didn't know how. But…she knew someone that could.

"The Advocate that got stabbed," Gail said to the doctor, "is he awake?" The doctor nodded, not understanding the relevance. "I need to go to him. Can you watch Crow and make sure she doesn't…get worse?" Without even waiting for an answer, Gail dashed out of the compartment and into the next car, and the next one. Finally she found the stabbing victim near the front car, laid out on a first-class bed conversing with a nurse nearby.

Gail dropped to her knees beside his bed. "Hello," she said quickly, "I'm Gail and I need your help. Are you an Advocate?"

The man looked at her with mistrust. "Why are you—"

"Are you an Advocate?" Gail asked again with additional urgency. "If you are I need to speak with your lord or lady and quickly. My friend is dying, and I need their help and I have something to offer them."

The man shook his head and appeared to be ready to send her away, but he suddenly froze, his eyes rolling back into his head. The nurse beside him scooted away, out of his line of sight. "I am Lord Dónal," he said in a low tone. "Who are you that wishes to make a deal with me?"

"My name is Gail. I was working with the Duke and Lady Clíodhna. Do you know them?"

"I do."

"Then you need to know that Lady Clíodhna made me an offer and I refused it. But my friend is dying and I don't know what to do, and I need magic to heal her or she'll die."

The man's eyes returned to normal, and he put a hand to his head for a moment as if he had a sudden headache. He spasmed again, his eyes rolling back a second time. "Lady Clíodhna knows you will not accept her offer." Gail shuddered again. "But she is merciful. She will grant your desire, for a favor."

"What favor?"

"One to be determined in time."

Gail didn't hesitate. She didn't regret. Not now, at least. "I agree. Now please—"

"Hold out your hand, child."

Gail lifted her trembling palm, holding it out. The man's mouth opened wide, and something lightning-blue and hot poured out of it, slithering down his blanket and leaping into her hand. It rested there like a ball of blue-hot fire, crackled and dissipated. Gail was gone in an instant, not even awaiting an explanation, dashing back through the train compartments. She practically barreled Nick out of the way as she came in.

"She needs a hospital now," the Doctor said again, standing up to face her.

The train jostled, and they could feel the brakes beneath them start to act. They were slowing on their approach to Columbia. Gail looked at her friend, the witch's face frozen in confusion, and her breath came in shallow waves. The train was taking far too long in its final approach. Gail scooped her up and headed for the nearest train door. "Leonard!" she shouted.

He was there instantly. "How bad is it?"

"Bad," Gail said, and as the train came to a stop Gail slammed her way through the doors and out into the street.

NINETEEN

"Hospital?" Gail called out to the passers-by on the train station platform. "Hospital? Please."

They ignored her. They all ignored her. She was now just one of many, needing help in a world that had turned its back on people. It had made people cold and unfeeling. Now, rather than risk wasting precious resources on a stranger, they passed on, eyes forward, as if she was invisible.

"Clinic," Leonard said, pointing to a wooden spray-painted sign near the end of the platform with an arrow. The injured Advocate was on a stretcher, and two Samaritans were already wheeling him that way.

Gail didn't hesitate. She ran after them, still cradling Crow in her arms. The witch was mumbling something and seemed to be slipping deeper and deeper into unconsciousness.

Columbia was flatter than Raleigh, Gail thought, as they exited the driveway leading down to the platform. A red boxcar at the end was plastered with a map. The clinic, marked prominently in yellow, was only a block away. She took off down the street, holding Crow tightly in her arms.

She could feel something in her hand—something tingly and electric—where it met the skin between Crow's shirt and trousers. It was as if Crow's body had become electrified, and then it was hot, and then cold. Then it was gone.

Gail's arms and legs burned as she continued to carry Crow down the street another block. Then another. She could hear the clanking of Nick's armor behind her, and kept her gaze focused on Leonard who ran ahead. They passed a surplus store and a park, and Gail's lungs ached.

"HERE," Nick said through his talking box, and Gail slowed just enough to allow him to take her. She didn't want to be separated but at the same time she knew that Nick was faster and didn't tire. He ran ahead, careening around a corner and past the Advocate on his stretcher.

She slowed and stopped, her legs aching and feeling like she might lose her balance. As she toppled forward, an arm reached out and stopped her. "Hey now. It's alright. I've gotcha."

"It's my fault," Gail whispered.

"It's not," Leonard said. "You could not control this. It is not your fault."

"I should have...reminded her..." Crow probably hadn't even noticed that there was any discomfort at all until it was too late. And she hadn't noticed because she couldn't feel pain. And she couldn't feel pain because the Mori had experimented on her to make more of whatever *thing* Gail was. It was her fault, on more than one level. She heaved great gasps and coughs as her body tried to keep up with the exertion.

"I saw what happened with the Advocate," Leonard said, and the compassion in his voice was suddenly gone. Gail looked up at him, her eyes wide.

"I—I didn't—"

He held up a hand. "I know why you did it. I'm here telling you it was officially stupid. You made a deal with the Mori, Gail."

Gail dropped down, clasping her knees in her arms. She was shuddering. "I didn't know—I didn't know what else to—"

"I know that," he interrupted, crouching down to meet her on the level of her eyes. "And I still think it was stupid."

Gail shuddered again and took in a deep breath of the cold October air. "She can't know," she whispered. Leonard was quiet. He was just staring at her, and she could feel his contempt and his judgment. It made her just want to melt away and get sucked down a sewer drain. Gail slowly stood up, still breathing heavily. "Leonard. You can't tell her. I am going to try and get out of it, okay? I don't know how yet."

"I believe you," he said, scratching his chin. And starting off around the corner to catch up to Nick, "I don't think for a moment that you're the kind to join forces with the Mori willingly. But I want you to know something. Some of these Advocates? I bet it started like this. A loved one in peril. Then they cut a deal with the Mori and they're in debt. And the debt gets bigger and bigger. I'm trying to warn you so that doesn't happen to you."

"It's one favor."

"That's one favor too many," he replied. "Some of the advocates do it for power—the Duke, for example—but some of them are just people who wanted to help others."

"*You* said they're betrayers of the whole human race," Gail reminded. "Why are you trying to convince me now that they aren't?" She shoved him. "Why do you keep changing sides? Whose side are you on, Leonard?"

"Because—" He stopped, searching for an answer. He didn't speak throughout the rest of their trip, during which time they made it another block and into a shopping plaza where the clinic was situated.

A sign indicated this used to be a women's health clinic. Now, however, it was a medical hub for travelers coming into town by train. Wheelchairs and stretchers were thrown about through the parking lot haphazardly, and people bustled in and out of the building here and there. The rotating door, still functional, led to a dim lobby with people waiting. Crow was not there.

Gail stormed up to the desk. "Hello, a woman was just brought in by a man in armor," She said through her heavy breaths. They pointed at a door and before the receptionist could have a moment to explain further, the redhead shot through it like a cannonball into the ward full of patients.

"HERE," came a familiar digital voice, and Gail rushed over to the bed. Crow was laying on her side, away from Gail, apparently asleep. Her shirt was pulled up, revealing the wound in her back. It was no longer red or bruised, and appeared to be much shallower than even the half-hour before.

The Mori had kept its end of the bargain.

Nick gestured to the wound. "It's healing fast. How did this happen?" he signed to her.

Gail didn't reply, walking around the bed to kneel down near Crow's face. The witch was snoozing rather soundly. A nurse joined them at the bed with a bandage he had apparently been fetching, and applied a topical ointment, along with the bandage, to Crow's back. "That should do it," the nurse said, patting the sticky bandage with his hand. "It probably seemed worse than it was. She does seem pretty dehydrated though; when she wakes up, make sure she drinks a lot of water." He smiled and moved on to the next bed.

Leonard approached the bed, glancing at the not-serious-at-all injury on Crow's back that, a half hour before, had been a deadly wound. He was stuffing money back into his pocket. "Bill's paid. Is she still out?"

Gail prodded the witch gently with a finger. "Crow."

Her eyelids fluttered a little bit and she opened them part of the way. "Hey. Did I fall asleep?"

Gail nodded. "You kind of…passed out. Nurse said you were dehydrated." Nick looked up at Leonard, and if he could show any expression Gail was sure it would be a questioning one. Leonard nodded knowingly to Nick, who said nothing.

"Shit." Crow wriggled her shoulders a little bit as if they were stiff and sore. "I'm sorry. I'm bad at taking care of myself."

"Yeah, you are," Gail stroked Crow's black hair.

Crow slowly began to sit up. "It's a good thing you're here to take care of me then." She laughed, and Gail felt her own heart sink; Crow didn't understand the irony of her own words.

◌

"Well, we're here in Columbia, Leonard," Crow said as they walked out onto the sidewalk. The chilly air stung Gail's face and she pulled the collar of her brown jacket up. "How far is Manning?"

"A couple days' walk," Leonard replied, trying, unsuccessfully, to light his pipe with a match and one good hand. "I figure we should grab supplies and head out tomorrow morning."

"Fair," Crow laughed.

They started off down the street, past empty, crumbling buildings. Gail reached out to touch the brick and it yielded to her touch, falling apart at the slightest pressure. "I've always wondered why buildings like this are coming apart," she remarked.

"The Ritual of Homecoming," Leonard said, having failed to light the pipe quite yet. Crow yanked it out of his mouth, put it into her own, and lit it before returning it to him. "Thanks. But yeah, it's part of the ritual the first part was the guns and the electronics and the infrastructure. But the second part is slower. It's literally tearing down buildings. 'Reclaiming them to the earth' or something."

Crow snorted. "That's stupid. And horrible. They're basically making the places where *they don't even live* unlivable for the people who *do* live there." She sighed and hiked up her bag over her shoulder. "So what are we going to Manning for, anyway?" she said, looking up at the hunk of walking metal.

"FUNERAL," he said.

"Whose?"

"MINE."

Gail explained what Nick had told her about delivering his remains home. Crow shook her head. "That's terribly morbid, Nick. I mean,

186

wouldn't you rather your wife knew what happened to you? She might understand. You—"

"NO."

"But what if she—"

"NO."

"Come on, Nick. She—"

"NOO." The third time he hit the letter O twice and it came out with a long "oo" sound that would probably have been hilarious if not for the context.

Crow didn't protest any further, and as she spotted the market up ahead she pulled her hood up and picked up the pace, eager to get out of the cold.

Columbia's market was at one time a nice cluster of businesses within a short walk from one another. Gail saw long-faded signs for coffee shops and restaurants all in a line, with a few apparel stores and small shops in between. Now, they had all come together, erecting a large and flat canopy across the street that used to be highway 1—a tabernacle of sorts, under whose vinyl roof a loud hub of commerce had been built. Gail recalled a phrase from her childhood—flea market—as she looked around at the tables covered in merchandise. It was a fitting term.

Leonard surreptitiously counted out the cash in his pocket. "Okay, I don't want to alarm anybody, but I'm running dangerously low on funds here." he displayed a few bills. "I might be able to make a bit this evening entertaining at a bar or something, but we have to be pretty careful about what we get. We need to prioritize."

They discussed the matter at length—or, rather, Leonard and Crow argued about the matter while Gail and Nick watched silently—and finally decided that food would be a priority, since they would not need their winter gear much as much as they continued south. Crow pulled out Bluejay's computer from her bag. "And I need to sell this, too."

"Let me—" Leonard reached for it, but Crow pulled it away. He coughed and regained his composure. "I assume you've reformatted it?"

"Yes."

"Ran a tool to make sure it's completely reformatted?"

"Yes!" Crow sounded like any answer to the contrary would be utterly preposterous.

"Okay then: *please* let me sell it for you. I guarantee I can get a better price than you can. It's literally all I'm good for anymore."

Crow narrowed her eyes at him, regarding him for a long moment before handing over the device. She snatched the rest of the money from Leonard's hand and walked away into the throng of shoppers in the market to buy supplies.

Gail followed closely behind the black cloak, pointing out things here and there that could be useful. Crow handed Gail some money and sent her over to buy new blankets, since the ones they had used to dry off after the river fiasco had been left behind in Dunn.

They finally regrouped at one end of the market, where Leonard handed Crow a large stack of bills as well as a small bag of bullets. "All yours," he said with a grin, and Crow couldn't help but smile as they headed toward a two-story brick hotel on the main street where Leonard had already reserved rooms for the night. "And this is courtesy of Nick, who offered to spend the night chopping firewood for them in return for the rooms. Thanks, Nick."

Nick waved his hand as if to say it was nothing, but Gail hugged him appreciatively nonetheless.

◌

Gail closed the motel room door and groaned, planting her face on the door as she dropped her bag—now heavier from extra supplies—onto the floor. It was warm in here, thanks to more steam-powered heat that was flowing out of a radiator on the wall, and Gail resisted the urge to just press her face against the hot pipes to get warmer. Lukather already had a similar idea, spinning around on the floor before collapsing in an instant sleep directly in front of the heat source. Gail had been fortunate, she thought, to have access to a fireplace in the mountain retreat, because the alternative was startlingly terrible.

"Hey," Crow said from behind her. Gail turned to see Crow, standing with a decidedly innocent look on her face, holding something behind her back. She had lit the coal oil lamp on the desk, casting the whole hotel room in an orange glow that threw Crow's face into just enough shadow that the only thing visible in her expression was a rather wry grin.

"Hey," Gail said, returning the smile and leaning against the door.

"I got you something at the market when I sent you off to get blankets. See, I *might* have found a wad of bills in one of the bags on the train."

Gail chuckled. "And to think, you used to rag on me for being a thief."

Crow's smile faltered a little; she looked like she found it a little less funny than Gail did. "Yeah. Well. Anyway." From behind her back, where she had apparently stashed it in her cloak, she pulled out a sword in a slick leather sheath. The hilt was a blackened iron color, and the handle was black with silver studs in it. "The salesman told me this is an arming sword from a renaissance festival and is actually made for fighting. No mall-ninja crap."

"Oh wow," Gail breathed, stepping forward to take it from her. She pulled it out of the sheath a little and examined the blade. It was definitely sharp. "You really didn't need to do this…"

"Well, I wanted to." Crow stood rocking on her toes awkwardly as if waiting for something—or deciding something. "And I wanted to tell you something…you know, before we got interrupted on the train."

"Mhm." Gail re-sheathed the sword and set it next to her bag before straightening up to face the witch eye-to-eye.

"I…I really hate wasting time, you know?" Crow said slowly, and her hands seemed to have somehow found Gail's hips.

"You might have mentioned it once or twice," Gail said. Her voice was shaky.

"Well," Crow continued, her face now very close, "I could waste lots of time with you."

Gail wasn't really sure what to make of Crow's lips, now pressed on hers. They were sweet, in a way, and despite the streaks of dirt and sweat that dotted her skin and clothes, Gail was quite happy to come to the conclusion that her first kiss was with the most beautiful girl in the whole world.

TWENTY

"So...what does this mean now?" Gail asked into the darkness. The coal lamp had burned all night, sending the room into shifting shades of amber and yellow for hours so that, by the time Gail and Crow actually got around to doing any sleeping, it was like a visual lullaby.

But now it was morning, despite the single thread of sunlight that was streaming in through a hole in the curtain, casting an upside-down image of the streets outside on the far wall, the room was still mostly dark and the two of them were not too keen to get up and greet the day just yet.

"What does what mean?" Crow asked, scooting a little closer and burying her face in the redhead's collar.

"All this. I mean...what does it mean?"

"Which...*part* exactly?" Crow looked up at her, her eyes still half-lidded.

"All of it, sort of," Gail said. "Like...are we still friends?"

"I'd hope so," Crow chuckled, her hand shifting to rest on the small of Gail's back. "I don't think enemies usually end up like this."

Gail hadn't really known what she was doing. Neither had Crow, though she appeared to have a little bit of a better understanding of

191

the general steps to the dance, even if, she admitted, most of her understanding was more theoretical than practical.

Gail sighed. "We've gotta get up though."

"Five more minutes," Crow mumbled, reaching up to plant another kiss on Gail's lips.

"You've said that twice now," Gail said, and despite the groan of protest from the loss of additional body heat, she slipped out from under the covers and went to the window. She pulled open the inner curtain, a wall of white suddenly filling the room with blinding light. Crow shielded her eyes and looked like she was about to dive under the covers, but the sight of Gail backlit by the window gave her pause and she stared for a moment before diving under.

Gail laughed at her and went to the bed, leaping on top of it and pinning Crow there beneath the covers. The witch stuck her head out. "Hey!"

"So what does it *mean*?" Gail asked again. "What are we?"

"That's up to you," Crow shrugged. "I think generally the term is 'girlfriend'."

Gail chewed on her lip for a moment, considering the word. "Seems to fit. Is that okay with you? Do you want to be my girlfriend?"

Crow pecked her on the lips. "Yes. If you do."

Gail pulled away and yanked the blanket off of her. Crow let out a squeal as most of her olive flesh was suddenly exposed to the cold air. "Okay," Gail said, throwing the blanket to the side, "now that we've sorted that out we need to get going."

"*Fine*," Crow said with such a sigh that it made her whole chest heave. "I'm not going to lie. I can't wait to get to Florida so I can get out of this stupid cold."

They dressed, only pausing briefly for a spontaneous amount of kisses, before they left the room. Leonard was already dressed and leaning against the wall near the stairwell. He had apparently been practicing the recovery of his dexterity, because he was able to light his own pipe with one hand as they approached. "Morning," he said, and his eyes darted for a moment to the pair's clasped hands. "Hope your—"

"Don't," Crow said, pointing a finger and narrowing her eyes. Leonard put his hands up in defeat and they headed outside, where Nick was being thanked by the inn's proprietor.

"This should be good for most of the winter," he was saying to the armored man. "For me and the neighbors. I've never seen someone work that fast, and so long, without even a break."

Nick shrugged. "ALL IN A DAYS WORK", he typed out on the Type-N'-Talk. "MAKE SURE YOU…KEEP WARM THIS…WINTER. TAKE CARE."

The innkeeper's wife threw a crocheted scarf around the Marine's neck, tying it gently. It was a tin-grey thing that, to be fair, didn't particularly match with the black-and-grey metal of the armored suit, but Nick reached up to touch it with his fingers tenderly. Gail wondered if he could feel the yarn in his fingers. "THANK YOU," he typed, and they started off down the street.

△

They took the south-west road out, clambering onto Route 48, and a few hours later Columbia was far behind them. The sky, a clear pool of azure above them, was like a sign that the troubles of North Carolina were far behind them, and that only positivity waited before them now. Gail and Crow led the group, clinging onto each other with smiles plastered on their faces.

And yet, Gail could not help but feel terribly guilty. Leonard and Nick were very quiet ten or twenty feet behind, and Gail wondered whether the two men had talked…and if Leonard had filled Nick in on the source of the magical healing of her wound.

But at the same time, seeing Crow not only healthy but also in an incredibly good mood, Gail found it hard to say that it wasn't worth it.

△

They stopped a few hours outside of Columbus. Signs along Rt. 48 called the area "Bluff Run", but whatever kind of town it might have been was lost. The Ritual of Homecoming had certainly 'reclaimed the earth' here, as the buildings had completely fallen into disuse. They appeared long abandoned—decades and decades of wear had swallowed them and covered them in vines and dirt, despite the fact that their disrepair was only, at most, 15 years old.

At the end of the day they decided to camp at an intersection at the southern end of Route 48. Here, another larger highway crossed them, and beyond that lay forest and woods. Crow checked her map and suggested they start south in the morning, since up ahead would be a river and it would be far easier to cross at the train bridge about a quarter-mile down the road.

Leonard tore open a bag of beef jerky with his teeth. "Why are you so keen to have your own funeral, Nick? Not trying to pry."

Nick shrugged. The armored suit sat down on the curb and looked depressed—at least, as depressed as an emotionless suit of armor could possibly be.

Crow watched him and chewed thoughtfully. "You don't have to do this, man. Like, none of us think you're dead. You're very clearly alive."

He shrugged again and knocked on his armor. "EMPTY," he typed into his device.

"That is not true," Gail said, rising indignantly to her feet. "You have been an immense help. You saved my life. You got Crow to the hospital. You even gave me relationship advice."

"He did?" Crow said, her eyebrows raised in amusement.

"Yes. And now you're sitting here saying you're 'empty'? Come on, Nick. I…I know it sucks to be you right now. But you are still a *person*."

"Not to mention," Leonard added, "that you being what you are is far better than the alternative."

Nick shrugged again, so hard it made his shoulder joint make a creaking sound. Leonard lit his pipe and picked up his bag. "Alright,

Nick. Your choice. But if we can help you, then please, please let us know."

Nick stood up, brushed himself off, and nodded.

⌂

They saw the first sight of Manning, South Carolina as they crossed a bridge over another highway. The clouds in the distance crowned the small town, and the raised signs on the horizon leered down at them like forgotten statues. Those signs had once been made to attract attention of passers-by, but now they were simply another marker of a place where people struggled to live.

Gail looked over the bridge's edge and saw, to her amazement, that it had once been painted with the number 95. "Wait a minute," she said, stopping to double check. "Is this I-95? It's my road!"

Crow laughed. "Fate keeps bringing you back to this road, doesn't it? Well, to be fair we'll have to take it to get to Jacksonville."

"And Orlando," Leonard added. Well, Nick, where are we off to?"

Nick pointed to a sign on the far end of the bridge. It was a faded blue color, with a symbol Gail had never seen before. Up close, she could see it was a sort of L-shaped ruler, with a geographer's compass situated over them. Beneath it read the words "AFM; 2ND MONDAY 7PM."

Crow tilted her head. "I feel like I've seen that before."

Leonard laughed out loud. "Oh! Know that that is." He patted Nick's shoulder. "Nick, you're a Freemason?"

Nick nodded.

"What's that?" Gail asked as they continued down the road toward town.

"It's sort of a—and correct me if I get this wrong, Nick—it's a religious men's fraternity. Really old. Like, biblical old, supposedly. Something about…building men up. Making them better. Sharing brotherhood. I didn't know they were even still around. Are you a member of that Lodge?" Leonard asked, jutting his thumb back toward the sound.

Nick nodded. "WHAT DAY IS IT?" He typed out.

Crow checked her watch. "Sunday. The 5th."

Nick signed to Gail. "I need to see my wife. And then, tomorrow, I will see my Brothers. In the meantime, you all just need to keep safe. Do research and things. We shouldn't be here more than a week." Gail translated all of these things and the others nodded. Nick turned to Leonard. "I will need your help."

⌂

Gail wasn't really sure what to expect when Leonard rang the doorbell. He had ditched his trench coat and bandolier and even his narrow-brimmed hat He had even swapped out his t-shirt for a grey button-down and slacks he had bought from a consignment store.

"I am not sure this is necessary," he'd told Nick.

"It is," Nick replied through Gail's translation. "It's the way these things are done."

"But the United States isn't even—"

Gail had put out a hand to stop Leonard. "We're going to do it, because he asked us to."

And so here they were, on an unfamiliar front porch. The girl who answered the door was younger than Gail had expected. She had to be in her late teens, maybe a year or so older than Gail herself. Her hair, a dark plait that ran down her shoulders, was a fine accent to her dark skin and chestnut eyes. She looked confused as she pushed the screen door opened. "Can I help you?"

"May I speak with Mrs. Tabitha Harvey, please?" Leonard's voice was crisp, and calm, and Gail wondered how exactly this man could possibly retain his composure in this circumstance. She wondered how she could do it herself. Grief wasn't something that she felt able to handle deep down inside her mountain girl heart—not yet, at least. It was so strange, to be surrounded by death and desolation on all sides, and yet she hadn't truly been able to grieve. Not for her parents. Not for M.

The girl disappeared inside and returned with, presumably, her mother. She was standing very tall—taller than Leonard, even—and her presence was fiery there in the doorway, like an indomitable tower of strength. Gail respected this woman the instant she laid eyes on her. The woman even gave Leonard pause. "I'm Mrs. Harvey."

"Ma'am," Leonard said, regaining his composure, "I have been asked to inform you that your husband has been reported dead at Camp Lejeune on June 1 of this year after an attack by the Mori. On the behalf of the US Military and the Secretary of Defense, I extend to you and your family my deepest sympathy in your great loss."

The woman didn't move. She didn't flinch. Her eyes slowly narrowed as she gazed into Leonard's eyes, and the storm that was brewing behind her face was almost terrifying to behold. "The Secretary of Defense?" she spat. "The same Secretary of Defense that signed over the United States' surrender 15 years ago? The same Secretary of Defense that kept the military running secretly, keeping soldiers and using them to carry out the Mori's plans? Your Secretary of Defense is a cocksucker, and I'll thank you if you don't reference that son-of-a-bitch Advocate in the same sentence as my husband ever again." She turned her gaze to Gail, who shrank from her, and then back to Leonard. She paused, considering her next words. "Thank you for telling me. I had suspected it when his letters stopped coming. But...thank you anyway. You can go now." She closed the door without another word.

Gail and Leonard walked back up the driveway where Crow, Nick, and Lukather were waiting at the curb. "That was fast," Crow said, standing up and putting an arm around Gail.

"Is the Secretary of Defense really an Advocate?" Gail asked, untying her hair that had been put up into a professional-looking bun.

Crow shrugged. "I've heard theories that what's left of the US government is all Advocates. Makes sense, too, but you never really hear from them outside of propaganda anyway."

"Your wife is a tough woman," Leonard remarked, patting his metal arm. "I wish you would have come though. It probably would have been nice to see her."

"If I had come with you," he signed, "I would have never wanted to leave."

TWENTY-ONE

"So what are they doing in there?" Crow asked, pouring an absurd amount of syrup onto a waffle. They were once again at one of the safe havens of the world, Waffle House, the following evening. Gail rested her head on Crow's shoulder, glad to see that she was eating once again. Across the street, they had watched Nick knock on the door of St. Peters Lodge #54, and was received by the people inside. Now, the door was closed and locked.

"No idea," Leonard said. "It's important to them, anyhow. And It's really important to Nick."

"I can't imagine how he feels," Gail said, closing her eyes. "He's been stuck in that suit of armor for how long now? Only able to talk to me except through that talking box. And then the fact that the suit's got his own corpse in it? That's...that's a mess. I can't even imagine how that must feel."

"Empty?" Crow said, recalling one of the words Nick had croaked out on his machine. "I can't imagine it would be anything but a really dehumanizing feeling."

"Well, he's human enough to us, isn't he?" Gail said, sitting up. "Shouldn't that be enough?"

Leonard raised an eyebrow. "Would it be enough for you?"

⌂

Nick came by later in the evening. He had been neatly polished, and the tin-grey scarf was neatly tied again around his neck. He explained that one of his Lodge brothers owned the local funeral home, and had helped to extract his remains from the suit of armor, leaving it an empty, but still functional, shell.

Gail couldn't quite place it, but something in his gait made it seem as though he were somehow sadder. She was up on her feet and her arms were around him in a big hug before he'd even reached the table. He patted her back gently.

"Are we staying for your funeral?" Leonard asked.

Nick shook his head.

"That's fair. Well, we've got a hotel stay all paid for, so I think I'm going to go find a bar." He grinned at Crow. "Coming?"

She considered it for a moment and a smile spread across her face. "Sounds good to me. We've got the money and we're ahead of schedule already. What's your drink of choice, Necia?"

Gail shrank in her seat a little. "I've never drank."

"Even better!" Crow laughed. "Fun times all around. Let's go!"

"Great," Leonard said clapping his hands. "But I'll need to borrow Lukather."

⌂

The last time Gail had walked into a bar, she had killed someone. She wondered if Crow realized that this was the source of her discomfort, but she also knew that Crow was not terribly apt at picking up on these things unless they were shoved into her face. Gail considered telling her, but Crow was now getting psyched up about the idea of having a celebration that Gail had absolutely no desire to deflate her balloon.

It used to be called the Yucatan, but the sign had been taken down and replaced with a hand-made one that said "The Berg." Gail didn't know what a 'berg' was but it clearly meant something to the

200

proprietor, who had slathered orange and black paint all over the walls and covered it in unfamiliar logos.

Leonard took a seat at the bar, spotting a young mousey-haired woman at the far end, and started to talk to her.

"Is that your dog?" she said, scooting over toward him.

"Yes ma'am," Leonard said, tipping his hat. "His name's Lukather."

"He's so *fluffy!*" The woman said, scratching the sheepdog behind his ears. Lukather, meanwhile, had no idea what was going on but he enjoyed the attention nonetheless.

Crow made a disgusted sound as she watched him.

"What do you have?" she asked the bartender, a burly man with long brown hair flecked with white.

"Cheap, strong, and tasty," he replied. "Pick two."

Gail slammed some of her money down. "Strong and tasty!" she laughed.

The bartender poured something dark, like wine, out of a jug. "Q's famous apple pie moonshine," he explained, and up-close Gail could see that it was actually cinnamon-colored. "Have fun, don't die."

Crow took the drinks and led the redhead to a booth in the back. Gail was still quite uncomfortable, trying to keep the image of Dirk, impaled on her sword, out of her head. Because thinking of that reminded her of Lillington, which reminded her that I was all her f—

"Drink," Crow interrupted Gail's internal crisis. "You'll feel better."

Gail sniffed the glass. "It smells really sweet."

"Damn right it is." Crow took a gulp of hers, let out an enormous sigh, and looked over at Leonard, who was still talking to the woman at the bar. "Gross…"

"What?" Gail finally took an experimental sip of her drink. It was cinnamon-sugary and had a warmth to it that filled her mouth and followed all the way down her throat.

"Leonard, over there, trying to pick up that girl. First, she's like ten years younger than him, and second, I think she's a working girl."

"Working girl?" Gail took another sip.

Gail looked at her with narrowed eyes. "I keep forgetting how little you know. It's endearing at times, I'll admit, but sometimes…" She shrugged. "She's a girl who gets paid for sex."

Gail choked on the moonshine. "Wait, so Leonard is trying to…uh…" she lowered her voice to barely a whisper. "…have *sex* with her? Why?"

Crow laughed. "I bet it has nothing to do with the two gorgeous ladies he's been traveling with for weeks, neither of whom he's had the chance to bang. And who recently started banging each other." Gail turned a really deep crimson shade. "I'm sorry, I get really crude when I drink."

Gail took a deep breath and swallowed a huge gulp of the moonshine. The vapors from it filled her nostrils and while she didn't cough from the smoothness of the drink, she did feel a distinct burning sensation that went down her throat like she had swallowed a lit match.

The woman and Leonard were now sitting closer together as she continued to pet Lukather and converse. Leonard was grinning from ear to ear; Gail couldn't quite read what he was saying, but from the looks of it, the woman was genuinely enjoying his company. It was possible, of course that it was a 'working girl' act, but Gail honestly didn't think so.

Leonard gestured to the back, where Crow and Gail were, and he headed over to them. "Hey folks. If I head out are you going to be okay?"

"The dog, Leonard?" Crow said with a raised eyebrow. "The dog trick?"

"No," Leonard said pointedly, and rolled up his right sleeve to display his scarred cut-off limb. "The dog trick *and* the wounded soldier trick."

"You're not a soldier. You're a pig."

Behind him, another guy had approached the woman and was now trying to get her attention. She waved him off, and he persisted, and as

Gail watched, he reached around to grab at her breast. "Hey, Leonard—"

Leonard looked back, saw the situation, and took off back toward the bar. Gail didn't see the knife come onto Leonard's hand, but the man immediately backed off as a rainbow-colored blade poked aggressively into his throat. Gail couldn't understand what Leonard was shouting. In fact, the whole room was becoming sort of staticky, and Gail was finding it a little harder to concentrate. "Crow…?"

Crow was laughing. "Oh my god, you really never have drank before, have you? Damn, these drinks are strong. It sure doesn't taste like it…"

Leonard's shouting had caused the man to back off and leave the bar. Leonard put his knife away and went to check on the girl, who was looking rather upset but grateful. Gail watched them, as if through a fog, as they stood up and walked out of the bar.

Gail leaned in to Crow and curled up against her. "I like you."

"I like you too, Necia."

Gail wasn't sure how much time had passed before either of them spoke again, but the bar seemed to dissolve at the edge of their booth, like they were floating through a dark space with dim coal-oil lamp lights and music played on acoustic instruments. The music and the lights swirled for a time and settle into ripples, like crashing waves on the shore.

⌂

In the morning, however, it was just pain. Gail's head felt hot and heavy as she woke up, and the rain outside was far too loud for her.

She was sprawled, fully-dressed, across the hotel blanket. Lukather was curled up by the door, looking somehow forlorn, and Gail wondered how he had gotten in, especially if he had been a companion to Leonard's late night escapade. Groaning, Gail half-rolled, half-flopped out of the bed and made her way to the bathroom.

The water was perpetually cold, but as it rushed over her skin it gave her a bit of a shock that helped her come to her senses. Little bits of the night previous were floating here and there in her mind but she couldn't string them together. She thought that she might have finished the container of apple pie moonshine, and she very vaguely recalled a particularly intense session of kisses with Crow that might have been slightly too inappropriate for the public. She also remembered Crow being frustrated and taking her back to the hotel room.

Once cleaned, dried, and dressed, Gail came to the realization that not only was Crow not in the room, neither was her bag. She had clearly gotten an early start to the day; Gail hoped that her own state of consciousness had not inconvenienced her companions too much.

She stepped out of the hotel room to find Nick, standing at parade rest next to the railing that overlooked the empty parking lot. He turned his head slowly as she exited. "Morning," she said cheerfully.

He turned to her and signed. "Almost afternoon, actually."

"Aftern—Oh no. I'm sorry, I didn't mean to sleep so long." She gave Nick a sheepish smile which he didn't acknowledge. His movements were a little stiff and she wasn't sure if it was the fact that he was getting used to not having a corpse inside his armor, or if something was wrong. "How did Leonard's date go last night?"

"I think she's still asleep in his room," he signed, gesturing to Leonard's hotel door. Then: "Crow's gone. Left early this morning with Leonard. Caught the morning train toward Charleston."

"*Gone?*" Gail gasped, putting her hands out against the railing. "Why? What happened?"

Nick didn't move as he thought for a moment on how to phrase the response. "You got very drunk last night very quickly. Drunk enough that you started getting very talkative."

Gail's stomach felt like it was suddenly packed with ice. "No…" she whined, putting her head against her hands on the railing. "How much did I tell her?"

"Everything," Nick signed, but there was sympathy behind his movements. "About how guilty you felt about Crow's experimentation. Then that led to you talking to her about the wound in her back. And, finally, you told her the truth about what happened in Columbia, and about your deal with the Mori. You told her that you didn't know if that meant you were an Advocate now."

Gail was shuddering. "Then what happened?"

"Crow took you back here. Made sure you were comfortable. Then she packed up and went to leave. Leonard stopped her; told her she shouldn't go out alone. When Crow was insistent, he offered to go with her. And I guess she agreed."

She was beyond words now, and Lukather was rubbing his side against her leg, sensing her pain. She saw the armored man approach from the side and take her in his arms; she relented to this and pressed her face against his green breastplate. She sobbed into him, wondering if her tears might make the metal man rust, but unable to stop herself.

INTERLUDE: THE MORI

"Please...My Lady..." The whimpered cry was muffled by the floor, as the Duke tensed and curled into a ball in his low bow. His arms covered his head, in the hopes that his beautiful mistress might finally see his total and complete regret and take pity on him.

The Mori were known to take pity on lesser beings. It was simply the civil thing to do when dealing with the ruffians—the barbarians!—that were humans. Humans that made strange noises and built tall buildings made of stone and metal. Humans that disrespected the earth beneath their feet, who shunned the ancient gods, and who knew nothing of magic!

Perhaps it was this last thing on that list, Bláthnaid Clíodhna considered while her servants continued to beat the Duke for his insolence, which caused her such disdain. The Magic was innate to the Mori; the use of it to, for example, solidify a cloud and turn it into the throne upon which Clíodhna sat was a trivial thing. They had possessed Magic for ages and it was simply a part of their existence, as much as breathing or thinking. The Magic was a power beyond even the Mori's true comprehension; the secrets of its origin were lost to the void of time and the fog of memory. The Magic simply *was*.

She held up a hand and her servants finally relented. "*Slave,*" she sneered, her voice carried only through the Magic, since this slave should not even deign to hear the perfection of her otherworldly voice, "*you shall tell me why I have punished you this day. You shall beg forgiveness for those actions.*"

The Duke pulled himself onto his knees and dropped into another bow, the back of his shirt glistening with fresh blood. "Oh glorious mistress, I beg of you, forgive me! I have embarrassed you by allowing a witch to steal your power and allowing the child Gail to escape from you! I am truly repentant and will do anything you could possibly desire if it would bring me your favor once again!"

"*You have done all of these things,*" Lady Clíodhna replied silently. "*And you shall be given a chance to do so. The girl now owes me a favor.*"

The Duke raised his head just barely in surprise at this revelation, but it was a motion that crossed an unspoken boundary. He saw stars as the whip struck the back of his head and forced his forehead to the floor. "You will…send her to me?" He asked, his voice barely a whisper.

"*I shall not waste such a favor giving her to you!*" Clíodhna screamed in the Duke's head, making him tremble violently on the floor. "*I shall not waste such a precious thing as a favor for your sake. You shall bring her to me by your own capabilities. When she is brought to me—then, she shall truly be mine. She belongs to me. She had belonged to me many months, and yet I have not possessed her. She will be mine, and she will serve me and her children shall be the New People of Mankind.*"

"We know where she is going," The Duke said, his face still against the floor. "We believe she intends to go to the Tower of Peace."

"*And why would she go there?*" Clíodhna asked. Her voice in his head had softened.

"Because she is with Leonard Bohr," The Duke said, and Clíodhna could not see it, but she knew that there was a smile on his face. "Marion's brother."

If it was possible for the telepathic link between the Mori and her slave to communicate a gasp, it was felt. "*This is interesting news,*" The

Mori whispered in his head. "*And it means we know that she is going to resist us. Your attempt to silence his co-conspirator also failed: you did not recover the blue witch's magic box and now it is in the hands of another witch.*"

"Because Gail—"

Clíodhna leapt to her feet, the cloud throne cracking with lightning behind her, her mouth emanating a deafening banshee screech that sent the Duke back into a ball as the force of the sound made him slide a few feet back across the floor. "*I will not tolerate your excuses, slave! You will recover the girl. You will kill the witch. You will recover the magic box before whatever their plan is can be enacted.*" She took her seat again on the throne, which calmed its stormy nature and returned to a delicate white. "*If you succeed, there will be no reward. If you fail, there will be no mercy.*"

The Duke cried, thanking her for this opportunity, and for not killing him or torturing him further. His terrified, pious cries echoed through the hall for a short while as he retreated across the floor, into the hall, and out the door.

TWENTY-TWO

It was another hour before Gail had calmed down enough to decide on what to do next. Leonard and Crow, they reasoned, would be in Charleston within the hour, and would probably get passage on a ship headed down the coast, in order to get to Jacksonville quickly.

"Do you think we could catch up to them?" Gail said. They were both leaning against the hotel bannister. No one from the hotel had come up to check on them all day, and Gail wondered how a place like this could still be in business. Then she recalled that saying it was "still in business" was quite the stretch of the imagination as it was, given the emptiness of the town and the state of the world.

"Two problems with that," Nick signed back. "First, they are a day ahead of us. Second, they have all the money."

"*All of it?*" Gail checked her bag and found only the last few small bills Crow had given her in the Columbia market. She was utterly broke. "Oh, this can't be happening. Why would Crow do this?"

"Because she's hurt. And I'm not saying that she's making the best decision," he said as Gail opened her mouth to protest, "but I am saying that she is expressing the hurt she feels in the only way she really knows how: she is leaving the problem behind and moving on."

"But that's stupid!" Gail cried. "We could have talked about it! She...she understands me." She sniffed. "At least, I thought she did."

"Something I learned in almost 20 years of marriage with my wife: communication is key. We didn't see each other for months at a time. At one point almost two years. But we communicated. We never stopped communicating. We wrote letters. And then, after all of this happened to me...I stopped writing. And to her, I am sure, that was the end of things. And then it was over."

"But that wasn't your fault—" Gail interrupted before Nick had even finished signing.

"It doesn't matter whose fault it is," he replied. "The point is that the communication broke down. Same here. You didn't communicate with Crow. She didn't communicate with you. And now you're both screwed."

Gail wiped her nose with the back of her hand. "Alright, well, what do I do now?"

Nick slowly stood up. "Do you still want to go to Sun City? We need to see Osbourne. We need Crow and Leonard. So the plan hasn't changed, really. We have just added an extra step." He gestured to Leonard's hotel door. "Someone should probably wake up Leonard's date, too, or she'll sleep all day."

Gail stood up and walked over to the door, which was slightly ajar. Pushing it open, she found the mousy-haired woman still asleep, stark naked, on the hotel bed. Gail walked over and prodded her shoulder gently. "Hello?"

She opened a bleary eye. "Hm? Oh, sorry, are you housekeeping? Because—"

"No, I just wanted to make sure someone woke you up," Gail said with a smile. "I'm a friend of Leonard's but he's left already."

She sat up and stretched. "Oh man, I haven't slept that well in a long time. Even though I'm *so sore* now with all the—"

"Details unnecessary," Gail said, looking away.

The woman started to pull clothes on from where they had been discarded on the floor. "I heard him leave this morning. Sounded like it was a rough morning with that other girl."

"Yeah," Gail replied absently.

"She your girlfriend?"

Gail shrugged. Had this been a break-up? It sure seemed like it.

"Well, if you're headed to Jacksonville I can help."

Gail snapped her head to look at her, who had now assembled enough clothes to be considered at least decent, "How did you know I was going to Jacksonville?"

She took a defensive step back. "Hey, now…Leonard said something about it last night. No need to get mad. I just thought—"

"How can you help?" Gail didn't mean to sound as crabby and impatient as she did. Oh god, she was slowly turning into Crow. She wondered when she would start gaining the urge to dye all her clothes black.

"You see," the other woman said, pulling on her shoes, "my husband is a merchant. He has a wagon headed that way later today."

Gail balked. "*Husband?*"

"Yeah?" the woman shrugged. "Don't you get all judgey with me, missy. You don't know my life. And I'm not the one whose girlfriend just ran off with a strange man."

"You're right." Gail ran her fingers through her ginger hair. "Sorry. So your husband. What kind of stuff does he transport?"

◌

Lukather was not happy about the goats. They were stinky, dirty, loud, and each and every one of them made guttural sounds at him no matter what he did. In the end, he hid, trembling, behind Gail in the corner of the covered wagon.

Gail was thankful for the cover, because the rain had come back. It slammed down on the canvas roof, making a constant din that made her incredibly appreciative that she didn't have to trudge through all of this mess on her own.

For his part, Nick was incredibly helpful. Gail went through several iterations of the same cycle of tears, regrets, and self-hatred as the long stretch of I-95 unfolded out the back of the wagon.

Nick was quiet. He had been very quiet since the city of Manning had disappeared on the horizon, and Gail wondered if the Marine had any intent to ever return. Perhaps, with the application of Mori technology, there was a way to recreate a body for him to download his brain into. The exact process by which the power suit continued to operate had never quite been explained, but since all technology, to Gail, blended into one single phrase called "magic" it seemed that nothing was truly impossible.

They stopped to sleep overnight near a city called Savannah. The city was one of the Mori's claimed cities, the merchant driver explained, and so it wasn't safe to camp too close to the city limits. It would, however, be perfectly okay to stop off on a side road a few miles out and get some shut-eye.

Gail woke rather suddenly in the middle of the night. The dream that had awoken her quickly slipped away into the annals of her subconscious mind, but she was trembling and sweating. Nick's arms were around her and he hugged her close. There was a strange warmth to his metal body, she noticed—not really a heat, but simply that the surface of the metal was not particularly cold, even here in the middle of October. It was just slightly warmer. Or perhaps it was just Gail's imagination.

⌂

It appeared that the farther she got away from Lillington and Campbell and Dunn and even Raleigh, the less real it all seemed. It was as though she was slowly waking from a vivid dream. And if it was a dream, she mused to herself, what was the waking world and was it any better than the desolate and crumbling land that now surrounded her?

Perhaps, if she tried hard enough, she could wake from this dream. She would be back in her quiet little mountain retreat, with a small pile of books and survival guides. She would have a nice overlook down a jagged cliff to some trees below. She would have several lovely paintings on the wall that she couldn't really understand. She would have Lukather to talk to every day, and play games with, and chase critters with. And she would have M—he would show up sometime during the week and make sure she was okay. He would give her an anecdote or a small story about something he had experienced in his travels. He would tell her no, she couldn't come with him this time…and he would brush her wavy hair and leave, telling her he would be back soon.

The first major sighting of Jacksonville came after crossing under an overpass of another highway. The land was wide and flat, much unlike the mountains of Virginia where she had started her journey. The trees, some of their leaves now beginning to change color in the brisk air, were growing more and more sparse as the road went on, and as the wagon pulled to a stop under the overpass, Gail could not help but feel like she was now in a completely different country than the one she had come from. "You're not in Kansas anymore," Gail recalled M saying once, though she had no idea where exactly Kansas was.

"I wanted to ask you something," Gail said as she pulled on her silver Doc Martens and hopped out of the wagon. "Do you feel better after doing all those things in Manning?"

Nick picked up Gail's bag and threw it over his shoulder. "I don't know."

They thanked the merchant, asked him to give their regards to his wife, and the wagon pulled away down another street. Nick and Gail headed southward, continuing along the yellow-striped road. "I was thinking—and you can always correct me if I'm wrong here—that you probably don't really feel like a person anymore. And I can't really know how that feels, at all. But I want you to know that when I look at you, I see a person who cares and is compassionate. And if there is a way to help you, I want to."

Nick didn't say anything in reply for a long time; he continued to stomp along in his armor. He stopped rather suddenly. "I can't feel anything," he signed.

"What do you mean? Like, touch? Pain?"

"Not that," he signed dismissively, "but something else. I don't feel sad anymore. I don't feel depressed. Or afraid. I just feel empty."

Gail crossed her arms. "I cannot, for an instant, believe that," she said. "All the time I have known you, you have been self-sacrificing, caring, and genuinely friendly to everyone you meet. You've taken every weird look thrown in your direction completely in stride. And you've made other people happy before yourself." She gestured to the scarf around his neck to accent her point. "Now, if you're so *empty*, where did all that come from, I wonder?"

He shrugged. "It felt like the right thing to do."

"Exactly," Gail said, jabbing a finger into his breastplate and withdrawing it because doing so had made her finger hurt. "You did it because it *felt* right. Maybe there's some kind of biological thing that makes us feel emotions, sure...but you feel them anyway. It's different, I suppose, but you still do these things because you know they're the right thing to do."

Nick was contemplating her words at length and he simply signed, "Thank you", and continued on. The spring in his step—the one he had seemingly lost after his visit to St. Peter's Lodge, was back, and Gail felt quite satisfied to have contributed to its return.

TWENTY-THREE

"I know it's an awful idea," Gail said, putting her unopened can of food back into her bag. "But I can't think of a single other way to find her."

Nick shrugged in agreement. They were sitting on a curb in downtown Jacksonville. Three days had passed since their arrival, and their queries about girls in black or men in narrow-brimmed hats had been a fruitless search. Now they were just wasting time. How much Crow would have hated it! She would have certainly thought up an alternate solution long ago, but Gail had never pretended to be the brains of the outfit, and so they had persisted in the plan, to no avail.

There were several major cell towers in the city, Gail reasoned, and there was a great possibility that they had not only been repaired but were also maintained by Crow's mother. If one of them were to malfunction…well, then it would be a simple matter of waiting for her to arrive to fix it.

There were two big problems with this plan. First, Gail had no idea what exactly could be done to disable the tower. Second, even if she did she would have no idea of how to damage it in such a way that it couldn't be quickly repaired. The idea was only to attract attention, not to knock out the New Internet for every witch in the city.

They got up off the curb, walked through an alley, and arrived at one of the tall towers. At the foot of it, a large grey and green box sat, a heavy padlock hooked around the door handles. Gail took hold of it, shaking it and trying to see if it might have rusted enough to come loose, but she was not so lucky. She looked at Nick with a grimace, hoping that there were replacement padlocks somewhere so that this place would still be secured after it had—*crunch*—been broken open in the armored man's grasp.

"Sorry," Gail said, as though the broken lock might be able to hear her, or tattle on her to Crow's mother. They opened the doors to find a series of switches marked with old, faded labels. One of them, she could see, was marked "MAIN".

Nick reached out and pulled the switch. The whole board of circuits shut off instantly.

"That was easier than I expected," Gail said. "Now we just have to wait."

They turned to leave the alley, a grin widening on the redhead's face. That grin fell immediately, though, as the only entrance to the alley was suddenly filled with several men, advancing with menace. Each one was armed with a knife, sword or a bow, and each one also bore the unmistakable sigil of the Duke of the East.

"Really?" Gail groaned, her new sword instantly in her hand. "We're 500 miles from Raleigh. Why does the Duke care this much?"

"Shut up," one of them shouted. "Drop your sword and come on. They're waiting for you."

"How did you even find me?" Gail demanded.

"We have been walking around town for a few days," Nick reminded her.

"Oh, screw off—" She shouted, and before they could throw any more annoying threats her way she cleared the distance to the nearest one and landed a solid kick square into the front man's groin. Nick flew past her, his armored limbs knocking weapons from hands and kicking the feet out from under the thugs.

Something had changed in Gail. No longer the scared, innocent girl she was back in Lillington, she now felt a burning anger deep in her stomach. The Duke—the Mori—had followed her along the yellow-striped road and now they were going to take her back. The image of the fancy room with the sprawling bed flashed across her mind and she decided that there was no room for guilt. Not right now.

She ducked into a roll, coming up on the side and slicing evenly through the air. Her sword met the plates of a jacket and dug into flesh; not a deep wound, she judged, but enough to slow for a moment. She turned the hilt of her blade and the next swipe dug into the back of a leg, sending the next bandit to the ground. She felt her side collide with something hard, like she had been hit, but there wasn't much force behind the swing of her attacker. Looking up, she saw several inches of crossbow bolt now sticking out of his chest. He dropped to the ground.

She didn't have time to think about this, however, as the edge of a large, diamond-shaped shield made out of a metal sheet labeled "WATCH FOR FALLING ROCKS" came swinging at her face. It caught her squarely in the jaw, and she staggered back; the split-second of pause let her change her grip on the sword and she rolled again to the side, the blade coming up in an arc that landed at his rump. Whether it actually dug into the flesh of his buttocks wasn't clear, but he seemingly made an instant judgment that this was not worth whatever reward money had been offered, and he turned to run. A moment later he was impaled on another crossbow bolt and slammed into the ground.

Gail stood up and looked around. Above her, on a roof adjacent to the alley, was a woman with long dark hair in braids that reached her waist, holding a crossbow. A quiver of bolts hung at her belt and she was staring down at Gail with a look of such contempt—contempt that, even from this distance, bore a resemblance to someone Gail knew well.

The woman climbed down from the rooftop, and when she straightened up she stared at the redhead with eyes that seemed to bore into her skull. "Are you Gail?" She said with narrowed eyes.

"Yes—" Gail jumped as the woman fired her crossbow again, at one of the injured thugs on the ground. He stopped moving. The woman pulled another bolt from her crossbow and reloaded it with one hand—a smooth, practiced motion that not only prepared her to fire again but also explained, without words, the expertise of the woman holding the weapon.

"Yeah. Leonard said you'd probably find a way out here." She sniffed derisively. "You going to fill me in on what's going on? Because she won't talk to me and Leonard keeps saying it's 'not his place' and it's driving me up a friggin' wall. I'm Dani, by the way. You must be Nick." She offered a hand to the armored combatant, who shook it politely. She didn't offer such a hand to Gail.

"Well, it's complicated," Gail said, trying to put all of her jumble of thoughts into words. "But basically I...I..." She took a breath and decided to just spit it out, half expecting her answer to elicit a crossbow bolt in reply. "I saved her life but had to make a deal with a Mori to do it."

Dani's eyes narrowed even further, making them look almost like arrow slits. "But you told her about it, right?" Dani clearly already knew the answer.

Gail flushed. "Not...as such...no."

"And she found out, and got upset, right?"

Gail nodded. Dammit, this woman was so much like Crow, especially in the way that, with a glance, she could steal your courage. It was infuriating.

"Then what exactly are you going to do about it?" Dani said, taking an aggressive step forward.

Gail realized that Dani was easily 6 inches shorter than her, but somehow she still seemed to tower in stature. Gail took a deep, steadying breath. "I want to talk to her and apologize, and get back to our plan to *stop the Mori*." Her last few words came through gritted teeth.

"So, are you going to talk to her because you need her? Or because you want to?"

Gail clenched her fists. "*Both!*"

Dani relaxed. "Okay. Two things you should know, then: first, I guarantee she is more upset that you didn't tell her the truth than she is about what you did. And second, she is *really upset* that you did what you did."

Gail nodded, but there was no longer shame in her face. "I understand. Now, please...where is she?"

Dani hooked the crossbow to her belt. "She's fixing the other cell tower. The one across town. See, you and her seem to both have this great idea that if you need me you should just go *shut my towers off*. At least you had the good sense to hit a switch, rather than cut a god damned cable." Dani put on a pair of rubber gloves and forced the "MAIN" switch back into its upright position.

"She cut a cable?" Gail tried to suppress her amusement, but from the icy glare she got in response it was clear she had failed to do so.

"Yes. She *cut* a cable. On *this* tower. You're probably lucky she did though, because I was just one street over finishing the patch-up."

Gail nodded with as apologetic an expression as she could manage. "Okay. Which tower? Can you direct me?"

⌂

Crow was nowhere in sight as they strolled up to the tower about a 20-minute walk across part of town. Gail was quiet, but Dani was rather talkative with Nick.

"I mean, it wouldn't be difficult if I could figure out where various sensors were in your head," she was saying. "Either that or maybe somebody could wire your Type-N'-Talk directly to your suit. The problem, of course, is that since your whole setup is powered by Mori tech, then there's really no way to configure it without the original researchers' notes." Nick nodded. "But I would be willing to try to cook something up for you. Maybe add some buttons for common phrases. That wouldn't be hard to put together and it might end up saving you time and trouble from typing the same things over and over."

Nick nodded again. "THAT WOULD BE...KIND OF YOU."

Gail slowed as she approached the tower, looking up at it. The nest of transmitters was dense, but she could just barely make out the shape of something black moving up there. As she was trying to figure out what exactly to do next, she heard a familiar sound from her bag. She dug through it, fishing through a few items before recovering the black radio. Staring at it like a lost treasure, she waited. Sure enough, it made another staticky noise as Crow apparently kept accidentally pushing the button.

Dani patted Nick. "Hey, let me walk you over to my place. It's not far." Nick nodded and the two of them walked off in another direction, Dani continuing to chatter about circuits.

Gail stood there for some time, just staring up at the nest of equipment with the radio in her hand. Finally, with a surge of courage, she pushed the button on the radio. "Crow?"

There was a clatter of surprise, and something dropped from the tower, landing with a metallic *thunk* on the ground below. "Holy— Who's there? You made me drop my wrench!" came the reply.

"It's me," Gail said simply, and up in the tower she glimpsed the witch looking around. Crow finally spotted her hundreds of feet below.

"No. I don't want to talk to you, Gail. We are done."

"You need to talk to me, Crow. I know you're hurt. I can't fix it if you don't talk to me."

There was a long silence. Then: "Fine. Talk."

Gail swallowed a massive lump in her throat. "First, I'm sorry I didn't tell you. I don't know why I didn't. I should have. I was...I was scared of what you would think of me."

"And what *exactly* do you think I think of you?" came the muffled reply. Gail shrugged and immediately felt silly doing so, knowing that

Crow couldn't possibly see her do it. "And don't you *dare* shrug at me, Gail. I want an answer." Oh.

She clicked the button a few times and tried to string some words together. "I think that you think I'm a traitor to the human race."

The silence over the radio was long, and painful. Crow didn't deny it, nor did she agree, but as moment after moment passed it became more and more painful. Finally, Gail heard the telltale static. "I don't necessarily think that."

Necessarily? Dammit, why did she have to be like this? "Ok then," Gail said indignantly. "What *do* you think then? Do you think I should have just let you die?"

The answer was instant. "Yes."

It was Gail's turn to not reply. She looked at the radio as if it was suddenly something utterly foreign to her—and in a way, it was—as she tried to figure out what exactly Crow meant by that. She should have let her die…why? Because she wanted to show that same sense of 'nobility' that had taken her dad from her? Because she didn't feel worth it? Gail trembled, and her stomach burned in anger.

Then, like a spark on sawdust, she exploded.

"And then what, Crow? I go back to being alone again? Go back to knowing that I found someone who understands me and doesn't care that I'm weird and that I don't know anything about anything? Someone who tells me things straight, without evading the question the way Leonard does. Somebody who talks and encourages to do the right thing—but without that detachment from humanity and self-loathing that Nick has. How about somebody that doesn't get along well with other people but somehow gets along with me, and I don't *fucking* know why. Where else am I going to find that person, Crow? Because you are all I've got, and I traveled hundreds of miles to get here and I wouldn't have had to if you had just stuck around and not run away like a *coward*. You hear that? *You're a coward who can't even communicate like an adult* with somebody you love. Yeah, I said it, *love*. And you have all the plans, and all the money, and you seem to be the only person in this group that has any semblance of holding it together, and the whole stupid 'resistance movement' needs you and Leonard and Nick do and I do too and you're a *stupid, cowardly, selfish bitch.*"

She was breathing heavily now, and her knuckles had gone white from her grip on the radio in her hand. Tears had spattered the speaker holes of the matte plastic and she now stared at it like she wanted to throw it as far as she could and never look back.

Crow's voice was weak. "That was a lot of words."

Gail stormed over to the base of the tower, seeing the now-bent steel wrench on the ground where it had not only impacted but had left a sizeable crater in the dirt. She picked it up and stuffed it into her bag before, on impulse, ascending the ladder.

"What are you doing?" Crow squawked into the radio.

"I'm bringing you your wrench," Gail replied.

"No, you don't have to do that, I can come down—"

"I am *bringing you* your *wrench,*" Gail said again, and dropped the radio into her bag as well. She reached the top of the leaning stepladder and continued upward. Gail had never had a particular fear of heights, she considered, but as the ground began to drop away rung by rung, she couldn't help but be unnerved by the slight swaying of the metal pole.

"Really…you don't have to come up here, Gail." Crow's voice was muffled in her bag. "You're right, I should have talked to you in the first place. You're right, I shouldn't have ran away. You're right, okay? Now you don't need to come up here." Gail ignored her and continued climbing. She was over halfway up now, and she forced herself to look only upward since she knew that the view down to the ground was probably not a particularly good one. The rungs were a little slippery, too, and she had to concentrate on keeping her grip on each one as it passed through her hands. Her shoulders and forearms were starting to burn and she started to feel a nagging regret in the back of her head as she slowly came to realize exactly how dangerous this climb had become.

"And you're right, I shouldn't have said that you should have let me die. That was pretty selfish and impulsive and…and…and you *really don't need*—" the radio crackled a little bit. "Well, dammit. I guess I can't stop you now, can I?"

Gail reached the top rung and planted her hands on the small grate that made up the cage at the tip, hoisting herself into a sitting position. Crow was there, her cloak hanging on a hook and her face red and flushed with what could only have been tears. She was wearing black mascara now, and it was smudged and streaming in several places. "Well, there you go," Crow said. "I finally get my hands on a bottle of mascara and the first time I put it on, you made me frickin' cry. And now you get to see me cry. Good job, Gail. You suck…so much…" she laughed and wiped some of the smudged makeup away.

Gail just sat there. She had said what she needed to say.

"There is something else. This whole plan to go to Sun City—it's kind of vague on a few key elements of what happens once we get there. I've been doing research in Bluejay's notes but the whole thing doesn't wash. And I have a bad feeling about it, and I thought…I thought maybe if I had an excuse to leave, then maybe you wouldn't follow me and you wouldn't get hurt."

"I told you I wanted to come with you."

"I know you did," Crow said evenly, "but you've got to understand that I've been suspecting this is a trap from the beginning. I'm a paranoid person. It's just how I am. You understand, right?"

"Of course I understand," Gail said, scooting closer to her. "But *you* need to understand that I want you—I *need* you here. And you leaving doesn't keep me out of danger. I literally got attacked by a gang of bandits an hour ago because the Duke is still following me. I'm not going to be out of danger just because I'm out of sight."

Crow sighed and put her face in her hands. "You're right. You're right, okay?" She leaned back against one of the handrails; Gail was surprised at how relaxed the witch could be here, hundreds of feet up. The redhead, meanwhile, was gripping tightly to two different hand-holds. "You need to understand," Crow said, looking up, "that I was always smart. I learned to read before any of my peers. I started to learn about computers when I was 4 and I was coding basic programs by 6. And then when I was 7, the Mori came and everything went to hell—but I had a computer and a massive downloaded library of information so I grew up learning everything I could about everything electronic or mechanical. To this day I am an expert on network infrastructure, radio communication, and mechanical engineering. I am *smart*, Gail."

Gail nodded slowly. "I don't think anyone ever doubted that."

"Then why," she said, scooting closer and putting an arm around Gail's waist, "do you make me feel like I don't have any brains at all?"

Gail let go of the hand-holds and threw her arms around the witch. "Please don't run away again," she whispered.

Crow squeezed her tightly. "I won't."

TWENTY-FOUR

Dani's house was on the corner of a street practically right in the middle of the three main cell towers of Jacksonville. It was white, once, but time had caused the paint to peel and crack in a way that somehow made it a little extra-charming. It had a wooden porch with a swing on it, and a small front yard with a fence, where Lukather was apparently already running himself into exhaustion as he chased chickens.

Crow pulled the front door open and hung her cloak on the hooks. Inside, the window shades were all open, filling the space with natural light. Nearly every wall was white, beige, or yellow, and the smooth hardwood floors were shiny to the point that it seemed brighter inside the house than outside.

Crow looked a little out of place here. Head-to-toe in black, she was darker than the darkest shadow of the house. She went to the hallway staircase and called up. "Mamá, I'm back."

"Ahorita bajo," came the reply, and Crow walked over to the kitchen, where Dani had apparently been jarring fruits for the winter.

The witch stole a piece of an apricot and popped it into her mouth. "Mom got a hold of Eagle. She's supposed to be here today sometime. So there's that."

"Eagle? Oh wow! Does that mean you're getting your authenticator back?"

Crow nodded with great enthusiasm. "Which means that hopefully, after we see this Osbourne guy we can start coordinating the plan."

"You have the plan?" Gail said, a grin bursting out across her face.

She hesitated. "Well, I only have part of it," Crow explained. "It was a joint plan between Dr. Glenn, Leonard, and Bluejay, and M. I don't know if Osbourne was involved yet, but I suspect he might have been."

"I think he was," Leonard said, coming down the stairs. "M told me that Bluejay had found 'more Partholónians' at one point but she didn't say where. I assume it's something Osbourne knows about."

Dani followed Leonard down the stairs and fixed Gail with a glare. "Did you two get everything sorted out?" She asked sharply. Gail nodded. "Good, then I don't have to kill you."

"Mamá!" Crow said through gritted teeth. "Deja de molestar a mi novia."

Dani raised a heavily-penciled eyebrow and crossed her arms. "Me da risa verla toda nerviosa."

"Eso es horrible," Crow said, throwing up her hands in disgust. "Eres una cabrona!"

"Where's Nick?" Gail asked Leonard as the other two continued to bicker.

"On the roof," Leonard said, straightening his jacket. "Keeping a watch out since you got attacked earlier. How was your trip?" He gave the redhead a hug that she heartily returned.

"Good. Nick kept me company. And…thanks for taking care of Crow."

"No big deal," he said, waving his hand as if it were nothing at all. "She's a good kid but if you let her out of your sight she'll get in trouble, ya know?"

"Did you guys take a boat down?" Gail sat down at the dining room table, a large round piece of furniture that was covered in blueprints and technical documents that Gail probably couldn't make heads or tails of if she had tried.

"Yeah," Leonard said. "The train from Manning runs down to the coast, so we jumped on a boat. This one," he gestured to Crow, "apparently gets seasick."

"Well, I've never been on a boat before, Leonard," Crow retorted, finding a reason to escape her quarrel with her mother. "How was I supposed to know it, like *moves* constantly?" She appeared slightly green just thinking about it. The witch turned back to the counter and opened a canvas bag, pulling out a dark, squat, hand-sized fruit. Grabbing a knife from the block on the counter, she cut it open revealing pale green insides and an unnecessarily large pit. Gail watched her, moving and slicing the flesh and passing it to a bowl, as Dani moved around her and pulled other things out of cupboards.

"What are you making?" She asked.

"Braised pork. See, Mamá does a lot around town here, fixing things and building things, so people tend to give her gifts. Like extra food. And since she's Mexican, she never refuses a reason to go through a bunch of it for her guests. So guess who got elected as her assistant chef?" She rolled her eyes and started peeling an onion. "Go on and make yourself at home. We'll be a while."

Gail nodded, getting up and starting to look around. The house was small, but had several rooms on the ground floor including a sitting room decorated with wall tapestries. Against the wall of the sitting room was a tall bookshelf and she let out an involuntary excited sound. "You have *books!*" She called out to the people in the next room.

"Dad collected them," Crow replied from the kitchen. "Any he could get his hands on. Any the Mori didn't destroy."

"It really seems like their whole invasion wasn't very efficient," Leonard said, taking the seat at the table where Gail had been sitting and removing a rainbow-colored knife from its bandolier. "Like, take the Ritual of Homecoming. It knocked out every single combustion engine in the world. It destroyed every single firearm. But then, it passed over a lot of electronics, and was only marginally effective on infrastructure."

"Because they don't understand us," Dani said, returning to the kitchen with another canvas bag full of more vegetables and a few slabs of pork. "They don't understand our technology very well. They think it is as much magic as their magic seems to be to us. They can understand things like combustion and fuel because those are mostly simple chemical reactions, but the intricacies of electronics confused them and it was far more hit-and-miss."

Gail picked up one of the volumes, a lengthy book entitled *The Best Years to Live in Medieval England* by Gilbert Cox, and carried it back to the kitchen, flipping through its pages. Back at the stove, Crow and Dani were in a flurry around each other, chopping and mashing and slicing things here and there.

Dani was slicing up some kind of thin green peppers and Crow stopped her. "Mamá. Podríamos no ponerle tantos serranos?"

Her mother looked confused. "Por que?"

"Mira a mi novia," Crow replied softly through gritted teeth.

The woman looked over at Gail for a moment. "Ah, claro! Es güera."

Crow made a snorting noise and almost lost her grip on the onion in her hand. Gail returned the book to the shelf and sat down to watch Leonard. "What are you doing?"

Leonard tried to flip the knife around his finger and it clattered to the table. "Trying to get used to using my other hand. Until I do, I'm useless in a fight."

Gail scoffed. "No way. When that guy was causing trouble in the bar, you were all over him with that knife."

"And you've been really good at avoiding fights altogether," Crow added, now chopping up wide green vegetables. "Which to be fair is a talent that both Gail and I lack."

Leonard considered these words, but before he had an opportunity to reply, there was a knock at the door. He glanced out the window, using a finger to separate two of the blinds. "It's a woman with a Mohawk," he said.

"Eagle," Dani replied, wiping her hands on a towel and walking to the door to let her in.

Eagle was nothing like what Gail had imagined for the "queen" of the New Internet. Beautiful and curvy, she wore a studded leather jacket over an orange-and-brown sundress, and her hair was a multicolored wave down the center of her head. Gail wondered if, when choosing bird names, *peacock* had potentially crossed her mind, but she refused to be so impolite as to let that thought escape her mouth.

Crow was grinning ear to ear as she crossed from the kitchen toward the door, where Dani was now greeting Eagle with a hug. Dani glanced over to her. "Eagle, this is my daughter. Crow, lávate las manos, you were just cutting peppers…"

Crow made a frustrated noise and dashed to the sink to wash up. Leonard had stood up and extended his left hand. "Hello, Eagle. I'm Leonard Bohr."

"*You're* Leonard Bohr?" Eagle replied, the trill of her tongue revealing a pierced tongue, "Great. How much of this mess is your fault? Because I have half the Internet talking about you."

"Me?" Leonard looked taken aback. "What did I do?"

"Well," Eagle said, crossing her arms, "the rumor is that you led a pack of Mori to Campbell University and now a hundred and forty-seven people—including Dr. Avery Glenn—are dead."

A hundred and forty-seven? Gail thought. That must have been two-thirds of the people at the seminar. She shuddered and interrupted before Leonard could start pouring out an explanation. "No, I led them there, by accident," she said, stepping beside Leonard. "The Duke was looking for me. He sent his thugs *and* some friends of his mistress."

"His *mistress?*" Eagle repeated. "So it's true? The Duke's an Advocate?"

"Seems so," Leonard sighed. "And we suspected it but didn't realize exactly how many pies he's got his fingers in. And now he's sending people all the way down here to Jacksonville to try and recover Gail. We can fill you in."

Crow had finished her washing and had materialized behind Gail. "Hello," she said with a shy smile. "I'm Crow."

Eagle's features immediately softened. "Hi, Crow. First off, I know how much it sucked to lose your token."

"I know. It's the rules."

"Yeah. And some people aren't as lucky as you are when it comes to being connected. But I've got a new one for you and I'll give it to you this evening. It activates at exactly 8pm and there's a sort of protocol to it."

Crow nodded, but Gail could see that she was a little disappointed that she couldn't get the token now and rejoin her online family.

"After dinner, then," Dani said, returning to the kitchen.

⌂

It occurred to Gail that she had not had a family dinner in 15 years. Her last memories of dinner with her mom and dad were fuzzy, and she could almost form an image of a bowl of spaghetti in her mind. But it was a fading memory, as the fog of time slowly encroached upon those things she kept secret in her heart: those memories of her life before. Not that she'd had much of a life before, but even so, the fact that these memories were slowly being lost to her was a terrifying and painful proposition.

It occurred to her, for example, that she could no longer recall the face of her mother and father.

She had started off her journey looking for her home. Her home, she figured, would be a place with family she had never met, who would subsume her into their lives and put her into a niche that had been left empty for over a decade. She had been convinced that there was somehow a place for her in the world that was just waiting for her to fill it. Since that time, she had given up on that dream because something greater had been found. Something that made her feel like she had found that niche for which she had so long wrought.

Gail was very quiet at dinner, as they passed around plates of pork and vegetables and delicious sauces—some of which Crow told her she should not have if she wanted to continue use of her taste buds—and listened. Crow and Leonard and Eagle all talked about programming and computers for a while and moved on to discussing the infrastructure of the New Internet with Dani and moved on to more subjects including their recent travels. Gail was happy enough to just listen and sneak pieces of pork to Lukather under the table.

And when the dinner was over, and the plates were being cleaned up, Gail felt something she could not really describe in words. If anything, she might have said it was a feeling that, around that dinner table, she felt more comfortable than anywhere she had been previously. And then, later, as she sat curled up with Crow on the sitting room couch and waiting for 8pm, she might describe it as a feeling that there was nowhere else in the world she would rather be.

If there is a feeling of being home, Gail thought to herself, *then this is surely it.*

TWENTY-FIVE

"First things first," Eagle said, opening up a bright pink backpack that had a faded image of a unicorn on it, "I am going to log in and activate the token just before 8. Then, just after 8, I will give you the token and you will log in. You'll be forced to authenticate twice, so you'll log in with the number on the token, wait for it to change, and then log in again."

Crow was raptly attentive. "Okay."

The dining room had a bit of an otherworldly feel to it, Gail thought, as the two witches sat across from each other. The coal lamps had been extinguished, so the only light in the room came from the screens of their computers. Eagle's computer was particularly compact—basically just a grey rectangle covered in smooth black glass on one side. Crow had asked her how she had managed to keep the internal battery running, and Eagle told her it was a trade secret.

Eagle looked at her watch and pulled a tiny grey number device from her bag. She looked at it, typed the digits in one-by-one, and waited. After a few seconds, she passed to token over to Crow, who took it with shaky fingers. Gail thought that Crow might actually drop her authenticator from the way she trembled as she typed in the next set of numbers, but she kept her resolve for the sixty seconds it took to refresh the authenticator and enter in the next code. She hit the final key and her screen filled with text from the other people on the New Internet.

"All done," Eagle said, leaning back in her chair. "Also, just in case you end up with more river adventures, this one's waterproof."

Crow attached the little device to her laptop. "So I'm good to go?" Eagle nodded and wiggled her eyebrows, which Gail suddenly realized were actually drawn on in little swirls. "This is great. I'll start putting together what I know of the whole plan and start coordinating everybody."

"Sounds good," Eagle said, resting her elbows on the table and placing her head in her folded hands. "Let me know if I can help. I'll be down here on the couch.

"Oh, you're staying here?" Crow asked, closing her computer with a snap. "Well, I'll be right upstairs. Ping me or whatever if you need me. And..." She stood up, looking really awkward in the shadow of her internet idol, "and thank you a lot. This means a lot to me."

"No big deal," Eagle dismissed. "Now get workin'. There's a lot of good people that can use that information." Crow nodded and skipped up the stairs to the guest room, where she stopped at the door, her hand pausing before grabbing the door handle. "Huh."

"What is it?"

Crow pointed at the door. "This is the guest room, where we're staying, right?"

"Right."

"And Nick's outside keeping watch, right?"

"I think so."

"And Eagle's on the couch, and Mamá is in her bedroom, right?"

"That sounds right..." Gail wasn't quite catching on yet.

"So where's Leonard?" Crow narrowed her eyes and eased the door open. The guest room was cozy and sparsely decorated but was also devoid of any one-handed tricksters.

Gail walked in and shrugged. "He could have gone somewhere." She lit the coal lamp next to the bed.

In the doorway, Crow was standing with her face contorted in suspicion. "When we arrived earlier, Mamá was upstairs…but Leonard was the first person to come down and greet us."

The redhead's eyebrows knitted together. "What are you implying?" Crow put up a finger and disappeared from the doorway. Gail could hear the patter of steps in the hall and the witch returned. She wordlessly closed the door and put her back against it, her eyes wide. Gail leapt to her feet. "What is it? What's wrong?"

"I think…" She swallowed hard. "I think that Leonard is in bed with my mother."

"No way!" Gail's reaction was to squeeze her eyes shut in disgust. "Okay. Ew."

"I know, right?" Crow took a step forward and faceplanted on the bed. "This cannot be my life."

◌

Gail woke up in the middle of the night. At first, she didn't know what had awakened her; she lifted her head and peered through the gloom of the room, straining her ears. Whatever it was, she heard it again—a low voice downstairs that she couldn't understand. Prying herself out of the bed as carefully as she could so as to not wake the witch still sleeping under the covers, she crossed the room and eased the door open. The voice was still unintelligible, but she recognized the speaker. It was Eagle.

Using every ounce of caution she could muster into her half-awake muscles, Gail crouched down and crept to the edge of the stairs and listened harder; she still couldn't quite make the words out. She put a foot on the stairs and made a measured step that didn't cause the wood to creak. She descended another step and another, pressing herself against the bannister.

"I don't want to do this," Eagle said.

Gail took a few more cautious steps down, and as she peered out from the stairwell she could see that Eagle was still seated at the dining

234

room table, her face illuminated by the computer screen. Eagle was typing something and stopped. Her eyes rolled back into her head and she spoke aloud. "Well, we are just waiting for her to give the information to us. Then all we have to do is let them carry out the plan."

Eagle's eyes unrolled. "What if we just make a fake plan, something to distract them, and we try to stop this rebellion peacefully? There's no need to—"

She stopped, and her eyes snapped back upward. "You know what the Mori do to those who rebel. The Reclamation must commence. This is the final answer. You understand, yes?"

"Of course I do," Eagle said as her eyes returned to normal. She went silent, typing a few things and she then perked up, as though she knew that she was being watched. Her eyes fell on Gail far too quickly, and she coughed. "Oh, hello."

Gail's first instinct was to run, but she resisted it. From the sound of the conversation, Eagle had not been too keen to follow the orders of whatever Mori was clearly speaking into her head. "Hi, Eagle," she said, taking a few more steps down the stairs. Her sword was hanging off the back of a dining room chair. She might be able to saunter over to it without arousing suspicion.

Eagle bit her lip. "You saw that. No point in denying it, or saying 'it's not what it looks like', right?"

Gail reached the bottom of the stairs. "I don't think so."

Eagle nodded, leaning back in her chair and considering Gail and this predicament for a minute. "You don't remember the Riots, Gail. I was there. I saw them happen. I watched people—millions of people—die a horrible death because they resisted. That's all they did. They peacefully resisted. We live in this world where everyone knows the Mori are evil and only a select few are doing anything about it. And those people, well…they're the ones who are going to get vilified. The college students that started the protest years ago were the ones blamed for all the deaths. The Mori narrative was that they were troublemakers and that they were the blame for all of the woes in the world. It was a perfect tool to use fear to control anyone who might think of resisting in the future."

Gail took a few steps to face Eagle from the other side of the dining room table. She was a step away from her sword. She started calculating in her head whether she could draw it in time if Eagle got up to attack her.

"And it worked, Gail. Because I saw it happen and I look at all these people on the New Internet and this idea of a plan to stop the Mori and all I see is death. The Reclamation...it's their response to all of this rebellion. People are becoming too much of a...a liability."

"What did you do?" Gail asked, feigning concern and interest.

"I made a deal with them, Gail. I..." She took a breath. "I did what you did."

Gail felt herself flushing red.

"Yes, I know about that. All the Advocates do. I did the same thing. They promised me that if I stop this plan from the inside, that they won't take it out on everyone else. I don't want anyone else to get hurt.

"Stop it from the inside? What do you mean?" Gail leaned against the hall doorway, her hand just inches from the iron sword's handle. "And what do you mean, 'anyone else'?"

Another voice piped up. "You alerted the Mori back at Campbell." Gail looked over to the stairwell, where Crow now stood, wrapped in her black cloak. Dressed as she was, she might as well have been a floating face making its way down the stairs like a ghost. "Bluejay was telling you everything about what was going on. She showed us on the screen."

Eagle didn't say anything. "I didn't want anyone to get hurt," Eagle said, putting her hands up evenly. "They were *supposed* to come in and frighten people; that's all it was supposed to be. A scare tactic. I thought if we could stop the rebellion, then the Mori would stop its plans to—"

"The Mori were *supposed* to live alongside us in peace. Then when they didn't do that, they were *supposed* to deal fairly with us and treat us

236

with respect. Then when they didn't do that, they were *supposed* to let us live independently outside of their cities. There are a lot of things they were *supposed* to do, and they didn't do because they don't keep their promises and they don't play fair!" The witch was shaking. "But there's two kinds of people that let them get away with it. There're people like the Duke, who openly and actively support this...this evil. There's the people like you, who defend them and try to make us believe your support comes from some *moral* high ground that the rest of us *sheeple* couldn't fathom. And there's the majority out there—the people who just let it happen and don't stand up and *do* anything about it. It will keep getting worse until someone stops it. We can't keep letting them take us apart piece by piece."

"A hundred and forty-seven people," Gail said, resting her hand casually on the hilt of her sword. "Dead because of you."

"I was trying to protect people!" Eagle protested, slamming her fist on the table. "The Mori are...they've got more influence and more experience and more firepower than we do."

"And Bluejay trusted you," Gail said. "And Glenn, and Leonard, and probably M too."

"Not enough to share her plans with you, though." Crow's face was a little smug. "She didn't trust anyone, and that caused you a problem when she died because all her plans disappeared."

"But we have them now," Eagle said, choosing her words very carefully, "and we can try and figure out a way to—"

"No," Gail and Crow said at the same time.

Eagle gritted her teeth. "Fine. Well, if you won't hand them over, then this gets a little more complicated." She stood up and produced a knife from her belt. "The Duke's on his way

. He'll kill all of you and I'll take your computer and the problem's solved. Because I'd rather give up the location of every witch in the United States than risk the Reclamation. They promised me if I stopped it, then wouldn't do it."

"And you *believed* them?" Gail choked.

"The computer...I locked with your token..." the realization on Crow's face was painful to see. "What is it, some kind of back door? And you're going to just...just *betray* everyone online? Everyone that trusted you?"

Eagle shrugged.

Crow sneered at her. "I can't believe this. I believed in you. Everything I thought you stood for was all—"

Lukather was the first one to sense that Eagle was going to make her move. As if from nowhere, the sheepdog darted out of the darkness of the house to land his jaws somewhere in Eagle's shin. She screeched and grabbed the lip of the table, throwing it toward Gail while she kicked the dog off of her leg.

The mountain girl tried to pull her sword free from its sheath, but the force of the furniture hitting her knocked her back and she hit the ground hard, trying to recover. With the laptop on the floor, the room was plunged into darkness and Gail could feel a pair of heavy boots walk right past her; she reached out to stop Eagle, but she had already thrown the door open and was escaping into the front yard.

Outside, the first dregs of the sunrise were beginning to fill the eastern sky with red and purple hues. Gail could see Eagle reaching the front gate, and soon she would probably be disappearing down the street.

There was a sudden thud that sounded like it came from everywhere at once. Finally no longer dazed, Gail pulled herself to her feet and looked to see that Eagle had halted right at the front gate. She slowly turned, and the head of a heavy crossbow bolt was protruding from her chest. A stain of crimson was now making its way rapidly down her sundress.

The source of the arrow, Gail realized, was Crow, who had pulled her mother's crossbow from under her cloak. Her face was like stone.

The night was silent, and the moment hung in the air like an hour. Gail could almost hear Crow's heavy heartbeat—or maybe it was only her own—as Eagle, her face contorted in a plea for sympathy or mercy, dropped to the ground and did not move.

Looking at the black-cloaked witch's face, Gail could see no regret for her actions. She could see nothing at all, in fact; Crow was stoic and calm as she took a deep breath and set the crossbow down on the floor. "Go get Leonard and Nick. We're leaving right now."

TWENTY-SIX

"After all this time, you had no idea?" The witch was rather sharp in Leonard's direction, but to his credit, he seemed to realize that she was under an immense amount of stress in her questioning and he remained calm in his responses.

"I didn't know. I promise. If I did I would have told you."

The road to Orlando was an incredibly smooth walk along the yellow-lined road of I-95. According to the map that they had consulted just before leaving, the road they had been affectionately calling "Gail's Road" would take them about two thirds of the way. Then, they would jump onto I-4 which would be a straight shot to Orlando.

Crow didn't mention what exactly she and her mother had talked about before they left, but Dani had instructed the group that they leave Eagle exactly where she was. The stern woman had hugged Crow tightly and whispered encouraging things into her ear while Leonard, Nick, and Gail packed their bags.

Crow grumbled to herself and kicked a rusted tin can that was in her path, watching it clatter across the dust. Her expression was perpetually angry now, and Gail was unsure of a single thing she could possibly do to console the young witch.

"What do we know now?" Leonard continued, counting things off on his fingers. "First: we know that Bluejay never told anyone about her part of the plan and there's so much data on that hard drive it might as well be lost. Second: We know that Eagle has been trying to break the whole thing up so even if we did know the whole plan, we might not have anyone who's willing to carry it out."

"Third," Crow added, "we know that if we can get into the tower, something might allow us to shut it down. That's literally all we know. This is terrible. And I can't, I can't—" she clenched her fists and punched the air angrily. "I can't *believe* Eagle was behind all of this. And she was manipulating me into doing the Mori's dirty work. And she cut a deal with the Mori." She glanced over at Gail. "And…uh…she didn't have a good reason."

"Didn't she, though?" Gail said, trying to hide the little sting in her heart that she felt whenever Crow ranted about people who made such deals. "She thought she was saving millions of people."

The witch threw her hands out wide. "I don't know. I don't know anymore. Everything used to make sense to me and now it doesn't."

Leonard slowed his pace a little bit, scratching his chin with his hand and taking the pipe from his mouth. "I used to think the Advocates were just traitors. But then I saw how easily—and please don't take offense here, dear—how easily Gail cut a deal. That's what they do, Crow. They make the sacrifices seem normal enough that by the time the big axes fall, no one bats an eye. You're *right* to be angry. But you should be angry at the situation that got us here. You shouldn't be angry at the people. And you…you did what you needed to do. You knew if Eagle got away that she was going to out every single person on the New Internet."

"You don't need to tell me what I already know," Crow seethed, pulling her cloak in around her. She gave the impression of a porcupine with invisible quills, and even Gail didn't come too close for fear of being the next target of Crow's wrath.

The landscape around them was changing. The farther south they went, the warmer it was, even though it was now getting to be almost mid-October and Gail was certain that North Carolina was turning into a frozen tundra. The Appalachian trees had turned into a dense swampland that appeared indivisible except by the mighty I-95 that had carved a path through the muck by some ungodly feat of strength and human ingenuity.

Her mind wandered back to her mountain retreat back in Roanoke, and she wondered if someone else had found it yet and turned the small mountain home into their own. She wondered if she could ever find it herself, if she was so inclined to go looking for it.

"Basically, we need to come up with a plan from scratch, then," Leonard was saying when she started paying attention again. "Hopefully this Osbourne guy can help. And basically, he's got to— because if he doesn't have any answers then I think we are officially up shit's creek."

△

They approached a strange establishment along the highway, about an hour north of the Highway 4 interchange. It looked, at first glance, like a gas station attached to an old restaurant, but as they got closer Gail saw the bright yellow letters that read "Travel Center" on a sign above the defunct gasoline dispensers. "What is this place?"

"Truck stop," Leonard said, leading the way across the parking lot toward the front doors of the building. "Beds, showers, food. The works. I wonder if they're still in business."

"And if not, whether they have anything useful," Crow grumbled.

"A roof is always useful," Leonard observed, pulling the front door open. "Especially in Florida."

Inside, there was no sign of life, and the section of the truck stop that used to be a convenience store was mostly ransacked and smelled like garbage and death. The back of the store, however, was a bit cleaner, and there was at least a little water pressure in the bathroom and showers. They all—except Nick, of course—decided to clean off and stop here for the night.

The shower room was one large, steel room with individual stalls. The women's side appeared to not be functioning, so Leonard, Crow, Gail, and Lukather all used the men's side. Crow didn't seem at all shy stepping into a stall next to Leonard and scrubbing herself, and Gail had a fleeting thought—wondering exactly how close the two had gotten on their boat-ride down the coast. She dismissed such stupid ideas, though, because she recognized that they originated in her own insecurity and stinging from their separation in the first place. Besides, that would be incredibly gross.

The water was cold, but with a little soap it was still effective at cleaning away the dust and grime that got into every crevasse and surface of the human body here in Florida. The air here was practically swamp gas and mosquitos, and it made Gail constantly feel sticky.

Once clean, they dressed again and headed toward the back, to a room containing a few battered mattresses on degrading frames. A sign on the wall reminded helpfully that this room was for short-rest and relaxation only, and that stays over 30 minutes were prohibited by management.

Gail stood up and moved to the cot that Crow was now lying on and scooted beside her; Crow stiffened as the redhead scooted into place and relaxed as the mountain girl put her arms around her. "Hey," she whispered in Crow's ear.

Crow turned over to face Gail. "Hey."

"You're not okay," Gail said. It wasn't a question. She couldn't see Crow's face, but her silence was a confirmation. She pressed their foreheads together. "And you're not having a good day. What can I do?"

It was a short while before she got a response. "Don't betray me. I'm running out of people I can trust."

"I won't," Gail promised. "I don't care if I owe them a 'favor'. I'm not working for them. I'm on your side."

"I'm tired of lies."

"I'm not going to lie to you."

"I'm tired of secrets."

"No more secrets from me. Promise."

Crow sighed and as Gail kissed her cheek she felt warm tears there. "What can I do for you right now?"

Crow sniffed, and her voice was barely a whisper. "Just hold me tight, please."

⌂

The lake that stretched out ahead of them from one side of the horizon to the other was called Lake Monroe. Its water was the deep green and brown of mottled jade. The shoreline, filled with trees with their hanging branches that swayed like curtains, stretched out as far as the eye could see, and despite knowing it was almost November, Gail might have easily mistaken it for summer with how green and lively the foliage appeared to be. Was all of Florida this green? Gail imagined green buildings and carriages and even green people, and the thought of it amused her immensely.

There was a wide bridge that spanned Lake Monroe along the I-4 Route, and as the party approached, they could see that it was not a simple walk across an empty bridge. Guard towers and barricades had been erected, with armed guards stationed everywhere.

"Keep calm," Leonard reminded them as they made their descent down the highway's grade toward the bridge. "I think I know what this is. We should be able to pass through just fine."

"Can't we go around?" Crow whispered.

He shook his head. "It would take days to go around the lake. We're—"

"Running out of time," Crow grumbled.

"Stop there at the line!" someone called out from the barricade up ahead. A thick white line had been painted across the edge of the bridge and they all stopped at it. "Where are you headed?"

"Orlando, then Miami," Leonard called back. Gail noticed that Leonard's accent was slightly different; he was mimicking the local twang of the guard.

"Orlando?" the guard repeated. "What's your business in Orlando? Harvest's over. Unless you're buying."

Leonard visibly stiffened, but he kept his polite but firm demeanor. "I've got business in Orlando," he called back. "I'd appreciate passage. What's your price?"

"Stand by," the guard called back.

Gail heard a familiar static coming from her bag. Glancing at Crow, she took a small step to half-hide herself behind Nick's hulking form. Opening her bag, she removed the black radio and turned the volume up a little. She could hear voices—the guards a few dozen meters away were using radios, too.

"What do they look like?" one of them said.

"Just a second." There was a static pause. "Female, redhead, white. Female, brunette, middle-eastern. Person in a suit of armor. Male, other."

Leonard grumbled. "Why can't white people tell dark people apart?"

"I know, right?" Crow replied under her breath.

The radio crackled again. "That's them. Get 'em."

Gail drew her sword. "Shit." She looked at Nick. "Think we can take them? There's, what. A dozen?"

"We should run," Leonard said back, and Gail could see him pulling a knife from his pocket.

But it was too late: the guards were over the barricade and running towards them in an instant. Nick stomped forward, his feet planting heavy strikes on the asphalt as be barreled in the attackers' direction. He made contact first, shoulder-checking someone hard enough to throw him back about 20 feet.

Gail was right behind. She met a down-swinging machete with her sword, deflecting it off to the side before landing her heavy silver boot straight into his groin. Her next swing embedded the tip of her sword into another guard's side, digging in a few inches and letting her shift her weight; she kicked out with her boot and connected with a face, sending a guard stumbling over the side and falling off the bridge.

She heard a massive thud and turned to see that a net had been thrown over Nick's hulking form; he was now thrashing about in it. She tried to dash over, dodging a crossbow bolt that went zipping through the air, but before she could get there she skidded to a halt—several guards had come out from the umbrella-like trees behind them on the path and had surrounded Leonard and Crow with weapons drawn.

A voice boomed out from the guard post. "Drop the sword."

They had grabbed Crow and Leonard, now, and were securing their hands—to her credit, Crow was giving them a lot of resistance, and lashed out with kicks and bites until one of them knocked her out cold with a sucker-punch. "Hey!" Gail cried out, but she stopped as a bowman trained his weapon on her instantly. Nick had stopped struggling in the net, and was looking at her through the heavy fibers. Sighing, she dropped the sword to the ground with a clatter. Two men were on her at once, grabbing her arms and wrenching them behind her back to tie them up. They dragged her backwards, toward the barricade, but she didn't resist them—she was watching Crow, unconscious, being carried over someone's shoulder toward them all.

Gail was pulled through a doorway and wrestled into a wooden bench in what looked to be a makeshift office. There was a desk, some chairs, and a coffee mug. On the wall was a flag that Gail didn't recognize.

Leonard was brought in to join her, seated with his arms tied together in front of him—the guards apparently not being able to find an effective way to handcuff or tie a one-handed man in a pinch—and he took in a deep breath. Crow came in next, the brief knockout from the punch having worn off enough that she was able to be guided around in a stumbling fashion. She was seated on Leonard's other side on the bench, and was mumbling curses in Spanish under her breath. All of the guards, save one, left the room, leaving the three of them feeling terribly foolish. Leonard patted Gail with his hand. "It was a good try."

Gail didn't agree; in retrospect she might have been a little too overconfident in her calculations that she and Nick could break through the guard station effectively. "You said you thought you knew what this is. What is it?"

Leonard slowly nodded, avoiding Gail's gaze. "If I'm right, we just walked into slave territory."

TWENTY-SEVEN

"*What?*"

"Florida's always had a bad slavery problem, even before the Mori," Leonard said, glancing to the guard to see if he cared if they talked. He didn't seem to. "Both labor and trafficking. Tomato and orange farmers were the big culprits. Well, after the Mori it just got worse, and Florida kind of became a big hub for slaves. And since it's a stone's throw from the Tower of Peace, well, nobody really came down to *do* anything about it."

"Any reason you didn't mention this before?" Crow hissed.

He shrugged. "I thought we might be able to avoid it."

Gail glared at him from his other side. "And avoiding it somehow makes it go away?"

Leonard grimaced. "That's *not* why we're here. And you know that."

The door slammed open and a burly guy with a thick, unkempt beard stormed into the room. He seated himself at the desk. "You're lucky none of my men are dead right now," He said, but he didn't look at any of them, "but they're pretty beat up. So when you get picked up I'm gonna have to tack on some fees to this…Duke guy."

248

"We didn't do whatever he says we did," Gail said. "He's been chasing us for hundreds of miles. And he's working with the Mori."

The man looked up. "'He's working with the Mori,' she cries. To me. Do you know who I am, little girl?"

"I know who you are," Crow interjected. "But then again I used to work on a horse farm. I know what shit looks like."

The man ignored her. "I guess you're not from here. Maybe up in the mid-Atlantic you deal with this Duke guy, but down here, in the south, you have to deal with Kalid."

"Who?" Leonard asked.

The man tapped the unfamiliar flag on the wall. "Welcome to the Kingdom of Kalida. King Kalid owns everything here. And while you're here, you're his loyal subjects. He owns the building, the food, the friggin' ground you walk on."

"And the people?" Leonard added with a tilt of his head.

The man shook his head. "He outsources the *people* to me. You can call me Boss. I provide more product to the Mori than anyone else in the States. You understand?" It was very clear exactly what he meant by "product". He leaned back in the chair, which emitted a creak of protest against his massive weight. "And you're mine now, for the next two days, until Duke gets here and puts hard cash in my hand."

A guard came in, carrying their bags. Boss cleared off his desk and watched as the assistant started emptying their belongings onto it. Gail's sword. Crow's computer and Dani's crossbow with which she had apparently been gifted. Leonard's knives and large wads of cash, which Boss promptly picked up and 'confiscated' right into his pocket. There were also packages of food and various pieces of survival gear and other things. It was almost embarrassing to see their only possessions laid out before them and analyzed, including things that Gail hadn't seen before. Leonard's bag had a rubber duck. Crow's bag had a lock of Gail's hair that the redhead hadn't remembered giving her, plus about a dozen bottles of nail polish—all of which looked to be the same shade of black except for one single bottle that was a pale yellow. Crow also had in her possession a curious-looking handheld device Gail had never seen before, the sight of which made the witch turn a deep crimson.

"It's a scare tactic," Leonard breathed so softly that Gail could barely hear it. "Makes you feel demoralized."

After picking through their belongings for the most immediately valuable things, the remainder were all stuffed haphazardly back into bags and tossed into a nearby trunk. Satisfied that he had waved his authority in their faces enough, Boss pointed his chin at the guard at the door. "This is Rob. Rob is your new best friend. Rob and his friends are going to take you to the end of the bridge and get you put up in our guest rooms. Welcome to the Garden." Boss smiled a big toothy smile while Rob pulled out a rope with multiple carabiners tied into it. He attached a carabiner to each person and led them out of the office where they were joined by more Kalida troops. Rob grinned and pointed up, where Nick, still in his net, was hanging from the roof of the guard tower. He didn't seem to be resisting while several of the guards threw things at him.

They went past the guard towers and to the far end of the bridge, where a large iron wagon lashed to a horse was waiting. After being pulled up and into the wagon, the door was locked and the rope secured through an iron slit to the front near the driver seat where rob and his friends sat.

"What's the plan?" Crow hissed as soon as they were alone in the back.

"Escape," Leonard replied.

Crow kicked him. "Yes, obviously. But how?"

"Don't know yet," Leonard said. "Right now, let's just keep our heads low."

The dozen or so people who had been stationed at the bridge appeared to be a very small part of the contingent stationed here at "the Gardens". They passed rows and rows of makeshift barracks, campfires surrounded by soldiers, and one large pit that they couldn't see into, but which bore the unmistakable sickly-sweet smell of death.

When the wagon stopped, they were met with more armed guards who led them down a footpath through the trees. Here, they crossed a small bridge over more swampy water and Gail glanced down over it to see something brown and scaly moving just under the surface.

At the end of the bridge, a large brown door marked "kennels" was unlocked, and the three led inside. Here, a beige hallway went down about thirty feet with cages on one side and doors to those cages spaced every few feet. With crossbows and swords still at their backs, the three were each led into a cage, their bonds removed, and the doors locked.

"Have a good day," Rob said, tipping his hat and disappearing with his goons out the door.

"Well," Leonard said with a sigh, "this is not a good situation."

"You think?" came the sharp reply from Crow's cell.

The door at the end of the hall opened again and another cell door was opened. Gail could hear a yap and some snarling before it was slammed shut again and the guard exited.

Gail went up to the door. "Lukather? Is that you, boy?" The dog whined, and Gail reached through the bars to the next cell. She felt a warm tongue lick her fingers. "I'm so sorry, boy. I hope you're okay over there." Withdrawing her fingers, she sat down on the floor and put her head in her hands, trying to calm her nerves.

The sound of her heaving breaths must have carried farther than she thought they would, because from the next cell she heard a rattling on the cage from Crow. "Hey Necia. Everything is okay. You are okay. We will get out of this."

"H-how?" Gail gasped.

There wasn't a reply.

◌

"Dammit." Gail could hear a scraping sound followed by Leonard cursing under his breath. "I broke it."

251

"Broke what?" Crow sounded exhausted. "And why are you trying to do anything in the dark?"

"I found a piece of straw," Leonard explained. "I was trying to jimmy the lock open, but it keeps collapsing and folding and then it broke."

"Eh," came the muffled reply, and it sounded like Crow might be lying face-down on the floor, "it was worth a try."

They sat in more silence for a few minutes. "Okay, Leonard. Real talk." She sat up and pressed her face to the bars of the door. "You and my mom. Her bed. Explain."

Gail could hear the embarrassed breath get sucked into Leonard's lungs. "Uh. Well. She offered to let me sleep on her floor because you had the guest room."

A long moment passed by, during which the man offered no further explanation. Crow cleared her throat. "And?"

"And I did. I slept on her floor for like, the first night or two."

Again, silence. "And?" Crow barked sharply enough to make Lukather jump.

"And then she offered to just share the bed because it was more comfortable."

Crow had apparently tired of his explanation, and rattled the door of the cage. "Answer me straight, Leonard. *Are you banging my mother?*"

Gail could almost hear him grin. "Not currently. I don't think this jail allows conjugal visits."

The door rattled some more. "You are! You god damned pig, you are!" Crow let out a frustrated sound and dropped back onto the floor.

Leonard cleared his throat. "Does it make it any better if she's the one who initiated the, uh, situat—?"

"No."

There was silence once again. No, not silence, Gail thought as she heard the sounds of sword and target practice outside. She wept silently in her cell, staring up at the ceiling that was too far away to see through the oppressive darkness. She reached through the bars, trying to see if she might be able to get her fingers over to Crow's cell, and she found that Crow was apparently trying to do the same thing at the same time. Without a word, they knitted their fingers together.

"You had a lock of my hair," Gail whispered. "Why?"

There was a pause. "I don't know. I hope that's not creepy. I grabbed it when you cut your hair back at Campbell."

"No, it's fine," Gail replied. "I hope it made you think of me."

◌

"The girls," came a gruff voice that woke Gail from her dreamless sleep. She was curled up, her hands clenched tightly in front of her. She relaxed them to find a few strands of thick black hair. Had Crow given them to her in the middle of the night? She couldn't remember.

The door of her cell was thrown open and a pair of hands yanked her to her feet. "Come on," the guard said, slapping a pair of metal cuffs on her wrists. "We're going to go make some use of you."

"What kind of *use?*" Gail replied in horror. Behind her Crow was being pulled out of her cell as well, but the witch was far less willing to go quietly. She kicked out with a boot and her heel made contact with the other guard's shin. The response was a sharp, closed-fisted blow across her jaw. The witch fell silent and immediately became more complacent.

They were led out, Lukather barking and snarling at the guards as they passed by. They crossed the reptile-filled river again and down back to the main road, where a set of collapsible targets had been set up. At the end of the target range, a group of Kalida waited with hatchets, knives, bows and arrows. Several Kalida troops were tying people—some of Boss's slaves, most assuredly—to the end of the range in between each target, so an errant projectile would almost certainly end up embedded in flesh.

"The biggest problem with accuracy," one of the guards was saying, "is that when the stakes are low the guys start slacking off. So you've gotta give them motivation. And of course you've gotta hope that the guy doesn't want to miss on purpose."

"This is utterly barbaric," Crow spat, as a knife went flying downrange and slammed into the painted wooden board.

"What's that?" Came a familiar voice. Boss was waddling down toward them. "Did I hear the girl say she volunteers?" the guards all laughed and started pulling her toward the target range.

"No!" Gail shouted, trying to pull herself free from her bonds, jostling and shoving the others around her that rushed to keep her under control. She couldn't escape, and she was forced to watch them tie her girlfriend between two targets near the center.

Once the downrange was clear of any Kalida troops, the knives and arrows started flying. One struck the target perfectly in the center, while a few here and there were somewhat off their-mark. An errant thrown knife swept through and nicked a slave's legs near Crow. Gail stared, unable to look away, as the troops took aim for another volley.

Gail had to do something. "You c-can't!" She pleaded with Boss. "Don't you want to collect her bounty?"

"The only one the Duke said needed to be alive was you, darlin'," Boss replied.

Another round of knives and arrows flew. Most of them hit the target, again, but an arrow ended up grazing the face of one of the slaves. He howled in pain.

Crow was stoic now. Gail knew that, even if she was hit, she would not feel the pain—but what would that mean in the long run? That she wouldn't feel anything as she died of blood loss?

"Please," she said, straining against the people holding her. "I don't know what you want, or what you're getting out of this. Please. Please, stop." Boss said nothing. Another volley went down the field, leaving more targets hit; a knife cleaved its way past Crow's shoulder and looked like it had torn her shirt. Gail could see blood. "Oh god, no…"

One of the troops, a pasty fellow with incredibly platinum hair, aimed his knife and prepared to throw it. Gail could see already that it was not aimed at a target, and from the way Crow had fixed him with a deathly glare, she had come to a similar conclusion. Gail screamed as the knife left his hand, and the moment seemed to stretch out. Her fingers dug into her palms, grasping the few strands of black hair between her fingers—

The knife stopped. It was a curious thing. One moment it had been flipping through the air on an unerring journey toward its target, the next it had plummeted to the ground as though it had been dropped straight down from its position a few feet from Crow's head. The target range went very quiet. Those who, like Gail, had ever seen a Mori stop dead in its tracks recognized that unnatural movement and collectively took in a deep breath. Several people began looking around for the source of magic that had terminated the knife's movement.

"Everyone back to work," Boss shouted, and the troops went to gather their projectiles from the target range as quickly as they could. Gail was pulled back and shoved toward the kennel again, and as they opened the door for her and shoved her back into her cell, she could not stop shaking.

"What happened?" Leonard said. "Where's Crow?"

Crow was brought in a moment later and practically thrown into her cell. One of the guards kicked her and slammed the door, eliciting not a sound from the witch but instead a string of curses from both Gail and Leonard.

"What happened?" Leonard asked again.

Gail leaned against the bars of her cell and explained what had happened with the knife. As she did, she looked down at the strands of black hair in her fingers. She had been clenching her hands so tightly that the delicate strands of hair had dug into and lightly cut the skin.

"Crow, are you alright?" Leonard asked. "And are you sure it was Mori magic?"

"Never seen anything else move like that," Crow said, and she coughed and sputtered. "Dammit, I think I have a broken rib. Hard to tell though, since I can't feel it."

"But there weren't any Mori?" Leonard asked. "Then how—"

"I think it was me," Gail said, spinning the strands of hair between her thumbs and forefingers. "Somehow, I think I did it. The whole...Partholón thing."

"It's possible," Leonard replied. You said your thigh healed itself after the fight at Campbell, right? I bet you did that, too. We both know you're capable of harnessing the Magic since you used it to heal Crow."

"But I don't know *how* I did it," Gail said, knocking her head back against the bars. "I mean...I'm glad I did, but—"

"For the record I am *really* glad you did," Crow said, and from the chatter of her voice it sounded like she might be shivering.

TWENTY-EIGHT

Gail looked up as the door that led to the cells opened. Wondering what the Kalida might possibly want with them now, she was unsurprised to see Rob strolling through the door. "Duke's here. Get up, y'all."

"Already?" Gail wasn't sure if she was emotionally ready to face him right now, but then again it wasn't particularly up to her.

"Shut up, stand up, face the wall," he ordered, and they all obeyed. In a minute the doors were open, the ropes and cuffs secured, and they were being led back out.

Outside, it was growing very dark; the western sky was a dazzling array of reds and oranges painted across swirling clouds. They were led across the bridge once more, and at the end of the path that led back to the bridge they were met with people who bore the unmistakable emblem of the Duke of the East.

Boss was there, too, stroking his bulbous chin while one of the thugs finished counting out notes. "It all looks good," he said, taking several bricks of money and handing them to an assistant. "Mister Duke, or whatever—they're all yours." He bowed low.

The man he bowed to was not the Duke of the East.

He was tall and slender, with mocha skin and hair that was done up in an impeccable pompadour. His teeth were dazzling when he smiled. "Good, good. Do you have their belongings?"

"Already loaded in your wagon," Boss replied, clapping his fingers together and practically dancing on the tips of his feet from the sheer amount of money he had just made. "Anything else we can provide you before we escort you back to the highway?"

"My dog," Gail interjected.

"Yes," the not-Duke said, raising an eyebrow. "Bring the dog, as well. Let me take a look here now…" He walked over to the three of them, his long brown coat sweeping behind him. He looked Gail up and down and moved on to Crow. "Oh, tsk tsk. This one's injured. Hopefully not by your hand…?" He looked back at Boss over his shoulder.

"Of course not," Boss protested.

"Liar!" Crow shouted. "Your men threw *knives* at me—"

The not-Duke shook his head. "Oh well, what's done is done. Off we go." He walked off, snapping his fingers to have the other people wearing the Duke's colors lead them off. Crow made a sucking noise in her mouth and fired a massive spit wad at Boss as she passed. Leonard hissed in passing to Boss that, by the way, he wasn't "other"—he was Polynesian, thank you very much. Gail said nothing and just looked at her feet.

They were led along the road, past cages that, from the wagon, Gail had not been able to see. Behind these cages were dozens of people with sunken eyes and matted hair, their eyes like dinner plates as they gazed out at them. So many slaves. So, so many slaves.

They were loaded into another wagon, this one with an open top. Nick, still in his net, was loaded into the wagon with them, secured with extra lengths of cable and rope to make sure he could not free himself. It was a small caravan—only a few wagons and some men on horseback—but it moved with efficiency as they pulled out of the slaver's camp and back onto I-4 toward Orlando.

"Why are we going toward Orlando?" Crow hissed. "I thought the Duke and lady whatserface were in Raleigh."

"That's not the Duke," Gail mouthed at her. Crow tilted her head and stared off, trying to make sense of it all. It wasn't possible, though—they were too tired, too hungry, and too weak. The world was becoming a fog.

The wagon stopped after what felt like hours, but it could just as easily have been a few minutes. Here, in the dark of night, it didn't really seem to matter. The not-Duke made his way to the back of the wagon, hopping up and pulling a knife from his belt. Gail looked at it. She didn't even feel afraid anymore. Her eyesight was fuzzy.

The knife came down and cut the rope around Gail's wrists and then Crow's and Leonard's. Two other people helped Nick out of his bonds as well. "We've got water," the not-Duke explained, and as soon as several canteens had made it back to them and were placed in their hands, the wagon was off again, the pompadoured man staying in the back and riding with them. "We'll get food as soon as we're sure it's safe to stop and we're not being followed."

The water was cool, and it smoothed the sticky feelings resting in the back of Gail's throat. Several packages containing food bars were divided, and the redhead nearly choked while tearing into one. It didn't fill her belly, but it made the pain subside. "You're not the Duke," she said as soon as she had found her voice again.

"No, I'm not," the man grinned. "I'm Magpie."

"Magpie?" Crow said, coughing on her water. "The witch Magpie? Second-in-command-to-Eagle?"

"Not anymore," he said evenly. "Your mother told us what happened, so in theory I'm in charge now."

"And how did you know we were here?" Crow said, her eyes practically boggling out of her head.

"Your mother said you were headed to Orlando. I know the Florida slave trades pretty well and had a feeling that if you were taking the interstate you'd probably run into slavers, and those slavers probably would have heard about the bounty on you. I started heading

259

out here and a source confirmed you had been captured. I got here as quickly as I could."

"But you're not the Duke," Gail said, gesturing to him. "What if someone who knew the Duke had seen you?"

"Unlikely. We live in a post-social media world. People don't know faces from people they haven't personally met, and the Duke doesn't really leave his kingdom very often."

"But he is coming, right?" Crow asked. "He's going to show up eventually, and then—"

"And then the Duke will be very upset that his prisoners-to-be were released to the wrong person, and Boss is going to be mad by then when he realizes all of those bank notes are fake. It's a lot easier to pass a pile of fake bills in the middle of the night, you know."

Crow put up a hand. "Hang on, hang on. So you're saying that you came out here, in person, to save us because someone online reported I might be in trouble? That…That goes against protocols. And this is you, Magpie. You don't break protocols."

"No, Eagle didn't break protocols," he corrected. "And I did what a first officer is supposed to do and I supported her decisions. She was the one who made the decision to kill your credentials. And in retrospect, I understand why. She needed access to your computer. So for what it's worth I'm sorry for the part I played in that." Crow didn't seem to know how to reply, or perhaps she was simply too weak to argue.

They rode in silence for a little while longer and pulled over to the side of the road. "I understand if you don't want to give me specifics," Magpie said, "but if you will trust us with the address, I'd love to get you exactly where you need to go. Dani said it was important and I trust her judgment. But what with everything that happened with Eagle…I can understand how you might not trust me."

Gail, Leonard, Crow, and Nick all looked at each other in search of an answer. Finally, everyone was looking at Crow, and she glowered at them. "Oh, I see. It's all on me, then." She sighed. "Magpie, I really, *really* appreciate everything you've done. You did all this for me—for us—and it just…I can't even…" She stumbled over some words. "But I can't. It's been too much, too recently. My…my capability to trust people has run out. So…no. Just drop us off in Orlando and we'll figure it out from there. Then you…you head to Sun City. We'll meet you there. I hope."

Magpie nodded slowly as he listened. "I can't refute that. And like I said, I trust Dani, and she trusts you." One of Magpie's people came up to the wagon carrying a large burlap sack. Upon opening it, they found most of their belongings and began dividing them back into the correct bags. Crow was reunited with her computer, and she hugged it like a long-lost friend.

"What about the slaves?" Gail said, stuffing a few items into her bag. "There has to be something we can do about the slaves. We were there two days and had bad things happen. I can't imagine what it's like for the people who have been there weeks, months, years—you have to be able to do something."

"We want to," Magpie returned. "But this close to the Mori capital, the slavers have practically unlimited resources. And the infrastructure for slave labor already existed here before they came. If you ask me, I think they put their capital out here for that reason."

Gail nodded in reply, sliding her sword into its sheath and strapping it to her belt. "All the more reason to shut it all down, then." She took a deep breath. "Let's go."

"Aw man," Crow said, examining the screen on her beloved computer, "they cracked my screen. It's still usable, but…man. I've been taking care of this thing for a long time and it gets taken from me for a *day* and it's cracked."

They climbed down off of the wagon. Their feet on solid ground, and their hand freed of bonds, the sense of freedom washed over them all at once: Crow and Gail embraced tightly and were joined by Leonard. The three of them in one large group hug must have looked terribly silly, but that didn't bother any of them. Tears were streaming down their faces quietly, and after a few long moments they separated again. Nick patted them on the shoulder and gave an encouraging nod.

Lukather, meanwhile, ran in circles, incredibly excited to be outside once again.

Soon, they had packed up some food from Magpie's supply wagon and prepared to leave. Nick looked very happy to again have with his Type-N'-Talk, and spent a few minutes testing the buttons.

Crow shook hands with Magpie. "Speaking of second-in-commands," he said, "when you're done with whatever you're doing out here—win or lose—I really could use one. I know you are exceptionally talented. Are you interested?"

"Sure," she replied, grinning widely. "But if I can be honest, if we lose I probably won't be making it back."

"That's fair." Magpie waved to the party before the convoy made a turn down another branch of the highway. In a few minutes they were out of sight behind a green tapestry of Floridian trees.

Crow stood there for a few minutes, watching after them. The words that had left her mouth seemed to be sinking in, and it was not only Crow who realized the truth of her words—they were walking right into the heart of the beast—with or without Osbourne's help and practically without a plan—and failure was certain death. Gail considered the solemn thought of death; she wondered if it was just darkness. She wondered if her family was there. She also wondered about Crow—would Crow feel death as it came? Or would she numbly shuffle off to whatever new place waited beyond?

There had to be a new place, she reasoned. Because the alternative would be that the only existence was simply this wasteland of death and destruction. And it was a wasteland, Gail mused as they started off once again along the side roads that led toward the mysterious Harry Osbourne, even if parts of it were as beautiful and green as the things out here in Florida. It was a reminder that despite the beauty and splendor of the landscape here before them, this world was still not a happy place. She heard something M had once told her echoing in her head: "The evil does not stop being evil just because you can't see it right now."

"It's incredible."

"I've never seen anything like it," Crow said. "Leonard?"

"Not one this big, or fancy," Leonard replied, lighting his pipe. "Nick?" The suit of armor shook his head.

A wide square of land unfolded before them. The grass was green, and the rolling hills were covered in all sorts of strange objects—cars, windmills, tiki huts, an even a downed airplane. The whole property was surrounded by a deep moat, in which floated several large log-like creatures that Gail was sure were looking up at them. Most importantly, and perhaps most amazingly, were the lights glistening all over the property—incredible, glistening lights that cast the whole street in a fiery orange flicker. A massive blimp lit with spotlights was the centerpiece of the display, illuminating nearly the whole block in a starry, otherworldly glimmer.

Leonard nodded. "Then it's agreed. This has to be the most amazing mini-golf course in the world." The others nodded in agreement—even Gail, who did not know what mini-golf was. "You're sure this is the address?"

Crow double-checked the file on the computer, the light from the screen making her look particularly spooky in the semi-light cast by the glowing yard. "Absolutely. And I mean, it has to be. Electric lights, Leonard. How do they even still work?"

"We'll have to ask," Leonard replied, starting to walk along the curb to look for an entrance. He spotted one, a large bamboo door with welcome signs that had all been crossed out and replaced with other ones that read "Go away" and "out to lunch".

Crow, growing eager and impatient, strolled right up the door across the tiny drawbridge and slammed her fists on it. The sound echoed across the park and into the darkness.

"I hope that didn't attract the wrong type of attention," Gail whispered, looking up and down the empty darkened street. "I don't think I could do anything in a fight right now."

A speaker, secured with silver tape to one of the doorways' bamboo poles, crackled to life. "It's the middle of the night. Who on earth—" there was a clattering sound. "—Who are you? What do you want?" The voice had a strange accent

"Hello," Leonard said politely, tapping the button on the bottom of the speaker. "We're looking for Mr. Harry Osbourne."

"No one here by that name. Good night."

Leonard pushed the button again. "Hang on, don't go anywhere. I have it on good authority that there is someone here by that name. And if he is, he was working with a friend of ours named Bluejay."

There was a long pause, and for a moment Gail thought whoever it was might not come back to the speaker at all. "Is Bluejay with you?"

Crow hit the button this time. "No, she's dead."

"Dr. Glenn?"

"Dead."

"How about—"

"Marion Bohr, Eagle, all dead, okay? You are literally the only person left who has any idea what is going on now, Osbourne, so get off your ass and *fucking let us in.*"

Another pause. "Who are you, then?"

Leonard pushed Crow's hand out the way and mouthed the word *finesse* to her before pushing the button again. "Leonard Bohr— Marion's brother. I'm here with one of the leaders of the New Internet, a member of the US Military, and a Partholónian."

There was a gasp on the line. "A Partholónian? Why didn't you say so in the first place? Where did you—how did you—ack!" Another clatter of something in the background drowned out words. "Come in, come in, quickly…" The large bamboo door clicked, loudly, and Crow reached for the handle to pull it open.

"Well," Crow said with a sigh, "here we go."

Gail was not sure what exactly to expect on the other side of the door. Bluejay's notes hadn't given any indication of who the man really was, so she was prepared for any manner of person to come strolling across the lawn of the mini-golf course toward them.

Osbourne—if this was him—was tall and somewhat lumpy, his silver hair tied back in a messy top bun on his head and his beard trimmed into a pointed goatee. His skin was golden and pale, and his eyes were dark and crinkled with glee.

He was a Mori.

TWENTY-NINE

The man walked toward them with a spring in his step and his arms outstretched, a wide grin spread across his face. That grin vanished a moment later as he was suddenly facing four people and a dog, all planted aggressively in the doorway with weapons drawn. His eyes moved from the sword in Gail's hand to the knife in Leonard's, to the crossbow in Crow's, and finally to Nick, who was clearly just a weapon himself. Even Lukather had suddenly crouched, growling between the two ladies. "Oh!" He said, putting his hands up. "I mean you no harm!"

"You're Mori!" Crow spat. "Where's Osbourne?"

"I am Osbourne!" the man said frantically. "I promise! I am on your side!"

"You expect any of us to believe that?" Crow replied instantly. "You have no idea of the hell we've been through to get here. But if you think we're just going to sit down and accept that you're—"

"I worked with Bluejay on a plan," Osbourne said, still keeping his hands up. "A plan to stop the Mori—Get every single one off this planet once and for all. That includes myself," he added. "But please, I truly mean you no harm. I have no Magic. I am defenseless. I am at your mercy." He contorted his face a bit as large droplets began to stream down his face. He let out a whine, and the sight and sound of this elderly Mori bawling in front of them was an incredibly pitiful sight to behold.

"I've never seen an old Mori before," Gail whispered. "I thought they stayed young forever."

"Me too," Leonard said. "If he really doesn't have any magic…"

"We can't trust him," Crow interjected. "Not even slightly."

Gail watched the man continue to bawl and felt an instinctual pull. She stepped forward and cleared the distance between the two so that the tip of her sword was directly in front of his face. "You know what the Parthólonians are." Crow walked up to stand next to Gail and she felt even stronger.

Osbourne nodded and made blubbering sounds.

"Then you know that I have the ability to kill you."

He nodded again. "You all do!" he cried. "I am completely devoid of Mori magic. I have none of the normal defenses that—" Crow's fist slammed into his jaw, knocking the old man back. He clenched his face and screamed.

"Crow!" Gail said, shocked.

"Well," the witch replied sheepishly, "at least he's telling the truth about his Mori defenses."

"Yeah, but now I feel like the bad guy here." Against her better judgment, Gail sheathed her sword and offered the man her hand. "Here."

The man, still sobbing uncontrollably, took her hand and half-stumbled his way back to his feet before burying his face in his hands.

"Alright, alright, calm down." Leonard had made his way over. "If you don't hurt us, then we don't have a reason to hurt you. But you *do* understand why we have no reason to believe a thing that comes out of your mouth."

"Of course I do," Osbourne replied, wiping thick tears from his cheeks. "It's the penance I pay for my crimes. But please…close the door, pray—and I shall tell you my sad tale." Nick, the closest to the door, reached over and pushed the bamboo door closed. Osbourne took a white handkerchief out of his jacket and tried to clean his face.

Crow hadn't lowered her crossbow. "Let's start with the—" She stopped as she caught Gail's gaze, then gritted her teeth and took a breath before finally lowering the weapon. "Let's start with the basics," she said in a much calmer tone. "You're Mori, but you don't have magic? Why?"

"I'm an outcast," he said. "Banished from their world and disconnected from their Magic. I live only because I have protected myself with the technology of Earth. The rest of the Mori believe I have taken up with witches, and they leave me alone. That is why I keep these lights on day and night, so they will think I am still protected.

Osbourne gestured to the building nearby, where an open doorway read *Dining and Arcade*. "Shall we go? I would like to answer your questions as best I can. There is much that I can do for you. And if, as you say, the others are dead…then I will do everything within my power to help you."

The interior of the dining hall was brightly-lit with strings of lights that ran across the ceiling from wall to wall. The electric light made the rest of the room seem to glow; blue and red tables and chairs littered the floor, many of which were covered in books and gadgets. Gail was briefly reminded of the barn where Crow had lived back in North Carolina—a place that seemed so impossibly far away now. She wondered briefly if Bart, the cat, had ever made it back to the barn unscathed.

Crow picked up one of the gadgets and turned it on. It made a musical sound and lit up. "All of this works. And the lights. All of this requires power…how did you get all this to work?"

Osbourne looked a little smug as he leaned against a table covered in books which appeared to be mostly about geography, navigation, and astronomy. "I have spent most of my life as a researcher. Among Mori culture we are called *spell-keepers*, and our job is to understand and utilize the Magic. I am a…magical technician, if you will."

"But it's not magic," Crow protested. "It's advanced technology. Why don't the Mori understand that?"

"Because we were born into its existence. The Magic is so far advanced to us that no person, Mori or otherwise, knows how it works, at least technically. It does the things we will it to do, and if it can't do those things, then we determine that such a thing is beyond The Magic's capabilities. It is a simplistic view, for a simplistic people. A few of us—myself included—don't accept this simple view, and we study The Magic. Can I offer you food?" he added, gesturing to the kitchen at the far end of the room. "I have many different things you can eat. I have discovered a fondness for a curious confection called 'funnel cake'."

Nick gestured to the kitchen, and after getting an approving nod from Crow he stomped off to see what could be found. Crow lowered herself into a chair, still holding the crossbow but pointing it at the floor. "So you know how The Magic works?"

"No," Osbourne said, running his fingers through his hair. "For a long time I was a theorist. Then, when the Mori came to this world, it became my task to study the magic here. One of my greatest fears was the witches—for I soon found out that the witches were able to do wonderful things. And I discovered that their magic was simple trickery! I was fascinated." Crow shifted uncomfortably in her seat. "And I come to discover the concept of *technology*. The evil magics that the Ritual of Homecoming was made to dispel were actually applications of the foundational laws of the universe. And you…humans. You have published many books on the subject. The idea of *science*—it's something unknown to the Mori."

Leonard waved a hand. "Step back here a moment. You're saying you don't know what the Ritual of Homecoming does? Like…you don't understand its purpose?"

"The way it is explained to us," Osbourne said, taking out a slender cigarette and putting it in his mouth, "is that the Ritual of Homecoming infuses the planet with the noble and glorious power of our people. It dispels the darkness and plants the seeds from which our magic grows." He patted his pockets and Leonard reached out to light Osbourne's cigarette with a match. "But it's all a humbug!"

Osbourne said after a long drag of the cigarette. "It's a lie. Now I know that the Ritual of Homecoming targets and destroys certain types of…of… *technology*. But how it does this I do not know."

"But someone must know," Crow said, finally setting her crossbow down on the table next to her. Gail sat down next to her and rested her head on the witch's shoulder. "Someone in the Mori must know the truth. I can't imagine a society like yours can exist for so long without science or research."

"And yet it does," Osbourne lamented. "The Magic provides us with all of our needs. We have become so reliant on it that we don't understand lesser…things. Perhaps the First would know, for they are the ones who move and direct the Mori's divine voyages across the stars."

"Who are the First?" Leonard asked. He lit his pipe from the same match.

"The First are the parents of the Mori. They are a greater species than us, and the Magic bends more greatly to their will than to ours. They command the Mori. It was the decision of the First to return to Earth and succeed where the initial voyagers had failed."

"Then it sounds like the First are using the Mori as pawns," Leonard mused. He caught sight of Crow's disgusted expression. "I don't mean in any way to sound like I am excusing the things the Mori do, okay? I'm just saying that in this case, there are people pulling the strings and giving the orders. The Mori are still guilty for following those orders. Having a different culture is no excuse for a lack of morals."

"Oh!" Osbourne cried, disposing of his cigarette and wiping his eyes which had grown wet again. "And that is truly the source of my woe. For as I learned about the human *science* and the human *technology* I came to realize that the people of this planet were not the lesser creatures that the First had told us you were. You must understand," he said with pleading eyes to Crow, "that we were told that you were like bugs. Like fleas or parasites, leeching off the surface of the planet. And the evidence was damning—buildings that spill toxins into the air and oceans filled with waste. It was an easy argument that the planet was in peril because of the creatures that were rapidly destroying it."

Leonard looked down at his feet. His eyes were moving back and forth, as though he was suddenly coming to a deep realization. "Oh no…Oh no no no."

"What is it?" Crow said.

"We caused this. We caused all of this. We did this."

"I wouldn't say that," Osbourne said, stroking his pointed beard. "But I think that the actions of human-kind made it very easy for the First to prove that you were not worth saving."

"I think it's a magnitude of difference," Crow said to Leonard. "And while I'm sure that someone out there *really* appreciates your sudden realization about how shitty human beings are, it doesn't help us now. So what about *you?*" she said, jabbing a finger toward Osbourne. "What happened after your change of heart?"

"I brought it to the ruling council at the Tower of Peace, and they called my words blasphemous. They said I had been taken in by the dark magic and the witches. They took The Magic from me and they cast me out and chased me down…but I had taken this place as a sanctuary. And by repairing and augmenting it I created a new fabrication against theirs. I told them I was a great and powerful wizard and that if any attempted to seek me out in my exile, that I would destroy them with my great wizardly magic. I have been…" He searched meekly for the words. "Making believe."

"Making believe!" cried Gail. "You're not a great wizard."

"And they believed you?" Crow said incredulously.

"A simplistic view, for a simplistic people," Osbourne said again. "They are like a…oh, let me think of a metaphor a human might understand." He tapped his chin, grabbed a book and flipped through it to search for a word. "They are like children, armed with 'rocket-propelled grenades', being told it's okay to hurt the children in the other school's playground. But they are still children and they will still act like children."

Leonard coughed. "That is an awful metaphor," he choked out. "But it's also terrifyingly accurate."

Gail ran her finger across the spine of one of the nearby books. "And you've been here ever since? Reading and studying?"

Osbourne hung his head. "Yes, yes. I had hoped to find something in the realms of science or technology that I might give to the humans to help them fight back. But the answer was in neither." He picked up a book. Its cover was long faded, but when he passed it to Gail she instantly recognized the face on the cover. "*Ancient Ireland: A Study of the Proto-History of The Irish Isle,*" She read. "*By Dr. Avery Glenn.* This is how you learned about Partholón and the Fomóraiġ!"

"Indeed," Osbourne said, and the smile had returned to his wrinkled face. "And from that myth I discovered an answer. You see, I had connected with the young woman, Bluejay, here in Florida, and through her I was connected to several others. They came here, several years ago—a pilgrimage to my safe place, where we put the pieces together and discovered the truth about the Partholónian lineage. Even the Mori did not know about it, which I find terribly amusing. Humans are just better record-keepers, it seems."

"M was here?" Gail gasped. "Marion. He came here to see you? He saw you, in person?"

Osbourne's smile fell. "I...no. No, they did not meet me in person. I was ashamed. So I...I communicated to them with trickery—smoke and mirrors, you might say. But that is another tale in itself."

"So they never knew you were Mori," Crow said, her eyes narrowing just slightly. "So why tell us if you didn't tell them?"

"Because you brought a Partholónian!" Osbourne said, jumping to his feet fast enough that Crow's hand jerked toward the crossbow. "And we can begin the plan." He beamed at Gail. "Oh, you are truly divine. The red of your hair, the freckles on your skin, your eyes that—" He stopped, catching a glimpse of Crow's still-angry face. "Ahem. Anyway. I have a plan to get into the Tower and shut it down. The Tower is an amplifier of the Magic, and if its functions are disrupted, then the whole thing will…well, to use a human science phrase—it will go into nuclear meltdown."

"Disrupted how?"

"If the legends are right, a Partholónian," Osbourne exclaimed, his voice becoming rapid and loud, "can use the Magic. They can harness it. And the tower…it is practically *made* of the Magic. A Partholónian, I believe, could turn the tower off. I don't know how. The Mori would be severely weakened. It could turn the tide, and the humans could send the Mori away. Perhaps, as in the legends, they would flee again."

"The last time they were here, though, they only tried to take over an island. What makes you think that toppling the tower would make them do it again? They have such an iron grip now."

"Simplistic people," Osbourne said once more. "I do not know what the Mori would do, or if they would stay and fight. I cannot promise that, if the tower falls, that the Mori will be defeated eventually. But I can promise that while the tower still stands, they never, ever will will."

Nick stomped back into the kitchen carrying a tray of steaming food: meat patties on bread, bowls of some kind of soup, and plates full of a strange and sweet-smelling confection covered in powdered sugar. He laid the platter down and made a little bow before typing on his device. "BON APETIT," he proclaimed—but the lack of the second "p" in the word *Appetit* made the Type-N'-Talk pronounce it rather inappropriately, eliciting amused snorts and chuckles from Crow and Leonard.

Crow grabbed a meat sandwich and took a few large bites and washed them down with water from her canteen. "So what are you going to do for us to help get this plan off the ground, then? What do you have to offer us? Unless you're expecting us to go storm the Tower of Peace, which is guarded by probably a thousand Mori and Advocates."

Well, Osbourne said, picking up a funnel cake and pointing at Crow, "I know a secret way into the tower. You are right that the outside of the tower is protected rather heavily, but if you were inside already, well…that's a very different story. I also have the plans for a very useful gadget—a hybrid of human and Mori technology—that will certainly prove useful. Oh, if they knew that I had been able to engineer the scary 'witchcraft' with the Magic." He chuckled and stuffed half the funnel cake into his mouth, swallowing it in a somewhat horrifying fashion. "I cannot imagine the things they might do to me then." Nick remained silent, but to the others it was clear what he was thinking—he knew exactly what the Mori would do.

⌂

It was very strange to try to sleep in a place with electric light. The most light she had ever seen in the night-time was that of a small coal-oil lamp, and it was somewhat unnerving to glance out the window and see so much bright glare.

Osbourne, for all his obliviousness about human behavior, was nothing if not hospitable. The windmill on the far end of the Mini-Golf range, situated near the massive golden blimp, was actually a furnished single room, which Crow "called dibs" on, for reasons she declined to reveal until they had bid their good-nights and securely locked the door with them inside—at which point she practically attacked Gail on the spot.

A few hours later, they were still awake, unable to get any sleep under the harsh glow of the electric lights outside, not to mention the knowledge that they were effectively inside the personal lair of a Mori regardless of how trustworthy he seemed to be. The careful and responsible thing was to stay awake.

Gail traced her fingers along the outside of the knife wound in Crow's shoulder, gently rubbing in some antiseptic ointment. "You cannot let this get infected," she admonished, and Crow, who was staring off into space, nodded absently. "I'm serious."

"I know you are," Crow sighed. "But who knows—maybe you'll learn new *Mori magic* and learn to heal things on your own." The words were not friendly on her lips.

Gail dug into her bag and pulled out a brush. She picked a few red hairs out of it and ran it through Crow's unkempt mane. The feeling startled the witch, and she almost wrenched away, but caught herself. "H-hey!"

"Your hair needs brushing," Gail said flatly, and continued her work. "It's a mess."

"It's always a mess," Crow explained. "It's part of the style." But she didn't resist Gail's attempt to untangle the enigma of black atop her head.

The mountain girl sighed. "You…don't approve of me using Mori magic to save you again?"

Crow shrugged, a movement that probably would have been quite painful to her shoulder if she had been able to feel pain. "I dunno. I used to think a lot of things about a lot of things. Now I don't know what I think anymore. I mean—thank you for saving me. Again. But it's weird."

She stopped brushing. "Will you stop liking me?"

Crow turned her head and her eyebrows pressed together. "For what? For using 'the magic'?" Her face was serious, but her voice was dripping with sarcasm.

The redhead nodded and fumbled with the brush.

Crow turned then, pushing Gail backwards and pinning her to the bed. "I like you a lot. I'm not going to stop liking you unless you start doing screwed-up things or start hurting people I care about. And as long as you're honest with me about things, you and I are *good*. Why would you even think that?"

"Okay. I'll be honest—I'm afraid that I'm going to accidentally upset you again, and you're going to run away."

Crow pulled back, letting go of Gail, and looked down at her hands, suddenly becoming very interested in her fingernails. Gail could not get away from the anxiety and the hurt that Crow had left in her departure, and it appeared that Crow had not yet fully grasped that kind of wound it had left. "I…I don't want you to feel that way. You know I'm not going to."

275

Gail nodded, and as Crow bent down to kiss her again, she tried her best to believe her.

THIRTY

Leonard, Crow, and Osbourne were moving around the table, conversing in soft voices about what 'the plan' was. So far, they had collected and assembled all of the pieces, but fitting them together was turning into its own disaster as they bickered over who would do what, and how.

"So where is the tunnel?" Crow asked, tapping the drawing; Osbourne had recreated a semi-detailed map of St. Petersburg out of an atlas. St. Petersburg was a small near-island on the west side of Florida's main peninsula, right across the bridge from Tampa. The majority of St. Petersburg was therefore surrounded by water, which made the idea of storming the Tower of Peace to be an incredibly silly prospect: the main tower was guarded by an army of slaves and Advocates and even Mori themselves, who were stationed primarily along the bridges and the across the place where the peninsula met the main land.

Osbourne circled a place on the main land that, on a similar map brought up on Crow's computer, was labeled *Tampa Bay Estuarine Ecosystem Rock Ponds Area*. "It starts here, and runs down through a set of old maintenance tunnels under the bay."

"Cockroach Bay," Leonard read off Crow's computer. "Fitting name for the home base of a race of cockroaches. Present company excluded," he added to Osbourne, who was nonetheless nodding in agreement.

Gail and Nick were sitting at a nearby table, playing with a set of arcade tokens they had found. They had divided them up and were now taking turns flicking coins across the table at each other, trying to knock the other person's coins off the edge. Gail was also using this game as a way to try and "harness the Magic", as Osbourne had called it. His instructions were incredibly unhelpful: "Flex the Magic like a muscle. Tell it what you want to do. And it will do it."

But the Magic, apparently, was did not want to be flexed like a muscle. Gail had not succeeded in moving a coin, or stopping a coin, or really doing anything at all. She was, however, winning the coin game.

"Why wouldn't they close down this tunnel?" Leonard asked. "It seems like a terrible security risk to have a backdoor like this unguarded. Like, this is Death Star levels of bad foresight."

"You are such a friggin' nerd," Crow said with a roll of her eyes.

"Well," Osbourne said, rubbing his chin, "It's not exactly *unguarded*. It's just less guarded because, first, no one is supposed to know about it, and second, most people would avoid it even if they did."

Crow crossed her arms. "Explain."

Osbourne twiddled his fingers a little bit. "The estuary and the tunnel were perfect for some of the Mori's needs when their new home was selected. You see, the Mori do not reproduce the same way you humans do. Our young are formed and grown by the Magic. And to do so they need a specific environment—cold and wet and shielded from the radiation of your sun."

"An underwater tunnel would fit that," Leonard agreed. "And this tunnel is a…what? An incubator? For more Mori?"

"Well, that depends—"

Gail stood up, an idea suddenly crossing her mind. "Osbourne, what do you know about the Mori's plans for the Partholónians?"

278

"Ah, yes." His face had fallen once again. "It was a plan to *improve* humans. I think they had the best of intentions—" Upon receiving most contemptuous glares from everyone in the room, he backpedaled his statement instantly. "It was a horrifying plan, I mean, inspired by their misplaced sense of morality. Not something I support, so we're clear. But it was all theoretical! The Mori were not able to get their hands on a single confirmed Partholónian descendant to test the application of the theory. Thank goodness."

Gail wished that Leonard and Crow would stop looking at her. The redhead suddenly found the floor's intricate designs to be particularly fascinating, and she wished that the burning red that she felt in her cheeks would subside.

Osbourne, whether out of sheer obliviousness or a desire not to pry—Gail was inclined to believe the former—continued on. "But as I said, it's not unguarded. The young Mori are guarded by the wet-nurse—a Mori specifically tasked with watching over the young."

"*The* wet-nurse?" Crow asked, crossing her arms. "As in, one? There's only one Mori down there?"

"You want there to be more?" Leonard quipped. "But Osbourne—I get where she's coming from here, okay? You're basically telling us that there's a secret entrance no one knows about and is mostly unguarded. I've never heard of anything that sounded so much like a trap in my whole life."

Osbourne's eyes almost looked like they might pop right out of his head. "A trap? Oh goodness, no, not at all. This is the plan we've all been working on. Bluejay and I discussed it at length, and sent a scout—"

"We don't have any way to believe you, though," Leonard reasoned. "You're asking us to rely on blind faith that this isn't another Mori plot to capture Gail or quash a rebellion. And we've had our share of traps already."

A tense silence fell over the table, while Osbourne's face contorted as he tried to figure out a way to refute the man's logic. Gail walked over to the table and laid her hand on the map. "We don't have a better plan. The alternative at this point is to pack up and go home. If you all want to do that, I understand…but I'm going. Even if it is a trap."

Crow took a deep breath. "If you're going, I'm going. End of discussion." She gave Gail a warm smile that was returned in kind.

Leonard fumbled with his pipe. "I'm going, of course. It's what Marion would've wanted me to do—to see this through with you until the end." He patted Gail's shoulder.

They all looked over at Nick. He gave them a thumbs up.

"Then it's settled," Gail said, feeling a surge of confidence welling up in her. "Let's start getting ready."

⌂

The next few days were a flurry of action peppered with brief respites for meals and sleep. Even in the dead of night, the bright electric lights of the Mini Golf compound was a daylight glow that made it easier to work later and get up earlier. The large golden blimp did very well at illuminating even the smallest crevasses of the compound, to such an extent that Gail began to suspect that Osbourne was afraid of the dark.

Crow spent much of her time sorting through more of Bluejay's files, searching for any additional information. There was so much, a lot of it incredibly technical, and Crow called the process "mind-numbing" and "endless" a few times. Gail spent a little time with her, resting her head on the witch's shoulder and staring with her eyes unfocused at the graphs and lines of unintelligible code as they crawled across the screen. Crow's part in the plan was majorly strategic—data analysis and communication. For the sake of security, she had not shared any part of the plan with the New Internet, including Magpie. She did, however, send him several messages letting him know that the crew had arrived safely at their destination in Orlando and that she would fill him in with more information as soon as she was able. Magpie, in turn informed her that he and some others had set up at Sun City and were awaiting further information.

Osbourne and Nick, meanwhile, were working on the "gadget" that the exiled Mori had mentioned. "It is an ingenious device, based around the concept of the nuclear reactions of a star," Osbourne excitedly explained. "Stars, you see, emit radio waves. This device emulates that process and creates a massive burst of radio and microwave radiation. One powerful enough to disable the Tower." The problem with this, of course, was the fact that the massive amount of radiation emitted would be deadly to anyone in the immediate vicinity. For this reason, they would set an internal timer and escape, leaving the device behind to do its work.

Leonard and Gail spent a lot of their time sparring. Leonard was becoming far more used to fighting with his off-hand, and his aim with his throwing knives was improving considerably. This, in turn, made him far more confident; his fear of being "useless" was quickly being proven wrong. Gail kept trying to use the Magic in combat, but every attempt not only produced no effect whatsoever but also caused her to pause and concentrate in the middle of a fight. Leonard theorized that the abilities she had used thus far were tied to her stress responses. Gail refuted this idea, since she had been in danger many times before without effect. In the end, they both agreed that there was little point in pursuing the use of The Magic until they had figured out exactly how it worked.

△

"Happy November," Leonard said, puffing on his pipe as they sat down to eat.

"It's November?" Gail asked, reaching out to cut a slice of a giant piece of bread from the platter. Cheese and black beans had been broiled on top, which Osbourne had concocted in the giant oven in the kitchen. He had called it pizza, but both Crow and Leonard had declared that it bore little resemblance to such a food, and that without sauce it was basically just a pile of cheesy bread with beans on top. Beans, apparently, were also not an appropriate pizza accoutrement and Leonard declared that some flavors should never get to know each other.

"As of yesterday," Crow said, checking her calendar. "That means people should be arriving in Sun City by now."

Leonard shrugged. "Unfortunately, they're expecting Dr. Glenn to give them some kind of direction. I'm assuming that the big plan's timeline was meant to be a little further forward than this."

"Well, we can deal with them after the tower." Crow closed her computer and stuffed it away in her bag. "We're heading out tomorrow."

"Tomorrow?" Leonard choked on his pipe smoke. "Why tomorrow?"

"Because we're as ready as we're going to be, and every day we delay is another day the Mori could figure out what we're up to. Osbourne—is the 'gadget' ready?"

Osbourne swallowed a massive chunk of 'pizza' he had been chewing on. "Seems so. No way to test it, of course, but in theory there's no reason it won't work."

Nick pulled out his speaking device and tapped a few buttons. "I'M READY."

Leonard sighed and took a long drag of his pipe. "Well, then tomorrow it is. I'm going to go get some sleep." Without finishing his food, the man stood up and stalked off toward a piece of the Mini golf scenery that was shaped like a tiki hut. Nick picked up some empty plates and walked to the kitchen to clean them, leaving Gail, Crow, and Osbourne to sit quietly.

"It's going to be a long walk," Gail finally said to break the silence.

"Walk?" Osbourne brightened. "Oh, you won't have to walk. We're taking the blimp." He gestured across the mini-golf compound to the massive illuminated balloon.

"Blimp?" Crow said, looking over at it in both wonder and, perhaps, a little bit of terror.

"We?" Gail asked at the same time. "You're going with us?"

"Of course!" Osbourne said, puffing out his chest. "I can't sit here forever and sulk. For the first time in a long time I feel like I have a purpose." Gail couldn't help but smile at him—he was childish, incredibly intelligent, and had shown a mature understanding of the deplorable actions of the Mori invaders. And yet, while he showed a wisdom and awareness that the other Mori seemed to lack, it appeared that he was still very simple in his thoughts and motivations. He was like an old but energetic puppy.

"If this is our last night here," Crow said, stretching a little bit and standing up, "I'd like to go for a little walk. I'm feeling cooped up. You said no one comes by here, right? Scared off?"

Osbourne nodded. "No one's lived within a few blocks of here for a couple years."

"Great, then we'll be nearby. Come on, Gail."

Gail felt a bit of a relief as they closed the faux-bamboo door behind them and stepped out into the street. Lukather was happy to escape the confines of the gaudy yard and took off a hundred feet down the road before running back a minute later looking very pleased with himself for no reason at all.

Even under the light of the massive blimp, the street was darker and as they made their way down the pavement, the night air had the slightest tinge of a chill. Crow relaxed. The bright lights—and the presence of Osbourne, no doubt—had made her very tense, but the darkness with which her black clothing blended put her at ease. They sat down on a bus stop bench.

"So, we're really going to do it," Crow said, leaning back and looking up at the stars.

"Seems so," Gail replied. She turned and laid down on the bench, putting her head in Crow's lap. A set of black-painted fingers started to gently tousle her hair. "We're probably going to die."

"Probably." Crow sounded completely ambivalent to the idea. Gail wondered if the witch's fear had been dulled in the same way her pain sensations had. "But we're doing the right thing, right?"

"I think so. We've sort of run out of things to lose."

Crow sighed. "I think it's important to have hope. And it's easier to have hope when you're hoping in someone else doing the right thing. I think it's a lot harder when you *are* the hope. But," she added, looking down at the redhead with a strange, unfocused expression, "I also don't really know whose hope we are. Who, right now, is hoping we succeed? Besides us."

"Your mom. Magpie. The other people on the New Internet. And when you think about it, everyone's hoping we succeed because they hope that *someone*, somewhere is doing something. They just don't know it's us specifically."

"That's the problem," Crow said, a frustrated grimace gracing one side of her mouth. "Everyone's hoping someone *else* will do it. They aren't standing up on their own."

"Because they're afraid. They've seen others try and fail, and they're scared to be the next ones to try."

They sat in silence for a short while, until Lukather's ears suddenly perked. At first, Gail didn't know what had caught his attention, but a moment later she heard the sound herself—a dragging set of footsteps coming down the street out of the gloom. They stood up and Crow started walking back toward the Mini Golf course. "Alright, we've spent too long out here already. Time to—"

Gail heard the clatter of something metal on the ground, and before there was a moment to react, the darkness was split by a terrible flash of light and a crack like thunder that sent Gail reeling and left her ears ringing. Her hand found her sword, and as she tried to make the world right-side-up again, she felt a hand grabbing her around the throat.

She was fairly certain the source of the hand was not Crow, and she kicked out with her silver boots, making contact with a stomach or rib and she spun, blinking to get the stars out of her eyes. Another set of hands came from behind, grabbing her and trying to wrench the sword from her hand. She reversed her grip and jabbed backwards, fairly certain she had struck something fleshy and driving her attacker backwards. Through the ringing in her ears she heard a howl of pain.

One of her eyes cleared before the other—she could just see enough to know there were three people here, and a fourth was now walking up to join them. She fixated on the fourth while her fist, still gripping the sword tightly, rammed into the face of another attacker who had seized Crow by the front of her collar and had struck her; Crow looked dazed and fell to the ground. Gail didn't hesitate now in stabbing him, though the sickening sound of the sword piercing his lung gave her absolutely no satisfaction.

Having dispatched the three first attackers, she turned her attention to the fourth, who was standing by, looking stoic. He looked disheveled, and his clothes were dirty and torn. His face was bloodied and his left eye swollen, but it was a face that had been seared into her mind.

The Duke.

THIRTY-ONE

"You're a long way from Raleigh," Gail remarked, having found her footing again standing to face off against the man who had pursued her. "You're never going to stop, are you?"

The Duke shook his head and pointed a dirty finger at Gail. "You belong to My Lady."

Gail looked the man up and down, his condition giving her pause. "What happened? I guess Boss wasn't very happy with you?"

"Shut up," The Duke snarled in reply, reaching down to pull a sword.

Gail shook her head. "What do I have to do to be free of the favor I owe the Mori?" She asked, as calmly as she could possibly muster. "Do I have to kill you, too? I don't want to kill anyone. But now you've forced me to."

"Shut up," he said again. "You're coming with me. I don't even need you alive." Without warning, he charged at her, his sword swinging wide. Gail easily sidestepped the overbalanced swing, and as the tread of her silver boots held fast against the concrete, she turned her weight and threw the flat of her blade up to block his errant backswing. It glanced easily off her blade, the sound of steel echoing down the street, but she paid it no mind. The Duke had recovered from his miscalculated charge and was panting heavily. There was no way he could possibly win in such a condition.

Then, he suddenly wretched, and his eyes rolled back. "You are mine," a familiar voice poured from his mouth. "If you will not serve me, then you will die." The Duke's whole posture changed; the slight sag in his leg from injury and the exhausted slump of his shoulders disappeared, so he was now standing, prepared to fight her, as though he was not injured at all. Lady Clíodhna, it seemed, could not feel the pain of the servant she possessed.

Gail let out a shout and took a step forward. Her sword went up once and she made two sweeping cuts across the possessed man's left side. She had hoped this might throw him off balance once more due to the gash on his leg, but in confirmation of her suspicion the blows were blocked easily and Clíodhna sent out a series of low jabs at Gail's legs. Gail scooted back, trying to be aware of the cracks and bumps of the ground beneath her. Lukather barked from somewhere in the darkness, and she put her hand out. "Stay back, Lukather!"

Clíodhna took advantage of the moment and sent a sidelong slice across in an attempt to sever that hand from its arm, but Gail spun to the side, bringing her arms in close, and missed the swing by inches. She walked her sword through a series of high and low cuts, keeping her body crouched and small. She was faster than the possessed body, but she knew that any attempt to tire him out would be a failed tactic. She wasn't even sure if, should she succeed in killing him, the possession of his Mori master would stop even then.

But she had to believe it would. She had to stop this man who hounded her trail and haunted her nightmares. She shouted again, rolling to the side and coming up with a cut that connected to flesh and dug into the bone of the possessed Duke's leg. Withdrawing the blade from the wound she parried another masterful chop from above, and her dodge was a moment too slow; the tip left a gash running from her left upper forearm to her elbow. It stung, but through the pain she gripped her sword's hilt and swung overhead.

But Clíodhna saw her maneuver and blocked it, the might of the strike sending Gail back on her heels. She found her balance, then, and as she threw the tip of her sword forward she felt it sink deep into the Duke's ribs. She followed this up with a swift kick and knocked him backwards onto the asphalt. Clíodhna tried to force the Duke to rise, but before he could get a handhold Gail's sword found him again, and the sheer force of the blow sent him backwards where a wooden pole was planted firmly in the grass beyond the curb. Gail was still not sure that the death of the body would stop the assault, so she took a few more steps forward and threw her weight into impaling the possessed man, pinning him to the wooden pole. He hung there, his face looking shocked as Clíodhna tried, vainly, to pull the weapon out from where it was lodged securely through the Duke's chest.

Gail slumped, dropping to a knee. The world was spinning a little bit from her adrenaline and her wounds. Crow was suddenly there, keeping her from falling down onto the blood-spattered road. "Gail. Gail, are you okay? Oh god…" the cut what had nicked her arm had apparently dug into the veins and arteries, and thick blood was oozing and spurting its way down her arm. "This is bad. You're losing a lot of blood."

Gail nodded, feeling very light-headed already, and tried to stand. Why had the ground suddenly become uphill in all directions? It was as if the road was turning to muddy water and she couldn't find her footing. "This is bad," she mumbled.

Crow put her hand over the wound, clamping down to keep more blood from pouring out. "We have to get back to the compound. Maybe Osbourne can—" she didn't seem to know what exactly Osbourne could do. "—do something."

Gail looked down and watched as pulse after pulse of sticky dark liquid made its way down her arm. "I…I don't think so."

"What?" Crow's voice was unusually high pitched. "Goddamnit…" She pulled on Gail, half-dragging, half-carrying her over to where the possessed body lay twitching. "You! Mori person! I'll do anything. Favors. I'll give you favors. Just—"

"No," Gail coughed. "It's not worth it, Crow."

The Duke's head was reeling, and Clíodhna made no intelligible reply. Crow let out a shriek of frustration. Gail was feeling unusually cold now. Wasn't Florida supposed to be warm year-round?

Then, something happened. It looked like a sparkle of light, like a firefly, that appeared for a moment in the air between them. Then another, and then another—each dotting into existence for a moment and vanishing. Then, beneath Crow's hand there was a crackle of electricity that sent a feeling of numbness shooting up Gail's arm. The numbness was replaced by warmth and, as quickly as it had appeared, it vanished.

Gail sucked in a breath. The fog over her mind was starting to lift, and as she looked down she saw that the blood was no longer dripping from under Crow's touch. As the witch lifted her hand, the gash across her arm was completely gone.

Clíodhna had suddenly become more focused, as she watched this happen right before the Duke's eyes. "No," the body whispered through a gargle of blood, and she stared at Crow with such a depth that the redhead was sure the Mori could see something that Gail could not. "The Tuatha…no…they couldn't…you didn't…" Then, as the Duke's eyes rolled back into place, he looked down at the sword that was pinning him to the wooden pole. He looked confused, and he whispered "My Lady?", his head tilting and his brow furrowed. Then, his gaze drifted upward to stare at Gail, and then they stared at nothing any longer.

◌

"The Tuatha Dé Danann," Osbourne said, tapping his chin with a long, twiggy finger. "That must be it. Clíodhna must be doing her research now that she knows what you are."

Leonard finished bandaging up another nick on Gail's leg. "I don't know that one. Can you fill us in?"

"Well," Osbourne said, starting to poke through his books for a certain volume, "the Tuatha Dé Danann were descendants of Neimheadh. Are you familiar with Neimheadh?"

"Yeah, from Dr. Glenn's seminar," Leonard replied, putting the extra bandage away in the first aid kit that Osbourne had dug up. Inside the blimp's basket compartment, Osbourne had created a strange study. While the furniture within was human, it had been arranged strangely--books on shelves, rather that stack side-by-side, were on top of one another, while the desk, littered with books, was sitting crookedly off to the side for no apparent reason. Not one piece of furniture matched, but they all had been painted—even the large cloth-upholstered couch—in a pale green color.

Below, there were grey clouds over the Floridian landscape as it slowly crossed their field of view. Here and there, through the mist of the morning, a bonfire could be seen, twinkling in the darkness. The trip, Osbourne said, would be just over an hour at the blimp's top speed, and would allow them to avoid any Mori who might now be on the lookout for Gail or Crow down on the ground.

"The Mori—er, the Fomóraiġ—fought with them, right?" Leonard continued. "They killed Neimheadh and enslaved all but one of his sons. And that son is the one who destroyed the Mori's tower."

"Conand's tower, yes," Osbourne said, finding the page in the book he had been seeking. "Depending on which myth you read, Fergus Red-Side—the last son of Neimheadh—gathered together allies before storming Conand's tower. Among them he reached out to the Tuatha Dé, who were at that time embroiled in a great conflict with another race called the Gaels—the druidic people who lived in Ireland. Dr. Glenn had theorized that they might have been a different group of invaders altogether, because they supposedly wielded magic and used it to ransom the Gaels for food and supplies."

"What does that have to do with me?" Crow said. Her voice was very weak.

Osbourne sat for a long time, thinking about the answer. Then, he came to a dawning realization. "Dr. Glenn and Marion both surmised that the reason the Partholónians have the ability to fight and kill the Mori is because they can resist the Magic, and somehow break through it…at least to some extent. We theorized that it was an ability to harness and use the Magic—but that assumption was based on the fact that Neimheadh's army used magic in the battle that destroyed Conand's Tower. But if we assume that the magic was *actually* used by the Tuatha Dé…well, what if the Partholónians don't have the ability to use magic at all?"

"Well I certainly can't, that's for sure," Gail breathed.

"The Partholónians," Leonard interjected. "They're not special at all. They're a—no pun intended here, Gail—red herring. And the Mori fell for it too."

"I don't think that's entirely true, either," Osbourne said. "because the Partholónians definitely have the ability to break through the Mori defensive spells and kill them. We—and the Mori, I assume, by extension—have been under the assumption that the Partholónians can *use* the Magic. In reality, I would ager that they can *absorb* the Magic. Disable it."

"When the Duke had me back in Raleigh," Gail said, recollecting, "and the Mori used its power to grab me, I felt like I was resisting it. The one woman…she said she had never seen anyone resist that."

"Like a dampener, or a heat-sink," Leonard added, and Gail nodded despite not knowing what either of those things were.

"But what does that have to do with me?" Crow repeated. Her voice had become higher and she looked to be on the verge of tears.

Osbourne pointed at a passage in the book. "If the myth is right, the army of Neimheadh wielded magic against the Mori. And if they were not able to wield the magic—like Gail—then that means the Tuatha Dé did. And just as Neimheadh was a descendant of Partholón, there may well be descendants of the Tua—"

"I'm not that." Crow's face was flushed. "I'm not using 'the magic'. You're wrong. There's another explanation. There has to be."

"Gail," Leonard said, stroking his chin. "You've only used—or thought you've used—the Magic a few times. When?"

"Well," Gail counted out on her fingers. "My thigh wound healed on its own sometime after I was knocked out at Campbell. I healed Crow. And then I stopped the knife that was going to hit her…"

"That means twice, you've helped Crow when *she* was in a time of stress. If we're going on this theory that Crow's the one using the magic, and not you, then Crow might have healed *herself* and we didn't realize it. And it's possible that she healed you, without realizing it, while you were unconscious."

"I didn't!" Crow protested. "I didn't do any of that. I don't have that magic." It was hard to tell if she was trying to convince the others, or herself.

"Here's another one," Leonard added over Crow's protests. "After she set off the radio tower that disrupted the Mori in Raleigh, Nick got knocked offline. And he didn't wake up until a little while after Crow climbed into the carriage."

"He was also stuck on the tracks in Lillington," Gail said excitedly, "until a little while after Crow examined him to see if he could be fixed!" Crow was now seething.

"Gail's had no luck trying to use the Magic," Leonard said. "Not one little bit."

"It warrants further study," Osbourne said, opening another book.

"—*I am not using Magic!*" Crow screamed, and the entire compartment fell into dead silence. She took a deep breath. "I'm not a descendant of whatever," she said in a much calmer voice. "It's a mistake. Gail's mistaken—she must have healed herself, just like before. I refuse. I don't want any part of it. Can we please stop talking about it? I don't want to talk about this, okay?" She was shaking, slightly curled up on the green couch.

Gail moved over to her and laid her hand over her girlfriend's hand. "Okay."

Osbourne moved over to the front of the blimp, where Nick was sitting in the driver's seat. Out in the darkness, the glow could be seen blooming across the horizon, and the unearthly, curved shape of the Tower of Peace became visible as a shadow against the light. The drawing that Dr. Glenn had shown during his presentation did not really capture the enormity of the tower; nearly the whole tip of the peninsula where St. Petersburg rested formed the base of the tower, which rose at least a mile or more into the sky. It was shaped like a flower bud, but thicker at the base, and the top of the tower was emitting some kind of light that was just visible against the sky as the blimp approached.

The four of them looked out at the tower for a short while, unable to say anything at all. They were all transfixed by its singular beauty and form, while at the same time disgusted by the massive destruction that was borne from the tower's otherworldly emanations. There was no turning back, now, they all agreed silently, because to give up now would only mean that no one else would ever succeed.

THIRTY-TWO

Osbourne brought the blimp down at the southern edge of the estuary. Dawn was preparing to break, and he hoped that the blimp might have evaded detection due to the low-hanging clouds over Cockroach Bay. There was no way to be sure, however, and all they could do was hope.

The estuary was also very close to Sun City. They sat for a little while trying to determine what the best course of action was—should they tell all of the people that had made it to Sun City the plan so they could prepare? Or should they wait until they had made it out before spreading the word of the weakened state of their oppressors? In the end, it was decided that they would wait; not only would they be less likely to tip off their attackers, but in the event that their raid was a failure, they would not inspire a false hope in the people who had shown up seeking it.

Osbourne elected to stay behind; he would pilot the blimp out over the bay and, when the tower fell, he would use the massive speaker system onboard to begin to spread the word.

"You're not coming with us?" Gail asked as they disembarked from the blimp's compartment and came to rest once again on solid ground—solid enough, anyway, for Florida's swampy terrain could hardly be considered "solid".

"No," Osbourne said, patting the side of the blimp's compartment. "I can do much more for humans from in here. While you're inside I'll be zooming around the bay causing a ruckus. With any luck, I'll provide enough distraction to keep you safe." Crow shook her head with derision. And Osbourne's face fell once more. "You still think I am leading you into a trap."

"Of course I do!" Crow snapped, but she held out her hand. "But I really hope not. So if you're not, good luck to you."

Osbourne beamed a wide smile and shook her hand. "And you, too. Be safe." He waved good-bye and boarded the craft once more, and a few minutes later the massive blimp was back in the sky.

Gail leaned down and patted Lukather—sweet, kind Lukather— on the head. "Stay here, boy. I'll be back soon. And if I'm not back soon, go get help." Lukather gave her the same wide dog grin he always had, and while he looked despondent at her departure, he did not move to follow her.

"Alright, let's go," Crow sighed as the golden balloon swept out of sight over the trees, "I hate wasting time."

"We know," Gail and Leonard replied at once.

They traipsed through the mud and swampy earth a short distance. Nick was particularly careful with his steps, as the weight of the power armor kept pulling him into the mud. Under two thick grey trees they encountered a small concrete building surrounded by a black fence laced with razor wire. Crow pulled out a pair of bolt cutters she had snagged from Osbourne's compound and started clipping away at the fence until she had cut a hole large enough for all of them to slip through. "So far so good," Crow said under her breath, pulling the hood of her cloak up.

The door to this small building was made of steel and was locked with a padlock. The bolt cutters went to work again, cutting it off with ease. Nick then pulled the massive door open, the sound of squealing metal rather obvious in the quiet morning, but there was nothing to be done about it.

The door led down into a concrete stairwell, but how deep it actually went was not immediately visible. Leonard pulled a hooded lantern from his belt and, after expertly striking a match, lit it and held it aloft. The stairwell went down a few feet and through a doorway; corroded metal signs about authorized personnel were visibly bolted to the concrete walls. "Welp," he said, pulling the brim of his hat down, "here we go."

Through the doorway, they entered into a series of short corridors and more stairs. The concrete walls were covered in mildew, a product of the perpetual wetness that seemed to permeate the air and every surface. It was a wonder that the concrete hadn't deteriorated at all over these many years of disuse, what with the constant pressure of swampy soil and sediment pressing in from all sides.

Finally, after several sets of stairs, they arrived at a long, wide chamber that went down as far as the lantern would allow. It was about 10 feet wide, with an arched roof and a steady stream of dripping water that came in through highly concerning cracks in the ceiling. Gail reminded herself that they were now somewhere under Cockroach Bay, and the fact that water was dripping in was a somewhat horrifying prospect.

On the subject of horrifying prospects, however, even more so was the contents of this chamber as they walked a quarter or a mile or so. As they moved forward through the oppressive darkness, they began to see equipment up ahead. Large metal boxes lined these walls each humming along almost musically with an electrical murmur not unlike the massive lights back at Osbourne's compound. As they drew closer, they could see that each of these boxes had a glass front, and were filled with marked shelves.

"They're all numbered," Crow said quietly, looking through the frosted glass. "What are they?"

"Embryos," Leonard said, pulling his hat down and moving on. "Viable embryos. More Mori children ready for the growing."

"Do you think—" Gail began, but she stopped herself as Crow put her hand on the redhead's shoulder.

"Don't think about it."

"But they're probably here," Gail said. "My—my—"

Her words were interrupted by a loud sound up ahead. Vaguely metallic, something had audibly scraped across the concrete floor and echoed all the way down the chamber. Leonard looked at the others and at Nick. "See anything?"

Nick's helmet clicked as he scanned ahead. "Something alive," he signed to Gail, who translated in a whisper.

They crept forward, Nick being especially careful to rest his heavy metal feet gently with each step, and discovered the source of the sound slumbering in the middle of the chamber. It was unmistakably Mori, what with its golden skin and flowing blonde hair, but what part of it was humanoid was that of a giant, with a head the size of Gail's torso. Where arms should have been there were only thick, rubbery tentacles, and in place of legs it appeared to have several crablike appendages with metallic, clawed tips. Despite its huge size, it was curled up enough to leave some space on either side of it, and the group began to signal each other rapidly as to whether they thought they could bypass the creature without waking it. They finally decided that they probably could, and one by one they tiptoed around the beast. Nick, in particular, took a while as he moved, foot-over-foot, to avoid making sound.

They breathed a collective sigh of relief once safe on the other side, and continued on. The machines here were slightly different: instead of shelves and shelves of labeled things, there were full-sized creatures in each machine. The glasses were heavily frosted on the outside, and despite a fierce glare from the witch, Leonard approached one and gently scraped some of the frost off with his jacket.

Inside was a child. If she had been human, Gail might have thought she was no more than six or seven years old. But she was Mori, her silvery hair short and cropped about her face and her eyes closed as if in slumber. A second look made him realize, to his horror, that her head and her torso were not connected and were resting on different shelves—it was like looking at a doll that had not yet been assembled.

Leonard shivered at the discovery and motioned that they should move on. As he went to move away, though, the boy's eyes opened. Leonard did a double-take. "What the—"

The boy screamed. But it was not a human scream—it was a screech that seemed to emanate from everywhere. The girl in the next container opened her eyes, too, and she joined in with the din. Soon, behind the panes of frosted glass, dozens of children were now awake and screeching, deafening and echoing in the stone corridor.

Gail knew what was going to happen next, and she turned to face the massive creature they had so carefully crept past. It was already moving, its thick tentacles pushing it up from the ground while the monstrous claws beneath it found their footing.

The children stopped screaming as the Wet-Nurse rose, for their part in what was about to unfold had been accomplished: they had awoken the beast that now leered down at them, impossibly large in the cramped space.

Gail started moving, not wanting to give the creature a moment to understand its surroundings. She dove and rolled under its massive torso, coming up on the other side with a slice aimed well at its back. The sword made contact, but it didn't sink as deep as she had hoped it would. She let out a grunt, planting her boots firmly and springing up to try and get the sharp blade of the sword to bite flesh again.

Off to her right, she saw something shoot past the creature's head—a bolt, fired from Crow's crossbow, to be sure—and the wet-nurse caught the movement and looked around. Gail took advantage of that brief pause and tried to hack her sword through one of the rubbery tentacles protruding from the creature's long torso. She missed, the swing sending her teetering off-balance, and it slammed the side of one claw into her instantly, throwing her back against one of the containers of embryos and nearly sending her head through the machine's glass front.

Nick grabbed hold of one of the claws, his massive armored hands trying to wrench any part of it free, but the monster simply shook its appendage to try and free itself of the metal pest. Nick held fast, his fist slamming again and again into the side of it in an attempt to break through the armored flesh there. Several throwing knives seemed to appear along the rubbery tentacle—Leonard's aim was perfect—but even the rainbow-colored blades which sunk deep into the skin barely registered to the monster.

Crow had loaded another arrow and took her time aiming this time. The only light was from the lantern held by Leonard who, having depleted his few knives, he tried to stay back and illuminate as much of the fight as he could for the benefit of everyone else. Crow saw an opening and fired it, sending the projectile deep into the monster's torso right where, hopefully, its kidneys might be.

The wet-nurse reeled, wracking itself so hard that it threw the armored Marine off of its leg; Nick had managed to form a large crack in the chitin, but the creature's legs were largely unmarred. Gail had to duck a swinging tentacle as it let out a screech that was more terrible and ear-splitting than that of the children, and it swung wildly with its arms and legs.

A thick black tentacle came straight for Gail's face and she swung her sword high; the force of momentum threw her of balance and onto her rear but it also succeeded in driving the blade of the sword straight through the blubbery appendage. She rolled, avoiding thick blobs of jelly-like blood that poured onto the floor.

Gail heard a strange sound that caught the creature's attention. Crow had pulled out the pink star wand from her bag and was now gesturing with it menacingly. "Be gone!" Crow screamed. "Be gone!" The creature took a few frightened steps back from the witch, and Gail used that moment to swing her sword again, cleaving into the creature's ribs.

Nick was up again, and he bypassed the cracked leg to climb atop the wet nurse, and in an instant a flurry of armored punches were delivered to the thing's neck and face. It appeared briefly stunned as the metal fist came in again and again. "Light up its face!" Crow shouted to Leonard, who lifted the lantern higher and cast a cone of light over the thing's head. Crow let loose another bolt, and its aim was true—it sailed up and lodged itself in the creature's neck, coating Nick's front with a spray of viscous liquid.

Gail back on her feet, rolled under the creature and tried to slice its underbelly. She found it more heavily-armored than she had expected, and an errant leg hit her squarely between the shoulder blades and sent her reeling. The creature bucked Nick off again and maneuvered itself to grab Gail's leg and pull her upward.

"You are the mother!" it screamed in her head. *"You are the Mother of the New People!"* It bared its jaws, preparing to pull the redhead into its gaping mouth. Gail could see it unhinging its jaw like a snake—

It stopped, its eyes going wide and scooting back. The creature slammed against the wall and let Gail go, causing her to fall to the ground hard. She blinked and looked up.

Crow had run out of crossbow bolts the weapon was at her feet, and her arm was outstretched, her fist clenched against the thin air. She twisted her fist and the creature stumbled again; it was clear that she didn't have a complete control over it, but she was throwing its balance off terribly. "I am the Witch of Raven Rock!" Crow screamed. "Go—fuck—yourself—"

Gail did not hesitate. She grabbed her sword, and leapt up, digging it into the creature's ribs over and over, making puncture after puncture and eliciting more screams that filled her ears. *"You are the mother!"* it shrieked one final time and it dropped to the floor and ceased moving.

Gail pulled her sword from the beast, wiping the blade off on its furry leg. Breathing hard, she straightened and coughed a little, trying to get oxygen in this sour, wet air. She looked to Crow, who was standing and looking at her own hands. She wanted to smile, and congratulate her, or even be as uncouth as to gloat about exactly how right she had been, but the look on Crow's face told her that she was not in such a mood. It was an unmistakable look of disgust, and self-hatred. She could almost hear Crow's voice in her own head, shouting obscenities about the utter truth—that she had used Mori Magic.

The witch finally looked at Gail, and she flushed a deep red, even visible in the near-darkness. "I...I didn't mean...I didn't—"

Gail was at her side. "You did a really good job. And you didn't do anything wrong, I promise." Crow had tears in her eyes and Gail kissed them away. "You are still the same person."

Crow shuddered and held her close for what felt like an eternity.

⌂

They were dirty, wet, and exhausted by the time they reached the end of the maintenance tunnel that ran under Cockroach Bay. The tunnel ended in another steel door much like the one on the other side, and as they pulled it open there was a wall of green and orange light on the other side.

When Osbourne had said that the tunnel went right into the Tower of Peace, he was not lying. They were near the circumference of the massive tower, as they came to discover as their immediate surroundings came into view. The tower was completely hollow; the shapes of the flower bud-like plates were now visible up-close to be floating green plates of glass, suspended in the air and overlapping like scale armor and extending up into the sky as far as they could see. The green glass cast everything inside the tower in slowly shifting shades of green.

There had been a city in St. Petersburg once—that much was clear. They could see the outlines of building foundations and streets extending out from them. They could see a few buildings still standing, even, here and there—but the majority of the city had been leveled, leaving only imprints of its former self as scorched outlines on the level ground.

"Where is everyone?" Gail whispered, and a sound from outside answered her question. It was loud, like thunder, and through the glassy plates of the tower they could make out the shape of Osbourne's golden blimp making wild circles out over the bay. But something was already wrong—smoke was pouring from the rear end of it, and Gail quickly realized that the erratic disposition of the balloon's trajectory had less to do with an attempt to evade its attackers, and more to do with retaining altitude after already being hit.

"No!" Gail cried out without thinking, and as they watched, another fiery strike from the Mori send the blimp into a spiral. It went down, down…they lost sight of it over the trees, but it was hard to imagine that it would recover after its fiery plunge into the bay.

"We have no more time!" Crow shouted, and they turned from the image of the doomed airship to make a run for the center of the tower. It was a straight run over relatively flat land, and Gail began to slow as they came closer to the center. As they approached the core, they faced a massive field of light, almost reflective, like a mirror.

Gail looked at it. "Okay. What now?"

"*Now,*" A voice echoed in her head, "*You belong to me.*"

THIRTY-THREE

Gail spun to see Bláthnaid Clíodhna sweeping toward them, flanked by several other Mori. "You belong to me, child."

"Gail!" crow choked out, and the redhead realized, too late, that the witch and the metal man, and Leonard beside her were all frozen in place.

The Mori blinked once. "*The children beneath the tower. You have seen them. They are yours. You are their mother. Will you abandon them? Will you kill them?*"

"You...you took them from me," Gail sputtered. "You...you *violated* me—"

"*You will not destroy the tower. You will not kill your children. Even if you had the ability.*"

The ability. Gail thought to Osbourne's explanation of the powers of the Partholónians. They were a heat sink for Mori magic. And Tuatha Dé, on the other hand, were able to use that energy to fuel the magic. If the two were together...

Gail didn't have a moment to think. She reached instinctively for Crow's hand and as their skin touched something happened that Gail could feel, now that she knew it was there. She could almost feel the swirling of the Mori technology. She could not understand code or algorithms or the flow of the alien program but somehow, in her head, she could suddenly see the structure of the magic as it coursed through her outstretched hand. In her head, she tried to pull it, to grab it and shake it loose like dust from a carpet, and as her head imagined these things, Crow unfroze. Gail had absorbed the spell and had transferred that energy into Crow. Somehow.

Crow, too, seemed to have a sudden understanding, and she shoved the air in front of her. One of the Mori was thrown backward, but it quickly recovered from the unexpected blow, and threw something that seemed like a ball of energy directly at the witch. Gail stepped forward, though, and took the blow herself—but it didn't hurt her. She understood it now, and the ball of energy dissipated.

Gail advanced on the Mori. "You took things from my body. You used them to grow new abominations and now you want me to be their mother." Bláthnaid Clíodhna waved her hands at Gail, and something that might have been a deadly blast of the magic once again dissipated on contact. "You...all of you, destroyed this world. But I won't stand for it anymore."

Gail was now face-to-face with the towering face of this Mori, who let out a scream of rage and lunged forward—but Gail was faster. She seized the Clíodhna by the shoulders, and at once the creature stumbled to the ground, completely powerless. She shrieked, flailing her arms about, but the Magic was not there anymore. Gail had stolen it from her.

She pulled the angry Mori into her own face. "You don't own us any longer. We are free." Slamming her forehead into the alien's face, she threw Clíodhna to the ground, unconscious, before advancing on the other Mori. They, having no idea what they could possibly do to combat a creature immune to their Magic, did the most immediately strategic thing—they each vanished before she could reach them. "Cowards!" Gail spat.

Leonard walked over to Gail, landing a square kick to the Mori's face as she went past. "Okay. There, that thing, the core. That's what we need to blow up." The four of them ran as fast as they could toward it, and quickly discovered that the dimensions of the tower made the distance to it seem far closer than it really was. Ever-so-slowly, the center of the tower came closer and closer, until the three of them stood, breathless, in front of the glowing power source of the Mori Magic. It was surrounded on all sides by a field of glowing green.

Crow gestured to the barrier. "You're the Partholónian. Can you…I don't know."

Gail didn't know either, but she walked, unafraid, up to the massive field. She could feel a kind of radiative heat emanating from it, and it tingled her skin. This, she reminded herself, was why a Partholónian was needed for this task. Tentatively, she reached out her finger and touched it.

The energy surged around her finger, and for a moment she thought it was about to disintegrate her from the finger outward, but as she concentrated, fighting back against the torrential pull of the power within the field. Slowly, it gave way and began to weaken, finally succumbing to her will and vanishing, absorbed into her body.

Gail dropped to a knee and Crow was at her side instantly. "Are you alright?"

She nodded. "I think so." And as Crow took her hand to help her up, the Magic surged suddenly between them and they both were knocked back by the sheer force of it. Reeling, they both stumbled to their feet. "Crow…"

Leonard helped her up. "Necia, Are you okay? I'm okay. Are you okay?"

She nodded. "I'm okay. That was…"

"Yeah."

Gail shook herself a little bit as Nick patted her shoulder. "Now what?"

Crow walked a few steps toward the core of the tower. It was hard to describe exactly what it was. The space in the center of the tower seemed both to be filled with nothing at all, while also filled with the potential for so many things. It was as if the center of the tower was nothing but a solid, tangible mass of kinetic energy, waiting to be tapped into and utilized. It was magnificent and terrifying.

"Leonard," the redhead said slowly, "What *is* that?"

He shrugged. "A massive power source. I can't even…I don't even know what I would call it. It's not really matter. It's like…it's like energy that's been turned into physical substance. At leas tthat's my guess because…shit, I honestly don't know *what* it is."

"Okay, this should be good," Crow coughed as they got a little closer to the invisible core. "Nick, where's the gadget thing?"

Nick didn't reply.

"Come on, Nick, we don't have time. Where's the device you and Osbourne worked on?"

Nick didn't reply again, and he picked up his Type-N'-Talk. It still had the last message he had plugged into it, over a day prior. "I'M READY."

The realization hit Gail like a ton of bricks, and she couldn't even find enough mental or emotional wherewithal to reply. Nick looked at her and pushed the button again. "I'M READY."

"Oh no." Crow, it seemed, had come to a full realization of everything Nick was saying with these two words. "You're ready because…because one we cut power to the Magic, it's going to knock you out, too."

"I'M READY."

"You're ready because you know that even if we stop the Mori, there's very little chance that we'll be able to put you into any kind of proper body again."

"I'M READY."

"You're ready because you've already said goodbye to your family and they've already said goodbye to you. Your wife. Your Lodge Brothers. They already know."

"I'M READY."

Gail could not stop the tears that were pouring from her eyes. "What, you're ready because you feel empty inside? But that's not true,

Nick! It's not true at all! You're as much a person as the rest of us. Please, believe me. You don't have to do this—"

"You're ready," Crow said with dawning realization, "because you are the 'gadget', aren't you? You're the bomb. Osbourne turned your…your power source into it somehow. And you let him do it."

"I'M READY."

Crow came up to the large metal man and gave him a kiss on the cheek of his helmet. "Nick, you have been just wonderful. Just…utterly wonderful. I cannot possibly repay you for your kindness. You have been a friend, and an anchor, and…and…and I will never forget you."

Nick removed the crocheted tin-colored scarf from his neck and put it over Crow's head. It looked so strange on her, contrasting with everything else that was black which she wore. And yet it also was fitting that the woman who had spent so long not trusting the metal man should be the one to bear the peculiar mark of his favor.

Leonard stepped in front of Nick and took a deep breath before throwing his arms around the metal man. Nick reciprocated this hug, and gently patted Leonard on the back. They broke apart after a long moment. "I'll miss you, big guy. It's been an honor. Give us twenty minutes to clear the area, okay?" Nick nodded.

Gail straightened up, her chest shuddering in heaving breaths, and she lifted her arms to sign. "You are more of a person than most people," she carefully expressed with her hands. "I love you and will miss you."

Nick did not reply with sign language. He simply pressed the button one final time. "I'M READY."

Gunnery Sergeant Nick Harvey stood at attention, and at that moment he seemed to be the most human he had ever been. Gail could almost see his pride for a job well-done, and a life well-lived. He stood there, unmoving, a metal statue in an empty field, and as Crow and Gail turned to run back toward the maintenance tunnel, Gail could not help but look back to see him, frozen forever in a field of green.

THIRTY-FOUR

The trip back through the tunnel felt longer, somehow, and as they reached the rows and rows of machines Gail slowed her pace. "Are we just going to leave them here? The wet-nurse is dead. They'll die."

Leonard gestured to the glass. "Look at them—disassembled. If I was to guess, these aren't Mori children ready to be born...at least not yet. In the meantime, these are just spare parts."

Gail opened her mouth to argue and her eyes fell on the refrigerators of embryos. "And what about those? What if they're...they're..." She tried to complete her sentence but could not.

Crow finished it for her. "Yours? If they're yours, they were taken from you without your consent. You have no responsibility for these things, Gail."

"There must be thousands," Leonard added. "What are you supposed to do, care for all of them at once?"

"And even if there weren't thousands," Crow continued, reaching down to pick up a crossbow bolt where it rested on the ground, "the answer is still the same."

Gail let out a whimpering sound and turned to dash past the refrigerators. Crow and Leonard followed, traipsing over the dead body of the wet-nurse, and caught up to her. The corridor ahead was dark and wet, and as they ran Gail realized that the eruption of the tower would probably sacrifice the stability of the tunnel itself. There was no time to delay.

But at the end of the tunnel, right in front of the steel door that led upstairs to the outside, they met a familiar face. He was scarred, and his skin was mottled blue and purple, but he was clearly alive once more

The Duke. The *fucking* Duke.

"My Lady demands your presence," The Duke said, and his voice was strained as though speaking was very difficult to him.

"It's too late," Gail said evenly. "Your Lady is upstairs, about to be finished. And I owe her no favors—she didn't heal my friend. My friend healed *herself*."

"Details, details," the Duke said, and his bloodied sword was already in his hand. "You are weak and I am strong. My Lady gives me strength. She gives me—"

Thunk. Crow, standing behind Leonard where she could be obscured by the darkness, had taken perfect aim with her crossbow. The bolt, sticky from the blood of the wet-nurse, still flew perfectly straight, and it met its mark deep in the Duke's eye socket.

The Duke dropped to the floor with a sickening crash, and before there was even a moment to reconsider, Gail had begun to hack the body's head off.

"Gail," Crow said, cautious about approaching while the redhead vented untold amounts of anger and despair into the body of the man who was once named Hamilton, "we need to go. The tower—"

"He's going to just come back!" She screamed back. Off came a hand, at the wrist, then the forearm, at the elbow. The sword, the floor, Gail's clothes—all were being covered in blood.

"When the tower blows up, he won't. Hey—" Taking a bold step forward, she put a hand up to stop Gail's next swing and fixed her with a gaze that was both firm and understanding. Somewhere above them, there was a rumble, like thunder. "Come on."

They scrambled up the stairs. Gail ignored the terrible burning in her lungs as they went up flight after flight, and when they reached the final archway and burst into the light it was like an escape from hell. They had not realized that the cement corridor was so smoky until they reached the mostly-clean air outside and could see greyish-brown gasses belching out of the hole behind them.

"We have to get out of here," Leonard advised. "This tunnel is going to be like a potato gun. All sorts of shit is going to come shooting out of it." They cleared the fence and were back out into the grounds of the estuary.

Lukather was waiting for them. While it looked like he hadn't moved at all, the mud on his belly and paws indicated that he had been excitedly awaiting their return by rolling around in the swampy mess at their feet. He was a lovely sight to behold nonetheless, and Gail hugged him for a long minute before they headed out of the trees and back toward the road.

Above them, the incredible Tower of Peace was crackling with energy. Gail could see the glowing flecks of light that might have been Mori floating about, trying to repair the damage, but the powers they held were rapidly diminishing already. All at once, the tower became entirely dormant, and the floating scales of glass began to fall.

The sound was like nothing Gail had ever heard before—a million tons of green glass struck the ground in a cascade, filling the air with a din that sounded eerily like static. The air was filled with nothing but this sound, and the three of them had to cover their ears as it happened. From the base of the tower, where everything was now collapsing, a plume of smoke quickly rose.

"Cover!" Leonard shouted, and he dragged the two girls over a hill and down a slope toward an abandoned RV park. Leonard didn't hesitate as he threw a door open and practically shoved the two women and the dog inside. He was not a moment too soon, as the moment he slammed the tiny RV's door shut, the entire landscape was covered in an endless snow of glass shards. They thundered like rain for a few minutes before it all stopped.

The three of them huddled there in the dirty RV for a short while longer, just in case there was to be a second shower of glass, but outside it was very calm. The three looked at each other. It was Crow that cracked the first smile of relief and they all burst into chuckles. Not one of them could have explained exactly what made them laugh then, but as they stepped out of the RV they all had wide smiles on their faces.

The ground, and every surface, was covered in a layer of greenish-white—tiny shards of glass that had found their way everywhere and cast the landscape in a glow that looked like snow. It was like a newfound purity, whitewashed across the grass and trees.

The tower was gone from where it had stood above the tree line, and the great space it left was now filled with the sun, shining brightly and reflecting off the glittering glass particles, illuminating everything around them in a blazing sparkle of light.

Gail picked up Lukather, hefting the sheepdog over her shoulder to protect his paws, and they started off down across the RV park, the ground making crisp crunches beneath their feet. All around them, RVs and mobile homes were littered in various states of disrepair, and if it were not for the blazing heat—made worse, certainly, by the glassy coating everywhere—it might have been much like a set of winter cottages Gail had once seen in an art book.

Up ahead, they could hear voices—confused, celebratory, angry, and frustrated—and they slowed their pace across the mud and glass. As they reached the end of one RV part and the beginning of another, they could make out hundreds, perhaps thousands of people, huddled under the awnings of RVs and cleaning glass power from their clothes and picking glass out of their hair and skin. Most had minor cuts on their hands and faces, and there seemed to be a general scramble to be sure no one was seriously injured.

Gail looked out at them. They were all different: where they came from, what they looked like, how old they were—and yet from the cuts on their hair and hands and faces the mass of people appeared painted a single color of mottled red.

From the crowd, a familiar face approached them, his smile gleaming widely. "Magpie!" Crow said, throwing her arms around the king of the New Internet. "You made it."

"And you..." he gestured vaguely to the empty space where the tower had been. "You did something."

"You bet your ass I did," Crow said with a wicked smile. She looked at Gail for direction. "What now?"

Gail set Lukather down on a patch of ground under an awning where the ground was not covered in glass shards. "Now," she said, taking Crow's hand, "all of the Mori are powerless. Now, we go tell people what happened. Now, we start fighting to take our home back."

EPILOGUE

Dearest M,

I don't know what strange designs led you to find me in the woods some thirteen years ago. Was it fate? Some astral coincidence? As I think about it and talk to Crow about it, we discuss the number of strange happenstances that led me here. A small number of people, armed with an idea to fight back, whose sacrifice to that end started a chain reaction. Maybe it wasn't some strange coincidence—maybe revolutions happen like that. They start with a small spark, and a few people, and they grow like a wildfire and expand. It's easy to squash out that revolution when it's just a spark, and it's just started. It's harder when the spark ignites something much bigger.

I'm on a train right now, headed up the east coast. I've passed my road a few times along this journey, the bright yellow double stripes keep reminding me of where I've been. This has been a long trip, M. But I hope I made you proud.

Crow is here. You would have liked her. She's sleeping now. We said good-bye to Leonard and Dani a few days ago. They are planning to storm southward and raid Boss and the other slavers. Leonard is particularly adamant about the idea of people enslaving people, and he aims to change that. He's starting a revolution of his own, I think. Magpie is going to help.

Now it's just the two of us again, as it was in the beginning. We haven't decided where we're going to go just yet, but I think we're going to try and find the old house in the mountains and stay there a while. Then, our next stop is New York. I don't know what I'm going to find there just yet, but I do know that as we head back through the Mid-Atlantic, I expect to see great changes in the power vacuum that the Duke left. I expect there to be bloodshed—I'd be stupid not to. But in the calm here after the storm, and before the next one, I am taking time to enjoy a little peace on my road home.

I don't know if you can hear this prayer, but I wanted to let you know that I'm safe, and everything is going to be alright.

⌂

"This way!" Gail was bouncing with excitement as she spotted a few of the landmarks she knew from her youth. Now she was back in her own territory, and she could walk these paths blindfolded. She seized Crow's hand and tugged the witch over a fallen log and through some shrubbery. Next it was a long stretch of path bending around an outcropping and, as they passed under a boulder, the mountain retreat came into view.

"Wow," Crow said, pulling her hood down. "It's beautiful. Small, but beautiful."

The retreat was square in shape. M had called the design "Minimalist" and claimed that this house was once built for people with absurd amounts of money. The house was built to settle right up against a jutting boulder in such a way that the house almost appeared to be a part of the landscape itself.

"Come on!" Gail let go of Crow's hand, darted for the door, and pulled a key from her bag. How long since she had used that key! And in a moment the door was open and Gail had disappeared into the darkness of the house.

Crow was left standing out in the front yard. She looked down, picking up a dry brown leaf from the ground and examining it. The witch hadn't decided yet if she was going to tell Gail about what she had discovered on their trip back. She didn't want to worry her, but at the same time, she *had* promised there would be no more secrets, right? It was a little frustrating to keep that promise at moments like this.

Fairly certain that the redhead was busy looking around to be sure the house was undisturbed, Crow took a deep breath and focused on the leaf. Nothing happened for a moment. Then, a crackle of electricity jumped between her fingers. It was small, and barely unnoticeable, but as she pulled her thumb away it was clear that there was a hole burned black through the delicate fibers of the leaf that had not been there before.

"Come on! Let me show you around!" Gail said, sticking her head out the door and giggling like a little girl.

Crow let the leaf drop to the ground and smiled, pushing her concern to the back of her mind, at least for a moment. There would be plenty of time to discuss the Magic later.

Afterword

The story of the Fomóraiġ is a real part of Irish mythology. Many of the stories and texts referenced in this book are real and are available in the public domain for your research. I have taken as few liberties with the story of these mythical people who ruled the Emerald isle with an iron fist until a revolution unseated them and sent them back to whence they came, but I have had to where necessary. Were they aliens? That's anyone's guess.

This book was made possible with the help of a number of experts and professionals. I would like to thank in particular:

Dr. Nima Afshar, M.D., Associate Professor of Medicine at UCSF for providing, with great detail, the most helpful information regarding injuries in a post-apocalyptic setting.

Dr. Thomas Lebesmuehlbacher, Assistant Professor for Williams College of Business at Xavier University for helping me build multiple social and economic systems that make sense throughout the world.

Dr. Michael Simonton, Director of Celtic Studies at Northern Kentucky University, who provided a plethora of incredible resources related to the mythology surrounding the mysterious Fomóraiġ of Irish mythology and whose contributions were integral to the story.

Pat Warner at Waffle House, Inc, for being an incredibly good sport and explaining that per policy, Waffle House "will be open after an alien invasion."

Steve & Keith at SKH Music as well as Steve Lukather of the band *Toto* for allowing me to give our favorite dog the best name ever.

I would like to also thank the friends and 'found family' who have made my life so much more meaningful by being a part of it.

About the Author

Sam Swicegood is a native of Baltimore. His prior titles include multiple fantasy and science fiction works including *The Wizards on Walnut Street* and *Cold Start*. He has been a freelance writer for over a decade.

He is an active member of Ohio Free and Accepted Masons, N. C. Harmony Lodge No. 2. He is a community activist, avid podcaster, internet dweeb, and redditor. His hobbies include running D&D games, complaining about Ohio weather, accidentally finding new ways to trigger his own anxiety attacks, and being a general nuisance.

He lives in Cincinnati, OH with his best friend, spouse, and fellow writer, Lexis.

Also from Dragon Street Press

The Wizards on Walnut Street
By Sam Swicegood

When a well-respected corporate sorcerer is murdered, his eldest child Andy moves to Cincinnati to investigate, discovering a magical society bubbling just under the surface of the mundane world. Encountering odd characters such as an Incubus barista, a knife-happy security guard, and an enchanted espresso machine, Andy uncovers a plot to overthrow the magical society's hierarchy.

Buy it on Amazon.com,
at Barnes & Noble,
and select Bookstores

For more information visit dragonstreet.press

"I can shake off everything as I write; my sorrows disappear, my courage is reborn."

Anne Frank